S O S

By Terol (T-Mac) McCullar

2023

Contents

LITTLE WHITE LIES

The evening light was submitting to the inevitable night. Eve disengaged the COM as the last frames of the alien Adam in the video disappeared from the monitor.

Eve smiled and snuggled back into Richard's arms. Richard peered into her eyes and brushed a wisp of hair from her forehead.

"That is worthy of a Pulitzer Prize in Journalism." he proclaimed with adoration.

She tilted her head and pursed her lips.

"You, my dear, don't get a vote."

"No, but I might have some pull to get it nominated." he smirked.

She backhanded his arm and threatened.

"Don't you dare!"

Richard feigned a broken arm, dangling it limply.

"Oww! Now, how can I hold you?"

She draped his limp arm over her shoulder, "Just like this." as she snuggled deeper into his chest.

The COM on the wall flashed an alert.

Richard sighed and said aloud, "COM; answer audio."

"COM audio engaged." was the response.

"Good evening." Richard said, Sal's voice probed the room.

"Richard?"

Richard recognized the entreaty.

"Okay Sal, you found me…so you go hide and I'll count to ten to give you a head start."

"You don't know how tempting that game would be if I could hide with the Alphas. Maybe then I could understand their real reason for sending the 'diffusions' to earth." Sal retorted, Richard

1

slightly furrowed his brows and leans up off of the bed while slowly untangling his arms that he had wrapped around Eve.

"Sal, this isn't going to be a 'We've been blindsided' conversation is it?"

"Well yes and mostly no." Sal said, Richard stood up and walked over to a settee. He took a robe that was draped on it and donned it. He walked over to face a monitor. He pressed a button and Sal appeared on the monitor. Richard sat down on a sofa and took a breath.

"Okay, Sal how bad is it?"

Sal wrinkled his face somewhat and began, "Let me back up for a bit. The Alphas have been totally forthcoming about the effects of the diffusions. We are suffering no ill effects from them. And their intent is totally humanitarian, or maybe I should say exo-humanitarian."

Richard's wrinkled face matched that of Sal's.

"I'll have to add that word to my lexicon when you give me the definition."

Eve joined Richard, wearing acceptable attire, and sat next to him on the sofa and nodded to Sal.

"Good evening Sal." She offered.

Sal smiled and returned, "Good evening to you as well Ms. Walker. I hope I'm not interrupting."

She smiled and replied, "I've grown accustomed to interruptions, Sal, and you know better than to call me Ms. Walker."

She settled back on the sofa.

"Please, I'm intrigued by your new word's explantation."

Richard chuffed, "Sal; quit hitting on my girl and give us the breakdown of your exo-discovery."

Sal shook his head, "Trying to one-up me Richard? I've got the rights to 'exo'."

Eve intervened, "Now boys."

Richard smiled, "Okay Sal, let's have it."

Sal paused and took a breath, "Okay, but it's a long walk down this road."

Richard asked.

"Are we gonna need some popcorn?"

Sal replied, "Yeah, and bring a drink too."

Richard shrugged, "I have my walking shoes on."

Sal nodded and began, "I've been hanging out at Hat Creek with Amir and Dominique, soaking up the signal data stream translations. I had them pull up some of the earliest data streams the Alphas had sent to other systems and retranslate them with the new technology. We were pleasantly surprised to learn that signals from various systems were found to be of credible intelligent design."

Richard said, "Okay but, I don't see a downside to that. That's great news."

Sal smiled, "Richard, we're still walking."

Richard waved his hands to continue.

"We found that the Alphas are also in communication with the Wolf 1061c, a planet thought to be similar to that of an early Venus.

Richard leaned up and started to utter a response.

Sal held up his hand, "Still walking."

Richard nodded and leaned back down.

"We only have one-half of the translation, the Alpha side. It implies that the Wolf planet would receive the almost the same 'diffusion' to their planet as earth, but only after earth received its diffusion."

Sal paused and Richard sat in thought.

Sal continued.

"On that information I have questions for the Alphas, but they haven't created an 'open channel' for several days. They have sent us their blueprints for their 'time-wave' technology but, we haven't been able to duplicate their technology to send and receive signals on our own time wave."

Richard cocked his head in thought.

"Sal, the implication on the surface is that we were guinea pigs, but I believe there is a reasonable explanation."

"I agree Richard, but I would not be a scientist if I did not seek an explanation."

"Have you told the President about this?" Richard asked.

"Yes, he was my first call and he is of the same mind that there is no nefarious intent." Sal related, "But the better news is that there is apparently more intelligent life on at least one other planet."

"You said the other planet that the Alphas contacted was Wolf something, where is it?" Eve asked.

Sal explained.

"Wolf 1061c, it's in the Ophiucus constellation 13.8 light years away and is in a habitable zone for exoplanets. But, one of the questions I have is, what connection is there between Earth and Wolf?"

Sal paused, "I came back to DC to pick up some of my equipment and then I'm sojourning to the VLA to follow-up on a strange report of sporadic contacts with the Wolf system by a reclusive star gazer using their array."

Richard interjected, "How does the VLA justify the expense of the allocation of their system? That's gotta be thousands of dollars worth of access time?

Sal wrinkled his nose, "That's the strange part; billionaire Robert Atwood has been paying cash for the access time for his associate to use the system."

Richard leaned up and asked, "Who is the guy using the system?"

"That's even more intriguing, apparently his name is Al and he is a part-time curator of sorts at the Astronomical Lyceum in Magdalena."

"I'll have the FBI check him out." Richard offered, "Way ahead of you there," Sal said, "I talked to Pepper and he had nothing on file. He was going to send an agent to check him out, but I told him I would go down there myself. I have to find out his story first-hand and why he's interested in the Wolf system."

Eve added her thoughts, "Sal, you sound like a dogged journalist chasing a story."

Sal smiled, "I can understand now, the 'rush' you feel when you uncover the layers of the unknown."

"Sal, speaking of the unknown… how long until we are able to create our own time wave portal?" Richard queried, Sal shook his head, "Richard, I'm not sure we will ever be able to duplicate their technology. Looking over some of the specs I don't believe we have the minerals, ores and the power source that are required to build such a device. One hope is that the Alphas can show us a workaround."

"Sal, I have faith in your teams ability to conquer anything." Eve said.

Sal smiled, "Thanks Ms…Eve, but sometimes one has to face reality."

Eve smiled and offered, "Sal, it wasn't so long ago we didn't know aliens existed. Every day brings a new reality."

Sal nodded, "Goodnight."

He disappeared from the monitor.

Richard leaned back on the sofa and put his arm around Eve.

He smiled at her, "Didn't know that philosophy was in your wheelhouse; I learn something new about you every day."

Eve raised her eyebrows and said as she tugged on the belt on Richard's robe.

"Maybe I can show you something else new about me."

Managing The Fallout

Tsirch sat at the Resolute desk thumbing through pages of reports and glancing up to one of the monitors on the desk.

A tone sounded and Tsirch tapped a button on the side of the desk.

"Yes Philip."

"Mr. President, Madam Secretary is here."

"Thank you. Send her in."

The door opened and Marilyn Richter walked in and closed the door behind her. She continued in and stood in front of the President.

"Good morning Mr. President."

Tsirch stood and smiled, "And a good morning to you Madam Secretary. Let's get comfortable." He pointed to the sofa area.

Marilyn turned toward the sofas and placed her briefcase on a table and waited for the President to sit and then she sat down.

At that moment, the president's Chief of Staff, Joel Mack knocked on the door and came in without an invitation carrying his VPC (Virtual Personal Connection device).

He scanned the room and saw that he had caught Tsirch's eye and nodded to Marilyn, "Good morning Mr. President and Madam Secretary, sorry I'm late."

Tsirch replied, "Good morning Joel."

Richter added her greeting. "Good morning Joel."

Joel deftly made his way toward the sofa area and sat on the sofa a short distance from Marilyn. Joel sat his VPC on the table.

"DHS Secretary Van Hook and FBI Director Martin are on their way, Mr. President." he stated then added, "The National Intelligence Director, Carol Brown, will be here in twenty-minutes and Domestic Security Commander, Colonel Narkiewicz, and CIA Director Jack Silver are standing by on a COM feed."

Tsirch smiled, "Joel, you've only been back for one day, you can't pack everything you missed in the past three weeks into one day."

Joel nodded and countered, "But, I was not here to help guide you through one of the most significant events in history; alien contact."

Tsirch shook his head, "Joel, we had daily contact while you were undergoing *your* most significant life event; ridding yourself of cancer. Don't think your part in the alien contact situation was insignificant even though you weren't physically here. You organized almost every meeting and COM call from your hospital bed."

Joel shook his head slowly, "But I wasn't there to witness, in person, Adam's earthly introduction."

Tsirch sighed, "But you will be there for any ensuing events." He paused. "Right now you are an integral component in our navigation of the varied human responses to the reality of alien contact."

Joel half-smiled, "Thank you Mr. President." and quickly continued, "Is there anyone else you would like to join us?"

Tsirch thought for a moment, "Yes, Dr. Uschin."

Joel cocked his head, "I thought you would like his input, but he is en route to the VLA in New Mexico and won't be available for a COM feed for at least four more hours. And also I included your press secretary, January Yee."

Tsirch chuffed, "See Joel, you are indispensable."

Joel stood, picked up his VPC put it in his pocket and asked, "So, if you and Madam Secretary are ready, we should make our way to the situation room."

Tsirch and Marilyn stood and Marilyn picked up her briefcase and they followed Joel out the side door.

The trio made a couple of turns and stopped at the elevator door and Joel pressed the call button.

The door opened and they stepped in. The door closed and it opened when the elevator reached the basement. They stepped out and made a couple of short turns and arrived at the situation room.

To many, the situation room is unexpectedly narrow but well appointed with comfortable swivel chairs situated around a long table. Several COM monitors were fixed to both side walls and a large COM was on the wall at the far end.

Joel was the first in the door and pressed several buttons on the wall beside the door. The COMs lit up and light showered the room. Tsirch followed him in and stood by the chair at the head of the table. Marilyn walked around and took a chair to the immediate left of Tsirch, and placed her briefcase on the floor beside her. Tsirch on seeing her sit, took his seat. Joel went over to a cabinet and opened it. He took out several thick folders and began placing them on the table at various seats beginning with the president.

There was a knock on the door and Joel completed his activity and then answered the door.

Kevin, the president's butler, was at the door with a serving cart. Joel held the door open while Kevin pushed the cart in and Joel closed the door and remained by the door.

Kevin guided the cart over to a serving table and began to transfer a few cold beverage pictures and three hot beverage containers from the cart to the serving table.

When the cart was emptied, Kevin pushed it back out the door to a waiting kitchen staff member. Kevin closed the door and turned around and went over to the serving table and stood.

There was another knock on the door and Joel opened it.

FBI Director John "Pepper" Martin and DHS Secretary Julia Van Hook stood at the door and Joel greeted them as he waved them in.

"Good morning Secretary Van Hook and Director Martin."

Van Hook smiled and nodded, "Good morning Joel."

Martin smiled and nodded also.

"Yes, good morning to you also, Joel."

The two made their way into the room, each carrying a valise, and Joel was about to close the door when he noticed two other participants coming down the corridor, National Intelligence Director Carol Brown, carrying a briefcase and Presidential Press Secretary

January Yee. Joel held the door and Yee stopped and offered Brown the first entry to which she nodded acceptance as she stepped in.

"Thank you Mr. Yee."

Yee smiled, "Of course Madam Director."

They both stepped in and Joel closed the door.

The four entrants stood for a moment and Tsirch stood and went to each one and shook their hand addressing them individually;

"Secretary Van Hook, Director Martin, Director Brown and Mr. Yee."

Each responded with their greeting, "Mr. President."

Tsirch was smiling and continued, "Ladies and Gentlemen you may sit anywhere there is a folder on the table and a pop-up display is available for your VPCs."

Tsirch returned to his seat.

Secretary Van Hook sat to the right of the president and sat her valise on the table and Director Martin sat next to Van Hook, placing his valise on the table also.

Director Brown sat her briefcase on the floor and sat next to Marilyn Richter, Yee sat next to Brown and took his VPC out of his coat pocket and put it on the table. Joel took the last seat next to Yee.

Tsirch scanned the faces at the table.

"Thank you all for coming this morning. While you peruse the documents in the folders, Kevin will take your beverage selection and lunch orders while we wait for our COM guests to make their appearances."

Kevin took his cue and walked over to the President and began with him.

"What will you have Mr. President?"

Tsirch smiled, "How about hot tea and an avocado and shrimp salad with clam chowder?"

Kevin nodded, "Of course, sir."

He pivoted to his left and took Marilyn's order and continued on down the table to Joel. After taking their orders he walked back around the table and took requests from Secretary Van Hook and Director Martin.

When he finished taking orders he proceeded to fulfill the beverage requests for each guest. When he finished taking orders and serving the beverages, Kevin left the room.

Joel stood and addressed the group.

"I've taken the liberty of sending each of you digital copies of the documents in the folder and reference materials."

Several of the attendees had already taken out their VPCs and activated the pop-up display that slid up out of a slot in the table. Joel sat back down.

Van Hook held her VPC aligning two fingers with the print readers on the device and held it up to her face and activated the facial recognition. The device vibrated in her hand and she sat it next to the pop-up display. A virtual keyboard appeared in front of the display.

Marilyn continued going through the hard copies in the folder and was the last to retrieve her VPC from her briefcase and aimlessly placed it on the table as one of the pages in the folder caught her attention.

"Mr. President," she said without looking up from the page, "this blurb from Lieutenant Smithy at Domestic Security... is her assessment of Segr8's connection to the Islamic State and FATA been verified?"

Tsirch looked earnestly at Marilyn, "Very astute of you to focus in on one of the major topics of this meeting."

Tsirch continued.

"Commander Narkiewicz questioned her sources and found that Silver had the same intel from his CIA operatives and it was verified by Homeland."

Tsirch took a breath.

"When they get on the COM you can dig into it."

Marilyn wrinkled one of her brows and slowly shook her head.

"This does not bode well." She looked across the table at Van Hook, "Julia, how extensive is this threat?"

Julia took a short breath, "It seems that the Indonesian collective, FATA, has been supplying black market thermite grenades to various subversive factions; Segr8, including the Hi-Hangers, Silkmates and the Anti-Adam movement."

She paused and looked across and nodded at Carol Brown, NID director, "Director Brown has coordinated with our department and with Domestic Security Commander Narkiewicz in tracking various shipments."

Director Brown picked up the dialogue, "In addition to Homeland, DOD General Porter brought Domestic Security to the table and they have been an integral part in securing High Value Targets from possible attacks."

As if they were listening, two COMs lit up and the video feeds of Commander Edward Narkiewicz, Lieutenant Brie Smithy and CIA Director Jack Silver were displayed.

Tsirch noticed the three guests and greeted them.

"Welcome Commander Narkiewicz and Lieutenant Smithy."

The two responded in unison.

"Thank you Mr. President."

Tsirch continued, "And you Director Silver, you are just in time to defend yourself."

The faces of the group as a whole showed a quizzical expression. Silver looked at the display on his monitor. The names of each participant displayed below the images. He scanned the faces on his display. He smiled and chuffed then he retorted, "Thank you Mr. President, but for me I need to know which skeletons in OUR past you are referring to, but you may have to explain your humor to the Commander and Lieutenant Smithy."

Tsirch smiled and chuckled, "You are right Jack; fortunately the records of OUR skeletons are sealed."

The mood of the group changed to that of relaxation.

Tsirch smiled and looked at the monitor addressing Narkiewicz and Smithy.

"My apologies to you both, Commander and Lieutenant, Director Silver and I have a compromised history."

He light-heartedly continued, "But, actually Commander and Lieutenant, you WERE the topic of discussion," he paused, "your part in the security of HVT's from the FATA, Segr8 and other factions was brought up."

The Commander replied, "We are ready to answer all of your inquiries, sir."

As each member of the group activated their VPCs, their name appeared above their pop-up display. Additionally, when they spoke, their name on the monitor of a COM viewer would highlight itself.

Marilyn spoke first.

"Thank you Commander," she paused as she looked at a page in the folder. "I see in your report Lieutenant that the FATA pipeline for disruption of communication arrays has extended to our domestic contingents. Have you identified the contacts or distribution points?"

"Yes, Madam Secretary," Smithy replied. "We have been coordinating with DHS, CIA, FBI and DOD and the Philippine Anti-terrorist Director Raul Mendoza to facilitate a 'catfish' network using FlashCom media wholly supported by its owner Abby Gonzales." Smithy paused and busied her fingers on her keyboard.

"We followed the money and she revealed the IP addresses and I am sending you the pictures to your sub-screen of the major players in this chain of subversion."

Several pictures appeared on a separate monitor and on each of the pop-up displays of the group.

Commander Narkiewicz interjected, "I would be remiss if I didn't give Lieutenant Smithy the bulk of the credit for taking the lead on this project."

Brie turned her head, shook it slightly, tightened one corner of her mouth, squinted at Edward and countered, "And you Colonel are just window dressing? I think not."

She continued, "As I was saying, these individuals are the focus of our attention: Parker Heiser of Seattle and David Poole of Little Rock, both head up Segr8 and are currently in custody, but yet run the group; Harvey Norman of Baltimore, the Hi-Hangers leader; Carrie Milton, the creator of the Anti-Adam movement; Silky Mason of Alexandria the leader of the US faction of the Silkmates; and the head of the snake, Alfaro Garcia the self-appointed leader of the FATA, Filipine Asian Terrorist Anarchists."

Smithy paused and continued, "Garcia is the supplier of the black market thermite grenades that have been successfully used in partially melting one of the telescope arrays in Jakarta."

She took a breath and continued, "FBI Director Martin has more information about the changes in tactics of the various subversives."

Tsirch looked over at Martin, "Okay Pepper, I guess you are in the hot-seat."

Martin smiled and began, "Van Hook and Director Brown can jump in at anytime. But for my part, it seems that there is a great amount of misinformation and disinformation driving the actions of those that would do harm to the people and facilities that communicate with the aliens. The recent attempts to stop communication with the aliens by coating the radio telescopic arrays with reflective paints or coatings for the most part were parried by law enforcement. In the few instances where they were successful in coating the arrays it had no effect on the actual communication. The coatings were removed without any resulting damage. There were other attempts to interfere with the holographic appearance of Adam by delivering EMP waves at the hologram but as you know that had no effect whatsoever."

Marilyn took advantage of Pepper's pause.

"Director Martin, we know that the wearing of tin foil hats and foil coverings are of no defense against alien radio waves, as the aliens aren't sending radio waves to infect the brains of humans, but why is that belief so pervasive. Who is disseminating that misinformation?"

Martin shook his head.

"I've been working with Abby Gonzales at FlashCom to identify the source but the viral nature of the misinformation makes it difficult to counter. People believe what they want regardless of evidence to the contrary. Science fiction yet prevails"

Marilyn continued her queries.

"Has Ms. Gonzales had any success in tracking the FlashCom sources of the thermite grenade deliveries or locations?"

Van Hook spoke up.

"I can help you there Madam Secretary. FlashCom has been instrumental in supplying the addresses of several accounts and Homeland with the help of the CIA, FBI and Lieutenant Smithy, have derailed six deliveries in the US and prevented several major shipments from Puerto Princesa on Palawan Island north of Brunei. One of the targets was the Parkes Radio Telescope in Australia and fortunately the CIA alerted the authorities and the perpetrators were apprehended along with the thermite munitions and prevented the attack."

There was a knock on the door and Tsirch said, "Yes come in."

Kevin entered the room.

"Mr. President, I was just wondering if anyone needs a refill."

Tsirch looked around the dais and several raised their hands and Kevin attended to their needs.

Marilyn queried Director Silver.

"Jack, has the CIA back-channeled the Chinese, Russian and Eurasian counterparts about the threats?"

Silver replied, "Affirmative Madam Secretary, even the Islamic community has sent out an advisory denouncing the attacks."

Marilyn was surprised.

"Really? That goes counter to their religious take on the aliens being a precursor to Islamic Armageddon."

Suddenly, another face appeared on the COMs. The Vice President broke into the conversation.

"Perhaps I can enlighten you on this subject."

Tsirch smiled and stifled a chuckle on seeing Richard on the monitor.

"Mr. Vice President, welcome to the conversation."

Most of the group was surprised by his grand entrance.

Marilyn smiled, "Why am I not surprised by your intrusion Mr. Vice President."

Director Silver commented, "Richard...er, Mr. Vice President, you are going to have to teach me how you do that."

Richard responded as expected, "Jack, I would love to tell you, but then, of course," Silver and Pepper Martin joined him in finishing the rest of the quote, "*I'd have to kill you.*"

Richard smiled.

Marilyn continued, "As you were saying Mr. Vice President..."

Richard shook his head and offered, "Okay, first of all let's call me 'Richard' for the purpose of this meeting."

He urged compliance by nodding his head and extending his hands to faces on his side of his monitor.

Most of the group nodded affirmative.

"Anyway, actually as I recall the term should be Islamic eschatology. That represents a series or signs that the 'end of times' are upon us. But many of the religious scholars are divided or more accurately scrambling for an appropriate application to ascribe this event to. Much of the discussion shies away from the usual final events as a divine intervention, as that would imply that the aliens are god-like, and that certainly is not part of a preordination in scriptures."

Tsirch smiled and imparted an observation, "Thank you reverend Natás for your dissertation."

Marilyn continued the thought line.

"There are many that seem to be of the same mind, Richard.

There is confusion that has bread distrust in applying religious dogma and that in turn angers those that deny reality."

Kevin had been listening to the conversation and tentatively asked, "Pardon me Mr. President, but would it be permissible to weigh in as an interested party?"

Tsirch smiled and asserted, "Kevin, of course your comments would be welcomed."

"Thank you, sir. I would like to say that I think that 'fear' is a major issue of the people."

Richard interjected, "Kevin, can you expand on that my friend?"

Kevin started slowly, "Well, uh. When I speak with my friends about the aliens, some seem to fear what they might be up to. Some want to stop them, some want to embrace them and their technology, while others just want to hide."

Tsirch asked, "And Kevin, what would you like to do?"

Kevin thought and smiled, "Me, I think it's kinda cool. I don't see them as a threat, as you have said Mr. President; We can't change what has happened. Just as the alien Adam said; we can only deal with the here and now. The future is coming whether we want it or not."

Press Secretary Yee smiled and nodded.

"Mr. President, I think you have found my replacement."

Tsirch chuckled and stated, "It would be a salary savings, Yee."

Tsirch smiled at Kevin, "My dear friend, if only your words could go viral on FlashCom our nation would rest much easier."

Richard smiled and commented, "Mr. President, if you're serious at all, I happen to know a journalist that could make that happen."

Tsirch glanced up at Richard and paused in thought, "I may take you up on that, Richard. But for now," he turned back to Kevin, "Thank you Kevin for your keen insight."

Kevin appeared somewhat embarrassed by his unsolicited audacity.

"I apologize Mr. President and to everyone, for the interruption."

Tsirch stood and replied, "Kevin we have had many personal interactions over the years and this is yet another pleasant and memorable conversation."

Tsirch held out his hand and took Kevin's hand and shook it.

"Thank you."

Kevin returned the smile.

"Yes, Mr. President."

He turned and when back to the serving table.

Tsirch sat back down and looked at Director Martin.

"Pepper, I see there were several attempts to attack a bio-lab in New York and an array at the Hat Creek SETI site. Do you have an update?"

Pepper nodded, "The attack on the bio-lab was limited to melting an external door and fortunately another device that had landed on the roof, failed to detonate." He paused, "The attack at the Hat Creek SETI site only burned some external wiring connections. I credit the local law enforcement and the National Guard for apprehending the Segr8 and Hi-Hanger activist involved in the attacks." He looked up at the COM at Commander Narkiewicz and Lieutenant Smithy.

"Thanks again to your soldiers, Colonel and Lieutenant."

The Commander replied, "We appreciated the recognition, Mr. Director."

Marilyn added, "I must say, Mr. President, the coordination of DHS, DSC, Homeland, local law enforcement and the CIA in these extraordinary times is unprecedented. And our foreign counterparts are to be commended also."

Tsirch nodded, "Their efforts will certainly be passed on to congress and to the people by Mr. Yee."

Yee nodded.

Tsirch added, "And please include the DOD in your commendation remarks."

Yee again nodded, "Of course Mr. President."

Tsirch leaned back in his chair and looked up at the COMs.

"Since we have our resident interloper gracing our meeting; what say you Richard regarding our alien entanglements?"

The Vice President took a modest breath and began, "I spoke to Co-Director Perry Evans at Hat Creek this morning and he is still coalescing the latest combined signal translations from several SETI sites. There are yet more unanswered questions about the alien's technology. Miss Soul and Mr. Hadad have been tirelessly working on retranslating the data over the last year to determine what we missed in what the aliens had sent us. My left-hand man, Lucas Makiev, has been a workhorse at Hat Creek assisting in retrieving old data."

Marilyn interrupted, "I have to ask about the status of the re-creation of the alien communication technology and the analysis of the diffusion particles."

Richard scrunched his face, "Susan Byers and her team have had a fare amount of success in the analyzing the microbes the aliens sent last week. They have found new combinations of minerals, and using the alien spores we found that we can greatly enhance our agricultural production. Additionally, they have combined the microbes that were sent during the Lunar Fall and found that it can scrub our carbon footprint by ten-fold, taking us back to 1930s levels."

He paused, "But as far as the instant communication enhancement…their technology is far beyond our current capabilities. Sal Uschin and many of the world's greatest physicists have been totally immersed in the alien 'quantum mechanics acceleration' quandary."

Richard resettled in his seat.

"There is a flicker of news from Sal though, as he told the President there is someone at the VLA in New Mexico who seems to be using the arrays to send signals to a planet, Wolf 1061c, that the aliens have also contacted.

He is on his way there now to find out more information."

Say Again! You Are Who?

The last time Sal visited the Karl G. Jansky Very Large Array was fifteen years ago. He was poring over documents using his VPC linked to the COM monitor on the back of the seat in front of him. He occasionally glanced out the window of the plane to get his bearings. The flight to Albuquerque was only three hours and he was taking, what he calls this 'quiet time', to recharge. The plane banked port-side as it glided down to the Sunport runway. As the plane came to a stop, Sal opened up his backpack, gathered his VPC and personal COM and put them in the backpack. He waited for the four passengers in front of him to get up and walk down the aisle. He stood up and opened up the overhead and retrieved his carry-on suitcase. He walked past the flight crew, thanked them for the safe flight and exited out to the walkway ramp. He continued into the terminal and immediately noticed his 'ride' standing to one side of the roped-off area. Robert Rudolph had a wide grin to greet his old friend. Sal went up to him and put his suitcase and backpack down and they both bear hugged each other for a long while. They separated slightly and Sal said with a broad smile, "Damn Rudy, it's so good to see you. I thought you were still at the McDonald Observatory in Texas."

Rudy replied, "I was until three months ago, when Honrí at the VLA suggested I help him with a project. And when Johnny called and said you were coming, I had to be the one to pick you up."

Sal chuckled, "Johnny told you I was coming? I just talked to her and she didn't say a word about it."

Rudy laughed, "She knew how much I wanted to see you."

Sal exclaimed, "Wow this is great!" They hugged again.

Rudy said, "Okay let's get you out of here."

He picked up Sal's suitcase and pointed the way to go. Sal picked up his backpack and sidled up to Rudy and put his hand on his shoulder as they walked. They spent the short walk to the terminal exit bantering back and forth like the college chums they were. They arrived at the valet booth and Rudy handed the valet a ticket and they waited for him to return with Rudy's vehicle.

Sal asked, "I hear you are still punching above your weight with Sasha. I don't know how she puts up with such an ugly mutt like you. I always thought she had poor eyesight."

Rudy countered.

"You're no prize yourself, and how that diva Congresswoman Walsh keeps her sanity hanging around you is unfathomable."

Sal reflected, "We gotta admit we both got the brass ring with our women."

Rudy nodded.

A vehicle pulled up to the curb and the valet hopped out, went around and opened the door and held it for Sal.

Sal looked with wonder at the transportation offered.

"Rudy; is this yours or did you steal it?"

Rudy beamed with pride, "It's mine."

"It looks like a '84 Dodge Duel-Hydro Car, but you've tricked it out to the max."

Sal tossed his backpack over the front seat into the back seat and stood in awe looking at the beautiful machine.

Rudy gave the valet a tip and went to the rear of the car opened the hatch and put the suitcase in and it closed automatically. He continued around and stood at the driver's door and urged Sal, "Get your ass in the car buddy."

Sal took a last look and eased in the seat and the valet closed the door. The patrons fastened their seat belts and the transport moved them quickly on their way. The initial sound of the combustion engine eventually gave way to a low whirling sound of the electric motor, most of which was drowned out by the wind funneling past Sal's arm extended out of the window.

Sal admired the accoutrements: Self adjusting bamboo/hemp seats duel HUD's (Head-Up Display), VPC COM displays and sun dimming windshield. Sal reached over and waved his hand near the dashboard and music eased into the cabin.

Sal whispered, "Play Erin Karris." and her song began to play.

"Wow!" Sal exclaimed. "This ride is tres sweet."

Rudy grinned.

"I love driving this car."

Sal smiled.

"I assume we are driving me to Magdalena and not taking another flight, it's about an hour and a half drive."

Rudy replied, "Hell no, this is Air-Rudy at your service. We should be there in sixty-eight minutes. I have a pilot's license."

The 'flight' to Magdalena was very smooth and time passed quickly with deep conversation between the pals. And true to his word 'Air-Rudy' pulled up to Rudy's place in Magdalena with a minute to spare.

Sal questioned, "Rudy, I have a reservation at a motel."

Rudy replied, "No, you have the run of the house at Rudy and Sasha's bed and breakfast."

"I can't impose on you bud." Sal said, Rudy countered and shook his head with a death stare, "You don't want to disappoint Sasha do you?"

Sal bowed his head in submission and whimpered, "No, I guess not."

"Okay then, get your fat ass out of the car and get into the house." Rudy smiled as he demanded compliance, Sal did as he was told and stepped out of the car. He closed the car door and opened up the back passenger door and retrieved his backpack and closed the door. Rudy recovered Sal's suitcase from the rear hatch of the car.

Sal followed Rudy to the front door and Rudy opened it.

He stepped in and announced, "Sasha put the shotgun away, it's me baby. I brought a homeless guy to stay with us for a while."

Rudy sat the suitcase down.

Sasha yelled from another room, "I hope he cooks and cleans."

Sal countered loudly as he entered the door and sat his backpack on a couch, "No, but he does eat and sleep…" he paused, "a lot."

He heard her laugh and momentarily she entered the room. She quickly ran to Sal and snugly embraced him.

She said, "I might have known Rudy would bring home someone as worthless as he is."

Rudy raised his hands in dismay.

"Hey…I'm standing right here."

She let go of Sal and shrugged at Rudy.

"Well, maybe you aren't that bad."

She went over to Rudy and eased into his arms and planted a big, long lip-lock on him.

Sal shook his head, "Okay you guys. Get a room."

They separated laughing.

She looked at Sal.

"Darn it's good to see you."

"Yeah, it's been about a year, but at least we've talked on COM." Sal offered.

"But that's not the same as an in person hug."

Sal agreed, "That's for sure."

Rudy picked up the suitcase. He put his hand on Sal's shoulder, "Let's get you settled in to your room."

Sal grabbed his backpack as Rudy guided him down the hall.

Rudy set the suitcase on the bed.

"Here you are bud. I'll go help Sasha with breakfast."

Sal put his backpack on the bed also and finished settling into his room. He went out the door and followed the voices into the kitchen. Rudy and Sasha were finishing up preparing breakfast.

Sasha said, "I know it's early for your 'jet-lag' to have breakfast but, 'hungry-man' here," nodding to Rudy, "said you need to get acclimated to the time change sooner or later."

Sal smiled, "I've become used to 'time travel' accommodations in my line of work."

"Yeah, I get the reference," Rudy said, smiling, "I've been wondering, myself, about the alien communication issue."

Rudy picked up a serving tray of food and Sasha picked up another tray of food.

Rudy stated, "Let's take breakfast in the dining room."

Sal followed them into the dining room.

Sal sat down and they placed the trays of food in the center of the table. Pitchers of water, iced tea and OJ were on the table.

Sal made his selections of beverage and breakfast options.

Sasha inquired, "Rudy tried to explain, but I don't really have a grasp on the concept of instant communication with the aliens that are light years away. How's that possible?"

Sal chewed on a bite of his pancakes and also on Sasha's question.

He took a drink and swallowed the food.

"You are asking the same question the whole community of physicists is fumbling with."

Sal shook his head and simply replied, "We don't know." He continued, "All of our understanding of how time works has been shattered. Trying to see time as linear and as a wave length while incorporating the 'string theory' is totally incomprehensible, and yet, it apparently somehow exists; if you are to use the explanation our alien friend 'Adam' described in his dialogue with Dominique."

Rudy made his observation, "I've tried to look at this whole alien thing as a "hoax", but the facts are what they are. There was an alien diffusion of particles; and there was a conversation with the alien; and we did see and hear a hologram of Adam all over the world." He paused. "This is giving me a headache."

Sal chuffed.

"Join the crowd."

He took a few more bites of his pancakes, "Okay where are the treasures? Robin's got to be seven and Tyler's nine, right?"

Sasha smiled and corrected Sal, "No, Robyn says she is 'seven and a half'."

Sal smiled, "Oh, pardon me, seven and a half."

"They're still in school. You forget, time change?" She noted.

Sal looked at his watch and nodded, "Yeah, it is only ten o'clock." Sal continued, "So Rudy, you said earlier that Honrí wanted you to help on a project, what kind of project?"

Rudy began, "I've been subbing for Honrí assisting a high roller using the arrays in bouncing signals to a Red Dwarf Star system in the Ophiucus constellation. It is peculiar to me that so much time is spent in collecting data being sent to and from one of its exo-planets from different sources."

Sal slowly nodded in recognition, "Okay, Rudy let me guess, the exo-planet is Wolf 1061c."

Rudy scrunched his brows, "And you know that because?"

Sal said, "Because… that is why I'm out here. That 'high roller' is Richard Atwood and he has had an astronomer collecting data from that planet, and that just happens to be the same planet the Alphas have been in contact with and had delivered similar diffusions to, as the ones sent to Earth."

Rudy exclaimed, "Wholly shit. What is the aliens' interest in that planet? And how does he know that they have been in contact with it? We have no way of tracking signals that quickly. It would take years to see the pattern, and Wolf is 14 light years away. Unless…" Rudy paused, "he knew what he was looking for."

Sal interjected, "That begs the question and reason I am here; who is this astronomer and how and what does he know about the Alpha's connection to Wolf?"

Rudy shrugged, "I've seen the guy for the past three months or so." He stopped and reflected his thoughts, "He started showing up," Rudy paused again and spoke in a deliberate meter, "beginning with the synodic periods that probably coincide with that of Wolf and Alpha Centauri." Rudy took a large breath, "Wow! This is really very intriguing."

Sal pressed again, "Who is this guy?"

Rudy related, "His name is Al. He's a reclusive type, long hair, beard and usually puts on tinted glasses when you talk to him face to face, that is, when he talks at all. He buries his self in his work."

"Is he there today?" Sal asked.

Rudy said, "I'm sure he is, lately he's been there until around 1600 hours."

Sasha interjected feigning exclusion, "Well, thanks for the talk guys."

Sal said, "I'm sorry Sasha, I..,"

She smiled and held up her hand in a 'stop' gesture.

"Hey I'm used to shop talk. You guys take off."

Sal sopped up some of the syrup on his plate with the last bite of his pancakes and took a drink of his orange juice.

He stood up, "Thanks for the breakfast Sasha."

Rudy stood up also and went over to her and hugged and kissed her as she sat.

"Thanks babe, love you."

Sal went to his room and retrieved his backpack and joined Rudy at his car. They buckled up and jettisoned to their next adventure.

The duo's conversation made the twenty-minute drive pass quickly. As they rolled past the iconic National Radio Astronomy Observatory, Sal soaked in its historical significance as one of the first of its kind. Moments later they arrived at the Jansky VLA.

The VLA consisting of twenty eight parabolic antennas (dishes) laid out in three equal directions from a center point for about twelve miles each. That design creates a virtual 'dish' of a twelve mile diameter, hence the name: Very Large Array.

They departed the vehicle and went to the door and Rudy used his ID card to gain entry to the complex. Sal followed him over to the director's office and opened the door. Honrí Foster was sitting at a COM watching it intently.

Rudy caught his attention and Honrí stood up.

"Honrí, I have the package you were expecting."

Honrí smiled and extended his hand to Sal. Sal took the handshake offered, "Honrí, it's good to see you again."

Honrí replied, "Sal it's been too long. What a year?"

Sal thought, "Yes; probably so. We were at the Frankfort symposium." Sal added, "Thank you for accommodating my intrusion."

"Are you kidding, I'm honored to have a scientist of your renown grace our site." Honrí paused, "I was surprised by your request, I'm not sure if my array will give you any extra boost than the signals at Hat Creek."

Sal squints an explanation, "That's not exactly why I'm here. I am curious about Atwood's use of your array to explore the Wolf exoplanet in the Ophiucus system."

Honrí replied, "Well Rudy, here, is the one to talk to about that."

Rudy stated, "I told Sal as much as I could, but he wanted to speak to the scientist gathering the data."

Sal added, "What do you know about this guy?"

Honrí explained, "Not a lot, he is likeable, but reclusive. Keeps to himself and is fanatical in his data compilation."

Honrí shrugged, "Rudy can take you to him. He's out on station seven."

Sal nodded, "Thanks Honrí."

Rudy turned and went out of the office with Sal following. They turned left and walked over to station seven."

The individual in question was sitting at the station and sternly focused on the screen on the COM and entering data on the keyboard, and didn't notice his visitors.

Rudy stood next to him and spoke, "Al, I'd like you to meet a friend of mine, Doctor Sal Uschin."

Al seemed to freeze his activity when he heard Sal's name. He started to reach for his dark glasses, but instead slowly turned his head, initially looking down then slowly looked up at Sal.

Sal looked at the long-haired, bearded man. He nodded at him, "Hi, I'm Sal; it's a pleasure to meet you."

Sal partially extended his hand to shake but, Al didn't seem to want to reciprocate the gesture. Sal peered into Al's face that seemed to grow more and more familiar the longer he canted his head and studied it.

There seemed to be a smile cracking under the beard. Al slowly stood and looked squarely into Sal's face. Sal began to grow more aware of his memory of this visage.

Al's smile partially disguised by his beard confirmed Sal's suspicion.

Al revealed, "Perhaps my old friend would recognized me if I told him my name."

Sal shook his head and announced, "No need, Refario Alvendo 'Gemo."

Sal scooped him up in a mutual bear hug.

Rudy's face displayed total shock, "Say again! You are who?"

Sal backed away and held 'Gemo by the shoulders. He reached up and tugged on his beard and long hair and exclaimed, "Wholly shit, this is real."

Sal began laughing.

Rudy, still perplexed asked,

"Are you saying this is Doctor 'Gemo?"

Sal nodded, "Yes, Rudy. Doctor 'Gemo, alive and well." Sal put his hand on Rudy's shoulder and corrected Rudy's pronunciation of 'Gemo. "Rudy, pal, 'Gemo is pronounced as a hard 'g' like as in 'game-o'."

Sal continued looking back at 'Gemo. "What the hell R.A., you don't write, you don't call."

A smile peaked through 'Gemo's overgrown facial hair as he answered.

"You know that if I made ANY contact with you, technology would track me down and my cover would be blown."

Sal slightly shook his head, "R.A., what or who are you hiding from?" Sal brushed his fingers through 'Gemo's beard, "And what's with this Robinson Caruso look?"

R.A. gave a shrug of obviousness, "Uh, disguise!"

Rudy had been listening to their verbal exchange, but got 'Gemo's attention and held out an anxious hand to shake.

"Doctor 'Gemo," he interceded using the correct pronunciation of 'Gemo, "I know we've talked many times, but I had no idea who you were."

R.A. took Rudy's hand and shook it as he replied.

"Rudy, my friend, I couldn't tell you as it would have hindered the progress of my project."

R.A. released his hand, "I can tell you, Rudy, that your assistance has been exceptional in your fulfilling all of my requests."

R.A. turned to Sal, "Did you know how much, Rudy here, knows about the history and composition of the galactic systems?"

Sal nodded, "Yes, he's my first call if I need to find a fresh perspective of a problem."

Rudy took exception, "My knowledge is of no comparison to your expertise, Doctor 'Gemo."

'Gemo replied and offered a request.

"Rudy, you can try to be humble, but we both know the breadth of your knowledge," he paused, "and please call me R.A. or 'Gemo without the 'Doctor'."

Rudy smiled and shook his head in awe.

Sal pressed on, "R.A., what are you doing HERE?" he asked spreading his arms and hands indicating the building, and then repeated, "What are you DOING here?"

R.A. smiled, "Which question do you want me to answer first?"

Sal offered an indignant pose.

"R.A.?"

R.A. sat back down in his seat.

"Okay, I'll combine your questions in my answer."

He paused and began, "When I returned from the moon after my lab exploded, I began to recreate my analyses of the diffusion from memory; since I believed as everyone else believed that my notes had been lost. I didn't want any distractions so; I scurried to obscurity to my friend Aldo's home in Aachen, Germany. And there I ferreted back and forth to the university for my resource infor- mation. Coincidently, I found that Aldo was an old school mate of Robert Atwood, who had been following my endeavors."

Sal smiled and sighed a connection of thought, "That's your secret benefactor. It's starting to come together now."

R.A. nodded, "Aldo contacted Atwood, who was more than willing to covertly fund any of my research cost. Initially I was focused on recreating my moon-lab analysis of the alien effects of the diffusion on the moon, but I became obsessed by the communi- cations with Alpha Centauri. So, I surreptitiously disseminated my research specs to your lab in D.C. and also the one in Hamburg so the research could be carried on, and I then could devote more time to the data signals and translation from the Alphas and their connec- tion to the Wolf 1061c exo-planet."

Sal shook his head, "You sneaky bastard, that's how we were making breakthroughs in the microbial data composition."

R.A. nodded, "With Atwood's electronic resources, I was spying on your data and compiling it with mine. Your team unknowingly helped me immensely in reconstructing my moon-lab research. I can't wait to get together with them."

As R.A. was speaking, both Sal and Rudy grabbed nearby chairs and rolled them up to R.A. and sat down facing R.A.

Sal settled in his chair and pressed on.

"So, what are you finding in the data streams between the Alphas and the Wolf system?"

"I was trying to dissect the similarities in the translation of the data between those sent to Wolf and those sent to Earth by the Alphas."

"What was your concern?" Sal asked.

"It seems that the Wolf system received almost the same diffusion from the Alphas that had been sent to Earth but, there were slight variances in the microbial makeup. I am trying to calculate the variances to ascertain the composition of the Wolf 1061c exo-planet and compare it to that of Earth."

Rudy tilted his head quizzically, "Such a process doesn't seem possible."

Sal put his hand on Rudy's shoulder, "That, Rudy, is the difference between us and the genius of quantum physics."

Rudy smiled and nodded.

Sal continued, "Okay, not that I can comprehend such a process, have you drawn any possibilities and how would that matter?"

R.A. explained, "If I can determine the microbial differences of the diffusion sent to Wolf 1061c perhaps I will be able to determine the composition of the planet. Then I can better understand the purpose of the diffusions, as it seems that Wolf, in some way, requested the diffusion from the Alphas."

Sal shrugged, "So, you are trying to find out why Wolf asked for the diffusion." Sal paused. "But 'We' didn't ask for a diffusion; we didn't even know about the Alphas or even what to ask for."

R.A. scrunched his face somewhat and continued, "Actually, indirectly we did ask."

Rudy smiled, "This, I've got to hear."

Sal joined Rudy in his quest.

"Okay R.A., tell us."

R.A. sighed and started, "You realize that the Alphas have been collecting our broadcasts for almost two centuries and I'm sure they are aware of how we screwed up our planet with radiation and carbon releases, not to mention our years of land and water mismanagement." he paused, "Haven't we broadcast over the air waves and into space, our problems and sought solutions?"

R.A.'s audience shrugged in agreement.

R.A. continued, "Well, THEY were listening."

Sal sat pensively for a moment.

"So… we effectively sent an SOS."

R.A. nodded, "And the Alphas answered."

Sal followed the logic trail.

"And when we floundered with our analysis of the diffusion waves, they decided to make contact with us and give us a nudge in the right direction."

R.A. shot an acknowledging look at Sal, then asked, "Sal…how in hell can they communicate in real time?"

Sal chuffed, "YOU are asking ME? You are more versed in quantum physics and the 'string theory' than I am. I've wrestled with that until my head hurt. Our mind-meld contingent; Barrett, Jung, Hafed, Karloff and I, have spent hours trying to comprehend the quantum mechanics acceleration process that the Alphas described in the data they sent to create a module. Our fusion power generation process is sufficient according to the schematics, but it doesn't create a 'time-wave' in computer simulations. We enlisted the CERN Large Hadron Collider to simulate the power source structure, and the Collider in Japan is also working on the particle theories."

Rudy added his input, "I've worked a different angle by using a 'black hole' to accelerate it in a time 'worm-hole', but it also failed in my computer simulations."

R.A. held up his hands in a 'hold-on' position.

"Okay, now I'M getting a headache just thinking about it. I've gotta give this a rest for a while."

Sal nodded in agreement.

"How about we call it a day and get you out of here?"

R.A. shrugged his shoulders and looked at his monitor and entered a few key strokes and the COM shut down.

He picked up his VPC and put it in a satchel. He took a deep breath and put his hand on his beard and groomed it.

"Yep, it's about time I came out of the shadows."

He turned to Rudy, "You know of any good barber shops around here Rudy?"

Rudy smiled, "If you want, I can use my hedge shears."

Sal countered, "Or, we can just light it on fire."

R.A. sneered and stood up, "Very funny. I'll opt for a barber shop." He picked up his satchel off the table.

Sal and Rudy stood also.

Rudy pointed to the sun glasses, "Don't forget your sun glasses."

R.A. shook his head, "Don't need them. Not hiding anymore."

Sal hugged R.A. again and they walked together toward the director's office. Sal stopped just before they got to the office. He looked at R.A., "You guys go ahead I've gotta call the President and Richard and tell them we found you before the news hits the street."

R.A. smiled, "I'd be surprised if the VP didn't suspect I was here, given Evelyn's ties to Atwood's niece, Mara Luchia."

Sal furrowed his eyebrows.

"Well, didn't know that." he paused and took his COM out of his pocket, "Okay, I'll give them a heads up."

Rudy and R.A. stopped at the door of the office and knocked. Honrí saw them through the glass door and waved them in. Rudy led them into the office and presented R.A. to Honrí.

"Honrí I'd like to formally introduce you to Al but by his real name, Refario Alvendo 'Gemo."

R.A. held out his hand to Honrí.

Honrí was temporarily stunned and took the offered hand and shook it. He uttered a long no, "Noooooo, YOU are Doctor 'Gemo? No shit?"

R.A. replied, "Sorry I kept my identity secret Honrí, but I needed to work without interference."

Honrí shook his head, "Really, you're Doctor 'Gemo? It's an honor to meet you." He continued to shake his hand.

"Thank you Honrí but drop the doctor title, just 'Gemo or R.A. is fine."

Honrí added, "I have so many questions about your work."

He finally let go of the handshake.

"Honrí, I promise I'll sit down with you and talk, but right now I'd like to unburden my facial hair and visit with my friends. I still have more research to finish and I'll be back tomorrow."

Honrí smiled, "Wow, doctor, uh…'Gemo. Thank you. It's a pleasure to actually meet you."

R.A. smiled, "Honrí you're a wonderful host and the pleasure is mine, and could you try to keep my being here between us, although this will come out sooner or later?"

"Of course, I'll wait until I hear it on the news."

R.A. replied, "Thank you Honrí." and continued, "I've open up my COM station so you can access my data. Use the password 'ADAM' all caps."

Honrí nodded, "Thanks I'll make it available."

Sal came back in the office and shook Honrí's hand.

"Thanks for letting me drop in, Honrí. 'Gemo's being here was a total surprise to us."

Honrí smiled broadly.

"Can't believe it either."

As they turned to leave the office, Honrí said to himself, "Wow Uschin and 'Gemo on the same day."

They continued down the hall and Rudy asked, "Sal, what did the President and the VP say?"

Sal said, "Ren Lang didn't seem too surprised and R.A. was right about Evelyn. She suspected that Atwood knew where R.A. was hiding."

The trio left the building and Rudy asked, "'Gemo where's your car?"

R.A. responded, "I usually call my driver."

"There's no need, Rudy can take us in his time machine."

Sal said as he pointed to the car.

R.A. smiled, "I've admired this vehicle every day and finally I get to ride in it."

Rudy opened both the passenger doors and his passengers entered and secured their bodies. Rudy took the helm and launched the carriage.

R.A. took his COM out of his satchel and dialed.

"Hey Marnie, I'm leaving early and I'm okay. I'm hitching a ride with Sal and Rudy." R.A. listened and continued his part of the conversation, "Yes, Uschin…, yes he knows…, it'll probably be late…, I'll let you know…, sure…, thanks bye."

R.A. hung up the COM.

R.A. noticed Rudy's stare in the mirror and Sal's glance back over his shoulder from the front seat.

They sat in silence for a long moment until Sal turned back to look at R.A. and started to speak.

R.A. held up his hand, "Yes, Marnie is my driver and bodyguard, we live together and, no, we aren't an item. She is twenty-eight, good looking and is one of Atwood's security team."

Sal turned back facing front and chuckled, "I wasn't going to ask."

R.A. scoffed, "Bull shit, that's exactly what you were going to ask. It doesn't take a genius to know what you guys were thinking."

Rudy took exception, "Hey, don't put me in with Sal, I wasn't thinking anything like that."

R.A. chuffed, "Rudy, more BS. You guys are two turds in the same toilet."

The balance of the short twenty minute drive was consumed with ribbing between the verbal combatants.

As they entered town, Rudy asked, "'Gemo you still want to hit the barber shop?"

"Yep, gotta get decent." Before Sal could say anything R.A. jumped in the repartee, "and Sal, that wasn't an opening for your comment."

Rudy smiled, "Guess he does know you Sal."

The car stopped in front of the establishment and Sal noted the name of the, Solon Le Barge, that stumbled in his mind. They all piled out of the car and entered the barber shop.

SOS

There were two COM monitors mounted on the wall both with news channels on the display. A man and a woman patron were being attended to by two other barbers. Rudy saw an empty barber chair and went over to the barber and noticed the name on his smock.

"Paul, we just picked up this derelict and want to see if you can make a man out of him?"

Paul ticked his head and went over to the empty chair and slapped the chair with an apron, "Doctor 'Gemo, it's about time you got rid of that stupid beard and that long hair."

Rudy was taken aback as was R.A.. Sal laughed.

R.A. cautiously walked over to the chair and sat down.

"You know who I am?"

"Of course," Paul said, "This is the only hair salon in this town and I know everyone and everything that goes on in this town."

He tossed the apron around 'Gemo and cinched it up.

"Okay Doc, you want to look like you did when you first came to town or better looking?"

Sal chimed in, "Don't think you could make this sad sack look good unless you do plastic surgery?"

Paul the unflappable countered Sal, "That coming from Doctor Uschin, who can't figure out quantum mechanics acceleration."

Sal's brows lifted in surprise and he looked at Rudy.

"Rudy, didn't know you had a CIA operative in Magdalena."

Paul replied, "Rudy the astronomer, works at Jansky and he and Sasha have two great kids and are relatively new to the town."

Paul added, "And, no I'm not CIA but I do read and pay attention. By the way Doc where are your sun glasses?"

Sal mumbled to Rudy, "Guess he does pay attention."

Rudy went over and sat down in a chair against the wall.

Paul grabbed a comb and scissors and began the transformation.

Sal gazed intently at Paul as he began shearing the locks off of R.A.. He meandered over toward the shelf behind the barber chair and grew a knowing smile as he absorbedthe framed photos displayed prominently behind Paul's station.

As portions of 'Gemo's detached mane fell to the floor, Sal asked, "Paul, can I call you Paul?"

Paul glanced at Sal, "Of course, Doctor Uschin."

Sal uttered, "It's Sal, please."

Paul smiled, "Of course, Mr. Sal Please."

Sal smiled and Rudy laughed quietly.

Sal gestured to one of the photos and suggested, "This must be a photo of you with your mother and father."

"Very good deduction." Paul smiled and said without looking up.

Sal continued, "And the other photo was taken last month after the holographic appearance of the alien 'Adam' at the Capitol."

Paul nodded and continued his work.

Sal looked over at R.A., "R.A. you aren't the only celebrity here."

R.A. replied, "Sal, if you want recognition, we can call the media."

"Not exactly where I was going with that," Sal said and added, "Did you know that you are entrusting the outcome of your appearance to the Honorable House Representative Paul Le Barge of the great State of New Mexico?"

R.A. tried to look over his shoulder at Paul.

"You're not a barber?"

Paul put his hand on R.A.'s shoulder and held him in place.

"Yes, Doctor 'Gemo, I am a certified barber. I'm covering for my Dad while he is on jury duty, and Mr. Sal Please, quit disturbing my customer."

Rudy leaned up in his chair, "Paul, you're a congressman"?"

Paul replied, "Guilty as charged."

Rudy asked, "Sal how did you figure that out."

Sal chuffed, "Duh, I'm a rocket scientist."

Paul laughed, "Rudy it doesn't take a rocket scientist to ascertain my real job, especially when Mr. Sal Please saw a picture of me with his main squeeze, my friend and colleague Johnny Walsh, on my shelf."

Rudy stood and went over to look at the photo. He stared at the photo for a moment, "Yep, that's Johnny and you. Damn! It's a small world. Is this solon your 'side-hustle'?"

Paul shrugged, "I grew up in this barber shop and learned the trade until my mom and dad kicked me out to college. I got a BA in Administration of Justice and ran for congress. End of story."

Sal shook his head.

"Not the end of the story, Rudy, Johnny tells me he is a major player in the Intelligence Committee, which is how he knows so much about the alien situation and the people involved."

Paul continued the snipping and shaving of his customer, "And you might recall I met both you and 'Gemo two years ago at a Fourth of July event in D.C."

R.A. spun in his chair to get a better look at Paul. He shook his head, "Sadly, there have been too many moons since then."

Sal added, "I don't remember that occasion but thinking back, I do recall your being at a dinner function for the Speaker."

R.A. changed the direction of the conversation, "So, Mr. Paul, you mentioned the quantum mechanics acceleration quandary, hopefully you have solved the glitch in our calculations for us."

Paul chuckled and cut another chunk of hair off R.A.'s head and held it in front of R.A.'s face and rubbed his fingers together dropping the hair.

"This is as closed as I get to that solution, Doc. However, my wife has tried to explain the dilemma to me, but I get lost when she gets to the fusion power source applications."

R.A. and Sal became intrigued and R.A. asked, "Your wife discusses that with you?"

Paul turned R.A.'s chair back around, "Doc, I'm trying to focus here." as he grabbed another lock of hair and cut it off. He continued the discussion.

"Yes, my wife. She's been a little obsessed with the quantum theory and time wave correlations since she heard about the alien's assertions."

Sal asked, "What does your wife do?"

Paul replied, "You already know her, she's the head of the physics department at New Mexico Tech in Socorro."

Sal raised his head and nodded in recognition.

"Your wife is Marie Barrett and not Le Barge?"

Paul shrugged, "Yes, she uses her maiden name. She's her own person."

R.A. also nodded.

"Sal isn't Marie one of the members of your think tank?"

Sal replied, "Yes, she's indispensable."

Rudy glanced at each participant of the verbal triad and decided to return to his seat against the wall.

Paul continued pealing his customer's hairy onion growth as he conversed.

"Mr. Sal please, Marie has spent a lot of time on the COM with your team, trying to unravel the quantum question. I wonder when I can get my wife back. It's tough splitting my time with house votes and committee work and having time with her, especially since the aliens invaded our alone time."

"Paul buddy, you realize you are lamenting your concerns to the other half of the equation? Johnny and I have the same difficulties."

R.A. fired his verbal engagement from his chair.

"Gentlemen, you are well aware that the infusion of alien contact has disheveled the lives of every human being and even if there was no more contact with the aliens, the fact remains as Amir Hadad affirmed, 'We are not alone', and from that time forward mankind has to deal with the ramifications and our metaphysical relationship with the universe."

There was a short pause in the discourse.

Rudy chuckled, "Okay, coming from the cheap seats, that's exactly what I was going to say."

Sal smiled and rolled his eyes. Paul paused his performance and looked at Rudy and stated, "Rudy, you need a haircut."

Sal smiled, "Yeah, and I'll hold him down for ya."

Rudy chuffed shaking off the remarks.

"The door to a new future has been kicked wide open. We have fantasized for centuries about this very possibility, and for all of our philosophical preparations; we are yet stunned by its reality. How many more 'unknowns' are out there?"

Paul nodded in agreement.

"I guess we have to follow our alien friend, Adam's advice; live today for life comes at you quick enough."

R.A. gave a supplement, "That's true but we yet need to use our knowledge to prepare for the possible future."

Sal stood pensively, "Yeah, but the problem I have is that, the more knowledge I have the more questions I have about what I don't know."

R.A. gave his suggestion, "Perhaps that's what our purpose is; to seek knowledge."

Paul spun the chair around to allow R.A. to check the reflection of his new visage and asked, "Okay Doc, you want me to leave the mustache or just trim it up?"

R.A. studied the options in the mirror.

Sal started to speak and R.A. glanced at him and Rudy in the mirror and verbally objected, "Ahhh, you and Rudy don't get a vote."

Paul awaited his choice.

Hat Creek Redeux

Amir sat entranced with the COM display while Dominique stood behind him with the same focus. The data and noise filter scans bounced on the display as Amir occasionally entered some keystrokes.

Amir asked, "Is this the same response you had, Dom?"

She delayed her answer, "Mmmmmm." then replied, "No, that is a decidedly different audio scan, but the data stream is the same."

"So…we are closer to opening a contact channel." Amir stated.

"It seems so." she said, "But, we still need to find a stable data stream."

"Maybe Perry can reach out to our SETI group and find the best frequency and spectrum that has the longest range for this data stream."

Dominique patted Amir's shoulder, "I'll go ask him."

She turned to the left and walked down the aisle to the director's office. She stopped at the door and knocked.

Perry Edmonds was sitting at his desk and saw her through the glass door and waived her in.

She opened the door and went over to his desk.

"Perry, we need you to reach out to the group to get a consensus on a stable frequency and spectrum for data stream 41273.4 Alpha."

Perry nodded slowly and glanced at a digital clock on his wall, "It's 1200 hours here, and we can get our western half to gather the info, but we'll have to wait till morning for Europe and the Asian half to wake up."

"Perhaps we can get Virginia Tech, Boston U or VLA to do a quick calculation." She asked, Perry shrugged, "I can try."

Dominique smiled and turned and left the office.

When she got back to her station next to Amir, "Perry was going to make some contacts with the group."

She sat down at her COM and began typing. Her display began changing with her keystrokes.

Amir leaned over from his station to her station, "Dom, did you get the same result from data stream 82557.6 Wolf?"

She thought for a second and entered some strokes on her keyboard. She studied the screen and tilted her head in thought.

"Well…yes and no." She entered a few more keystrokes.

She slid her chair over to allow Amir to move his chair next to her.

"See here, the data stream is the same but the frequency seems to fluctuate."

Amir slid over next to her and studied the screen.

"Could it be it is due to a 'send and receive' variance?"

Dom thought as she scanned the screen.

"But why would the data stream be the same?"

Amir rolled his chair back to his station and looked at Dom.

"There has to be some sort of sub frequency within the same spectrum."

Dom looked back at Amir and shook her head.

"If there is, I can't see it."

Perry's image appeared on the corners of each of Amir's and Dom's COMs.

"Hey you two, Boston and Virginia are compiling their data and it should be available soon, but I got a cryptic response from Honrí at the VLA. He said he's sending his data, but he also has an encrypted message to send but he's waiting for confirmation."

Amir shrugged, "What the heck is that about… encrypted message?"

Perry replied, "Don't know, but he was excited for some reason."

Dom smiled, "Well if he's excited it must be good news. Guess we'll have to wait for it."

*****

Rudy guided his carriage into the driveway and brought it to a stop. The three trailblazers ejected themselves from their capsule. R.A. was smiling as he collected his satchel.

He opened his door and stepped out and closed the door.

"Okay Rudy, I gotta drive this machine."

Rudy dropped his brows and replied, "Well, maybe. I was going to say you have to be a rocket scientist to operate the controls, but I guess you qualify."

Sal posed a query as he walked around the car carrying his backpack, "Rudy, better ask him when is the last time he drove a car. Wait! R.A., do you even have a driver's license?"

Rudy quipped, "He's probably been grandfathered in."

R.A. scrunched his face, "Okay, I can see where this is going. Maybe your wife will take pity on me."

Sal chuckled, "Don't count on it."

Rudy led them up the walkway toward the front door. The door swung open and Tyler smiled at Rudy and hugged him at the waist.

Rudy pressed him against his side, "Hey Buddy, guess who's here?" as he waved toward Sal.

Tyler continued to smile as he moved toward Sal.

Sal dropped his backpack to the ground and squatted down to receive Tyler into his arms.

"Good to see you Tyler. You still have that vintage Tony Hawk skateboard?"

Tyler nodded and continued as he separated from Sal's embrace, "Sure do, but don't ride it much. I have to hide it, cause Robyn wants to ride it. Don't want it to get broken…parts are hard to find."

"Doesn't she have her own board?" Sal asked as he stood up, "Yeah, but she likes mine better. Last week, I caught her with it raking down the hand rails at the park."

"She's pretty good huh?"

"Yep, she's a showoff."

Rudy continued into the house and called out, "Sasha, we have more company."

R.A. yet stood watching the conversation between Sal and Tyler.

Sal put his hand on Tyler's shoulder and aimed him at R.A.

"Tyler this is a friend of mine, Doctor 'Gemo, but I call him R.A."

R.A. held out his hand to shake and Tyler took it and firmly shook it. He looked at R.A. pensively, "I've heard of you. You are a scientist too."

R.A. replied, "Yes sir, Tyler, it's a pleasure to meet you."

Tyler said, "Thank you, Doctor."

R.A. replied, "You can call me R.A."

Tyler smiled, "Okay, you can call me Tyler."

Sal picked up his backpack, "Tyler, how 'bout we head into the house?"

Tyler nodded and let go of R.A.'s hand and went through the door with Sal and R.A. following and R.A. closing the door behind him. Rudy and Sasha were exchanging a hug and broke apart when the saw Sal and R.A. came in.

Rudy made the introductions, "Doctor 'Gemo, this is my lovely wife, Sasha. Sasha, Doctor 'Gemo."

Sasha smiled and stepped up to meet R.A.'s outstretched hand and firmly grabbed his hand with both of hers.

"Please call me R.A."

Sasha grinned, "I shall, but I want to remember this moment… meeting Doctor 'Gemo." she paused and somewhat in awe, said, "and call me 'very pleased to meet you', and also call me Sasha." She was still holding his hand but slowly released her grip. "I'm sorry but, having both you and Sal here is somewhat overwhelming. Rudy and I have discussed the alien/time conundrum but we fall short in our understanding. Maybe now we can get a few more reference points."

R.A. smiled and nodded, "Sasha my dear, your input would be greatly appreciated as every scientist's mind is boggled by the alien's quantum mechanics acceleration quandary."

She added, "Rudy told me you've been hiding out at the VLA."

He nodded, "Yes I have. I needed to work on some alien radio transmission technology without being interrupted."

She asked, "You have any success?"

He smiled and chuckled, "It's a work-in-progress."

She sighed, "Well, maybe some dinner will give you some energy to make more progress."

R.A. held up his hand, "I don't want to impose on you."

She shook her head, "No imposition, it's my pleasure to serve you and Sal in exchange for some 'timely' conversation."

R.A. turned to Rudy, "Rudy; is she always this inquisitive."

Rudy started to answer but both Tyler and Sal spoke up simultaneously, "Yes."

Rudy shook his head and laughed.

"Okay, let's give the inquisition a rest."

He looked at R.A., "R.A. you can put your bag down anywhere."

R.A. took his satchel off his shoulder and sat it on the sofa.

Rudy said, "You guys can sit in here for a bit or we can head on into the dining room."

Sal said, "I'll put my backpack away first." and went down the hallway and Tyler followed him.

R.A. waved his hand to Rudy, "Lead the way."

Sasha and Rudy turned to their left and went toward the dining room and R.A. followed them.

Rudy pointed R.A. to a chair as they enter the room, "You can sit here if you want."

R.A. obliged and sat down. Sasha and Rudy continued on into the kitchen.

Sal went into his room, put his backpack of the bed and stepped out of his room and heard some guitar music coming from a room next to his. The door was partially ajar and he peaked in and saw Robyn picking on a guitar. He knocked lightly on the door. Robyn slowly looked up and saw Sal. A big smile came over her face.

"Sal." she exclaimed. She put the guitar on the bed and ran to the door and opened it.

Sal bent down and received her hug.

"Mom said you were here."

Sal smiled broadly, "Yes, I came all this way to see my little princess."

She backed away slightly and put her hands on each of his shoulders looked into his eyes and expressed with slight exasperation, "Sal, I'm seven and a half, I'm not a little princess anymore. I'm a young girl."

Sal took a modest breath put his hands on her shoulders and softly replied, "I'm so sorry. I didn't realize until this very moment that you are in fact a young and pretty girl."

Robyn's face beamed as she hugged him, "Thank you for noticing." she said in a prim and proper voice.

Sal's face turned serious, "But even young girls want to take on the half-pipe at the skateboard park." he said as he tickled her ribs.

She wiggled and giggled saying, "Yes."

Sal stood, "Okay let's go eat and then you can play some guitar for me later."

She smiled, "Okay"

Sal ticked his head saying, "Come on."

They turned and went down the hallway.

Tyler and R.A. were seated at the table talking when Sal and Robyn came into the dining room. Sal led Robyn over to R.A. to introduce her.

"Doctor 'Gemo I'd like to introduce you to Robyn." R.A. pushed his chair back and stood.

Sal continued, "She used to be my little princess..." Robyn turned her head up at a slight angle, furrowed a brow and displayed a slight scowl at Sal. Sal continued, "but, as you can see now, she is a young girl of seven-and-a-half." Robyn's face molded back into a smile.

"You're Doctor 'Gemo the scientist?" She asked, R.A. bent his head to one side and pursed his lips, "Sal, I believe you are mistaken, I see a young lady, wise beyond her years." he added, "Yes, but you can call me R.A."

"My mommy and daddy said that you were lost." she said.

He chuckled, "Well actually, I was just sort of hiding so I could do some special work."

"Were you hiding from the alien, Adam?" she asked.

He smiled, "Actually, Robyn, that's who I've been hoping to meet."

"Yeah, me too, I have a lot of questions for him." She replied.

He smiled broadly, "We are going to have to have a long talk, young lady."

Sasha interrupted, "Robyn, let's have dinner before we take on the world's entanglements."

"Okay," she said, "Can I sit between R.A. and Sal?"

Sal pulled out the chair next to R.A., "It will be our pleasure to dine next to you."

*****

Dominique and Amir were pouring over the latest frequency and spectrum data from Boston, Virginia and the latest data from VLA. Amir spied the new data on his COM.

"Dom, do you see this new data from VLA, it has data streams from Alpha AND Wolf that matches the frequency and spectrum from the last fourteen months."

She was also looking at the COM, "I see that, but why wasn't this included in the last update?"

Amir added, "Yes, but who compiled it and what made them compare these data streams? This is so suspicious."

Dom punched in some keystrokes and pushed the 'print' key.

"Well, I'm printing it out and taking it to Perry."

"Good idea." Amir agreed.

When the print sequence finished, Dom deftly pealed it off the printer and she and Amir stood and walked down the aisle toward Perry's office.

Perry was sitting in his chair pondering the day's events.

He saw Dom and Amir coming toward his office. He waived them in even before they got to the door. Amir pushed the door open and held it open for Dom to enter first. The door closed slowly behind them. Dom spread the printout on the desk in front of Perry.

"Perry, can you explain why this information is just now showing up? It opens up a whole new approach to the data analysis we've spent weeks trying to unravel."

Perry gave cursory glance at the printout took a breath, exhaled, "You two, grab a seat."

Amir and Dom gazed at Perry then rolled a couple of chairs over to front of his desk and sat purposefully.

Perry began in a reserved but excited manner, "I've been waiting for the go ahead to give you the news, but it has yet to come…but I have to tell someone. If you promise not to say anything to anyone until I tell you it's okay, I'll let you in on the news."

Dom and Amir looked at each other and shrugged agreement.

"This came from Honrí at the VLA. There has been a rogue scientist working on a secret project there for several months.

Dom asked, "What do you mean by rogue scientist, a saboteur?"

"No, hear me out. He's been compiling data from the Alpha and Wolf systems in an effort to link them to the diffusion sent to earth and a diffusion sent to Wolf from the Alpha system."

Amir's face wrinkled, "Earth and Wolf both received diffusions from Alpha?"

"Apparently so, and I don't have all of the details, but the kicker is that the rogue scientist is none other than…"

Dom said the name at the same time as Perry, "Doctor 'Gemo."

"It all makes sense." she said, Amir nodded, "Certainly, who else would have the capability."

They all sat quietly for a moment.

Dom asked, "Okay, where is 'Gemo now?"

"He's at the VLA in New Mexico. Sal found him and they are taking a breather before they break the news of 'Gemo's return."

Amir said, "Well it's no surprise that 'Gemo's been working underground. He attracts too much attention."

Dom added with excitement, "I, for one, can't wait to meet and talk to him…I have a lot of questions."

Amir added, "As do we all."

Assistant Director, Mike Mitchell hurried into the complex carrying a flashing COM. He went past the main office and made a sharp turn into the security office. He sat down at the desk and watched the monitor carefully as the Alpha drone swept to the east in search of the suspicious intruder.

"Security One, base."

"Go for Security One." Darcy Blaine replied.

"The Alpha One drone is probing the east tree line, its infrared picked up some movement in Section 3." Mike advised.

"I should be in your view coming from section 2."

Mike followed the screen display and eventually saw Darcy in his view.

"10-4, I see you now, head a little bit to the left."

Darcy maneuvered the four-wheeler slightly to the left.

Mike saw that she was on Target and continued to watch as she neared the infrared alert sighting.

As she approached the tree line she slowed and chuckled as she veered away from the speckled faun huddled in the tree line.

"Mike, I've got your intruder, a baby deer patiently waiting for its mother to return."

"Copy that, thank you."

Darcy made a sweeping turn and headed back to section 2.

Alpha One drone paused and scanned the tree line, then elevated to a thousand feet above the trees and then went west toward the RV Park and paused at the half-way mark. It scanned the Highway a couple of miles to the west. It turned northeast and flew past the SETI site and eyed some hang-gliders floating toward the Institute. Security Two, Juan Gozicr, was watching the same hang-gliders as he sat on his four-wheeler in section 1. He pulled his COM out of his pocket and opened the display transmitting from Alpha One. He enhanced the visual of the hang-glider. He noticed the glider had a remote guidance system and some sort of satchel suspended from the bar. He took the two-way radio off of his belt and keyed it up.

"Base, Security Two."

Mike was still in the security office and heard the call. He picked up his two-way radio, "Go for base."

"Mike, Check out the Alpha One camera. I have a rider-less, self-propelled, remote controlled glider headed your way. It appears to have a small payload hanging from the bar."

Mike sat down and looked over at the security screen and saw the glider's image. He intently studied the image, and zoomed in on the payload.

"What's the location of the glider?" Mike asked, "It's about two miles northeast of the complex."

"Okay, stand by I'll activate protocol one."

Mike swiveled his chair to the left and pressed a red button that was on the desk. The COM screen to the left lit up. Momentarily a female officer's image appeared on the screen.

On her screen she could see Mike's image. "Domestic Security Command, Cheyenne Mountain, Lieutenant Smithy, at your service Mr. Mitchell."

"Thank you Brie, I have a probable protocol one. If you access my Alpha One camera you'll see my problem."

She visited her fingers on a keyboard and she got the visual of the Drone's view. She studied her screen for a moment, "I agree it looks like a protocol one to me."

She entered some more keystrokes and looked over at another screen.

"I've engaged GPS and see it's approximately two miles from your location, and moving at three miles per hour. What is your choice for removal?"

Mike took a breath as his face pondered the situation.

"I don't think shooting it down would be an effective option. How about we slice and dice the payload and let it drop to the ground. I might be able to drop it in the riverbed."

Smithy nodded her approval, "Sounds like you have the plan, Mike. You want to do it or you want me to take control?"

"I think my security guy, Gozier, can handle it."

Smithy smiled and queried, "That wouldn't happen to be Juan Gozier, would it?"

Mike chuckled, "Yes, do you know him?"

"Sure do, he was a crew chief on an old Huey I used to fly. He's more than capable of doing the job."

Mike smiled, "I'll tell him you gave him the go-ahead."

"Copy that. Tell him I'm watching."

Mike keyed up the two-way, "Security Two, base."

Gozier keyed his mic, "Go for Security Two."

"You have a go from Lieutenant Brie Smithy to slice and dice to payload off the glider, and be advised she is watching."

Juan smiled and took control of the Drone.

"Can you try to drop it in the river bed?" Mike asked.

Juan got a naked-eye visual of the glider and calculated.

"I'll have to get a closer look, it might be close."

He drove his four-wheeler closer and stopped in the middle of a field. He watched the movement of the glider for a minute and decided to move closer to the riverbed. He looked up and down

the riverbed and moved his hands as if he was guiding the drop. Satisfied with his calculations, he turned and sped back to the middle of the field.

He keyed his mic, "Okay Mike, I think I can do it, I want to stay clear in case that shit blows up."

Mike smiled and looked at his screen and entered some keystrokes on the keyboard. He held his hand above the enter key, "Okay Juanito, let me know when you're ready to take control of the Drone."

Juan stabilized the COM on his four-wheeler and replied, "Okay, in 3…2…1…go." He took control of Alpha One and maneuvered it into position. He looked up at the glider and mentally measured the trajectory of the drop of the payload.

Watching the COM screen he deftly guided the Drone blades toward the strap of the payload.

Juan squinted his face, keyed his mic, "I hope the guy controlling the glider doesn't see the Drone."

Mike sighed, "Yeah, that would be a fubar."

Juan bided his time and chose wisely. It wasn't perfect but the strap was cut and he banked the Drone quickly away, and the payload took a full fifteen seconds before it bounced on the edge of the riverbed an exploded. Juan's clearance from the explosion was sufficient. The sudden release of the payload from the hang glider caused it to jet upwards and the remote operator struggled to keep it aloft. Eventually the glider regained its balance and seemed to be searching for the source of the weight loss. It made a few turns and took a dip toward the smoke below. Realizing the payload was no longer available, the remote operator guided the glider back to its original starting point.

Mike in the security office and Lieutenant Smithy at Cheyenne Mountain, DSC, both cheered at the result.

Juan heard a four-wheeler pull up beside him and Darcy hopped off it and held up a hand for a high-five. Juan smiled and obliged. Mike nodded at Smithy on his screen.

Smithy nodded back, "Now my work begins, I have to get FBI agents Knox and Lane on board to track down the perpetrators. I'll try to track the glider back to its source and give them an update."

Mike said, "Yeah, they should be by later for their check-in."

Smithy replied, "This looks like the work of Segr8. They were responsible for the same kind of attack in Berkeley"

Mike said, "Thanks LT."

Smithy replied, "No, thank you Mike. Keep your head on a swivel out there."

"Copy that." Mike said.

Mike's image disappeared from Smithy's screen and her fingers conjured up the icon images of special agents Frank Knox and Robin Lane. While she waited she engaged in other keyboard and another COM screen lit up. A list of locations and small maps appeared on the screen. She took metal note of the screen's content and turned her view the primary screen. Across the room she saw Commander Edward Narkiewicz seated at his desk engaged with someone on his COM. The primary screen came alive with images of agents Knox and Lane.

"Good afternoon a special agents, I trust things are going well."

"The day's been okay so far but hopefully you can make it better." Frank said with a smile.

"You know me too well, just trying to spread more sunshine." She said, "Okay LT, then make us smile." Robin added, "We just had an incident at Hat Creek. It seems that a hang glider carrying an explosive device was possibly enroute to the SETI site. It was summarily dispatched by Security Two, Juan Gozier. It seems that Segr8 wants to destroy the Alpha connection."

Frank's face grew serious, "Was anybody hurt?"

"Negative, he dropped it in the riverbed." she replied.

"Way to go Juan." Robin touted.

Brie nodded, "Yeah, he did good."

Frank asked, "So you think the target was the SETI site?"

"Yes, it was on a trajectory to it."

"If that's the case were going to need some support." Frank said.

"I already got you covered. I pulled two squads of National Guard from Redding and I'm putting one in the RV Park and the other will cover the perimeter of the SETI site. They should be arriving by Hilo within the hour."

Robin inquired, "Are there any dignitaries of note at Hat Creek that could be the target?"

"Actually Hat Creek itself is a target due to his notoriety and at least one major target Dominique Soul and possibly Amir Hadad are there. Either one would be a feather in their cap should they take out one or the other." Brie explained, "Maybe we should take them to a safe house." Frank suggested, Brie sighed, "That's a nonstarter they have to work there, but I'm working on a couple of options. Until then, we have to concentrate on neutralizing the threat."

Brie looked over at her other screen and scanned through the list and maps.

"It seems that most of the players in your area are yet indisposed, except Parker Heiser."

"Actually Arlin Harper is available as a suspicious participant." Robin added, Brie raised her brow and continued, "Well in any case it appears that the source of the hang glider was the paragliding complex to the northeast of the SETI site."

"Perhaps Frank and I can pay them a visit and see what's …up." Robin said with a smile.

Brie grinned, "You're not getting that one by me."

Frank shook his head and smiled, "Well, I guess you're UP to the task."

"Okay 'Agents-Special', you guys do your thing and let me know what's UP." Brie retorted, They both smiled and Frank replied, "I copy that."

The screens went dark.

What Do Aliens Drink?

Sasha and Rudy seemed pleased as they watch their guests clearing their plates of food. R.A. divided up his last two asparagus spears with his fork and guided the morsels into his mouth.

"Okay we have apple strudel and rocky road ice cream for dessert, who is up for it?" Rudy advised his guests.

Sasha looked across the table at Sal and R.A., "Sal, R.A. what's your pleasure?"

Sal sucked in his cheeks in thought, "I'm ready for strudel."

R.A. looked over at his young lady companion, "Robyn what would you suggest?"

Robyn smiled and delivered her choice for R.A., "I think you should have both."

R.A. smiled and furrowed his brow, nodded and announced, "Since I am a guest, I'll have a little of both."

With a sideways glance, R.A. asked Robyn, "And you young lady what would you have?"

She tilted her head slightly and softly said, "I would like some strudel please."

Sal looked across the table at Tyler, "Sir Tyler, let me guess, you will have a double portion of both."

Tyler shook his head slightly, looked at his dad and replied with a wry smile, "I'm on a diet…I'll just have the rocky road ice cream."

Sal sat and chuckled.

Sasha chimed in, "He's been listening to his dad complain about his pants shrinking while they were hanging in the closet."

Rudy countered, "That's true, but those pants were from six years ago." he looked at Sasha and continued with a smirk, "Do you have a dress you can fit into from six years ago?"

Rudy scrunched his face as he knew he had stepped in it. He looked over at her svelte figure and hung his head in defeat. He shook his head in shame and announced, "Okay, I guess I'm skipping dessert." he said as he chuckled.

Sasha smiled as she visibly bit her tongue hanging out the side of her mouth.

The meal rotation went smoothly despite Rudy's angst.

Sal took the last bite of his strudel and looked down at his dining companion, "Okay young lady, how about you plinking on the guitar for me?"

Robyn smiled, "Okay."

Sal stood up and pulled Robbins chair away as she stood. They turned and Robyn led Sal out of the dining room.

R.A. saw Tyler pick up his plates and utensils and carry them toward the kitchen.

R.A. stood and reached down and picked up his dessert plate and put it on his dinner plate. He put his dining utensils on top of the plates and picked up the plates and started to take them toward the kitchen. Sasha caught him mid-step, "Oh no you don't." as she quickly moved to relieve R.A. of the plates.

"These can wait till later, we have much to discuss before we participate in menial tasks."

R.A. shrugged and took a breath, "Okay you're the boss…your house, your rules."

Sasha nodded, "You got that right. You can retire to the living room."

"Yes ma'am." R.A. obeyed and walked toward the living room.

Sasha set the plates down and picked up a few of the serving dishes of leftovers and took them to the kitchen. Rudy in complement picked up the remaining leftovers and took them to the kitchen. Sasha returned and scanned the table for any necessary culinary attention and saw nothing of urgent need.

R.A. entered the living room and sat next to his satchel on the sofa.

Tyler entered the living room and walked over to R.A., "Could I sit next to you, R.A.?"

"It would be my pleasure Tyler."

Rudy came into the room and Sasha followed in short order.

Rudy looked at Sasha and R.A. and asked, "How about I get us something to drink?"

He walked over to his bar and grabbed a bottle of scotch.

"This is bound to make our math fuzzy."

R.A. took note of bottle of scotch and stated, "More than likely it will serve to dampen our memory of the rest of the evening."

Rudy recovered one of the several glasses on the bar and poured two fingers of scotch and handed it to Sasha.

"Thank you sir." She said as she curtsied.

He gathered another glass and duplicated the two fingers of scotch and walked over to R.A. and offered its delivery which R.A. accepted with a nod.

Tyler looked up at his dad and said with a smile, "I'll have the same thank you."

Rudy nodded graciously, "But of course young man."

He returned to the bar retrieved another glass and promptly filled it with two fingers of scotch. He pivoted and faced Tyler and held it to toast position, "This, young man is yours…" There was an intentional pause, "perhaps in twelve years."

R.A. looked over at Tyler, "Has that ever work before?"

Tyler smiled and replied dejectedly, "Not yet, but apparently I have twelve years to practice."

R.A. leaned up from the sofa and raised his glass and stated, "Here's to Tyler's future success."

Sasha and Rudy raised their glasses and they all said, "To Tyler!"

Tyler smiled and leaned his head toward R.A. and said quietly, "I prefer iced tea anyway."

R.A. responded, "A better choice."

Tyler stood and headed for the kitchen.

Rudy took a few steps over to an armchair and sat. Sasha strolled over to the sofa and sat next to R.A.. She turned to R.A., "So my new celebrity friend, hopefully the meal has loosened your tongue sufficiently to relate what you have been up to while hiding at my husband's place of work?"

R.A. leaned back on the sofa, "It's good that the night is still young and I yet have sufficient decorum to deliver an explanation." He raised his glass and took a drink.

Rudy interrupted, "Sasha, at least let the doctor sustain a good buzz before your verbal encounter."

R.A. smiled, "It's okay Rudy, I don't often get to engage with views from a different perspective other than my driver/bodyguard, Marnie."

Sasha was in mid-drink and gulped on hearing his declaration.

Her brows raised in surprise and words came out of her open mouth.

"You have a bodyguard?"

At that moment Sal came into the room from the hallway. His attention was garnered by Sasha's question. He entered the conversation, "Oh yes, about the bodyguard… Sasha you need some background on this, she is not only his driver and bodyguard but she yet lives with him. And he admitted she is twenty-something and is of pleasant appearance."

Sasha pursed her lips in understanding, "Do tell R.A., how much of your body is she guarding?"

Rudy wrinkled his face in intrigue and Sal lowered his head slightly and his forehead wrinkled in curiosity awaiting an answer.

R.A. displayed a blank face that eventually squiggled while taking a deep breath.

"I don't deny the veracity of Sal's statement, but I should add it's a business and professional relationship that became necessary in light of our recent contact with the aliens. As you know there are those who take issue with the concept of alien involvement in Earth's religious and human socio-economic status quo. Additionally it was required by my benefactor Robert Atwood."

R.A.'s glance bounced between the participants in his rendition and pleaded, "Let's put this to rest; okay?"

Sasha nodded slowly and leaned back on the sofa and stated, "Okay, but I've got to meet Marnie." as she took a drink.

R.A. shook his head

Rudy stood up and went back over to the bar and picked up the bottle of scotch and held it up toward Sal. Sal nodded and Rudy grabbed another glass and two fingered the scotch. He walked it over to Sal and delivered it. He turned and took the bottle back to the bar and set it down then returned to his seat. Sal scanned the living room and spied a chair to land on. He made his way to it and sat down.

Sasha leaned up and looked at R.A., "Okay Doctor 'Gemo, uh," she stumbled in her speech and continued, "oh, uh R.A., I will not be dissuaded by the revelation of your living arrangement. What say you about your search for alien technology?"

R.A. tilted his head toward Sasha in curiosity, "Are you an astrophysicist major?"

She shook her head slightly, "Nope just a housewife."

Rudy laughed, "R.A. she's lying to you, I met her at New Mexico Tech and she graduated with a Space Studies degree, she's the town mayor and she runs the state's wounded Warriors program."

Sasha shrugged, "Other than that I'm just a housewife, so as you were saying…"

R.A. smiled and took a breath, "Okay, I got your number."

He reached into his satchel and pulled out his VPC and placed his thumb and fingers on the print recognition sections of the device. He sat it on the coffee table in front of him and the virtual keyboard opened up. He looked up at the monitor on the wall and then at Rudy, "Is your monitor COM capable?"

Rudy nodded, "It is but, I don't have a COM connection with a security clearance." He took the COM, off of a shelf and pressed a button. The monitor lit up.

Sal set his drink down stood up and stated, "I can fix that." as he headed down the hallway.

R.A. entered some strokes on the keyboard and a virtual screen popped up in front of the keyboard. He studied the screen and commented, "It seems that Honrí received some queries from Dominique Soul and Amir Hadad about the streaming data I disseminated prior to leaving the VLA this afternoon."

He paused and continued, "I guess I should explain the data to them."

Sal came back into the room carrying his backpack. He walked over to his chair and set the backpack on the floor next to him.

He looked around and saw a table with a plant on it a few steps away. He walked over took the plant and placed it on the floor and said to the plant, "Sorry plant, I need this table."

Sasha saw his maneuvers and chuckled.

He moved the table over in front of his chair.

He took his COM and VPC out of his backpack and engaged both of them to operating mode and set them on the table.

Momentarily, a virtual keyboard and screen appeared on the table. He typed in several keystrokes and gave a voice command,"-Good morning Johnny."

The members of the group smiled on hearing his command.

The monitor flashed several times and a caption appeared on the screen, stating, "Security status acquired."

Sal's image was displayed on the upper left corner of the screen.

Sal looked over at R.A., "R.A. what icon do you use?"

R.A. smiled and responded, "It's the same as it's always been."

Sal smiled and entered some more keystrokes, "Okay R.A. it's your turn, search for Sal on your screen and engage it."

R.A. looked at his screen and saw Sal's icon and selected on it.

R.A.'s image appeared next to Sal's image in the upper left corner of the screen.

Sal asked, "Rudy, do you have a multi-scan room camera?"

Rudy replied, "Yes, it's function three."

Sal entered some keystrokes and the icons disappeared from the monitor and the screen once again flashed several times.

After a few seconds the images of R.A., Sal, Sasha and Rudy appeared on the screen.

Sal announced, "Looks like we have all the players ready."

Sasha asked, "Rudy did you know it could do that?"

Rudy replied, "No, I didn't. I gotta learn that trick."

Sal asked, "You want to see if we can get Dom and Amir to join us?"

R.A. responded, "Sure, have yet to meet the celebrities."

Sasha added, "Yes, we've only seen them on the news."

Sal looked on his virtual screen and typed in some more commands. He searched the screen and entered some more keystrokes. The room monitor displayed Dom and Amir's flashing icons.

Sal took a breath, "Let's see if they answer."

*****

Amir and Dom were busy at their workstations when each of their screens displayed Sal's flashing icon. They both looked at each other and Dom said, "Wow, how about that we were just talking about Sal. Let's see what he wants." Amir nodded and they both accepted the COM.

Almost simultaneously Amir and Dom's images replaced their icons on the monitor screen at Rudy's house.

Dom and Amir looked at their screens and saw numerous images.

Dom realized it would be difficult to COM on their small screens, so she announced, "Hold on, I'm going to transfer to the larger screen."

She visited her fingers on the keyboard and soon the images were transferred to the four foot monitor above their workstation.

On seeing the plethora of people both Dom and Amir were intrigued.

"Okay, is this a group intervention? Whatever it is, it's Dom's fault." Amir stated with a chuckle.

Dom looked over at Amir and softly punched his shoulder.

Sal responded, "You guys must've done something very bad to feel guilty."

Dom gazed at the large monitor and noticed a curious image.

"Oh my, that's Doctor 'Gemo. Honrí said you surfaced; wow this is great."

Amir added, "Yeah, this is fantastic. We've been waiting for the chance to talk to you."

R.A. replied emphatically, "Me, I finally get to meet the world famous celebrities, Dominique Soul and Amir Hadad."

Sal interrupted, "Okay, before this winds up in a mutual admiration society, let me introduce all of our participants.

Sal pause momentarily and continue, "Dominique Soul and Amir Hadad, it's my pleasure to introduce you to Sasha Rudolph and her other half Robert Rudolph a.k.a. Rudy. I'm sure you all can figure out who is who on your respective monitor screens."

Sal paused again and continued, "Rudy is a new resident astronomer at the VLA and Sasha is the mayor of Magdalena and has a degree in Space Studies from New Mexico Tech."

Sasha spoke first, "It's great to meet you even though it is Via COM, Rudy and I have great admiration for both of you for your work."

Dom replied, "Thank you, but Amir and I realize we are the fortunate part of the great work of those who came before us.

We just happened to be in the sequence of events that anyone could have encountered, simply by chance."

R.A. took exception, "I beg to differ, your interaction with Adam was par excellence and Amir, there may have not been a discovery of the alien data stream corresponding to Dom's conversation and there would have been no verification of alien contact had you not presented it."

Sal interjected, "So, you both have to live with being rock stars."

Tyler came into the room with his ice tea and walked over and sat next to his mother on the sofa. The multi-scan camera automatically added Tyler's image to the monitor. Rudy noticed Tyler's image and stated, "Excuse me, you may have noticed a new addition to the discussion, this is our son Tyler."

Dom smiled at his image, "It's a pleasure to meet you Tyler and my friend here, is Amir."

Tyler responded, "Thank you, I've seen you both on the news, you found the aliens."

Amir replied, "Actually Tyler, the aliens fortunately found us."

Amir pause momentarily then rolled into his inquiry, "Doctor 'Gemo, we were working on the supplemental data stream that we believe was sent from you, and have questions about the relevance of the data from sent to Wolf and the data sent to Earth."

R.A. nodded and busied his fingers on his keyboard. He looked at his screen and began, "I was trying to establish what the data differences are that represent the diffusion's to both Wolf 1060c and earth. If I can determine the type of diffusion and what the differences were between the two, I may be able to determine reason for the diffusion and what the apparent needs of each planet were to be addressed by their diffusion."

Sasha took a small breath and leaned her head back and then forward, "While I have so many questions for you, Doctor 'Gemo, I will try to stay on track. It seems that you are suggesting that both planets have deficiencies or needs that were recognized by the Alphas." Sasha paused and continued, "How could they possibly comprehend the needs of the ecosystem of those planets?"

Sal's head nodded slowly as he added, "R.A., I believe we have someone of like mind to include in this and our future discussions."

R.A. replied, "I agree and these questions hopefully will lead to possible answers and further questions to present to our alien friends; the Alphas."

R.A. continued, "That was one of the questions I have, dear Sasha. But one of the greater questions is how we can best use the diffusions that they have sent to us?"

Rudy placed a pensive hand on his chin, "If I may change the course of the discussion; are we any closer in our understanding of the Quantum Mechanics Acceleration, QMA, that the aliens used to communicate in real time from light-years away?"

R.A. looked at Sal, "Sal has a better grip on that subject having offered that discussion to his think tank contingent; Jubal Jung, Carmen Hafed, Marie Barrett and Aldo Karloff."

R.A. continued, "And Sal, you may be surprised that Marie Barrett's husband lives here in Magdalena and he is a contemporary of your Ms. Walsh and serves with her on one of her committees."

Sal's head bounced in query, "I did not know that there was a Barrett on any of her committees."

R.A. smiled, "It may be that you did not know Marie kept her maiden name. Her husband is Paul Le Barge."

Sal took a knowing sigh, "Just when you think the universe is so enormous it's tidbits like this that makes us realize how small relevance is."

Sal was curious, "How did you come by that information?"

R.A. began his explanation, "It so happens that his family has owned the Salon Le Barge in Magdalena for years and you have Paul to thank for transforming R.A.'s appearance from a caveman to the clean-shaven indigent you see before you. And by the way he convinced him to discard his handlebar mustache."

Sal smiled, "I shall discreetly discharge that information to Johnny at an inopportune time."

R.A. looked at Sal, "Okay, have you and your cohorts made any headway in your comprehension of the 'time wave' quandary."

Sal took a modest breath and began, "We have had many conversations and poured over the data the aliens have sent that was supposed to enable us to create a real-time communication channel and however our computer simulations have left us with only theories. Our discussions have involved; the HESS, high energy stereoscopic system; observance of the diffusion from the Fermi Gamma ray space telescope; and Quantum Entanglement.

We did discover a tidbit from the use of the LHC, Large Hadron Collider, that, Muons have been found to interact with matter at a higher charge without ionization. We are not sure what that means relative to the increase in microbial concentration or the development of biofuels.

As far as building a device to enable QMA, the power source might have to include fusion energy, either direct or alternating."

Sal took a breath, "So, if any of you have any suggestions or questions, we are open to any and all theories regardless of how illogical they may be."

Tyler took a drink of his iced tea, looked at it, "Can I ask a question?"

Sal looked over at Tyler, "Of course Tyler."

"What do aliens drink?"

The smiles and easy laughter were plenty as the interaction took a needed respite.

Sal responded, "Well Dom, that's one question you did not ask Adam. Perhaps you or someone else, who has the pleasure of such conversation, should put that on the list of questions."

Dom replied, "Tyler, if I were so chosen, I shall endeavor to place that on my list of important questions."

What, No Gunships?

Colonel Narkiewicz, at Cheyenne Mountain, was monitoring the progress of the Hat Creek incident and keeping an eye on the resurrection of Doctor 'Gemo.

The flashing icons of FBI agents Frank Knox and Robin Lane appeared alongside of Honrí Foster at the VLA.

Brie Smithy was engaged at her station, in a conversation with Vice President Natás.

The conversation began while in progress, "So, Mr. Vice President, are you in contact with Doctor Uschin?"

"He is on a COM with Hat Creek originating from Magdalena, New Mexico. He is at the residence of Robert Rudolph and Doctor 'Gemo is present there also."

Smithy continued, "Have you spoken to Doctor 'Gemo about his plans?"

"Not as yet, but I will keep you apprised or possibly include you in a COM with him."

"Thank you Mr. Vice President."

His image disappeared from the screen and the lieutenant went over to the Colonel's station. The Colonel noticed the Lieutenant's presence and they both sat down and took a breath together.

"The VP said he will contact Doctor 'Gemo and apprise us of his plans. He should be getting back to us shortly."

Edward sighed, "I hope that it's soon, as I am concerned about Doctor 'Gemo's safety as well as for those who he is in contact with." He paused and then continued, "What do you think about Hat Creek director's suggestion to house Ms. Soul and Mr. Hadad on grounds?"

Brie nodded her head slightly, "It's a better option, and perhaps the only option given their importance in contacting the aliens."

"I agree. Do you have any suggestion about handling the logistics of their housing?"

"Yes sir." She paused and visited her fingers on Edward's keyboard and a layout view of hat Creek appeared on the screen.

"I researched the availability of modules to be placed on grounds by 1000 tomorrow. I've also included two other modules, one to house the director and assistant director, and a third module for the necessary security personnel. The National Guard troops can be encamped in areas as needed. I've addressed the needs of power, water and sewage, by tapping into the power grid and sewage access that are already established, and the placement of an above-ground water tank to supplement the water supply. I have also included two 10,000 kilowatt generators and a 500 gallon reinforced fuel tank as a backup." She paused for a moment and continued, "Our Chinook's can drop all of the equipment needed and the modules can be delivered by the National Guard. Additionally I have ordered nine sets of bedroom furniture with bedding and three sets of kitchen tables and accessories and assorted bath accoutrements from Burleson's, Hassan's, and Y-Kroft furniture in Reading that will be delivered in three vans."

She entered some more keystrokes and a different view of the map appeared on the screen and she pointed to locations as she continued, "As you can see the placement of the modules would be as such, due to the location of the power, water and sewage sources."

Edward looked at the display and thought for a moment.

"What about pizza delivery?" He said in sarcastic humor.

Brie retorted without hesitation seemingly ignoring the comment with a straight face, "That's what Hueys are for."

Edward looked away and raised his brows knowing he had been bested.

Brie saw him look away and dropped her head and stifled a chuckle and then looked back feigning interest in the display on the screen.

Edward looked over at Brie as she added, "And Sir, I did order two gunships."

Edward tossed a sly look at her and laughed.

Brie succumbed to laughter also.

Finally, the flashing icons of agents Knox and Lane changed to their images.

Edward greeted them, "Good afternoon Special Agent's, have you been in contact with Perry concerning the hang-glider package explosion?"

Frank responded, "Yes, he advised us of the situation and we've also been in contact with his security personnel."

Edward asked, "Can I be of any assistance in ferreting out the perpetrators?"

Frank said, "It appears that the origination of the hang-glider is from the paragliding site to the northeast of Hat Creek, and there are two known persons of interest, Arlin Harper and Parker Heiser. We believe that other associates, Alan Landry and David Poole are yet being detained in Redding. Is that still the case?"

Living up to her a.k.a., Lieutenant 'fast-fingers', she applied her expertise to the keyboard and a status report appeared on the screen.

Brie related the update, "Yes, at the moment they are yet in custody." She paused and entered some more keystrokes and continued, "Are you aware that Jan Wheeler may be an additional person of interest?"

Robin entered the conversation, "Affirmative, but we are lacking her last known address."

Brie replied, "I'll send you all of their last known addresses to your COMs."

"That would be of great help." Robin replied.

Edward stated, "Agents, we believe that Segr8's purpose of the attempted attack was to destroy the connection to the aliens."

Robin shook her head in exasperation, "I'm sorry, but this SETI site is not the only SETI site connection to the aliens, there are dozens around the world."

Edward replied, "Yes, but this was where initial contact was made and that is seen as the primary threat."

Edward continued, "We've assessed the situation and have determined that in order to keep the personnel safe it would be best for them to live on site. We are in the process of delivering modules as living quarters. Lieutenant Smithy has worked out the logistics of that implementation."

Frank asked, "Are Ms. Soul and Mr. Hadad on board with the arrangements?"

Edward replied, "I have yet to engage with them on the plans and I would like to include the director and assistant director in the living arrangements. This will alleviate much of the security risks involved in their traveling from their residences to the SETI site."

Robin added, "That's a big ask of them. It would be like living in prison."

Edward nodded, "Given the circumstances, but, perhaps they would see it more as witness protection, and hopefully it won't last too long."

Edward paused for a moment and continued, "Sadly, it may be necessary to duplicate these arrangements at another SETI site."

Frank shook his head and stated, "This is beginning to look like a cluster fuck." He paused and continued, "What is the time-frame and security needs of this operation?"

Edward answered, "The modules should be operational by tomorrow evening, but the security needs, until then, will be handled by the SETI security and the National Guard."

Robin and Frank looked at each other and she said, "If you would like, I believe Frank and I could sit on them until we get a couple of agents on a more permanent basis."

Frank looked over at Robin and nodded in agreement.

Edward thought for a moment, "I'll have to check with director Martin and see what can be done. I certainly appreciate your offer. Thank you."

Edward took a deep sigh, "Okay you two I'll let you do your agent thing and I'll get back to you."

Frank and Robin nodded and Robin said, "Copy that, Colonel."

Their images disappeared from the screen.

Edward turned to Brie, "Can you put Dom, Amir, Perry and Mike on the queue for me? I messaged both Perry and Mike about our security plans but they have yet to get back to me." He looked at the screen, "I think you can take Honrí off of the queue.

Brie nodded and attacked keyboard. Four flashing icons requested by Edward appeared on the monitor and Honrí's icon disappeared.

Edward looked over at Brie, "Should we be concerned about the budgetary costs of this project?"

Brie wrinkled her nose and raised her brow slightly, "The president has given us carte blanche for all needs related to domestic security and the preservation of alien contact."

Edward nodded slowly, "Yes, but depending on Doctor 'Gemo's plans, this may just be the tip of the iceberg. His reappearance has added a new dimension in the overall structuring of our security basis."

Brie asked, "Have you received any updates on the incursion in the Parkes Observatory in Canberra?"

Edward turned and looked to his left at another screen and entered some keystrokes on the keyboard below it. He studied the updated screen for a moment, "The Australian Defense Force has surrounded the insurgents, but unfortunately, one array was partially damaged and fortunately there were no injuries on either side."

"Have they determined which faction may be responsible?" She asked, "They are not sure but indications are that it was a group supporting Anti-Adam." He replied, "It seems that the dissidents are becoming more and more violent." She stated, "The more organized they get, the more potentially violent they become. One group's success, however small, can serve to embolden another group." He stated in a factual tone.

*****

Dom and Amir were yet engaged on the COM with R.A. and Sal, when Mike and Perry came up to their stations.

Mike said, "I'm sorry to interrupt your COM, but we need to talk to you both."

Dom looked up at them, "What is it Mike?"

Mike looked up at the screen and saw the COM participants,"Actually, what I have to say might involve all of you."

Sal looked up at his screen, "Okay Mike you have our attention. What's up?"

Mike began with somewhat urgency, "I'm not sure if you heard it but there was an explosion a mile or so from our site. It appears that there was a threat to detonate a bomb at this complex. A remote controlled hang-glider, carrying an explosive device, was taken down by our security."

Amir looked at Mike with concern, "Wow, I didn't hear anything. Was anybody hurt?"

Mike related, "No, but Colonel Narkiewicz at DSC has some security concerns for us here at Hat Creek and also for Doctor 'Gemo."

R.A. was somewhat surprised, "Me? What makes me a target?"

Sal turned to R.A., "You know old buddy, for a genius you can be pretty dense at times. The knowledge of your reappearance, itself, makes you a target. For, as a scientist, you are guilty by association. There are conspiracy theorists that will connect your sudden reappearance to the alien contact and see you as responsible."

R.A. thought for a moment and started to reply, "But," he paused as his logic caught up with his thoughts,"Okay, I guess there are those who would see it that way."

Mike continued, "Okay, for now you should take your COM conference and connect with Colonel Narkiewicz at Cheyenne Mountain."

Sal nodded, "Okay, I can make that happen from here. Thanks Mike for the update."

Perry inserted himself into the conversation, "By the way Doctor 'Gemo, welcome back from the abyss."

R.A. replied, "Thank you Perry, it's good to see both of you again. We'll have to get together in person."

Perry replied, "Looking forward to it."

Sal manipulated the keys on his keyboard and the screen flashed several times. The icons of Edward and Brie flashed briefly on the screen and their images replaced their icons.

Narkiewicz and Smithy's screen changed to the images of the plethora of people from Magdalena and Hat Creek.

Edward commented on seeing the group on his screen, "Wow… didn't expect to be invaded."

Sal smiled, "Thought we'd make this a community social call."

Edward looked at the screen curiously,, "Your community has some new faces."

Sal nodded, "Sorry Colonel, but given the situation, their presence is unavoidable."

Sal looked around the room, "I'll make the introductions. Colonel Edward Narkiewicz, Lieutenant Brie Smithy, these fine people are; Sasha Rudolph, Mayor of Magdalena; Robert Rudolph, a.k.a. Rudy, the new resident astronomer at the VLA; and their son Tyler; and Doctor 'Gemo."

During their introductions each of them nodded as their names were announced.

Edward said, "Doctor Uschin, I trust you can vouch for your group's discretion during our conversation."

"Yes Colonel, I believe our national security issues will not be breached."

Brie entered the conversation, "Welcome to all of you, it is a pleasure to meet you." She took a breath, "Doctor 'Gemo, if I may single you out, your dissertation about government distrust and political conspiracies, some years ago, was eye-opening."

R.A. smiled, "Thank you for your compliment."

Brie nodded and continued as she visited her fingers on the keyboard and spoke, "I'm sending secure messages to you, Ms. Soul and Mr. Hadad, concerning our security proposals. If you will open these and look over the proposal and map, I will give you a moment to do so. Meanwhile, Doctor 'Gemo, since we wish to include you in our security protocol, we would like to know your immediate plans for residence and/or movement."

R.A. pursed his lips and thought for a long moment. Finally, he took a breath and answered, "I have an apartment here in Magdalena, and have a live in driver/bodyguard, and I am working on a project I have going at the VLA. I'm not sure of what further security needs may be necessary."

Edward added, " It is our concern that you may be attacked at your residence and/or enroute to the VLA. Additionally, the VLA may become an enhanced target due to your presence."

R.A. paused again in thought.

Edward asked, "Doctor 'Gemo is it possible that you can continue your project at another SETI site that is more secure?"

Dom had finished looking over the proposal and map that Lieutenant Smithy had sent and offered, "Doctor 'Gemo, I believe we have the necessary resources for you to continue your project at our Hat Creek facility and if you wouldn't mind bunking with Amir and I, that may be a solution."

R.A. again paused for a long moment and thought.

"Wouldn't that present the same problem of the possibility of being attacked going from the residence to the site?"

Amir included himself in the conversation, "The proposal that was sent to us would have us living on grounds in a more secure environment. As Dom suggested it would be more than acceptable to have you as our roommate."

Sal nodded, "It seems that it would be advantageous for everyone to have three great minds engaged in one cause."

R.A. thought and weighed the suggestion, "I hesitate to intrude on your youthful cohabitation."

Dominique smiled and somewhat blushed, "Doctor 'Gemo, thank you for your concern, but Amir and I are simply the best of friends."

R.A. looked at their images and read their faces, "Ms. Soul, I will take you at your word. However, my years of observation and life experiences lead me elsewhere." He paused, "I accept your invitation."

Edward and Brie shared a collective sigh.

Edward stated, "Thank you, this will make our security concerns much more manageable."

Sal shrugged, "Well, Colonel, are there any other world problems you wish us to solve?"

Edward smiled and quipped, "No Doctor Uschin, I believe the head that wears the crown will sleep easy tonight. Thank you."

Sal smiled and chuffed, "Lieutenant, I believe you have a literary connoisseur in your presence."

Brie smiled and replied;

"Now you know what I have to deal with."

Edward added a final touch, "And to all…a good night. Cheyenne Mountain, out"

Edward and Brie's images left the screen.

Sal leaned back in his chair. He swayed his head cockily, "Okay R.A., I'm curious as to how your bodyguard/driver Marnie will take the news of your moving out. Did you both sign a pre-nup? Or are you going to just rip the Band-Aid off?"

R.A. displayed a disinterested face and turned to Rudy, "Rudy, my dear Sir, may I trouble you for a ride, so that I may avoid further verbal dismemberment by my colleague here?"

Sasha took exception, "But R.A., you were just about to give your thoughts on the time-wave connection with quantum mechanics acceleration."

R.A. shrugged and relented, "I don't believe that my assessment of QMA and its relationship to time, as a wave-form, carries any more weight than yours."

Sasha replied, "I understand that, however you related that the Quantum Entanglement theory supposes an instantaneous action of one form of matter with another." She paused for a moment, "If that is the case, isn't that a form of time-travel?"

Sal added his perspective, "The possibility of time-travel has been linked to black holes, dark matter and the void between physical matter, as being the key to understanding the possible mechanical link of instantaneous connection of all matter. But unless we can discern the connection between what we understand as time being relative to the speed of light and the alien's de facto use of time as a waveform, that conflict will yet exist.

Dominique listened and brought her query, "When Adam talked about jumping from the top of one wave to another it didn't seem logical, as I perceived there was a bottom of the wave. But, what if the QMA erases the bottom of the wave and leaves only the top."

Amir added, "Yes, but even if there were a type of energy that would do so, that in itself would have to be instantaneous energy."

Dom thought for moment and replied tentatively, "This may make the case for the actual existence of negative energy."

There was a long pause as each member of the group engaged the faces of other members.

Rudy broke the silence, "Okay R.A., I'll fire up the chariot for you and; we be off."

R.A. nodded and disconnected his COM as did Sal.

Dom saw that the party was breaking up and delivered her parting words, "For me, this was immensely enjoyable and enlightening."

Amir added, "I agree. This day, I will mark my calendar as exceptional."

Sal looked up at the screen, "Thank you both for your attendance. I'll see you in a couple days."

Dom said, "Looking forward to it Sal, good afternoon."

Their images disappeared from the screen and Rudy disconnected the COM.

Sal retrieved his backpack off the floor and placed his COM and VPC inside and set it back on the floor. He picked up the table he had moved earlier and put it back in its designated spot. He placed its former occupant 'the plant' in its original location.

R.A. collected his COM and VPC and placed them in his satchel. Tyler stood up and took his iced tea glass back to the kitchen. Sasha and Rudy followed Tyler into the kitchen. Sal stood and stretched out his arms and shoulders, bent down and retrieved his backpack from the floor and walked down the hallway toward the bedroom.

R.A. sat watching them navigating their departures. He looked around the living room and noted the decor. A picture on a shelf caught his attention and he stood and went to take a closer look. While he consumed the picture of a happy family, his mind wandered to his past. A memory of R.A. as a teenager, comfortably sitting on a rug sidled up to a coffee table reading a book while watching his parents sitting together on a sofa holding hands and talking. Sasha's return to the living room interrupted his vision.

She walked over to R.A. clasped his hands, "I enjoyed your visit very much and you're always welcome back anytime."

R.A. responded earnestly, "I haven't enjoyed an evening like this for some time and it will certainly be fondly remembered."

Rudy entered the living room and turned to Sal, "Okay partner, or is it copilot? Are you ready to depart?"

R.A. nodded and sighed, "Yes, but I need to say my adieus to Tyler and Robyn."

Sasha smiled and announced down the hallway, "Robyn, Tyler, come and say goodbye to Doctor 'Gemo."

Some voices and noises bounced out of the hallway, followed shortly by the two summoned.

R.A. bent down to receive Robyn's hand at eye level, "Robyn, young lady, it was a pleasure to dine with you. You must bring your parents some time and come to visit with me."

Robyn smiled and replied warmly, "Of course and next time, maybe I'll have two desserts."

R.A. smiled, "Of course you shall."

He pivoted to Tyler who offered his hand to R.A. and shook it firmly, "Doctor, I hope you get to meet Adam in person."

R.A. smiled, "That would be my hope also, Sir Tyler."

Sal meandered out of the hallway into the living room. R.A. stood and received a brotherly embrace from Sal.

"R.A., my friend, I'll certainly be seeing a lot of you in the future." Sal said, R.A. replied as they separated from their embrace, "Yes, apparently I'll be spending much of my time at Hat Creek with Perry, Mike and the youngsters."

Sasha gave R.A. a quick hug and he turned toward Rudy, "Okay Rudy, let's tempt fate in your machine."

Rudy chuffed, went to the door and opened it and announced, "Up, up and away."

R.A. retrieved his satchel off the sofa as he exited out the door.

When they got to the car, Rudy asked, "So, good Doctor, since I don't know where you live, would you like to drive?"

R.A. grinned broadly and nodded his head as he rounded the front of the car, opened the door, and snuggled into the driver's seat.

*****

The five minute drive took somewhat longer as R.A. savored the joy of the drive. As he pulled into the parking space he noticed Marnie coming to meet them. He stopped the car, stepped out and retrieved his satchel from the rear seat. Rudy exited his side of the car and proceeded around to the front of the vehicle.

Marnie came up to R.A. said, "Good evening Doctor, I trust you enjoyed your visit."

R.A. replied, "I certainly did." He turned to Rudy, "Rudy, I like you to meet Marnie Grayson."

R.A.'s previous description of Marnie was accurate; young and attractive.

She held out her hand and Rudy received the firm handshake, saying, "I'm very glad to meet you. R.A. speaks highly of you."

She chuckled, "Thank you but, you know how fractured the cognitive ability of the elderly can be."

Rudy laughed, "R.A., I can tell you're in good hands, this girl's got game."

Marnie replied, "I have to keep on my toes, as the Doctor can be demanding." She looked intently at his face, "How many of you had to hold him down to shear his locks?"

Rudy smiled, "Oh, that's right you probably haven't seen the clean-cut Doctor in a while."

Marnie nodded, "He was getting a bit grungy looking."

R.A. interceded, "I can't tell if this is a pity party or an intervention. You two can compare notes some other time."

R.A. grabbed Rudy's hand and shook it, "Thanks for letting me pilot your rocket."

Rudy chuckled and offered, "Maybe next time I'll let you kick in the afterburners."

R.A. replied, "I'll take you up on that."

Rudy turned to Marnie and shook her hand, "Again, Marnie, it was a pleasure to meet you."

Marnie returned, "And you."

Rudy went over to the car door and opened it, "Hey R.A., let the stars be your guide."

R.A. waved, goodbye, and Rudy entered and ignited his rocket, backed out and exploded out the driveway.

Red Rover

As the afternoon sun waned behind them, Agents Knox and Lane scanned the skies in search of an errant hang-glider. The many twists and turns of Bidwell Road presented its own navigational problems. Robin was on a COM with Lieutenant Smithy getting directions to the last known position of the suspected hang-glider.

"You should be within two miles, south, of the last known GPS coordinates." Smithy related on the COM.

"That puts it to the north of us." Robin stated.

Frank interjected, "What are the chances that our target is headed for that lumberyard where we picked up Landry a week ago?"

Robin smiled and nodded her head, "I'd say it's worth a shot, since this is the only road leading to the paragliding complex and we haven't run across anyone yet."

Frank slowed down and completed a U-turn on the narrow road and headed for Cassel Road. Robin asked Brie on the COM, "LT, can you pull up a satellite view of Cassel Road and follow it to the first farm on the east side of the road? You might find some activity at an old logging company."

Brie responded, "Standby."

Robin waited patiently for her response.

"Okay, I have what appears to be a truck and flatbed trailer at that location." Brie advised.

"Are there any other vehicles parked nearby?"

Brie responded, "Ten-four, there are two vehicles nearby."

Robin replied, "Copy that LT."

Robin reached over and picked up a two-way radio and keyed the mic.

"Break, any County Sheriff Deputy, FBI agent Lane, please respond."

Robin waited for a response. Not having any response she keyed the mic again, "Any County Sheriff Deputy, FBI agent Lane, please respond."

Finally the radio carrier broke the silence, "Agent Lane, this is Deputy Ariza, how can I be of assistance?"

A smile came over Robin's face as she responded, "Ariza, why am I not surprised you're on the air? Can't think of anyone else I'd rather hear from."

"I copy that, I'm ready for more good times. What do you have for me?" Ariza replied.

"Apparently, it's a déjà vu request, how close are you to the lumber company you assisted us with last time?" She asked, "I can be there in twenty minutes, you having problems?"

"Knox and I are looking for some backup in case things go south." She stated.

"Ten-four, my partner, Deputy Wallace, and I will meet you at the turnoff to Cassel Road."

"Copy that. Give me your COM ID and we'll switch to COM."

"Ten–four, read it as Sam, Sam, Ocean, four, two, three, nine." He replied, "Ten–four, copy, Sam, Sam, Ocean four, two, three, nine, initiating."

She entered the code, SSO4239, in the COM and Ariza's icon flickered and her image appeared on the COM.

Robin sighed as her image appeared, "That's better."

Ariza smiled, "See you there in twenty."

Robin put the COM aside, "That Ariza is a solid cop."

Frank nodded, "Yep, she's got what it takes. We're lucky to have her back us up."

As they continued toward the rendezvous, Robin kept track of the satellite view on the COM. Ariza and Wallace were waiting for Knox and Lane when they got to the cutoff point.

Ariza walked over to the car and Frank rolled down his window.

"I did a preliminary scan of the yard with my binoculars and recognized Parker Heiser and Jan Wheeler. Heiser is pretty reasonable but Wheeler is a loose cannon and can't be trusted."

Frank said, "How loose is that canon?"

"She carries a forty-five S&W and has access to explosives."

Ariza added, "I don't know how he got out, but David Poole is also there." Ariza paused and waved at her partner to meet Knox and Lane. Wallace leaned down into the window and shook Frank's hand, "Hi, I'm Bart Wallace; Ariza's said a lot of good things about you two."

Frank smiled, "I hope we live up to the hype." He motioned to Robin, "Wallace, this is Agent Robin Lane."

Bart looked across the front seat, nodded, "It's a pleasure to meet you."

Robin smiled, "If you're riding with Ariza, then you have my respect."

Frank looked at Ariza and Wallace, "So, in summary we have to expect that the explosives were supplied by Wheeler and Poole was sprung for the job by Heiser."

"Okay, how about you and Wallace peel off around the backside and wait for Lane and me to make our way to the truck and trailer? I'll keep my mic open on the two-way so you can hear what's going on. I will have Lane turn hers off so there won't be any broadcast." Knox paused for a moment, "You still have your rifle in the trunk?"

Ariza smiled, "Yep, I still got it and Wallace here has one also, but I have to admit, he's a better shot than I am."

Frank squinted, "Guess you'll have to swallow your pride, but I'll bet on either of you."

Ariza sighed, "Just hope no one has to collect."

Frank nodded, "That makes two of us. Okay let's do this."

They adjourned their meeting and Ariza and Wallace got in their unit and drove up the road and around to the backside of the buildings. They each retrieved their rifles out of the trunk of the vehicle and picked key observation points. When they got into position Ariza keyed his two-way mic. "Ariza here, we are in position."

"Copy that, we're on our way."

Frank drove up to the complex, pulled in and parked at a forty-five degree angle to the truck and trailer. They noticed two other vehicles parked several yards behind it. They saw Heiser and Poole adjusting straps on a hang glider that was sitting on flatbed trailer. They had no visual on Wheeler.

"Ariza, I don't have visual on Wheeler you have her twenty?"

Frank was asking for her location and Ariza replied, "Negative, could be in one of the vehicles."

Robin asked, "Okay, what's our plan?"

Frank replied, "Let's see if we can ease our way out of the car without a confrontation."

Robin opened her door and started to step out when Frank saw Wheeler and Frazier open up the doors of one of the vehicle to the rear of the trailer and step out.

Frank reached over and stopped Robin and spoke into the mic to Ariza.

"Ariza, you have a line of sight on the two that stepped out of the vehicle?"

Ariza replied, "Ten–four, and it appears that Wheeler has a sidearm under her shirt, but Frazier doesn't appear to be carrying."

Frank replied, "I don't see Frazier as an issue but you may be right about Wheeler."

Frank and Robin watched as Frazier and Wheeler walked toward the trailer in a less than threatening gate. Robin looked over at Frank and offered, "How about we wait to see if they get in one group so we can watch them?"

Frank squinted his face said, "Yeah, let's do that, and hopefully they won't scatter when we step out."

Poole and Heiser had noticed that Frank and Robin had pulled up in their vehicle and it appeared that Wheeler and Frazier were also aware they had arrived.

Ariza's voice entered the silence, "Have a visual on the suspects and only see one weapon, the one on Wheeler."

Frank responded, "Thanks for the 411."

Robin sighed, "Well, let's see how this plays out."

Frank nodded, "Okay partner let's do it."

They slowly egressed from the vehicle, but left their doors open. They cautiously walked toward the trailer keeping an eye on Wheeler's hands. Heiser spoke as he neared the trailer.

"Well, if it isn't agents Knox and Lane what brings you here?"

"Mr. Heiser," Robin began, "We are investigating the explosion of the device dropped from a hang-glider near the creek on Bidwell Road, and since this is a hang-glider it's only reasonable that we check it out."

Heiser nodded slowly, "Do you have a warrant?"

Lane shrugged her shoulders and looked at Knox, "Agent Knox, do you have a warrant?"

Frank checked his shirt pocket and patted his pants pockets, "No, I don't have a warrant, but Agent Lane as we drove down this public road, didn't you notice from the road that there was a hang-glider on this trailer?"

"You're right Agent Knox, I believe it was in plain view and I don't think we need a warrant."

Robin took her personal COM off her belt and began videotaping the trailer and hang-glider.

Heiser shook his head, "What makes you think this is the hang-glider you're looking for?"

Frank shrugged his shoulders, "Well that's why we have forensic experts to make that determination. So, I guess we'll have to wait till they get here and process the hang-glider."

Frank turned toward Wheeler, "Excuse me ma'am, I didn't catch your name, but I believe you have a weapon and I'd appreciate it if you allow my partner to secure it for our safety."

Wheeler took a breath, flexed her fingers, "Yes I have a weapon and a CCW for it."

"Of course you do," Robin replied, "but it makes us uncomfortable when there are other weapons around."

Wheeler returned, "You both have weapons, so why can't I have one?"

Robin agreed, "Yes ma'am you may have a right to legally carry one, but we are not sure about your intentions. Given that, if you insist on keeping your weapon I would request that you get in your vehicle and leave the area with your weapon so there is no question about your intent."

Wheeler thought for a moment and walked over to Poole and whispered something to him. Poole nodded and Wheeler did the reasonable thing, she turned and walked back to the vehicle, got in and drove out of the area.

Deputy Wallace slung his rifle and walked toward the road to see which direction Wheeler had gone. He saw that she had stopped on the road out front and stepped out of her vehicle and went to the rear lift-gate and opened it. She opened up a suitcase and reached in and was setting up what appeared to be a COM like device. Wallace hurried back to the sheriff unit and approached Ariza.

"Kerrie, we may have a problem, Wheeler stopped on the road out front and seems to be preparing some sort of electronic device.

Ariza squinted concern and reached over to the two-way and clicked the mic several times. Frank heard the clicks on the radio and garnered Robin's attention, "I have to get something out of the car." Robin nodded and Frank walked back to the vehicle and sat down in the seat. Covertly he spoke into the two-way, "Ariza, you got my attention."

Ariza responded, "It seems that Wheeler stopped on the road and is operating some sort of electronic device from the hatchback of the vehicle."

Frank took a breath, "Copy that."

Poole walked over to Heiser and had a private conversation with him. Heiser took a sudden breath and nodded. He leaned over to Frazier and whispered something to him.

Robin saw the exchanges and looked back as Frank stepped out of the vehicle and was making his way back to Robin when Heiser Poole and Frazier began running away from the trailer.

Frank ticked his head at Robin and thumbed his hand toward their vehicle and they both hurried away from the trailer toward their vehicle.

They jumped into the vehicle and Frank backed it out toward the road. Wallace and Ariza on seeing the actors fleeing away from the trailer, took cover behind their sheriff's unit.

The precautionary actions of all involved were decidedly justi-fied as the hang-glider on the trailer, exploded in a ball of fire.

Ariza and Wallace quickly placed their rifles in the trunk and got back into the patrol car. Ariza started the car and slid the car around and headed toward the road. Wheeler was replacing electronic device back into the suitcase and was starting to close the hatch when Ariza and Wallace pulled up behind her and exited their vehicle with their guns drawn.

Wheeler turned toward the deputies and on seeing their guns drawn, raised her hands above her head.

"Keep your hands raised." She did as ordered.

"If you have a weapon, keeping your right hand raised, reach down to your shirt with your left hand and lift it up to expose your weapon."

Following the orders she pulled up her shirt and showed the firearm in a holster on her right side belt area.

"Thank you. Now, with that left-hand un-snap the holster and with two fingers, slowly remove the weapon from the holster and slowly place it on the ground in front of you and then keep your hands raised."

Wheeler paused for a moment and took a breath and retrieved the weapon with two fingers and placed it on the ground.

"Please take three side-steps to your left and stop."

Again she did as ordered.

"Do you have any other weapons on your person?"

She shook her head, no, and Ariza asked, "If that is a "no", then say so."

Wheeler sighed, "No, I have no other weapons on me."

"Take two steps forward and turn around facing away from me."

Again, she did as ordered.

"Now, slowly lower yourself down to the ground and lie face down with your hands out to each side; palms up; your legs out straight; cross your ankles." Wheeler performed each maneuver as directed.

At this point Ariza looked over at Wallace said, "Cover her part-ner and I'll cuff her."

Wallace nodded and walked at an angle off slightly to the right following Ariza as she approached Wheeler. As Ariza got close she holstered her weapon and as she reached down and grabbed her wrist with her left hand she ordered her to look away from him. She looked away and Ariza grabbed her left wrist placing her thumb on the back of her hand, putting pressure on her wrist and folding her arm against her back as she slid her left foot against her arm. Maintaining her balance she gently rested her knee on her shoulder blade locking her arm to her body. With her right hand, she retrieved her handcuffs from its pouch and cuffed her left wrist. She securely grabbed the open cuff with her left hand and did a quick pat down of the waist area feeling for weapons. Having found no threats she told her to give him her other hand and place it behind her back. As she complied she firmly gripped three of her fingers including the little finger and cuffed her other hand. She released her left arm and grabbed her right arm with both hands, "I'm going to roll you over on to your butt and you can fold your right leg under your left and I will stand you up."

The transition was smooth and Ariza brought her to a standing position. She finished searching the rest of her outer clothing and ankle area for any contraband and removed a full magazine from her pocket and put it in her coat pocket. Wallace saw that the search had been completed and holstered his weapon. Ariza escorted her over to the front of the patrol car and waited as Wallace opened the rear passenger door. Ariza took her flashlight and shined it up her nasal area and then into each ear. She asked her to open her mouth and say, "Ahh" and stick her tongue out. She complied and Ariza put her flashlight away and retrieved her cuff key and double locked the handcuffs. She walked her back to the opened passenger door and guided her head and body into the backseat and closed the door.

Wallace and Ariza walked back over to Wheeler's vehicle and Wallace retrieved the weapon from the ground. He removed the magazine and extracted a live round from the chamber, locked it open and put it in his jacket pocket.

Ariza keyed her mic, "Knox, Lane do you copy?"

Robin quickly replied, "Ten-four, you guys okay?"

Ariza responded, "Yeah, we're okay, how about you?"

Robin said, "Yep, trying to secure this cluster. Apparently Lieutenant Smithy was tracking our activities and noticed an explosive event on her COM. She took the initiative to engage a squad of National Guard and direct them to our location. They should be here shortly to help locate the scattered suspects."

She paused, "You guys have any luck locating Wheeler?"

"As a matter of fact you will be pleased to know she is in our custody without incident." Ariza touted and continued, "We secured the vehicle and expect your forensic team would like to take control to preserve any evidence."

"Affirmative, but we're not sure how long it will take for them to get here. Give me your twenty and we'll take over until the NG's get here."

"If you backup onto the main road and peak to the south you'll see us." Ariza advised, Robin smiled as she stood outside the vehicle and walked a few steps toward the roadway. Indeed she saw Ariza waving at her from the distance. She called out to Frank, "Frank, come over here you might want to see this."

Frank moseyed over and stood next to Robin and saw Ariza and Wallace waving from the distance. He smiled, "Well, let's go say "hi" to the rest of the team."

Robin nodded and they walked back over to their car and got in. They backed out onto the roadway and rolled down the road to their partners in crime.

They stopped and got out of the car and eased over to the crime fighters and they exchanged handshakes and fist bumps.

Ariza began, "As I was explaining to your partner we have Wheeler in custody and are rolling out the red carpet for your forensic team to go over her vehicle."

Frank took a deep breath, "I gotta say that if it weren't for you two, we might have been dry-roasted."

Ariza offered, "I think we all played a part in this scenario.

Robin replied, "Yeah, that might be but I think you two had the heavier load."

Wallace interjected, "Well, that can be a discussion we might have on several occasions."

Frank nodded and suggested, "Well, if you guys are up for it, when forensics gets here we'll adjourn for a bite to eat at an establishment of your choice."

Ariza stated, "The only thing we have to do now is to transfer custody of our prisoner to the FBI on the suspicion of detonation of an explosive device in connection to a possible terrorist act."

Robin agreed, "Yes, and hopefully the guardsmen can gather up the others as co-conspirators."

Frank held up his hand, "Just a moment, I gotta bring Smithy in on this." He went over to his vehicle and retrieved his COM and set it on the hood of the vehicle. He entered some keystrokes and her image appeared.

"Lieutenant Smithy, our gang wants to thank you for keeping an eye out for us and for expediting the response to this incident."

Smithy collected the view from her side of the COM, "I think there's enough thanks to go around, as we all shared in a successful conclusion with no injuries."

Frank replied, "That may be, but we yet wanted to include you in the celebration."

Brie smiled graciously, "That is much appreciated and you should expect the squad of National Guard to arrive within fifteen minutes. You guys be safe." Her image disappeared from the screen.

Wallace took a deep breath, "I guess we all played a role in a real-life game of: Red Rover, Red Rover, send the next player over."

SAFE AND SECURE…shhh…Secret Talks

Agent Anji Rayner was practicing due diligence as she peered out the windows of Dominique's apartment. The apartment complex, although unremarkable, was well-kept with adequate security and a well lit parking area. Dom was finishing the packing of her suitcase with the necessary clothing for a long vacation. A smaller suitcase of personal items lay on the bed as was her purse and her briefcase. She took a quick look around the bedroom and spied her bed pillow. She zipped up the suitcase and reached over and secured the bed pillow and placed it on top of the suitcase. She picked up her briefcase, purse and the smaller suitcase and carried them to the living room and set them by the door. Agent Rayner saw her place the items on the floor, "Is that about it, Ms. Soul?"

Dom smiled, "Yes, one more trip, but please call me Dom."

Rayner smiled also, "Okay, Dom, and you can call me Anji."

She nodded her head, "Deal?"

Dom returned the smile, "Deal."

Dom returned to the bedroom and retrieved her suitcase and pillow, "Okay, this should be it."

Anji relieved her of her suitcase and pillow and opened the front door and made her way to the rear of the car and opened up the hatchback and placed the suitcase and pillow inside and closed the hatchback. Dom looked around the living room as if to say goodbye. Anji returned and picked up the briefcase and the smaller suitcase and went back outside to the vehicle and placed them inside the rear passenger side of the vehicle. Dom picked up her purse stepped out of the door, closed it and locked it. Anji scanned the parking lot and opened the passenger door for Dom to get in. Anji saw the apartment key in Dom's hand, "If you give me the key, I'll make a copy so one of the agents will be able to check on the security of your apartment."

Dom handed her the key and got into the car. Anji closed the door and walked around the vehicle, got in, and started the vehicle. They drove a short distance down the parking lot and arrived at Amir's apartment. Agent Ron Johnson was standing outside of Amir's apartment and saw their vehicle pull up. He walked over to their vehicle and Anji rolled down her window.

"How was your night?"

"Probably about like yours, uneventful." He replied.

"Is Mr. Hadad about ready?"

"He's making one last walk through as we speak."

Amir came out of the door and closed it and locked it. Agent Johnson went over to a vehicle and opened the passenger door for Amir. Amir walked over to the opened door and got in. Johnson closed it and went around and got into the vehicle.

As the cars made their way out of the complex both Amir and Dom watched as it disappeared from their view.

The agents drove their charges through the new checkpoint set up on the road to the SETI complex. As they arrived, Dom and Amir saw the new module units being secured in their assigned locations near the main SETI building. Mike and Perry were sitting at a picnic table in front of the complex when the cars containing Dom and Amir pulled up. Amir got out of the vehicle and went to the rear and opened the lift gate and retrieved his valise walked over to the picnic table. Momentarily, Dom joined them at the table carrying her purse and briefcase.

Amir looked up at the cloudless sky said, "I'd ask, but I'd say you're sitting out here enjoying the early morning sunshine."

Perry smiled and said to Mike, "You know Mike; I knew we didn't hire him just for his brains, he has common sense too."

Dom caught the conversation, "Amir, I think now's a good time to ask for a raise."

Mike chuffed, "Now you stepped in it Perry."

Amir looked over at the modules being set up, "Looks like we're going to be neighbors for a while." Amir paused, "Shall we draw straws or flip a coin for choice on our new digs?"

Perry looked at Mike, "Actually, we thought we'd wait until Doctor 'Gemo arrived and let him choose, it doesn't appear the units will be ready anytime soon anyway."

Dom nodded, "Sounds like a plan to me."

Amir added, "As long as I can get a hot shower at the end of the day, I'm good with whichever unit we get."

Dom heard a ringing tone coming from her purse. She reached in and retrieved her VPC, put her fingers on the print recognition and answered the device. The vice president's icon flashed on the screen.

"The vice president is calling," she paused and connected the COM. "Mr. Vice President, can you hold on until we get inside where I can connect to a larger monitor? It's difficult to see my screen in the sunlight. "

Richard smiled, "Of course Dominique, I'll wait."

She picked up her purse and briefcase and walked toward the office with the rest of the group following. They made their way over to a larger monitor and Dom transferred the COM to it.

The image of the vice president appeared on a monitor and the collage of colleagues gathered several chairs and placed them in front of the monitor and they all took their seats.

Dom finally began the conversation.

"Mr. Vice President, we weren't expecting your call."

Richard replied, "I had a break in my schedule and thought I would call to see how the accommodations were going. I trust that Lieutenant Smithy has her usual efficiency well underway."

"Yes Mr. Vice President, things are progressing very well."

"Dominique, it's just us on this call and you and the rest of you can call me Richard."

"We'll try Mr…" She paused and continued, "Richard, Sir."

"Thank you. I hope that this inconvenience will not last too long even though it's been less than a month since we verified our alien contact. Unfortunately the dissident factions are becoming more organized, as it seems negativity has its own breeding ground. Having said that, it is my hope that I, with the help of domestic security, can keep a buffer between you and the dissidents, so that you can devote your time to overcoming the obstacles to our communication issues with the aliens."

Perry made his observation, "We'll do our best with the information we have but the heavy lifting in the actual design of the communication aspects will probably have to come from Doctor Uschin's international think tank, and those chances have increased with the addition of Doctor 'Gemo."

Richard replied, "We're on the same page with that, Perry. If any of you can think of anyone else we can add to the team, then I'll make it happen."

Richard paused, "Okay, I have a meeting, enjoy your day and be safe." His image left the screen.

Dom disconnected her VPC and placed it back in her purse.

Amir left the group and went back outside to retrieve his valise. Dom went over to her workstation and placed her purse on the floor and her briefcase on the table. She heard a tone coming from her purse and took out her VCP and aligned her fingers with the print lock. A small text box appeared on the lower right hand part of the screen and she read the words that appeared, "We need to talk."

Dom smiled and entered some keystrokes and replied in the text box, "Yes, tonight." The text box disappeared.

Dom stood up and went back outside and received her luggage from the vehicle. Amir did the same and they both took their luggage into the main office.

Agents Rayner and Johnson after assisting Dom and Amir with their luggage, stopped for a moment and Ron stated, "Okay, let's take in their vehicles to the compound yard and drop them off and pick up our vehicle. They each got into Dom and Amir's vehicles and left the SETI complex.

*****

Richard stood up and collected his VPC and walked out the door of the communications room and went down the hall and walked into the president's secretary's office and greeted Philip.

"Philip is he available?"

Philip held up his hand and a hold motion and pressed a button on his desk.

A voice responded on a speaker, "Yes Philip."

Philip replied, "The vice president is here to see you."

The voice replied, "Please send him in."

Richard nodded to Philip and went in to the Oval Office.

The president was sitting on the couch in front of a COM monitor talking to Doctor 'Gemo.

Richard walked over and nodded to the president, "Good morning Mr. President."

Tsirch replied, "And good morning to you Mr. Vice President."

Richard turned toward the monitor and stood looking at Doctor 'Gemo's image and sucked in his cheeks and said nothing. R.A. saw Richard on his monitor, standing looking at him without talking. R.A. took a breath, "Okay, Richard let me have it."

Richard finally spoke, "You drop off the grid with barely a heads up and dive into a secret project funded by Atwood."

R.A. replied, "Come on Richard you knew I was going under so I could follow the breadcrumbs left by the aliens without interference."

Richard sighed, "Eventually I tracked you down, but you didn't make it easy."

R.A. responded, "I knew that there were those who were tracking your efforts to find me and that could compromise my cover."

Richard replied, "I get that but next time give me a little more warning."

R.A. responded, "I promise, but if I get beamed up by the aliens, all bets are off."

Richard said, "What makes you think the aliens would want you?"

Tsirch smiled and shook his head and interrupted their exchange saying, "Enough of your bantering, I need a situation report."

Richard half-smiled, "Other than the report from Domestic Security and Homeland I read this morning, I have no new developments."

R.A. offered his input, "I spent most of the morning going over data with Sal and preparing for my move to Hat Creek. We are going to COM later with the think tank and compile all the data we have so far."

Tsirch inquired, "Has Sal and his bio-scientist counterparts made any progress in determining how the latest diffusion enhances our food production and reduces the negative effect on our environment?"

R.A. replied, "From what I gleaned from our conversation there is a conversion process that can be used to reduce greenhouse emissions, while increasing food quality and production while greatly stemming our carbon footprint."

Tsirch asked, "This, conversion process, did they have any idea of the equipment and location needed for the process and the timeframe involved?"

"The equipment needed, is still being discussed as is a possible location. As for the timeframe, the International Science Foundation is still digesting the data." R.A. explained.

Tsirch continued, "I know you've been working on a project for Atwood, but I don't understand your endgame."

R.A. took a short breath, "It's somewhat difficult to explain but suffice to say that it relates to the difference in the type of diffusions sent to Earth and also one sent to and an exo-planet in the Wolf system."

Tsirch shrugged, "Do you see that as a priority when compared to the alien communication dilemma?"

R.A. sighed, "The diffusion differences are interrelated to the understanding of the diffusions sent to Earth. However, the need to communicate with the aliens will be my priority moving forward."

Tsirch took a breath and nodded slowly, "Well, I don't pretend to know the full effects of the diffusions, but it seems that getting answers from the aliens would be my first step."

Richard finally sat down on the couch a little ways from Tsirch, "If there's anything I or my resources can do to help, all you have to do is ask."

R.A. nodded, "I think your Domestic Security personnel have much of my situation under control for the moment. Lieutenant Smithy is a 'take control' asset of exceptional worth."

Richard smiled, "She is that."

R.A. thought for a moment, "There is one thing I would like to ask, whichever one of you could make it happen. I would like to have Marnie Grayson to continue as my security."

Tsirch and Richard look each other and each shrugged their shoulders and Tsirch said, "That's no problem."

R.A. smiled, "Thank you." He paused and continued, "Well, I have places to go and things to do. Thank you both."

R.A.'s image disappeared from the screen.

Tsirch leaned back on the couch and looked over at Richard, "Well, that solves the security situation for R.A., but we yet have to talk Sal into his security needs."

Richard sighed, "Sal is a curmudgeon and will resist anyone tagging along in his daily activities. However, I believe I have just the person he will accept for his security needs, but it will take your approval."

Tsirch tossed a curious look, "Don't tell me you have someone who will put him in restraints and a ring in his nose to make him comply."

Richard chuckled, "The one I have in mind just needs to smile and tell him what to do."

Tsirch chuffed, "The only one that can do that is Congresswoman Johnny Walsh."

Richard nodded, "That's true, but I have someone else in mind."

Tsirch replied, "Okay, who is this necromancer?"

Richard took a short breath, "I was thinking of Special Agent Natás."

Tsirch wrinkled his brow and thought, "Well, she may be one of the few that could keep him under control."

Richard looked over at Tsirch and questioned with two open hands, "So, yea or nay?"

Tsirch replied, "Richard, we didn't have to dance around, you could have just told me who you had in mind."

Richard smiled, "And miss a chance to jerk the President around?"

Tsirch chuffed, "If I could fire you I would."

Richard laughed, "So, we've come full circle."

Tsirch got up and walked over to his desk and pressed the call button. Philips voice responded, "Yes Mr. President."

Philip, give me the director of Secret Service Annice Potter on COM."

"Yes Mr. President."

*****

Marnie finished adjusting her shoulder holster over her blouse and reach down and retrieved her M&P 40 off the bed. She removed the magazine and pulled the slide slightly back to expose a visible round in the chamber and slid it back into position. She checked the magazine to ensure it was fully loaded, put the safety on, reinserted the magazine and put the gun in her holster. She picked her extra magazine off the bed and checked its capacity and placed it in the magazine holder in her holster. She put her jacket on and picked up her modest suitcase and stepped out of her room. She walked over and placed her suitcase next to the front door. She looked down the hallway and looked through a partially opened door and saw R.A.'s movement in the bedroom.

She walked toward the front door and opened it and scanned both directions. She picked up her suitcase stepped out and closed the door. She walked over to her vehicle and opened the driver's side passenger door and placed her suitcase inside and closed the door. Once again she scanned the area went back into the apartment.

R.A. was coming down the hallway toward the living room carrying a suitcase and a satchel and placed them on the floor by the door.

Marnie asked, "You ready Doc?"

R.A. nodded, "Yes, I'm ready. And I want to thank you again for agreeing to continue as my security."

Marnie smiled, "Doc, I got used to being around you and besides who else would put up with you?"

R.A. nodded, "Yeah, anyone else would have put duct tape on my mouth and put me in leg irons."

Marnie smiled, "I still might need the duct tape."

R.A. shook his head, "Okay, get my suitcase and we can start our new adventure."

She opened the door, picked up R.A.'s suitcase and offered R.A. the first exit. R.A. picked up the satchel and went out and got into the passenger side of the vehicle. Marnie closed the front door and followed him out. She opened the rear passenger door placed his suitcase in the rear seat and closed the door. She scanned the area and walked around the vehicle and got in the driver's seat. She buckled her seatbelt, started the vehicle and they drove off.

*****

Sal slung his backpack over his shoulder and took his cup of coffee and half eaten sausage sandwich off the table and walked toward the front door. He held the coffee in one hand and put the sandwich in his mouth, reached in his pocket and retrieved his door keys. Awkwardly he opened the front door with his door keys in his hand. He pulled open the door with his foot, wide enough to make his exit. He pulled the door closed with two fingers and securely grabbed the keys to lock the door. Put his keys back in his pocket and turned to go down a couple of steps and was abruptly met by a figure that put two hands on his shoulder. He backed away to get a better look at his accoster. He was surprised by a very familiar face.

Jennifer Natás chuckled, "Uncle Sal, I gotcha."

"Jen, what the hell are you doing?"

She put her hands down to her side, "Obviously, I'm keeping you from running over me."

Sal shrugged his shoulders, "No, what are you doing here; did we have an appointment?"

"No, but from now on we're joined at the hip."

Sal shook his head in confusion, "What's that supposed to mean?"

She smiled, "I, uncle Sal, have been assigned by the highest authority to watch over you."

Sal chuckled and looked from side to side and up in the air and back at Jen and finally said, "I don't see any higher authority than if you mean a deity, I don't answer to them."

She smiled and explained, "Perhaps I should have said the highest political authority, the POTUS."

Sally replied, "Well, now you need to explain, am I under arrest?"

She sighed, "Technically, no, but you are under tight security."

Sal was yet confused, "And what does that mean?"

She explained, "I have been assigned as your personal security."

Sal wrinkled one eyebrow, "I don't need personal security."

Jen continued to explain, "Okay, my seemingly oblivious rocket scientist, perhaps I should explain to you in layman's terms.

Since you are connected to the alien contact events, there are those who have been engaged in violent attacks on places and people anyway involved in alien contact." She paused, "Therefore, I have been assigned as your first line of protection. So, in a nutshell you either have me or a couple of other agents underfoot."

Sal thought for a moment, "Really, whose idea was this?" He paused for a moment, "Oh, wait, it doesn't take a rocket scientist to know your dad is behind this."

Jen smiled, "It only took you two minutes to put it together, for a minute there, I thought you were going senile."

Sal took a group, "How long is this protection going the last?"

Jen responded, "You are the rocket scientists you tell me."

Sal sighed, "I guess the answer is; as long as it takes."

Jen nodded, "Unfortunately, that's the truth." She paused, "Okay, where are we going?"

Sal responded, "I gotta go to my lab."

Jen replied, "Okay, since I can park anywhere, I'm driving."

Sal smiled, "Now that's the best thing you've said since you got here. That's fine with me, let's go."

Jen turned around scanned the area and began walking toward her vehicle while Sal followed.

*****

Agent Anji Rayner pulled up to the new checkpoint at Hat Creek and rolled down her window and stopped the vehicle. Although they had been here earlier she noticed there had been a shift change with new guardsmen. She displayed her secret service credentials and her partner agent Johnson displayed his also.

The guard walked up to the window, "Good morning."

Anji noticed his rank and last name said, "Good morning Corporal Lester, I'm agent Anji Rayner in this is agent Ron Johnson." She handed the Corporal her identification and agent Johnson reached over and gave the Corporal his credentials also.

Another guardsman came out of the guard shack pushing a mirror mounted on a roller and meticulously guided it under the vehicle to view the undercarriage. Corporal Lester looked carefully at the IDs and matched them with the agent's faces and went back into the guard shack and spoke to someone on a COM. The other guardsman continued around the vehicle checking the rest of the undercarriage. He stopped at the driver's window, "Could you pop the trunk and the hood for me?

Anji noticed his rank and name also, "Of course Corporal Moya." She reached down and pushed the trunk release button and pulled the hood release lever. Moya looked into the back seats as he continued back to the opened trunk and inspected it, looking for unauthorized passengers. The presence of two assault rifles, Kevlar vests and a case containing chemical agents did not concern him. He closed the trunk and went back over to the opened hood, looked into it and closed it. He continued over to the driver's window, "Thank you." He reached down and reacquired his rolling mirror and returned to the guard station.

Corporal Lester returned with their IDs, "Thank you agents, you're clear." and handed the ID's back to agent Rayner.

"Thank you Corporal. Be safe."

The Corporal nodded and Anji handed Johnson his ID, started the car and continued to the SETI complex.

When she got near the complex she noticed several modular units placed on pier blocks with electrical, water and sewage lines being attached to them. She continued driving on around to the front parking area and stopped the car.

Anji looked over at agent Johnson, "Well Ron, we're here. Let's check out the lay of the land and get acquainted."

They both exited the car and closed the car doors. They stood and scanned the grounds and walked toward the end of the parking area. Together they walked around the entire perimeter of the buildings taking note of possible hiding places and vulnerable structures. They stood for a few moments watching the modular's being connected to the utility grid. They returned back to the parking area and took out their notebooks and COMs and documented the types of vehicles and license plate numbers. They finished the perimeter check went up to the main building and inspected the entrance keypad. Johnson made several attempts to unlock the door and it failed to open. He took out his VPC and activated it. He looked at the screen and entered some keystrokes and then press the enter key. He entered some numbers on the keypad and the door unlocked. Anji smiled, "Guess we'll have to change the parameters for access."

Ron nodded in said, "Yeah, anniversary dates will get you every time."

He took a step into the building and Anji followed him in. They looked down the walkway and saw what appeared to be in office and walked toward it. Perry looked through the glass windows of the office and saw them approaching. He stood up and met them at the door. He shook their hands, "You must be the agents Dom and Amir were talking about. I'm director Perry Edmonds and the assistant director Mike Mitchell is over in the security office. It appears that we are all going to get to know each other real well, at least until the alien contact stigma works itself out."

Anji replied, "We'll try to stay in the shadows as much as possible."

Perry snickered, "Well, for me, I welcome the company. We have only six scientists and two on-call maintenance workers here."

Ron replied, "Yes, we've already vetted your two other staff and we're working on the maintenance workers.

Anji added, "Can we get everyone together for a little powwow so we can work out some logistics?"

Perry nodded, "Sure, let's go over to the break room."

Anji replied, "Sounds good to me. Lead the way.

Ron and Anji backed away from the door and allowed Perry to come through. He led them down the walkway and into the break room toward the end of the building.

Perry said, "Wait here and I will get Mike, Dom and Amir, the other two associates are not here today." He turned and left the break room.

Ron and Anji nodded and looked around the break room and to their surprise it was more than just a break room. It had a decent size refrigerator, an oven with a stovetop, a countertop and several cabinets for storage and of course a sink. There were also two four by six tables with chairs and an oversized COM on the wall.

Ron turned to Anji, "This is more than I expected."

Anji nodded, "Yes, this should make things easier."

Shortly, Mike came into the break room followed by Dom, Amir and Perry.

Mike approached Ron and Anji, "I'm Mike Mitchell. You two must be our keepers." He said with a grin.

Ron chuckled and said as he extended his hand, "Let's just say we're new additions to the family."

Mike took his hand and shook it and accepted Anji's handshake also. Dom and Amir smiled and nodded to Ron and Anji.

Ron address the group, "You can have a seat if you wish."

His audience each took a seat at a table.

Anji began, "We realize that this is a somewhat unique situation having all of us in virtual quarantine. Ron and I and other security personnel will do our best not to interfere with your daily routines." She paused, "After seeing this break room which is more like a dining room and kitchen, we believe that this will mitigate some logistical obstacles. Although from what I understand the residential units also contain small kitchens, this area could also be an alternate meeting and/or dining area to break up any monotony we may face.

As far as grocery supplies, some of you may have special needs and desires for certain foods, so please make a list and we will make every attempt to fulfill your wishes."

Ron stepped forward, "Surely you're wondering who's going to do the cooking."

Snickering was heard among the crowd, and Ron continued, "We may make arrangements to bring in a cook, however I can offer some of my culinary skills and Anji says she can also boil water." Anji grinned and tossed a sly look at Ron, "Additionally, I was told that Doctor 'Gemo's security, Marnie Grayson is also a decent cook."

Anji added, "While it is possible to order takeout, the possibility of intentional contamination makes that somewhat unlikely, but it remains an option."

Ron continued, "You will yet have the opportunity to maintain your own supplies in your cabinets and refrigerators and prepare your own meals."

Anji took a more serious tone and began, "You realize that you are here, voluntarily, because of possible threats to your safety. And we are here because those threats have been assessed as credible. Your safety and the security of this facility is the reason for these extreme measures. While on the surface it may appear that you are prisoners, "Anji smiled, "but you are free to leave at any time. However, we strongly suggest that if you plan to travel, outside this facility, you be accompanied by security personnel." Anji paused.

"Of course you may have visitors, but they need to be cleared by our agency." Anji looked over at Perry, "As I understand none of you are married, but if anyone requires some overnight visitors they also would need to be vetted, just supply us with their names."

Dom and Amir shrugged their shoulders and Perry looked at Mike and turned back to Anji with a grin, "We don't have any names, but if you have any suggestions were open to it."

Mike elbowed Perry in the side and laughed, but said nothing.

Anji smiled and raised her eyebrows, she looked at Ron, "We'll take that under advisement." She took a breath, "Other concerns will be addressed as they arise. Are there any questions?"

Ron and Anji looked around and saw no takers.

Ron nodded, "Okay, we do have a security concern that involves all of you and that is the access code you use on the keypad at the entrance door. Each of you will have to modify your code by creating an individual access code. We will direct you on how to do so, one person at a time. So, if you will follow us to the entrance door we'll get this first task out of your way."

Anji nodded and began to walk out the break room with the entourage following.

*****

Marnie stepped out of the chartered flight carrying her suitcase and walked down the steps to the tarmac at the Sacramento airport.

R.A. followed her down the steps carrying his suitcase and valise. Marnie scanned the area and spied a Huey helicopter idling on the edge of the runway. She looked back at R.A. to ensure he was following and slowed down her pace until he caught up with her. Together they walked toward the Huey. When she got close to it she stopped and showed her credentials to the pilot. The pilot looked at the ID and yelled above the engine noise, "Welcome aboard Grayson."

Marnie also nodded, "Thank you, but I need to see your ID also."

The pilot seemed surprised but complied with her request and retrieved his ID off his vest and gave it to her. She looked closely at the ID, it read, Chip Barker, and returned it to the pilot.

"Thank you, but I needed to verify your identity before we got on the chopper."

Barker nodded, "Yes ma'am, I understand."

Marnie assisted R.A. in securing his suitcase in the chopper and helped him inside. She walked around to the other side of the chopper and put her suitcase in, secured it, and settled in the seat next to the pilot. R.A. and Marnie placed headphones on and Barker said, "Okay, buckle up, will be there in about an hour. There will be no snacks served and no restroom breaks."

Both R.A. and Marnie chuckled loudly. The lift off was smooth and they began their journey. Barker pointed out interesting tidbits as they made their way past the Buttes and portions of the Sacramento River. They glided their way along various mountains and flew toward a Cinder Cone enroute to the destination.

Soon Barker made radio contact with Darcy Blaine, Security One, at the Hat Creek SETI complex.

"Security One, this is Chip, my ETA is two."

The radio crackled, "Copy that Chip. I am 10-97 at the LZ now."

Chip replied, "10-4."

As the complex got into view, Barker swung the chopper in an easy half circle and made a soft landing near the parking lot.

Darcy was standing next to a sedan watching the touchdown. Marnie gave Barker a fist bump and removed her headphones.

She unbuckled her seatbelt and stepped out of the Huey, grabbed her suitcase and walked around to the other side of the Huey and sat her suitcase down. She helped R.A. unbuckled his seatbelt and motioned to him to remove his headphones. R.A. took off the headphones and stepped out of the flying machine. Marnie pulled out his suitcase and handed it to R.A.. She waved once again to Barker and picked up her suitcase and walked toward Darcy standing by a vehicle. R.A. clutching his satchel and carrying his

suitcase, followed Marnie to the car.

Marnie and R.A. walked up to Darcy and Marnie extended her hand to Darcy, who shook it and Darcy transferred her handshake to R.A.,"I'm Darcy Blaine, Security One, it's a pleasure to meet both of you. Let's get you to the complex." Darcy walked to the passenger side of the vehicle and opened the rear passenger door. Marnie and R.A. followed carrying their luggage and they placed it in the rear passenger side seat and Darcy closed the door. Marnie opened the front passenger side door and offered R.A. entry. R.A. accepted and got in holding his valise. Marnie walked around the vehicle and got into the driver's side rear passenger door. Darcy maneuvered the vehicle to the left a short distance through the parking lot up to the main building and parked.

She got out and assisted her passengers in retrieving their luggage out of the car. Anji saw them approaching and opened up the office door and waited. R.A. was carrying his valise and started to pick up his suitcase, but Darcy grabbed the handle,"I'll get this for you Doc."

R.A. smiled, "Thank you."

Marnie grabbed her suitcase and they walked up to the office door where Anji was waiting. Anji initiated a handshake with Marnie, "Welcome, I'm agent Anji Rayner, but just call me Anji."

Marnie smiled, "Thank you, I'm Marnie and you may know Doctor 'Gemo already." She said as she motioned at R.A..

Anji shook her head, "Actually no, we've never met." She extended her hand to R.A..

"Doctor 'Gemo it's a pleasure to meet you. Call me Anji."

R.A. shook her hand and replied smiling, "Thank you Anji, but drop the 'doctor' and call me R.A.."

Anji smiled, "I'll try to remember that R.A.."

She noticed the luggage, "Come in and we'll find a temporary place for your luggage." She backed into the office to allow them to come in. Marnie waved R.A. in first and Darcy followed him in carrying his suitcase. Marnie took her turn for entry.

Anji led them down to the break room and asked them to place their luggage against the wall. After Darcy placed R.A.'s luggage with the other luggage and R.A. had deposited his valise there as well, she turned to R.A. and Marnie, "Once again welcome. I'll leave you in good hands." She continued out of the break room.

Anji looked around the break room, "There may be some coffee or drinks and maybe some snacks available, if you want anything."

Marnie and R.A. waved off the offer.

Anji said, "Okay, I guess I should take you to meet the other residents."

Marnie and R.A. shrugged in acceptance and Anji led the way out of the break room and walked toward the office. Perry and Mike were seated in the office talking to agent Johnson and saw the trio enter the office. They both stood and walked toward the new guests. Johnson was the first to greet them.

"I would guess that you are Marnie Grayson and Doctor 'Gemo, I'm agent Johnson but it's Ron to you." He shook both, R.A. and Marnie's hands."

Marnie replied, "I'm Marnie and Doctor 'Gemo prefers to be called R.A.." R.A. nodded, "Please to meet you Ron."

Ron nodded and stepped aside.

Mike took a couple of steps toward Marnie who offered her hand and Mike shook it saying, "I'm Mike and this is Perry," he said as he stepped aside for Perry to also shake her hand.

Perry said, "Welcome to Hat Creek."

R.A. stepped forward smiling at Mike and Perry. He heartily shook both their hands, "It's good to see you both again, it's been several years."

Perry returned, "Yes, the last we saw you was at the Frankfurt conference."

R.A. nodded, "Yeah, it's been a while." He paused, looked out through the windows into the complex, "So, where are the celebrities?"

Perry smiled, "If you're inquiring about Dom and Amir, they are out at their desks." He pointed out the office windows into computer stations area. "I'll have them come to the office."

Perry stepped over to the desk, leaned toward a COM, pressed a button, "Dom and Amir you have visitors in the office."

Dom and Amir were busy at their stations and heard the call. Amir looked toward the office and turned to Dom, "We are being summoned, m'lady." Dom smiled, "Yes, it appears so." They both stood up and walked toward the office.

As they neared the office they noticed the new arrivals. Smiles on their faces grew with recognition. They stepped into the office and immediately gravitated toward R.A.. They both avoided R.A.'s offered handshake and each gave him a hug. Amir released his hug saying, "I'm sorry Doctor 'Gemo for the personal hug, but we both feel we already know you from our COM meeting."

R.A. smiled, "Yes, but there is no apology necessary as I feel the same way. However, I am disappointed."

Both Amir and Dom appeared hurt by his comment. Dom asked, "I'm sorry we offended you Doctor 'Gemo."

R.A. smiled, "I'm offended that you called me Doctor 'Gemo and not R.A.."

The relief on their faces was felt by everyone, as they all stifled their laughs.

R.A. turned to Marnie and introduced her to Dom and Amir.

"Marnie this is Dominique Soul and Amir Hadad, scientists extraordinaire."

Marnie shook both their hands, "I'm Marnie. It appears that we all will be spending some quality time together."

Dom looked around the office and captured each face in her mind, "Yes, and although our gathering is the result of safety concerns, I don't think I could've chosen better companions."

R.A. sighed, "How about we take this meeting to a more comfortable setting, possibly in the break room?"

Perry nodded, "Spoken like a true rocket scientist,"

R.A. chuffed, "It's more like a weary traveler looking for a place to rest."

Perry smiled and motioned his hand toward the door. Ron was the closest to the door and led the exit to the break room.

As the group filtered into the break room, Ron said, "You can forage for any beverage or snacks you can find in the cabinets and fridge."

Most of the group opted for a beverage and then settled into their seating choices.

R.A. took a deep breath, "I hesitate to start with a work-related issue, but has anyone heard from Sal?"

Perry nodded, "Yes, Sal said he would be on a COM at 1100 hrs."

Ron offered, "I'll speak for Anji and me, we are not going to be put off by your scientific interactions, as we actually were chosen because of our educational background in astronomy and biological science."

Marnie chimed in, "And as for me, R.A. and I have had many a discussion about his work."

R.A. smiled, "Well, you might say it seems that the stars have aligned for bringing us together for this moment."

Anji took a short breath and offered, "Thinking about the stars it reminds me of the possibilities of intelligent alien life presented in the Drake equation. Of all the millions of galaxies and stars and planets it seems that of all the possibilities of "N" in the equation, all that matters is the result being "1"."

R.A. smiled, "That's very astute of you Anji, and in this case the chances of there being extraterrestrial intelligence are 100 percent."

AGAINST ALL ENEMIES...

Edward was looking over a list of agents on his COM. Brie was on a COM next to him talking to Jennifer Natás.

"Have you assigned any agents to Congresswoman Walsh yet?"

Brie replied, "Edward is looking at the list of available agents as we speak."

Jen replied, "Thank you, Sal was getting stressed out."

Brie said, "I understand his concern, but while she's at the Capitol she has security. We are working on assigning her a personal security detail. Let Sal know she will have coverage before she leaves the Capitol."

Jen replied, "Okay thank you." Her image disappeared from the screen.

Edward's screen showed six flashing icons; five agents and Congresswoman Johnny Walsh. The Congresswoman's icon disappeared and her image took its place.

Edward spoke, "Congresswoman Walsh, this is Commander Narkiewicz, how are you this morning?"

Walsh replied, "Doing well Commander, how can I help you?"

"It is what I want to do for you Ms. Walsh." Edward replied, "And what is that?" She asked, "I found it necessary to assign an agent to Doctor Uschin for security purposes. And while discussing it with him, due to your personal connection with him, I find it necessary to assign an agent for your security also. I realize you have security while you are at the Capitol, but your safety may be at risk when you're not there. I have a list of five agents available that you can choose from for your personal protection."

Johnny paused and thought, "Actually, I have an agent in mind that I've dealt with before, Darlene Gordon; is she available?"

Edward smiled as he looked at the screen, agent Gordon's icon was one of the choices.

He replied, "Yes she is available; I'll have her meet you in the rotunda in thirty minutes."

Johnny smiled, "Thank you, she is perfect."

Edward said, "Very good, enjoy your day and be safe."

Johnny's image disappeared from the screen.

*****

Faizan Badie was in the driver's seat and Jason Orr was in the passenger seat, as they waited in a parked, dark gray Chevy, on the street near the exit of the Capitol garage. Jason was watching a COM of the live feed from the Capitol. The committee meeting was adjourning for the morning and he watched intently and saw Congresswoman Walsh leaving the chamber. He reached down and grabbed a Kel-Tec carbine and unfolded the stock. He inserted a magazine and charged the handle. Faizan smiled, "Perhaps this will send the proper message to Doctor Uschin."

*****

Johnny had time to kill, so she went to her office and called Sal on a COM. Sal's image appeared on the screen and he spoke on seeing Johnny's image.

"Hey hon, did you get a call from Edward?"

She smiled, "Yes, but I don't really think it's necessary to have a bodyguard."

Sal sighed, "I didn't think I would either until I was shown the chatter on the dark web."

Johnny's face showed concern as she asked, "There was chatter; about what?"

He replied, "Segr8 has stepped up its activity and is partnering with the Islamic State. They have been attacking the primary sources of alien contact and attempted an abduction of a family member in Australia, and the same thread is linked to the DC area. And the attempted bombing at Hat Creek yesterday is evidence of the credibility of the threats. "

She responded, "Yes, I received a security notice that there was a thwarted delivery of a bomb by a hang glider and their tightening security around the complex."

Sal added, "Yeah, but did you know that R.A. is going to live at the complex with the other scientists with on-site security agents?"

She replied, "Really? That's got to be a big change for him going from being inconspicuous at the VLA to a target for terrorists."

She paused, "So, who did you draw for security?"

Sal portrayed a look of guilt, "Well, first of all I didn't choose her, but you shouldn't be concerned."

Johnny keyed on his suspicious demeanor, "Okay, what are you *not* telling me?"

He shrugged, "It shouldn't matter that she's young and good looking, and sworn to protect my 'body'." He attempted to change the subject, "So, dear; who do you have for security?"

Johnny smiled and shook her head and said sternly, "You're not getting away with that; who do you have guarding your 'body'?"

Sal laughed, "It's agent Natás."

She chuckled, "So, you got Jennifer! That's hilarious. You know that she won't let you get away with anything."

Sal responded, "Yeah, I guess I'll have to let some of my girl-friends go."

Johnny laughed, "Oh, poor baby."

They shared laughter and Sal asked, "So, who's guarding your 'body'?"

Johnny feigned urgency, "Oh, that reminds me I have to meet my tall, handsome bodyguard in the rotunda. So, I'll catch you later honey. Bye." She ended the COM.

Sal smiled as her image disappeared from his COM.

Johnny picked up her purse and put her VPC in it and picked up a briefcase off the floor. She opened the office door stepped out and closed and locked it. She walked down the hallway some distance and arrived at the rotunda. Agent Gordon was waiting in the rotunda and saw Johnny walking toward her. Johnny swung her purse on to her shoulder and extended her hand to agent Gordon.

Johnny shook her hand, "I'm glad you were available Darlene, it's good to have someone who knows my quirks."

Darling smiled, "Congresswoman, you have fewer quirks than anyone I know. But your wit and sense of humor are a challenge."

Johnny smiled and slowly shook her head.

Agent Gordon asked, "So, what are your plans; where we going?"

Johnny took a breath, "Well, I have some calls to make and a few COM's, but I can do them from home, so I guess I'm going home."

Darlene asked, "Okay, I know you have your car here, but since we're going together you can leave your car here and I'll drive my vehicle."

Johnny nodded, "Sounds good to me, it's better than me fighting the traffic."

"Alright, I'll go get my SUV and meet you at the garage exit. It'll take me about fifteen minutes."

Johnny nodded, "Okay, I'll see you there."

They parted ways as Johnny had to check out at the main security entrance. She made her way to the elevator, stepped in and selected the main floor option, and the elevator door closed.

*****

Agent Gordon exited the security service elevator and made her way to her assigned vehicle. She opened up the lift-gate and reached in and opened up a large gun case. She took a visual inventory of the weapons and munitions. She reached to her side and drew her service weapon and removed the magazine to check to ensure it was at maximum capacity. She pulled back the slide on the weapon slightly to verify there was a round in the chamber. She replaced the magazine and holstered her weapon. She reached to her magazine pouch and checked the two magazines to ensure they were loaded. She closed the gun case and reached into a bag and pulled out an extra Kevlar vest. She closed the hatch-back and went to the driver's side and tossed the vest on the passenger seat and got in.

She started the vehicle and navigated down several ramps and headed toward the main exit.

She drove up to the exit and stopped behind the guard shack. She waited for Johnny to make her appearance.

*****

Faizan was scanning the garage exit with a monocular, looking for Congresswoman Walsh's vehicle to come out.

Jason was tapping his fingers on the dashboard impatiently.

Faizan reached over and pressed on Jason's fingers to stop the tapping.

He looked over at Jason, "Patience my friend, you shouldn't hurry fate."

Jason huffed, "Why; when these heathens are trying to destroy our faith in God, in your Allah, by colluding with the invisible devil. We can't allow the pollution of our earth with their evil infusion." Jason became more agitated, "We must resist the poisoning of our minds with their electronic signals being sent down into our heads."

Faizan nodded in agreement and added with more fervor, "And let's not forget the government using their military to suppress our religious ideas. They are no more than pagans in their worship of aliens."

Faizan began pounding on the steering wheel with his hand and Jason complemented Faizan by banging on the dashboard.

The verbal rout was interrupted when Faizan saw Congresswoman Walsh in the monocular, walk up to the exit.

He exulted, "There she is!" and handed the monocular to Jason

who became excited as he focused in on Walsh as she neared the guard shack. Jason smiled as he watched.

"She's walking; this is going to be easy."

Walsh disappeared from his view as she walked behind the guard shack. Agent Gordon saw her in her mirror and stepped up of the car. She reached in and grabbed the Kevlar vest and walked over to Walsh. She held up the vest, "I know you don't think you need it but while you're in the public I would feel more comfortable if you would wear this."

Johnny looked at the vest and wrinkled her face, "Really!"

Darlene nodded, "You can wear it under your jacket and it won't be that noticeable."

Johnny relented and handed her purse and briefcase to Darlene. She took off her jacket and put the vest on over her blouse and then put the jacket on. It was somewhat awkward to wear, but she seemed to accept the inconvenience. She took her purse back from Gordon.

Jason had partial view of Gordon as she opened up the rear lift-gate and put the briefcase in and closed the door. Johnny came into his view and she opened the rear passenger door and got in. Agent Gordon got in the driver's seat and started the vehicle. She drove around some road cones into the exit lane and stopped at the guard shack. Jason watched as she punched in a code and the exit gate opened up. Jason handed the monocular back to Faizan, "They're coming out now in the black SUV. Faizan acquired a visual and watched as she drove out of the garage. Jason opened his car door, "I'll have to get in the backseat because she's going to be on the passenger side and I won't be able to get a good shot at her from the front seat." Jason got out and got into the back passenger seat and closed the door. He positioned himself in the center of the seat so he would have access to either side of the vehicle.

Darlene pulled out of the garage and scanned the vehicles along the street taking note of any vehicles with occupants. She looked both ways and pulled out into the right lane of the three lane one-way street.

Faizan was parked on the left side of the street and had to wait for two cars to pass before he pulled out. Gradually, he got into the center lane and began to maneuver closer to the SUV. Agent Gordon continued down the one- way and made a right turn onto another one-way. Faizan moved from the center lane to the right hand lane and also made a right turn.

Gordon watched her rearview mirror and moved to the center lane for two blocks then moved to the right lane and made a right turn into another one-way street. Faizan followed the movement of the SUV and made a right turn. Gordon saw the vehicle mirroring her movements and made another right turn into a one-way street.

Faizan also made a right turn. She noticed the same vehicle also make the last right turn. Gordon looked in the rearview mirror at Johnny and told her, "Lay down in the floorboard behind my seat."

Johnny was aware of security protocols and did as directed.

Gordon activated her car COM said, "Agent Gordon badge 3119, I have a 10-33. Dark gray Chevy sedan in pursuit of protective custody Congresswoman Walsh, westbound on thirty-fifth, enroute to DC PD."

Agent Gordon was very aware of the grid layout of the streets and where they went. She made several turns from one-ways to two-ways keeping at least two cars between her and the car following her. Faizan did his best to get close to his target and Jason was getting impatient.

Gordon was four blocks from the Police Department lot and took advantage of a break in traffic and quickly accelerated in and out of traffic and completed a full slide into the parking lot, and came to rest against the barrier with the passenger side of her vehicle facing toward the street. She got out of her vehicle, opened her door and stood behind the door and drew her service weapon and leveled it over the roof.

Faizan had been keeping pace until the last two blocks when another vehicle interfered with his chase. Faizan saw his target had stopped in the parking lot but made the fatal mistake of exposing his driver's side to the target.

Jason rolled down the rear driver side window and was sliding into a shooting position and started to point his weapon out the window toward the SUV. Gordon saw the glint of the weapon in the morning light, and saw a single flash from the muzzle and fired two sets of three rounds into the back seat. She assessed the situation and saw no movement from the backseat. She changed her focus to the driver. Faizan unadvisedly pointed a handgun out the window toward the SUV and discharged two rounds and Gordon traded two more sets of three rounds toward the driver.

Within seconds several capitol police descended upon the scene. Gordon raised her weapon and pointed it toward the sky with her finger off the trigger and held up her wallet badge and ID in front of her, all while keeping her eyes on the other vehicle. She peeked into the backseat and asked Johnny, "Are you all right?"

Johnny was yet prone on the floorboard and slowly looked up to Gordon, "I think so," she paused, and did a self assessment, "Yes, I'm okay thank you."

*****

Colonel Narkiewicz and Lieutenant Smithy were on separate COM's as another screen displayed the breaking news.

Congresswoman Walsh Targeted by Religious Dissidents; was the headline splashed below the video of the incident, edited from CCTV, DC Police Department and various individual COM videos.

Johnny's first COM was to Sal, assuring him she was not harmed.

Edward used his spy technology and hijacked the COM between them. Their images were on his screen along with that of agent Gordon.

Sal was in mid conversation with Johnny, "Are you sure you're okay? I can be there in twenty minutes."

Johnny replied, "Sal, there's no need; I'll be going to my place soon with the police and Secret Service escort."

Edward patched in Agent Gordon's image next to Johnny's image on their COM and Gordon said to him, "Doctor Uschin, I assure you she will be taken care of. There are two other agents going to accompany her in addition to the police escort."

Sal asked, "You're not going with her?"

Darlene replied, "I will be with her later, but I have to go before the shooting review panel."

Sal replied, "But you saved her life, what's there to review?"

Darlene smiled, "Doctor Uschin, you of all people know there are always standard operation procedures and this is one of them."

Sal nodded, "Anyway, thank you, thank you."

Edward interrupted, "Sal, we understand your worry that you have, but you have to trust she's in good hands with our agents."

Sal took a deep breath, "Okay, but Johnny, I'd feel better if you came to my place instead."

Johnny thought for a moment, "Okay Sal, I'll come to your place."

Sal replied, "Okay I'm on my way home now."

His image left the screen.

Edward said, "Agent Gordon; agents Holtz and Elliott should be there in ten minutes to escort Congresswoman Walsh wherever she wants to go."

"Ten–four commander, I'll wait until they arrive and give them a Sit-Rep." Gordon replied, Edward became serious, "Agent Gordon, you did great work today. Your country very much appreciates you."

Agent Gordon straightened her shoulders, "Thank you sir… Against all enemies," she paused and snapped a final emphatic, "Sir!"

The COM's went dark.

*****

Tsirch sat watching the monitor as his press secretary, January Yee, engaged the media in a press conference about the morning's attack on Congresswoman Walsh.

"Yes, according to the reports, videos of the encounter, statements from witnesses at the scene and the agent's statement, there were a total of fifteen shots fired during the incident. The first shot was fired by one of the assailants and the agent returned fire with six rounds. The second assailant discharged two rounds and the agent responded with six more rounds."

Several hands raised in the audience and Yee chose the next questioner.

"Bob Helton, Daily News; Have they identified the shooters and their motive for the attack?"

Yee replied, "One assailant was named Jason Orr, residence unknown, and was a known member of the group called 'Segr8'. The second assailant was Faizan Badie, residence also unknown, and was a known associate of the radical arm of the Islamic State. And I will add that both of these attackers succumbed to gunshot wounds at the scene."

Yee selected his next choice, "Kylie Mills, Boston Herald; Do you have the agent's name involved in the incident?"

He responded, "Yes, we have the agent's name, but we decline to divulge it, as that's why it's called 'secret service'." He ended that statement with a stifled grin.

The next question was presented, "Iris Toole, Southport Press; While you gave us the names of the dissident groups associated with the attackers do you know of any specific motive for them to attack the US Congresswoman? And can you preface that with Congresswoman Walsh's medical status?"

Yee leaned toward the microphone said, "I'm pleased report Congresswoman Walsh suffered no injuries and is resting comfortably at an undisclosed location."

He leaned to one side of the podium and began, "I, uh," he wrinkled his face and paused in thought, "You know, I was not given a prepared answer for the question about a motive, but I will give you my assessment of possible reasons for the recent violent encounters."

He placed both elbows on the podium and began, "Mankind has never had to face the real truth, that we are not alone in this universe. And that fact is not acceptable to everyone. There are those who have an unfounded apprehension that the aliens wish us harm and intend to destroy humanity. The evidence does not support that. On the contrary; everything I know about the aliens leads me to believe that they only have our best interest at heart. Yet, there are those willing to kill and die for their personal convictions. I am saddened by the fact that war and violence is brought by those who would force others to believe as they do, and to not accept what is."

Yee backed away from the podium, shook his head and finished with, "I'm just tired." He paused, "Thank you." then turned and left the dais.

Tsirch continued to watch the monitor as Yee left. He took a slow deep breath and half-listened as several alert tones emanated from his desk and he also watched as several icons flashed on his COM monitor.

For the moment the president chose not to respond. He leaned back in his chair and smiled. The president was pleased.

*****

Agent Joe Wong slowed to a stop, rolled down his window and displayed his ID to agent Paula Drake at the doorway to the entrance building. She inspected the ID, nodded at Wong and peered into the rear passenger seat and smiled at Eve. Joe reached down and popped the trunk lid open. Paul walked to the trunk looked in and then closed it. She walked back to Wong, "Thank you Joe."

Joe nodded, "Paula."

He put the car in gear and continued on the short drive to the residence. He stopped the car in front of the front door steps and exited the vehicle and opened the right rear passenger door.

Agent Bret Riley was in a vehicle following agent Wong and pulled up behind Wong. Riley exited his vehicle and scanned the area, looked at Wong and nodded, "Clear."

Agent Wong gestured to Eve, "You may exit now, Ms. Walker." She stepped out of the car carrying her briefcase and headed toward the door. She opened the door, stepped inside and closed the door. She walked down the foyer and turned into the living room and sat her briefcase on a coffee table. She turned back around and went out of the living room into the hallway and went into the kitchen. Richard was standing at the counter pouring a cup of tea. He saw Eve come in and held the cup in an offer to Eve.

"Okay, here you go dear, have a cup of tea and I'll explain."

Eve's face showed slight exasperation, "I heard about the attack, but I had security at my office."

Richard sat the cup down on the counter and offered a hug which she gladly accepted. The hug molded into an embrace and a modest kiss. They separated but yet held hands and Richard said, "Okay me first." He paused and guided her to a chair at a table and sat beside her. He explained, "Yes you have security at your office, but since the attack on Johnny was so quickly carried out after it appeared on FlashCom and on the dark web, I found it necessary to counter similar threats against you and family members of the major players involved the alien contact."

Eve somewhat agree but offered a different tact, "But Richard, aren't you overreacting somewhat?"

Richard curled a cheek, "Well, if it were just me I might agree, but this was strongly suggested by the president himself."

Eve was partially surprised, "Ren Lang actually pushed for this?"

Richard nodded, "Yes, he had a COM meeting with the Heads of State and made the same suggestion to them."

Richard paused and continued, "The tipping point for me was when your name appeared on the dark web."

Eve settled in her chair, "I heard there were other attacks and attempted abductions, but," Eve paused in introspection. Richard put his understanding hand on hers, "I know what you're thinking; what were all thinking." He paused and continued in a metered pattern, "When and how, will this all end?"

*****

Agent Randy Holtz secured the solar powered video surveillance camera into its base that was attached to the eve of the roof.

A voice emitted from his earpiece, "That's got it Randy."

He climbed down the telescoping ladder and released a lever and the ladder collapsed down to thirty inches. He picked up a case off the ground, grabbed the ladder and walked toward the front of the house. Agent Lee Elliott was watching the monitor on the dash of the vehicle. Six separate video boxes displayed six views of cameras that were attached around the eve of the house.

Randy walked around to the rear of the vehicle and opened the lift-back and set the case in the rear of the vehicle and closed the door. He walked over to the already opened driver's side door and sat down. He joined Lee and watching the monitor and looked approvingly at the display of the six camera views.

"Yeah Lee, the coverage looks good to me."

Lee nodded and picked up his COM off his lap and activated it. Randy reached down to the console and picked up his COM and activated it also. They each scanned through the video feeds on each of the surveillance cameras.

Lee said, "Okay, we need to connect this to the network." He reached down and entered some strokes on a keyboard and smiled.

Randy pivoted out of the car seat, stepped out and closed the car door. He walked toward the front door and took a couple steps up to the door and knocked.

Jennifer was in the kitchen fixing several cups of tea and Sal was sitting on the sofa next to Johnny holding her hand when she heard the knock on the door. She called to Sal saying, "I'll get the door Sal." She left the kitchen and walked to the door, looked at the monitor to the upper right side of the door. She saw that it was agent Holtz and unlocked and opened the door.

Jennifer backed away to let Randy in and closed the door after him. Jennifer asked, "You have things squared away?"

Randy nodded, "Yeah, all I need to do now is to check the surveillance feeds on the monitors."

Jennifer nodded and walked back toward the kitchen. Randy turned and checked out the monitor beside the door and pressed some buttons that allowed him to scan through the surveillance camera views. He pressed another button, "Lee, you copy?"

Lee's voice returned, "I copy." He stood for a moment and continued down the hall to the bathroom and verified the signal reception and voice on that monitor. Lastly, he went to the bedroom to ensure that monitor was working properly. Satisfied he turned and went back down the hallway to the living room.

Jennifer had returned to the living room and had brought a tray of tea cups and set it on a sofa table.

Randy walked over to Sal and Johnny who were sitting on the sofa, "Okay, the cameras are all online and with a voice connection. There are automatic sensors in each area and the cameras have an anti-laser protection." Randy took a breath, "You need to tell me what you want to use as a verification word."

Sal shrugged his shoulders, "How about; 'sweet pea'?"

Johnny looked at Sal and smiled curiously, "How'd you come up with that term of endearment?"

Sal replied with a wry smile, "Every time I think of you."

Johnny chuckled, "You are such a romantic."

Randy shrugged his shoulders and opened up his COM, "Verification word; 'sweet pea'."

Jennifer smiled and chuffed, "Uncle Sal, 'sweet pea'? I won't let you live that one down."

Randy put his COM away, "Anything else I can help you with Doctor Uschin?"

"Yes Randy; it's Sal."

Randy nodded, "Sal it is, then." He turned and went out the front door. Jennifer walked over and locked the door.

Randy was walking down the steps when he saw a vehicle pulling up behind his vehicle. Initially he started to reach for his weapon, but noticed that the driver was agent Gordon.

Lee had seen the vehicle pulling up behind him and had stepped out of the vehicle with his weapon drawn, but dangled it beside his leg. He also noticed there was no cause for alarm and re-holstered his weapon. Darlene stopped the vehicle and got out and closed the door. She was smiling as she approached their vehicle as she was aware of their temporary distress. Randy walked down the steps and met her.

"You guys seemed a little jumpy when I drove up." She stated.

Randy smiled and went up to her, shook her hand and gave her a half shoulder-hug.

"Good job today. Can I have your autograph?"

Darlene playfully slapped Randy's chest, "You shit-heads. I'll bet you two have been waiting all day to give me some crap."

Lee had walked around the front of the vehicle and went up to Darlene and shook her hand saying, "You know we only do that because we love ya." He paused and said in a sincere tone, "Really, you did us all proud today. We are glad you're okay."

Randy added, "I'll say this; my shorts would've been full if it had been me."

Darlene sighed, "I didn't really have time to think; I just reacted."

Lee replied, "I'd like to think that I would've done the same, but hopefully I'll never have to find out."

Randy shrugged, "Yeah, and she had four rounds left just in case."

Lee asked, "Thought you would be taking some personal or administrative leave after today."

Darlene replied, "I promised Congresswoman Walsh that I would continue as her detail for as long as needed."

Randy said, "Well, she's inside and she will probably be glad to see you."

Darlene asked, "Are you two assigned as temporary backup?"

Lee shook his head, "No, it seems that this is our gig for now. We just put six surveillance cameras and sensors around the house. It should be accessible on your COM on the security channel."

Darlene added, "Well, it seems that the threat assessments have expanded. I expect that the security at the Congresswoman's residence will be enhanced also."

Randy nodded, "You're right, her residence is our next stop. Since there are two of you here we can head on over there and put the cameras and sensors up."

Darlene replied, "Okay, I'll probably catch you over there if she goes back home tonight."

Lee added, "Yeah, but I guess everything is subject to change, given the situation."

Darlene sighed, "Okay, gonna go inside and see what's up."

He gave the guys each a fist bump and headed toward the door."

Randy and Lee returned to their vehicle got in and left.

Darlene went up the steps, knocked on the door and announced, "Friendly at the door."

Jennifer was sitting in an armchair and heard the knock on the door and smiled on hearing a familiar voice. She stood up and went over to the door and verified the voice by looking at the image on the screen beside the door. She unlocked the door and opened it. She stepped aside and allowed Darlene to enter. Jennifer closed the door and reached down and grabbed both of Darlene's hands and held them to her chest, looked into her eyes and said in earnest, "You, woman, have had one helluva day." She released her hands and gave her a long bear hug. They separated and Jennifer asked, "You okay?"

Darlene took a deep breath, "Yeah, I'm getting there."

Sal had been sitting on the sofa next to Johnny, but had stood up and was waiting for his turn to embrace Darlene. Jennifer stepped aside and Sal swallowed Darlene like the tentacles of an octopus. As he swayed her from side to side he said softly, "Thank you for keeping my girl safe."

Darlene accepted the long embrace and her face fought off a tearful emotion. She took a deep breath and gathered her composure as she grabbed Sal's shoulders, leaned back, "I'm glad that everything turned out okay."

She let go of Sal looked over at Johnny sitting on the sofa and went over to her. She reached down and clasped one of Johnny's hands, "Congresswoman, are you doing okay?"

Johnny stood up and put her other hand over Darlene's and looked into her eyes. She smiled, "I know I said thank you before, but I need to say it again; thank you."

Johnny sighed, "I think you've earned the right to call me Johnny."

Darlene scrunched her face, "How about I call you Ms. J.?"

Johnny raised her eyebrows in thought and replied with a smile, "Sure, I'd like that."

Darlene smiled.

Contact...With Caveats

ike and Perry were walking around the perimeter of the three modular buildings that were being assembled by the National Guard construction brigade. Each unit had a Sergeant supervising the installation of water, power and sewer lines in each modular.

Lieutenant Carlson was talking to a Sergeant in charge of one of the buildings. She noticed Mike and Perry and walked toward them. Mike and Perry saw her approaching and they met her halfway.

Mike said, "Well, Lieutenant, it looks like the project is progressing well."

Carlson nodded, "Yes sir, these crews are the best at what they do."

Perry noticed furniture being carried in to one of the units, "It looks like most of the furniture has been unloaded and placed in the units. Do the occupants have any preference of where the furniture is situated?"

Carlson smiled, "Funny you should ask, I was just coming to get you two, to see if you would like to make any adjustments to the placement of your furniture. Ms. Soul, Mr. Hadad and Doctor 'Gemo have already made their choices; would you like to tour your unit now and make any changes while the crew is here?"

Perry nodded, "Sure, since we're here. Let's do it."

Carlson nodded and led the way to their unit.

R.A. was finishing setting up his station that was next to Dominique's, when she suddenly reached over and grabbed R.A.'s forearm. She was staring at her monitor and exclaimed, "Doctor, uh, R.A., what do you make of this?"

R.A. saw that she was referring to her monitor and rolled his chair over to get a better look. She pointed to various lines and symbols on her screen and R.A. followed along.

Amir heard the excitement in her voice and slid his chair over to get a view of the monitor also. The trio watched the monitor intently and R.A. was the first to speak.

"Did that just now pop up on the screen without any input?"

Dom replied, "Yes, and no." She paused, "What I mean to say is I entered a data array but I haven't pressed the enter button yet."

They all stared at the words on the screen which were, "Beginconversation now."

R.A. looked over at his counterparts and shrugged his shoulders. "Well, my dear, start a conversation."

Dom took a slow breath and typed.

"Who is this?"

They expected a long wait time but the response was quick.

"Adam"

Each member of the crew shared glances and took long, deep breaths and soaked up this historic moment.

Dom thought for a moment and began typing.

"Who do you wish to contact?"

The response was immediate.

"You, Dominique."

Dom formulated a careful replied, "Why do you think this is Dominique?"

The reply was, "You are on the same device which we communicated on last time."

Dom started to type but the words on the screen interrupted her intent.

"We don't have much time. Can you open your COM for voice contact?"

Dom tossed side glances at Amir and R.A. requesting their approval. Both R.A. and Amir shrugged and nodded.

She reached down to the panel and pressed the COM button.

The speaker system blurred loudly with temporary static and the automatic sound level mechanism brought down the decibels to an acceptable level. She waited as the speakers had gone silent. Dom broke the silence, "Adam, are you there?"

"Yes, thank you Dominique, this is much better." Came the response, Dom remembered Adam's voice, but this time it seemed to be more personable. She continued her interrogation, "Are you the same Adam I spoke to before?"

"Why do you ask?"

"I'm concerned that you may not be a life form but an artificial intelligence."

There was a short pause prior to the response, "I understand your concern and accept your trepidations, and I will endeavor to ally your concerns in a candid repartee if you so choose. I recall that I expressed to you that I was using enhanced algorithms to make our conversation more natural. While that is true, I can only offer, what you may call, 'my word' as a pledge that I am undeniably an individual life form."

R.A. was listening to the exchange and asked Dom, "Ask Adam why he said he didn't have much time?"

"That must be Doctor 'Gemo speaking."

The response brought surprise to the listeners.

R.A. responded, "You can see us?"

Adam explained, "No, I have yet to solve the video communication aspect, but I'm able to use the stereoscopic properties of audio communication. And so, I determined the person to Dominique's right used the logon unique to Doctor 'Gemo and the person to her left is probably Amir Hadad. However, to answer your initial question about the shortage of time, you Doctor 'Gemo should certainly comprehend that the rotation of my exoplanet and your planet during this timeframe will be limited to seventy-four of your minutes of alignment access."

All three members of his audience nodded in comprehension.

Amir joined the conversation, "Now I understand the lack of response to our data streams delivered to your frequency and spectrum."

"Exactly, Mr. Hadad, which brings us to one of the reasons for this communication. I am sending you a data stream that can enhance our communication on a more consistent basis. If you convert the data stream into your computer language, you can upload it to each of your communication satellites that will enable worldwide communication between our planets whenever alignment is achieved."

Amir responded immediately, "That would be an exceptional achievement. Am I to assume the communication would be in real time and that access could be initiated by either of us?"

Adam explained, "The communication would be in real time but, unfortunately, your technology is not yet enabled you to clear a pathway to initiate communication."

Dom interjected her understanding, "Am I to understand that by clearing a 'pathway', you are comparing what we call a 'carrier' in the transmission of our radio waves?"

"Very similar to that process, Dom."

Amir questioned, "Then how is it we are communicating now without us creating a pathway for communication?"

Adam replied, "Our technology allows us to create a two-way pathway, in that it is sending and receiving simultaneously."

R.A. followed the logic and expanded the conundrum, "And that is the same quandary we find ourselves in the development and use of quantum mechanics acceleration relative to what we understand is your theory of time as a wave."

Adam uttered an audible chuckle, "Doctor 'Gemo you do realize that until your think tank unravels the design and power source dilemmas of quantum mechanics acceleration, or comes up with an alternate plausible explanation, you are yet left with an Occam's razor."

R.A. smiled, "Touché."

He swallowed, "Regarding the implementation of our satellite systems for communication, we may have a problem."

Adam replied, "As I understand your technology, you are totally capable of using the satellites for global communication."

R.A. pursed his lips, "You are absolutely right, we have the technology, but the human factor presents obstacles that must be addressed."

"Now Doctor, you have me at a disadvantage, please explain."

R.A. began, "Surely you have followed the recent unrest caused by the discovery of extraterrestrial life."

Adam conceded, "Yes, and our database is replete with the historical significance that greed, hatred, religion and love have brought death, destruction, and also rejuvenation and hope for the future of your planet. I, and I should say, we as a species, have had our share of such crises in the past, but have outgrown those propensities."

R.A. smiled, "That is a philosophical discussion that is best left for another time. Since we, humans, have not moved past our propensities, we have to yet deal with the political and religious divisions that stand in our way. If we opened up worldwide communications without restriction, we have those who would see that as a threat to Earth and try to destroy the satellites. However, I'll present your offer to my counterparts, both political and scientific and try to find a reasonable solution. "

Adam paused for the first time in his response.

To Dom the pause was significant. It showed her an introspective side of Adam. Her wrinkled brow of thought was pervasive.

Adam replied, "I think I'm beginning to understand what your humanity is and how important it is to your existence."

R.A. changed his tact, "I must assume that your database includes our research and theories of quantum entanglement, quantum gravity, our Fermi gamma ray space telescope, Large Hadron Collider, hydrogen fusion and of course quantum mechanics acceleration. If at some point you can offer your perspective on any of these subjects, I, we, would greatly appreciate any direction you might have."

R.A. paused, "Additionally, I have been engaged in a quest to discover the reason for the difference in the diffusions you sent to earth and to what we call Wolf 1061c."

Adam responded, "Yes, Doctor 'Gemo, we are aware of your research and theories relative to spatial relationship between gravity, quantum energy, and your theories of relativity and your concept of time travel possibilities. It may surprise you to learn that your theories, research and technology is not much different than ours. While we may appear to be extremely advanced comparatively, we certainly do not have all the answers. Concerning the diffusions sent to earth and the Wolf system, I can offer a short version of the need for the diffusions. We discovered, somewhat by accident in our scan of planets with possible intelligent life forms, that the Wolf system was in need of components to act as a catalyst to revitalize chemical imbalances and inert gases. I, we, would very much like to discuss many of the issues you brought up with your select group of scientists. Surely all of us would benefit from such a joining of intellect, theories and opinions.

R.A. sighed and took a long breath, looked at Dom, "I'm sorry Dom I've monopolized our time with your guest. You probably have many questions of your own."

Dom smiled, "It's quite all right R.A., I've been mesmerized by the conversation."

She posed a question to Adam, "Amir and I were wondering if you can send a detailed list of the components you sent in the diffusions. It would make Doctor Uschin's research in the biochemical uses of the microbes much more effective."

Amir posed his forehead in wrinkled thought, "Adam; Dom and I curious about your use of QMA, quantum mechanics acceleration, to communicate in real time and to send holograms and diffusions across the distance and yet, as far as we know up to this point, you have not transported a living being."

Adam's pause was decidedly longer than before and Dom interjected, "Adam, are you there?"

The pause continued and eventually there was a response, "Yes, I'm still here, and I only hesitate an answer, as it has been an ongoing discussion among my species. Yes, we have done those things you have stated, but although we are an advanced civilization relative to earth, we yet have our own internal conflicts and limitations. Advances in technology, as you well know, does not happen overnight, it comes at a cost; time, resources, disappointments, failures and often lives are sacrificed. Our capabilities of sending animate lower life forms and holograms have been developed through several of our centuries and at great cost. Our society has tried to safeguard the ultimate cost : loss of life. We have not solved the issue of time travel, but the virtual instantaneous movement of particles has been a major step forward to that end.

We can conceivably send a life form across the expanse, but we have yet to attempt a retrieval of the life form. That technology is still in development."

R.A. interjected his assessment, "If I may be so presumptuous to read between the lines, is there an underlying sentiment that we may be able to assist in such a technological development that would be advantageous to all?"

Adam answered in a matter-of-fact, "Doctor 'Gemo, that logic has not escaped us, but I assure you it was never our intent to be subversive. Our directives and reasons for contact were initially to assist your planet in reversing past damage to the environment. Fortunately, your advanced intellect presents the possibility of joint technological enhancement. For this I will not apologize."

R.A. smiled broadly, "Adam, I am delighted to say that you could not have presented your case in a more 'humanitarian' manner. I judge you as a man of honor."

Adam replied, "I thank you Doctor 'Gemo for those words. I judge this conversation a success. However, the window in our conversation is closing for the moment, and the next available contact window is in sixty-five hours and thirteen minutes by your time calculations. I thank all of you, Dominique Soul, Amir Hadad and Doctor 'Gemo.

Live your life.

R.A. responded, "Thank you Adam."

There was no response as it appeared that Adam had ceased communicating.

Dom reached down and disconnected the COM. She turned to her counterparts and verified, "And yes, I did record the entire conversation."

Amir replied, "I had no doubt she would record it."

R.A. leaned back in his chair tilted his head back as if to stare at the stars. He took several slow breaths, "I don't know about you two, but I am spent."

He smiled and offered, "We talked to an alien. It is just now sinking in."

R.A. swiveled his chair around to make eye contact with Dom and Amir.

Dom spoke, "I have to say this was more exhilarating than our previous conversation, as at that time I was not sure I was talking to an actual alien. But now, the realization has set in, there is life out there"

Amir swiveled his chair side to side, "I'm still processing." He turned his chair toward Dom and R.A., "So many questions I didn't ask." He sat up quickly in his chair, "What if we never get a chance to talk to him again?"

Dom replied casually, "Well, at least we got this recording."

Amir rolled over and elbowed her on her arm.

Dom busied her fingers on the keyboard. Shortly the printer began spitting out documents.

R.A. turned to Dom, "I assume your printing the copies of the screen print out and the voice transcripts of the conversation."

Dom nodded and cavalierly added, "Certainly did and also sent the entire transcript to the secure COM."

She leaned back in her chair and looked toward the office searching for Mike and Perry. Having seen no one she took a deep breath, "Okay, shall we all go find Mike and Perry and share the news?"

R.A. slowly nodded and replied

"We can start there, but of course we have to kick this up the chain and shake some trees while we're at it and see what falls out of them."

Amir sighed, "We've got a busy but exciting afternoon ahead of us."

Dom took her VPC off her desk and opened it up. She entered the call code for Mike and Perry and waited.

Shortly there was a response from Mike, "Hi Dom, this is Mike."

Dom replied, "Can you and Perry come to the office for some good news?"

Michael replied, "Always in the mood for good news, we'll be right there."

The soon to be famous trio got out of their chairs and headed for the office. They went inside and chose comfortable seats and waited for Mike and Perry. Shortly Mike and Perry entered the complex and made their way into the office. The group said nothing to them as Perry made his way to his desk and sat down. Mike walked around the desk and leaned against a credenza. Still the group said nothing. Mike looked down at Perry and shrugged his shoulders, "Well, haven't heard any good news yet."

R.A. looked at Dom and Dom in turn looked at Amir and nodded to him.

Amir said, "Well, I guess I'm elected. Could you please open the secure COM and play the latest file from Dom."

Perry shrugged his shoulders and engaged the COM and selected the file. At first the screen appeared normal until they saw the prompt, "**Begin conversation now**." which captured their interest.

They watched the screen as the conversation unfolded and the audio played in addition to being subtitled.

As the file played Mike and Perry occasionally glanced at each other while smiling. When the session completed, Perry was speechless and Mike was shaking his head.

Mike spoke first, "This is amazing. No, actually it's more than amazing. It's incredible."

R.A. spoke first for the group, "We haven't shared this with anyone else, but obviously the president, vice president and of course Sal is on the short list of recipients."

Perry nodded and stood up, "I agree; we need to get this to all of them right away."

R.A. made a suggestion, "Why don't we go down to the break room where the COM screen is larger?"

Perry nodded, "Let's go."

The entourage filtered out of the office and made their way to the break room. They moved chairs around a table facing the COM screen and sat down.

R.A. looked over at Dom, "Ms. Dominique Soul, I believe you should have the pleasure of using your COM ID to initiate this important call.

Dom took exception, "But, I am not the head of this facility."

Perry interjected, "I agree with R.A., this is been your baby all along."

Dom looked around and saw the encouraging nods from her peers.

She reached over to the console and activated the COM, paused, "I can't summon the president he won't to pick up my COM"

R.A. smiled, "My dear Dom, obviously you're not aware of how much sway you really have."

Dom shook her head, "Okay, but I'm telling you, he won't pick up."

She entered a request to the president using the console and waited.

The President was on a COM with Commander Narkiewicz when he saw the icon of Dominique Soul flashing on his screen. He paused his conversation saying, "Commander, I have a COM request from Dominique Soul. I'm going to add her to our COM."

The commander nodded, "Of course Mr. President, as you wish."

Tsirch said, "COM, answer; Dominique Soul."

His monitor not only added Dominique's image, but the four other participants.

The Hat Creek group was surprised to see the president and Commander Narkiewicz's images on their screen.

R.A. smiled and leaned over to Dom and whispered, "See."

The president was somewhat surprised to see the images of the Hat Creek contingent filling his screen.

R.A. elbowed Dom and said quietly, "Dom, it's your show."

Dom stood up, "Thank you, Mr. President for taking my COM."

The president smiled, "Of course Ms. Soul, I will always take your COM, and you need not stand. Please have a seat."

Dom obeyed and sat down. She visibly swallowed and started, "I'm sorry to interrupt you Mr. President, but we have some important information for you."

Tsirch looked at the faces and offered, "By the looks of this gathering I would assume nothing less." He paused, "What do you have for me?"

Dom began, "We have a file on the secure COM, under my name, we would like you to look at. It is a little lengthy and you can watch it at your leisure."

R.A. interjected, "Mr. President if I may, Ms. Soul is rather new at this process and I would like to continue on her behalf."

Tsirch smiled and leaned back in his chair, "While I appreciate your willingness to cut to the chase, Doctor 'Gemo, I rather enjoy the novice approach. Please continue Ms. Soul."

Dom gathered her composure, "The alien Adam initiated contact with us. The file is a recording of our interaction with him."

Tsirch leaned forward with undivided attention.

"Ms. Soul, I'm beginning to believe that you are an irreplaceable magnet of historical significance. I'll view the file and get back to you."

R.A. interjected, "Mr. President before you go, should we share the file with the vice president and Doctor Uschin?"

Tsirch thought for a moment, "Actually, I will have them view it with me. Thank you all." The COM went dark.

The gathering took a collective sigh of relief.

Mike stood and stated, "Well, that made me hungry. How about we fix an early dinner? We have stuff for salad and Anji and Ron said they could make soup and spaghetti, so how about it?"

The consensus was in the affirmative. Amir added, "Now, if we only had some French bread."

Perry stood up in a hurry, "I think I can take care of that, at least I'll try."

He turned and walked toward the office. When he got there he took his COM off the desk and activated it. He selected Lieutenant Carlson as the recipient. He turned and went back toward the break room as the call was being connected.

"LT, this is Perry, you have anyone in town at the moment?"

Carlson replied, "Yes."

"Okay, stand by."

He entered the break room, "Is there anything else we need, I can have one of Lieutenant Carlson's guardsmen pick up what we need?"

R.A. added, "I could go for some dessert also."

Amir looked at Dom and chimed in, "Yeah, count me in for dessert."

Dom looked over at him and gave him a sharp elbow in the ribs.

*****

The afternoon blended into the evening and the meal consumers were digesting their satiated appetites, while outside, construction of the modules approached completion. Lieutenant Carlson noticed another flatbed approaching with a large container on it. She made his way over to the driver, "Corporal, I don't recall another delivery being made. Who ordered this?"

The Corporal handed the Lieutenant the paperwork. Carlson read it over and opened up her COM and stepped away from the transport. When the connection was completed she said, "Lieutenant Smithy, I received an order for a 2832 safe room, with your signature on it. I don't see it or its location on the plans."

Smithy replied, "This is a request from the president personally. I'm assessing a proper location for the placement, but it will require a backhoe and special connections. I will send you the documentation within the hour. I realize the placement will not fit on this schedule, but its installation is scheduled for completion within forty-eight hours."

Carlson replied, "Thank you for your clarification. We'll take care of it."

*****

Agent Grayson and Perry were clearing the dishes out of the dish drainer and putting them away. Perry turned to Marnie, "You didn't have to stay around and help put these away, Mike and I could've done this."

Marnie replied, "Well Anji and Ron did the cooking and it's only right that I pull my weight. I don't want the Secret Service thinking that I can't handle the job."

Perry's smiled, "I didn't think that doing dishes was one of the criteria of the protection detail."

Marnie replied, "R.A. and I always fixed meals and cleaned up together. It helps in taking my mind off the job."

Perry nodded, "Yeah, I think that Mike and I could use the same therapy. This complex used to be somewhat of the doldrums, but since we've made contact with the aliens there is always something going on, either with the data streams or certainly now with the security issues."

Marnie put her hand on his shoulder, "Well, don't worry about the security issues, you concentrate on the arrays and keeping the stations running."

Perry nodded, "Yeah, that will be a big help, thank you all for being here."

*****

R.A., Amir and Dom were checking out their new quarters. R.A. opened up the refrigerator and saw that it was operational and starting to get cold. He went over to the table and unwrapped the packages of plates, cups and silverware and started putting them away. Dom and Amir were making some final adjustments in the living room uncovering the sofa and easy chairs. Amir went over to the coffee table, "Dom, how about we move the coffee table at an angle to give us more room to walk around?"

Dom looked at the placement of the table and nodded, "Yes, I think that will work better." She reached down and grabbed one end of the table and Amir grabbed the other and they moved it out of a walkway. R.A. came around the corner out of the kitchen and saw the furniture placement.

"You guys have made the furniture arrangement more accessible. Good job."

Dom smiled, "I'm glad you like it, but everything can change if we find something works better."

Amir asked, "How is your room looking, is it to your liking?"

R.A. nodded, "I've never been one for creature comforts, but it's more than I expected. I'm glad I brought my own pillow."

Amir and Dom laughed and Dom said, "We brought our own pillows too, great minds think alike."

Dom added, "The Sergeant said that you chose the bedroom at the end of the unit. You could have taken one of the two at the other end if you wanted."

R.A. smiled, "When I saw the layout I chose the one closest to the kitchen."

Amir bunched up one of his cheeks and nodded suspiciously, "Sure you did, you just didn't want to deal with the back-and-forth between Dom and me."

R.A. wrinkled his nose, "That may have been part of it, but this old man likes to have the option of a midnight snack and I don't want to disturb anyone. But, as I said before I don't want to intrude on your privacy."

Dom shook her head and started to speak, but R.A. grinned and held up his hand to stop her, "Dom, it's okay, I was young once or twice before."

Dom looked at Amir who sighed and raised his eyebrows and said nothing.

R.A. heard his VPC alert coming from the kitchen. He turned and hurried around the corner to the kitchen. He picked up his VPC and activated it. The virtual screen showed Sal's icon. He accepted the call, "Sal, I guess you're calling about our contact with Adam." R.A. began walking back into the living room and joined Dom and Amir.

Sal replied, "Well, that's part of it. I would like to discuss that with you, Dom and Amir, but I would like to see if you three are available for a call with the think tank."

R.A. looked at Dom and Amir, "Are you two up for a discussion with the group?"

Both Dom and Amir nodded in agreement.

R.A. said to Sal, "Sure, we can do that, but why don't we take the COM on a big screen we have in our break room in the complex?"

Sal replied, "Okay, I'll set it up, you can call me back."

R.A. disconnected the call, "I'm going to get some different clothes on and I'll meet you in the break room."

Dom and Amir nodded and walked toward their bedrooms.

R.A. left the unit and walked down toward the SETI complex and saw Mike coming out. He stopped Mike, "Hey Mike, Sal called and wants to discuss the contact with Adam and is also going to summon the think tank for a mini conference. Did you want to join us?"

Mike replied, "I may come by later if you're still on the group COM, but right now I'm going to meet with security to go over a contingent security schedule."

R.A. replied, "Okay, we'll catch you later."

They went their separate ways and R.A. made his way into the break room. He went over to the tables and set up some chairs for the meeting. Dom and Amir came into the break room and helped R.A. with the chore.

R.A. turned to them, "I'm going to pour me a glass of wine, you guys want anything to drink?"

Dom replied, "Sure I'll have a glass."

Amir raised a single finger and pointed toward R.A..

R.A. smiled, "Gotcha, two more glasses coming up."

R.A. selected a bottle of wine from the counter and collected three glasses and brought them over to the table and sat them down.

Amir popped the cork out of the wine bottle and began to pour.

R.A. activated his COM and the screen on the wall lit up.

He conjured up Sal's icon and selected it. The icon flashed for a short while but finally Sal's image appeared on the screen.

R.A. asked, "Sal, I forgot to ask, is Johnny doing okay? She has to be at least a little disheveled after the incident."

Sal replied, "She's doing well. We've decided that we have to play the hand we're dealt. What we do is too important for us to bury our heads in the sand. It's not going away."

R.A. nodded in agreement, "Is she there with you or did she go back to her place?"

Sal replied, "She's here for now, but she'll go back to her place tomorrow since they've added extra security."

Sal busied his fingers on a keyboard and queued up several icons on the screen. He offered up an observation, "I've never had a conference with this many attendees, but we'll see how it goes. We will all have to take turns and make sure we identify ourselves when we speak.

R.A. looked at the possible attendees, "Yeah, we will have a crowded screen."

Sal said, "Before we start, I want to express my admiration to all three of you for the way you handled the conversation with Adam. The whole thing was enlightening. The president and vice president were extremely pleased with all of you. While they understand that you were thrust into the limelight, you each have to realize this has made you a bigger target for the anarchists and terrorists. We have to tread carefully when we release any information to the public. The president and vice president are trying to determine how much and what kind of information they should share with other heads of state in the name of transparency. Homeland security, Domestic Security, CIA and the FBI may have to increase their threat status up two levels when this information gets out. We have to accept that this new alien contact will get out, regardless of it being a top-level security issue. Other SETI sites and Bio-Labs are being fitted with appropriate security housing and security personnel. Your site in particular is being fitted with an underground safe house."

The three listeners were surprised at the news.

Amir said, "We are getting an underground safe house?"

Dom added, "I guess things are more serious than we thought."

Sal said, "The president himself made this request."

R.A. replied in a matter-of-fact tone, "Ren Lang, huh? Looks like we're in this for the long haul, guys."

Dom and Amir sighed.

R.A. asked, "You have any more shoes to drop?"

Sal paused and bit his lip, "Actually, Richard was trying to reach Dom's sister, Elsa and her parents, and also Amir's parents. Do either you know where they are?"

Dom began to show some stress at the question as did Amir.

R.A. interjected as he turned to them both, "Dom, Amir, you don't have to worry about your family members as I have taken care of their security."

Dom asked, "What do you mean?"

R.A. put his hand on her hand and looked over at Amir, "When I heard about the attack on Johnny I made a call to a friend of mine who is making arrangements for anything they need. Your sister, your parents and Amir's parents have been given the option of moving to a secure location or staying where they are with heightened security. If they so choose, they can go wherever they want to go and stay at no expense to them. It's a lot like witness protection but without the government involvement. Your family members will contact you tomorrow and let you know what they decide, but for now I assure you that they are safe."

Dom's brows dropped in concern, "Who did you call that can do this?"

R.A. smiled, "Their benefactor is the billionaire Robert Atwood. I realized that the dissidents would have no compunction about leveraging your family members anyway they could. So, you need not worry about your family for as long as it takes."

Sal added, "You could have let me know about their family members and saved the vice president's concern."

R.A. replied, "Sal, I made the call to Atwood after the attack on Johnny and then we had the contact with Adam shortly after, so you see I was a little busy."

Sal replied feigning anger, "Okay, but next time; give me a heads up."

R.A. laughed and changed the subject, "So, how is Adam's suggestion about uploading the alien's global communication link to the satellites going to be handled? Surely, that would make satellites a target and further irritate the dissenters especially the anti-Adams. Even if our second contact with the aliens were to get out, that itself would incite more unrest."

Dom was listening to the exchange, "Maybe I'm missing something, but I don't see how we can hide this contact."

Amir added, "Yes, but I think they're between a rock and a hard place as it were. The news of the contact is going to come out, but I think they're trying to find a way to soften its release to dampen the likely effects."

Sal nodded, "I'm trying to decide how much I can even tell the think tank about the conversation. While I can tell them about the conversation, I hesitate to tell him about the possible alien satellite link to enable more communication. While I trust the group's integrity it seems inevitable that that information would yet get out."

Dom reasserted her statement, "Okay, it seems to me that there is only one solution. I don't see how the conversation in its entirety should not be released. My assessment of the president and vice president is that they are believers in the truth. I have to believe that anything other than telling the truth, or even a partial truth, would go against their nature, regardless of consequences."

Dom's words resonated with her peers as evidenced by their silence.

Sal sighed, "Well, I can't argue with your logic, Ms. Soul. Why don't you will stand by for a moment, I'll be right back."

Sal's image left the screen.

Dom asked, "Is it something I said?"

R.A. smiled, "Yes my dear, it was what you said."

Dom shook her head, "I only said what I thought."

Amir put his arm around her shoulders, "Dominique, you are precious."

Dom asked, "What do we do now?"

R.A. looked over it at them and grabbed his glass of wine, "We drink." He held up his glass in a toast.

The group took a few sips of wine and R.A. took the bottle and refilled the glasses. The screen flashed and Sal's image reappeared.

"Okay, let's see what the group has to say about our most recent conversation with Adam."

Dom asked, "So, what should we tell them about the conversation?"

Sal informed, "While I was away I spoke to the president and explained your suggestion, Dominique. He sat in silence for a long while and came to a decision."

R.A. smiled, "Pray tell, Doctor Uschin what was the decision?"

Amir smiled and interjected, "Let me guess, the president said to let it all hang out."

Sal laughed, "Amir, that wasn't his exact words, but the translation has the same result. In effect he said in a quote from Admiral David Farragut, 'Damn the torpedoes, full speed ahead'."

*****

R.A. walked up to the housing unit and opened the door for Dom and Amir to enter. R.A. followed them in carrying an almost empty wine bottle. They were all carrying their wineglasses and they sat down at the table. R.A. divided up the remaining wine from the bottle in each of the glasses and tossed the empty bottle in the trash.

R.A. asked, "Well, what do you think about our discussion with the group?"

Amir said, "I thought it went well. At least we have a consensus on the questions to ask Adam."

Dom said, "Yes, and I enjoyed Sasha's insight on the possibility of the aliens sending a living being through the pathway."

R.A. sighed, "Well, I think we got enough for this night. This guy is going to hit the hay."

Dom nodded, "Yes, I'm ready too,"

R.A. stood up, and carried his wineglass over to the sink and rinsed it out.

He turned, "Good night."

Both Amir and Dom said, "Good night."

R.A. left the kitchen and went down the hall to his bedroom.

Dom looked over at Amir, "You want to shower first?"

Amir said, "No, you take yours first."

Dom replied, "Okay, but we need to talk."

Amir said, "Yes, we certainly do."

Dom went down the hallway and went into her room. Amir followed her down the hallway and went into his room.

*****

Amir finished his shower, stepped out of the bathroom and went into his room. He turned out the light walked over to the window and turned the blinds open ever so slightly to allow some more light from the light on the power pole outside the window. He walked around the other side of the bed and took off his robe and pulled the sheets back, fluffed his pillow and lay down on the bed. He snuggled into the new bed and moved his foot slowly over touching her warm ankle. He gently caressed her shin with his foot and rolled onto his side. The light from the window filtered onto her nakedness. Dom lay still and spoke softly, "Are you ready to talk?"

Amir reached over to her stomach and gently and slowly ran his hand up to her breasts and said softly, "Yes, and I've got a lot to say."

Dom rolled over onto her side to accept Amir's embrace.

She sighed and softly said, "Let's talk."

Truth V. Dissention

Chief of Staff, Joel Mack, sat watching Tsirch deliver a COM meeting from behind the resolute desk. Tsirch delivered his summary to his audience, "And so, my fellow leaders, you have a copy of the entire conversation involving, whom we believe to be the alien Adam and our scientists. There will be a White House press briefing, shortly, that will be available on all COM's. May this day bring you health and safety. Good day."

Tsirch sat back in his chair, "Okay Joel, how many heads of state were on that COM?"

Joel replied, "There were sixty-seven available for a live feed and the rest have been sent a copy of the alien conversation file."

Tsirch reached over and pressed a button on his desk.

In the outer office, Philip, saw a green light appear on the wall beside the door of the Oval Office. He stood up and entered the oval office, "Mr. President the requested attendees have arrived in the Cabinet Room."

Tsirch nodded, "Thank you Philip."

Philip turned and went back to his desk.

Tsirch looked over at Joel, "Who is going to be present and who is going to be on a COM?"

Joel replied, "Your press secretary, January Yee, DHS Secretary Van Hook, FBI director Martin and DOD General Porter are in the cabinet room. CIA director Silver, Commander Narkiewicz, intelligence director Brown and the vice president will be on the COM."

Tsirch took a slow breath and stood up, "Okay, let's do this."

Joel stood also and went over to the door and opened it and allowed the president to exit first. They walked out the door and continued down a short hallway and made a left into the cabinet room.

Tsirch said good morning to the room and walked over to the seat at the head of the table. Joel closed the door and took a position at the other end of the table next to Press Secretary Yee. Yee, Secretary Van Hook, FBI director Martin in General Porter stood as he entered. Tsirch nodded, "Thank you, have a seat."

He sat down and looked up at the COM screen and saw the images of CIA Director Silver, Commander Narkiewicz and National Intelligence Director Brown and Vice President Natás on the screen.

Tsirch looked around the table and then up to the screen, "I trust everyone has seen the video file of the alien Adams's conversation with Ms. Soul, Mr. Hadad and Doctor 'Gemo."

The guests at the table and on COM screen replied with scattered, "Yes, Mr. President."

Tsirch continued, "I will open this to all of you without calling on each individually; I would like your response and impression and/or any concerns about the conversation."

Commander Narkiewicz was not shy and began, "Mr. President, in the short time the conversation has been made public; we have documented an increase of negative response on both the FlashCom social media and Dark Web dissidents. While the percentage is rather low at twenty-seven percent it is yet a concern. Director Martin and Secretary Van Hook are aware of the increase and we are requesting increased security on SETI site's and Bio-Lab locations in addition to the protection which you have already authorized for the personnel at the sites."

Tsirch looked up at the screen, "Mr. Vice President, since I have given national security response within your purview, are we prepared to meet such a request?"

Richard responded, "Yes Mr. President, I have been working with the Commander, Secretary Van Hook and General Porter in anticipation of the increased security needs. National Guard and Coast Guard units have been deployed as temporary security at the SETI site's and Bio-Lab locations until local law enforcement agencies are established. If it becomes necessary such deployment of those units may be extended. Placement of housing modules and construction of roads and structures is being coordinated by Lieutenant Smithy."

Tsirch looked up at Narkiewicz, "Commander, where is your illustrious Lieutenant?"

Narkiewicz responded, "As you would expect, Mr. President, she's a little busy.

Tsirch smiled, "Why am I not surprised?"

Tsirch looked up at Richard, "Mr. Natás, I noticed you are solo on this COM, is Ms. Walker not available?"

Richard responded, "She's available, but I hesitated to include her without your invitation."

Tsirch smiled, "The lack of invitation was my error. Ms. Walker is always welcome, although she is a journalist, she is also a de facto White House attorney by my proclamation if she so accepts."

Richard smiled, "As you wish Mr. President, I shall summon her." Richard stood up and left the screen momentarily and returned with Eve in tow. He and Eve sat down.

Eve said, "The vice president said you wish to ask me a question."

Tsirch replied, "Yes Ms. Walker, I would like to engage you as White House counsel."

Eve looked over at Richard. Richard shrugged his shoulders urging a response. She paused and thought for a moment, "Mr. President, you realize I have been retained by the Vice President as his counsel."

Tsirch responded, "Yes, but since the vice president is under the umbrella of the White House, I believe this would make that position as an extension of that position."

Eve asked, "And my obligation and discretion as a journalist, would that change?"

Tsirch replied, "Your duality as a journalist and attorney would not change."

Eve said, "In that case Mr. President I accept." She quickly added in banter, "Do I get a car?"

Tsirch rolled his eyes and shook his head, "How about a moped?"

Chuckles were heard throughout the room.

Secretary Van Hook recovered from her reserved laughter, "Mr. President, I have a question or concern, about the implementation and use of the global satellite system to expand communication with the aliens. Is there a jurisdictional assignment for the protection of the satellites?"

Tsirch thought for a moment, "I would expect that every department, Homeland, FBI, DOD, CIA and domestic security would share information and responsibility in the protection, since the threats could originate within any of your areas of responsibility. It is imperative that we protect the means of communication with the aliens while also protecting the citizens of Earth. Make no mistake if there is a choice between the two, then the citizens of Earth are the priority."

Van Hook nodded, "Message received, Mr. President."

Tsirch scanned the room and the COM, "Does anyone else have something to offer?"

Eve made her foray into the conversation, "Mr. President, it was stated during the conversation by the alien Adam, that the next window of opportunity for contact will be in about forty-five hours. If contact is made at that time, I would expect you have a contingency plan for media inclusion in the possible event."

Tsirch nodded, "Your correct Ms. Walker. Mr. Yee will be delivering a press conference shortly and he will announce a lottery for any interested media from which two representatives will be selected to document the conversation. The event will be recorded, but there will be no live broadcast. Relative to security needs of a possible contact, I have placed the entire West Coast air defense on alert. Commander Narkiewicz, you are tasked with the ground and air protection of the SETI site. You have carte blanche for any needs to complete this operation."

Eve added a request, "Mr. President, unless you require counsel during that timeframe, I request to be present, both as White House counsel and as a journalist."

Tsirch partially smiled, "Having anticipated your request, Ms. Walker, arrangements have been made for both you and the vice president to witness the conversation."

Richard nodded and Eve replied, "Thank you Mr. President."

Tsirch pursed his lips, "Although there will be no live broadcast, we will monitor the conversation and make real-time decisions about any changes in the release of its content."

Tsirch sighed, "I realize this is a world event and I will endeavor to maintain transparency as much as the security needs will allow."

Tsirch stated, "Unless anyone has anything else…" He looked around the room and at the COM monitor and saw no takers.

Tsirch said, "I thank you for your participation and I greatly appreciate your continued diligence in your civic duties."

He stood, "Mr. Yee and Mr. Mack please come with me to the Oval Office."

The members all stood as the president was leaving and Joel disengaged the COM as he left. Yee and Joel followed the president out the door, down the hall and into the Oval Office.

Tsirch sat behind his desk and Yee and Joel took seats on chairs in front of the desk.

Tsirch asked, "Mr. Yee, are you ready to meet the throng?"

Yee nodded, "Yes Mr. President, I believe you have prepped me well.

Tsirch nodded, "Very good Mr. Yee, I have every confidence in you. Do what you do."

Tsirch extended his hand and he accepted it and shook it. Yee turned and left the Oval Office and made his way down the hall to the press briefing room. Without hesitation he entered the room and went directly to the podium. He was carrying a folder and set it down on the podium and opened it up. He took a short breath and began.

"Thank you for coming, I'm sure most of you know of or have seen the video of yesterday's conversation between three scientists and the alien called Adam. Although there are those of you who doubt the credibility of our having had contact with aliens, this video was presented at face value. I'm sure there are many questions so let's get at it."

A deluge of hands and voices filled the room. Yee chose one of the hands.

"Thank you Mr. Yee, Allen Hughes, Charleston Gazette; I understand that the conversation took place at the Hat Creek SETI complex, and that was the same place where an explosion occurred near their recently. Given the explosion and yesterday's attack on Congresswoman Walsh, do you expect more attacks at that location or on the scientists?"

Yee responded, "The short answer is yes; there are those who use violence to express their distrust of the government and scientific community. The president and his staff are dedicated to protection of every possible target, be it a location or its personnel."

Yee made another choice.

"Nyla Harp, Bay Area News; according to the video, another conversation may be taking place in a couple of days; will it take place at the same location and will it be televised?"

Yee smiled, "Thank you for that question. In the event that there is another conversation, it will be a delayed broadcast. However, I'm pleased to announce that the president has made room for two media representatives to attend the event. The selection will be made by lottery. Following this conference Chief of Staff, Joel Mack, will supply you with the details of the selection process."

A heavy buzz of voices consumed the room. He selected another media representative.

"Pierce Inuit, Alaska Daily; during the exchange in the conversation, the alien suggested the possible use of global satellites to facilitate more frequent and longer contacts between our planets. Has such a connection been established linking our satellites?"

Yee replied, "As of now the link has not been established, but I would expect it is a possible alternative."

Another questioner was selected.

"Aaron Copeland, Missoula Press; what do you say to those who see contact with the aliens as a danger to humanity? The aliens have said that they sent, what we call a 'diffusion', to earth. How can we trust that they have not exposed the earth to alien poisons? And how do we know if there are aliens and everything isn't a big hoax?"

Yee took a short breath, put both hands on the podium and replied introspectively, "You know; I don't know that I can prove to you, that the aliens aren't a danger to earth. I do know that I can prove to you that the diffusions, they've sent to earth, are not poisonous.

But, for arguments sake let's say both of those are true. How would you suggest we stop the aliens? They are not physically here. Should we cut off all communications and bury our head in the sand?"

Yee shifted his balance at the podium, "What I can tell you is that scientists have been working on the content of the diffusions and have discovered that the elements delivered have enhanced the earth's chances of recovering from decades of abuse. This suggests that the aliens are not a danger to earth, and if it is all a hoax, then the only danger is in your mind."

Yee paused, "But I choose to deal in reality and what *is*. I believe the aliens exist and we cannot afford to let an opportunity to learn about other life forms pass us by. We are in control of our own destiny."

Yee paused and leaned on the podium with one elbow, "I would like to share what the president said just this morning. He said that if there was a choice between our maintaining communication with the aliens or protecting the citizens of earth, then the citizens of earth are the priority."

Yee pulled away from the podium and continued, "Okay, if you will stay here for a moment, I'll go get Chief of Staff Joel Mack to come out and give you the details on the lottery process."

He turned and walked toward the exit door and stepped out into the hallway. He motioned to Joel, who was in the hallway, and said to him, "Joel you're up, your audience awaits."

Joel smiled and nodded as he passed by Yee, "Thanks Yee, for warming them up."

Joel walked into the briefing room carrying a folder and took his place at the podium. He opened the folder and placed it on the podium. He took a breath and began.

"I know you all have questions about the lottery selection process, so let's go over it now."

*****

Vo Chen and Royce Pyle sat at a table watching the press conference on their COM. Royce shook his head, "Can you believe those bastards are not only encouraging contact with the aliens but are promoting it with a lottery?"

Chen added, "What does he mean he has no proof of an alien threat? What the fuck was the diffusion about then?"

Royce huffed, "They're dragging our asses deeper into this evil alien shit. Don't they realize the aliens want to destroy the earth by enslaving all of us?"

Chen took an angry breath, "Now, they want to give the aliens a chance to spread more of their lies to the whole world. We have to stop this broadcast."

They sat and stewed in their anger for a long moment. Royce leaned back in his chair and wrinkled his four head and thought. Chen joined him with his personal reflection.

"Okay, we've tried to bomb the place and we can't get close enough to take out their satellite dishes, so we've gotta think of another way to disrupt the broadcast."

Royce bounced his idea, "How about if we get someone into the meeting and blow it up from the inside?"

Chen said, "Come on Royce, we'd have to have one of our reporters win one of the lottery slots and even if we get that damn lucky, there's no way we can get a bomb inside through all the airport and SETI site security."

Royce smiled, "What if there was a way to get one of the reporters to take it in for us?"

Chen shook his head, "That's a longer shot than winning that lottery. Even if they did take a bribe or even if we threatened them and they agreed, there are still the security checkpoints to deal with."

Royce replied, "Maybe there is a way. We need to enlist Jan Wheeler; I'll bet she has a way to beat the system. She is tech savvy and is always messing around with electronic gadgets."

Chen nodded, "Yes, she did have a good idea about using a drone that we haven't tried."

Royce took out his personal COM out of his pocket and selected Jan Wheeler's icon. He waited for a connection. Eventually Wheeler answered, "Jan this is Royce, I need you to come over so we can pick your brain."

Royce listened to her response and disconnected the COM.

"Okay, she's on her way.

*****

Royce and Chen were still watching the lottery process on the COM, when there was a knock on the door. Chen got up and opened the door. Jan Wheeler stood on the other side and Chen nodded and shook her hand.

"Welcome Jan, it's good to see you again. Come on in." Chen stepped aside and Jan came in. Royce stood up and went over and shook her hand.

"Jan, thank you for coming so quickly, we need to find a way to stop this alien contact at Hat Creek. I'm sure you've been watching the news about the lottery selection."

Jan nodded, "Yes, I'm still fuming over the government's cover up of their conspiracy with the aliens."

Royce nodded in agreement, "I've been trying to think of a way to get a bomb into that meeting."

Jan nodded, "I was talking to one of our reporters about the lottery selection, and unfortunately none of our people were selected to witness the conversation. But I did get a rundown of the process the participants have to follow."

Royce asked, "Do you have any idea of how to stop the meeting?"

Jen smiled, "I think I do and I will need your help."

Chen said, "You can count me in all the way."

Royce added, "Whatever it takes."

*****

Lucas Makiev pulled up to the curb in front of Sal's residence. He stopped his vehicle and stepped out and went to the driver's side passenger door and opened and retrieved his briefcase and closed the door. Agent Holtz was sitting in his vehicle and saw Lucas drive up. He stepped out of his vehicle and waited for Lucas to approach. He nodded to Lucas, "You must be Lucas Makiev; Sal said you were coming."

Lucas smiled and held out his hand expecting a handshake.

Holtz nodded held up one hand and a stop motion, "Sir, I'm agent Holtz and I don't mean any disrespect, but could you hand me your ID and set your briefcase down and present yourself for a cursory search?"

Lucas' face showed surprise but he did as he was asked. He set his briefcase down and gave Holtz his ID. Holtz took the ID and carefully studied it and looked back up at Lucas. He placed the ID on the top of his vehicle, "Sir, could you turn around and face away from me?" Lucas again complied. Holtz performed a cursory body search and when it was completed he patted Lucas on the shoulder, "Thank you sir, you can turn around." Holtz handed Lucas his ID back and picked up the briefcase and took it over to the hood of his vehicle and opened up the briefcase. He quickly did a search of its contents and closed it. He went back over to Lucas and handed him the briefcase. He held out his hand, "I'm sorry Mr. Makiev, although I recognized you from a picture Sal showed me, I actually have never met you. I'm very pleased to meet you and I understand you have been unequaled in your dealing with the alien contact situation. Everyone, including Sal and the vice president, speaks highly of you."

Lucas accepted the genuine handshake from Holtz, "Agent Holtz; may I call you by your first name?"

Agent Holtz smiled, "Of course, I'm Randy."

Lucas replied, "Randy, call me Lucas. I guess the security measures are the new norm, considering the recent attacks and threats."

Randy nodded, "Sadly, it appears that not everyone is receptive to our contact with the aliens. Again, it's a pleasure to meet you, Sal is waiting for you."

Lucas smiled, "Thank you Randy."

Lucas continued up to the door and knocked. Shortly the door opened and Jennifer Natás stood and nodded at Lucas.

Lucas smiled, "Well, look at you; very special agent Jennifer Natás."

Jennifer chuckled and pulled Lucas in for a bear hug.

She released her embrace on Lucas, "Lucas, you know better to use that special agent shit with me."

Lucas smiled, "Jen, I couldn't resist."

Jennifer shook her head, "Okay, come on in."

Lucas stepped in and Jennifer closed the door.

Sal came out of the hallway and went directly to Lucas and they shook hands and exchanged shoulder hugs.

Sal said, "Damn, I'm glad you're here. I need someone to help me navigate these new events."

Lucas took a short breath, "Speaking of new events, how is Johnny doing after her ordeal?"

Sal shook his head, "She's dealing with it, unflappable as usual. I think I am more upset about it than she is."

Lucas said, "Yeah, I can only imagine how I would react if Ari or the girls were subjected to an attack like that. It's difficult to understand why violence would be an answer to something that has not been shown as a threat to you."

Jennifer added her thoughts, "But Lucas, that's the point. Some people see it as a serious threat to their way of life, their religion and in many ways it's the fear of change and the unknown."

Sal responded, "Okay Lucas, see what you've done. You've awakened the philosopher part of Richard's daughter. I didn't think philosophy was a course taught at the FBI Academy or in Secret Service training."

Jennifer feigned a scowl, "What; can't a girl have an opinion?"

Lucas laughed, "And I thought you were just another pretty face."

Jennifer chuffed and punched Lucas lightly on the shoulder.

Lucas sat his briefcase on the coffee table.

Sal asked, "Lucas you want anything to eat or drink, lunch or breakfast?"

Lucas replied, "Actually, yes. If you have any avocados, I'll make me an avocado toast sandwich and if you have orange juice, I'll take that too."

Sal replied, "I'm sure we have both."

Lucas started to head for the kitchen.

Jennifer looked at Sal, "Sal, you can't let your guest fix his own meal."

Sal replied, "Well, his legs aren't broken and he is perfectly capable of preparing his own food."

Jennifer sneered, "Okay, the little woman knows her place and will dutifully engage her culinary skills and let the grown-ups talk." Jennifer tossed her head up and purposefully walked out of the room.

Lucas laughed, "Is she always like that?"

Sal sighed, "You don't know the half of it."

Lucas smiled, "Good help is hard to come by these days."

From the other room Jennifer said, "I heard that Lucas."

Lucas replied back to Jennifer, "Thank you Jen."

Sal smiled and walked over to the sofa, "Alright Lucas, let's get ready for the meeting. I think everyone is going to make it. It's going to be a full house." He grabbed his COM and activated it. Together, they sat down on the sofa. The large monitor on the wall flashed. Sal began entering some keystrokes on his COM's virtual keyboard. One by one, icons began displaying on the monitor. Icon pictures of R.A., Marie Barrett, Jubal Jung, Carmen Hafed, Aldo Karloff and Sasha Rudolph populated the monitor.

As connections were made pictures of the attendees replaced the icons on the screen. When R.A.'s icon was replaced it included Amir and Dom.

R.A., Dom and Amir were waiting in the break room at Hat Creek waiting for the meeting to begin. The same icons appeared on their COM monitor, except that a picture of Sal included Lucas in the lineup.

At Sal's residence, he waited for all of the contacts to be established. Aldo Karloff was the last connection to be made and Sal activated the COM and started the meeting.

"Welcome to all. I believe everyone knows all the participants, except that some may not know Sasha Rudolph a graduate of New Mexico Tech in Space Studies, the mother of Robyn and Tyler and the wife of astronomer Robert Rudolph of the VLA. She is also the mayor of Marie Barrett's hometown, Magdalena. And for Sasha's benefit I gave her a short bio of each of the participants."

A sound wave of 'welcomes' was heard from the group.

Sal continued, "This gathering is larger than our normal meetings and we will try to give everyone a chance to engage in every aspect of a wide range of topics. Is there anyone that has not heard or seen the two audio files of the alien Adam?"

Sal scanned his monitor and neither saw nor heard any negative responses. Sal said, "Very good." and leaned off of the sofa and began the session.

"Over the years our meetings have involved the use of technology and theoretical applications of science and physics to the betterment of our planet. Since the discovery of the first diffusion some six months ago and the recent diffusion, we have endeavored to explore the effects and uses of the components of those diffusions. Recently, with the discovery of intelligent life forms other than our own, and subsequent actual conversations with an alien being, we call Adam, and the seemingly impossible holographic appearances; we find ourselves in uncharted but exciting times of discovery."

Sal took a short breath, "I, for one, have been overwhelmed by the reality we now face." Sal leaned back on the sofa, "At the same time, I am excited and have a sense of breathless urgency to finally get answers that have weighed on not only my mind, but humanity itself." As Sal spoke, his adrenaline leaned him forward. Sitting next to him, Lucas smiled and put one hand on Sal's shoulder. Sal glanced at Lucas and took a deep breath and leaned back on the sofa, "As you can tell, self-containment is not my strong suit." Sal paused and Lucas removed his hand, "So... I have sent to you, several topics of discussion, but I'm sure all of you have your own topics to present.

One of my primary concerns is the preparation of questions for our host in the pending contact. You have my topics that I would like to hear what your concerns are." Sal waited for a response from the panel.

Jubal Jung opened the discussion, "Thank you Sal. I'm sure others have the same questions about the Quantum Mechanics Acceleration plans that were included in some data streams. Our scientific contingent is yet having problems with computer simulations, without having sufficient power source data. It seems that regardless of the type of power source we use, it lacks consistency that is described by their fusion power generation. As you know we do not have that capability."

Carmen Hafed added her concerns, "We had the same problem trying to develop a prototype of fusion power based on the blueprint received in the data stream. And we are yet conflicted about the use of what is described as direct or alternating fusion energy."

Sal listened and took notes of the questions.

Jubal echoed Carmen's quandary, "Yes, that concern came up in our group assessment also."

Sal listened and looked up at the screen, "Aldo, I heard that your group was building a prototype that might be able to contain fusion energy combustion. Has that group had any success?"

Aldo replied, "We used computer simulations that combined rare earth minerals using a collider to change the molecular structure into a solid. Some of the solids created held sufficient ionic denaturation bond but none have yet survived the necessary heat containment threshold. But we are still working on the project."

Sal nodded, "Thank you Aldo, I wish you success."

At Hat Creek, Dominique and Amir were taking notes.

Sal brought R.A. into the mix, "R.A., have you had any success with deciphering the variance of the diffusion sent to earth compared to the diffusion that was sent to Wolf 1061c?"

R.A. leaned up on the palm of one hand, "It's interesting that you asked, as I did have one hypothesis."

Sal smiled, "Okay, we're all on the edge of our seats. Spill it."

R.A. started, "I found some similarities in the diffusions that imply a correction in the balance of microbes and archaea that may be degrading each planet. My assessment seems to lead that the Wolf 1061c planet is in danger of toxic destruction."

Sal asked, "How does that equate to our planet's level of decay?"

R.A. said, "While our planet is on the decline, it seems that the alphas discovered deficiencies in our ecosystem and the diffusion they sent was, in their assessment, and attempt to stop or reverse the damage that has been done."

Sasha asked a question, "I read the notes from your previous 'whiteboard' assessment of the effects of the diffusion involving the archaea, algae, microbes and possible metallic antigens, but did not see that there was a likelihood of permanent change or reversal of damage to our eco-system. Has that assessment been updated, and are those contained in the same diffusion sent to the Wolf system?"

Sal looked over at Lucas, "You know, I think we should let Lucas field that question as I've subscripted him to collate my data and R.A.'s data with his collection of the data from the samples he has gathered over the past six months."

Lucas sort of chuckled, "Oh my, wasn't expecting this."

Lucas took a short breath and began, "Well, R.A. and Sal laid all the groundwork for assessing the data and fortunately I was able to fill in the gaps with what I've collected. I'm happy to report, that since the first diffusion and the second diffusion, there has been a marked reduction in our carbon footprint and our ozone layer has stabilized. Indications are that the ozone layer may be increasing."

Sasha followed up, "So, does the same diffusion have a positive effect on the Wolf system?"

R.A. took this question, "While the diffusions are slightly different, it seems that the alphas modified the makeup of the diffusion to better suit the Wolf ecosystem. This leads me to believe that the Wolf system is in urgent need to inject various components to help save their planet."

Sasha questioned, "Does it appear that the diffusions sent to the Wolf system will correct the damage?"

R.A. squinted, "That's a question I will have to ask Adam."

Marie took a different tack, "I must bring up the elephant in the room; I am no closer to understanding the Quantum Mechanics Acceleration, described by the alphas in their assessment of time as a wave and QMA's use to communicate in real time from 4.3 light-years away." Marie paused and took a breath, "I've tried to theorize, hypothesize and mesmerize various aspects of this apparent reality. My group has bounced possibilities of using quantum entanglement, gravitational fields, wormholes, black holes, dark matter and Star Trek reruns to explain the unexplainable. I'm sure that ninety-nine percent of the scientific world is of the same mental quandary. And perhaps the other one percent understands this and is not telling anyone about it."

Various chuckles, stifled laughs and even outright laughter erupted from the ensemble.

Dominique also had to stifle a laugh and decided to add to the discussion, "Marie I believe we are all of the same mindset, but in my absentmindedness I have pondered a solution."

Maria smiled, "Dom; I recognize absentmindedness as my self-medication plays a part in that state of mind. But, pray tell any semblance of understanding of this seemingly impossible theory."

Dom smiled, took a breath, "Okay, just bear with me… How about if we just accept time as a wave and jumping from the top one wave to another instantaneously is possible, by using a catapult, explosive device, generated black hole or wormhole. If we can some-how accept what is, maybe we can work backwards to discover that possibility."

Amir looked over at Dom somewhat incredulously and smiled, "You know, most of the time, Dom and I are on the same wavelength, but I have to admit, after hearing what she's saying, I momentarily thought she was living in a Star Trek moment. But, knowing her as well as I do, I cannot deny her absurd logic. As for me it makes sense, but I'm at a loss to understand where we go from here."

Don looked over at Amir and casually said, "Well, thank you Amir."

More laughter in chuckles ensued.

Sal interjected, "Dominique, your observation is as good a place to start in understanding the time wave theory that I've heard lately."

Sal looked around at the faces on monitor, "How about we table this discussion and have further questions to ask our friend Adam, be sent to R.A., Dom and Amir to put on our long list for the interrogatory."

Sal stood up, "If there are no urgent questions or concerns, then I wish you all safety."

Sal looked around and smiled. He raised his right hand, split his middle finger from his ring finger, "May you live long and prosper."

The session ended.

THE WORKAROUND – DOMINOES

At Royce Pyle's house, Jan Wheeler sat at his kitchen table talking on her COM.

"Yes, I caught that, but, who else is going to be there?"

She listened for the reply, wrote down some names, "What are the types of recorders that are going to be permitted?

She waited again, "I see, and they might be able to use the video on the recorder, correct?"

She listened and spoke again, "So, they're flying to Sacramento and then take a chopper directly to Hat Creek?"

Once again she listened, "Okay thank you."

Jan disconnected the COM and studied her notes. She sat thinking, as Chen and Royce waited impatiently for her to offer her thoughts. Finally she looked up from her notes, "Okay, that was my contact, Milton Hamm at the Raleigh Post. I found out that Dale Parsons of the Pittsburgh Gazette and Ellie Hemengway, of the Austin Express, were selected to take part in documenting the alien conversation. They can take their own recording device, but as yet, video recording may not be allowed due to security concerns. There are no restrictions on the type of recording device, but of course it will have to be subjected to screening. They will fly into Sacramento airport and then take a military chopper directly to Hat Creek."

Chen shook his head in disappointment, "Shit, neither of those reporters is on our list of supporters."

Jan nodded, "No, but I didn't expect one of our supporters to be chosen."

Royce shrugged his shoulders, "So, we don't have any access to the event."

Chen pounded his fist on the table and exclaimed, "We're shit out-a-luck."

Jan wrinkled one side of her face, "No, I have a workaround, but you two will have to do some traveling."

Chen huffed, "Just tell me where to go."

Royce added, "I'll go get my toothbrush."

Jan held up her hand for Royce to wait, "Hold on to your toothbrush for a minute."

She opened up her COM and entered some information on the keyboard and found the target of her search, Hy-Mark Media Corporation, and scanned through the site. She focused in on the sales personnel and wrote down some information on a tablet. She smiled and nodded, "You guys will have to wait until I set up some dominoes so they fall just right."

Chen's face showed confusion, "What about fuckin' dominoes?"

Royce shook his head, "Chen, it's just a figure of speech, there are no dominoes. She means she has to get things ready, before we put the wheels in motion."

Chen scrunched his eyebrows, "What wheels?"

Royce shook his head and smiled, "Okay, Jan what can I do right now?"

Jan replied, "I need you find out where Dale Parsons and Ellie Hemenway are staying, so I can contact them, and Chen and I are going shopping for recorders."

Chen nodded, "I'll go warm up the car."

Several hours later, Chen and Jan arrived back at the house. Chen stopped the car and got out and went to the rear of the car and opened up the hatchback. Jan got out of the passenger side and went to the rear also. Jan picked up a box of electronics, a roll of shrink-wrap and Chen took a case of six recorders out of the car. Chen closed the hatchback and they carried their treasures into the house. Jan went back outside to her van and opened up the rear doors. She reached in and picked up a large wooden chest by its leather strap handle and set it on the ground. She also took out a cloth handled canvas bag and closed the doors. She retrieved the chest off the ground and walked back up the stairs and kicked on the door. Chen heard the kicking sound at the door and opened it. He saw Jan with the chest and bag, "Here, let me help you with that."

Jan nodded and lifted the wooden chest up to Chen's waiting hand.

Chen accepted the chest and stepped aside to let her in then closed the door.

They made their way to a large coffee table and Chen sat the wooden chest on the table. Jan sat her bag next to the chest.

Jan cleared the rest of the items off of the coffee table and looked around the room and saw the box of recorders. She looked up at Chen, "Can you bring that case of recorders and the box of electronics over here?"

Chen said, "Sure." and walked over and picked up the case and set it on the floor next to the coffee table. He went back and picked up the box of electronics and brought them also, and set them on the coffee table. Chen scanned the boxes, "Jan; why do you need six of the same recorder?"

Jan smiled, "Chen, you remember you were asking about the dominoes earlier?"

Chen said, "Yeah, but Royce said there were no dominoes."

Jan began to explain, "Well Chen, you have seen dominoes lined up in rows and if you do it just right, when you push one what happens to the rest of them?"

Chen shrugged his shoulders, "All of them fall down."

Jan nodded, "Well, after I change a few parts and modify these recorders, and if I get them to the right people and they are put in the right places, then at the right time I can press a button and the alien communication is no more."

Chen grinned, "That's what I'm talking about."

Jan smiled and reached over and lifted the hasp on the chest and lifted the lid back. Inside were several bricks of C-4 explosive. She slid the chest to one side and opened the lid on the box of electronic parts. She reached over and opened the canvas bag and took out various tools; screwdrivers, small wrenches and sockets, cutters, a soldering iron, electrical meters and gauges and placed them on the table.

Chen watched as she arranged her workplace and recognized the C-4 explosive. He showed surprise, "That's C-4, is it safe to have it in the open like that?" Chen wrinkled his forehead, "You had me carried it in, I could have bumped it on the table or something."

Jan smiled, "If you're asking if it will blow up, then the answer is no. It doesn't blow up just by bumping it against something. It needs something to ignite it."

Chen looked at Jan incredulously but said nothing.

Jan reached over and opened up the box of recorders and took one out. She carefully sliced open the shrink-wrap surrounding the package and slid the recorder out. She inspected the packaging and carefully eased open the adhesive seal on the flap. Having been successful with minimum disturbance of the packaging she slides the recorder out of the package and set the packaging aside.

The 3122 Hy-Mark Media Pro was the top-of-the-line technology in recorders. It was highly sought after by every journalist and reporters. Jan smiled and went to work opening the battery pack enclosure. Inside there were six battery canisters. Jan carefully removed five of the canisters and set them aside. She reached over into the wooden chest and took out a brick of C-4 and molded it into space created by the canisters she had removed. She reached into her electronics box and took out some wire and various electrical components. She carefully connected the wire and components to the battery. Satisfied with the work she took out some heavy plastic wrap out of her bag and placed it over the C-4. Then she sprayed the plastic with lemon scented air freshener to help disguise the smell of the C-4. She put the battery pack enclosure back together. Next, she removed an extension microphone from its holder and opened up its housing. She became more focused as she modified connections of the microphone inserting microchips and a receiving and sending Wi-Fi chip. The process was time-consuming but well worth it.

Chen watched for a while and got bored and went into the kitchen.

When Jan had finished her modifications she carefully replaced the recorder back into its packaging and sealed it with shrink-wrap in the same manner it came from the factory. She sat her finished product aside and began to create another masterpiece. She heard Royce coming in the door and stopped her project momentarily. Royce came over to the coffee table and admired Jan's work in progress.

Royce joked, "So, what you got going here? It looks like you don't like the way these recorders are put together."

Jan replied, "Actually, just trying to improve on it."

She paused, "I'll catch you up, but, did you find out where Parsons and Hemengway are staying?"

Royce nodded, "Yes, both are staying at the Sheraton near the airport."

Jan said, "Good, I've got to deliver them each a present."

Royce asked, "You want me to go with you?"

Jan replied, "That's what I'm thinking; you can drive so I won't have to try to find a place to park. But I got a little more work to do on these recorders.

Royce said, "Okay, let me know if there's anything you need and when you want to go."

Jan said, "Actually, I would like you and Chen to do something for me."

Royce replied, "Okay, what is it?"

Jan said, "I need you to call all of the media and electronics stores from Redding to Hat Creek and anyplace in between or near Hat Creek."

Royce shrugged, "Okay, what you want from them?"

Jen said, "Ask them if they carry the 3122 Hy-Mark Media Pro, and while you're at it call the Hy-Mark company sales division and ask for all of their distributors in Northern California."

Royce agreed, "Will do."

She took a breath and went back to her project.

Royce made his way back to the kitchen to let Chen know about their assignment.

After making the calls to the retail outlets and the parent company, Chen and Royce compiled their list of vendors in the Redding area. Royce looked it over, "Chen you did good work. I don't know what her plan is but, let's take the list to her."

Royce turned and he and Chen headed toward the living room.

Jan was leaning back on the sofa scanning the recorders on the coffee table and mentally checking her work in her mind.

Royce and Chen walked up and stood patiently, waiting for her to acknowledge them.

Finally Jan looked up, "Well, this is the first domino, so let's see where the other dominoes are."

Chen smiled and said proudly to Royce, "Jan told me about the dominoes, and now I understand."

Royce smiled wryly. He looked down at Jan, "Okay, we have the list of the vendors who have the recorders in stock."

Jan asked for confirmation, "And you specifically asked about the model 3122 Hy-Mark Media Pro?"

Royce and Chen both nodded and handed her the list.

Jan carefully perused the list and smiled broadly.

She picked up her COM and began entering information into it. She waited for a response and received it. She leaned back on the sofa, "Well guys, this is great news. Our plan may just work."

Royce said, "We would like to be excited also, if we knew what the plan was."

Jan leaned up off the sofa and began to explain, "I've modified the recorders; four with explosives and modified microphones, and two with modified microphones only. My plan is to offer a free recorder to both of the reporters who are going to witness the alien conversation."

Royce asked, "How do you know they will want to use this recorder instead of their own?"

Jan smiled, "Because this recorder costs $4500 and is the best on the market and is usually out of the price range of most reporters. I'm going to pose as a representative of Hy-Mark Corporation and give them a song and dance about my company wanting to be the first to record the alien conversation. Additionally, the media they represent will get free publicity and their name will be forever etched in the annals of time if they use our product."

Chen thought for a moment, "You know, I'm not the sharpest tool in the shed, but you know they're going to turn it on and try it before they get to Hat Creek. Won't it blow up then?"

Jan smiled, "Chen, you're thinking ahead; good for you."

Royce added, "Vo, I must be slower than you are, because I was going to ask the same question."

Jan laughed, "Well guys, I'm only going to give them the recorders that have a modified microphone and not the one with explosives, for as you know the explosives would never get through airport scanners and the reporter would try it out first."

Royce cocked his head inquiringly, "So… What does a modified microphone do?"

Jan continued, "I've inserted a receiving chip in the microphone that will, on my Wi-Fi signal, malfunction. And I will wait to send the signal until the reporters are on the chopper on their way to Hat Creek or maybe when they get to at Hat Creek."

Chen looked at Royce and Royce asked, "Okay, so now, since the recorder isn't working properly. What now?"

Jan added

"I will give them my business card with my personal COM address and I will instruct them to contact a local retailer and have someone pick a replacement up and deliver it to them at no cost." Jan paused, "This is where another domino comes in. I need someone to go to the two local retailers that sell the 3122 Hy-Mark recorder and purchase all of their stock."

Chen started to say something but Jan held up her hand to stop his thought and continued, "So, you ask if there are no recorders to buy what happens then? Well my dear sirs, after they purchase the stock from the retailers they will get buyer's remorse and return one of the recorders which will happen to be my modified version." She held up her hand still anticipating more questions. She continued, "When I get a call that the recorders are malfunctioning, I will instruct them to contact either of the stores to replace the malfunctioning recorders. My modified version will be delivered to the store waiting to be picked up or delivered to Hat Creek. And since it came directly from the store it will not be subject to scrutiny and will be delivered directly to the reporter. My Wi-Fi signal will activate the modified recorder, which will work perfectly until as such time as I deliver a detonation signal; and at that point what happens…?"

She used a sweeping hand gesture and directed it toward Chen. Chen responded emphatically, "Boom!"

Jan smiled, "Exactly."

Jan looked at her watch, "Okay, we have to pack up those four recorders back in the box," pointing to the recorders at the end of the coffee table. She gathered the two remaining recorders, "and I'll take these recorders with me."

She paused, "I got hold of a local pilot, Brad Stevens, and he will meet you, Chen, at the Wilson airport and he will fly you in his private plane to Northern California at my friend, Josh Frazier's farm. Josh is already on his way to the two electronics stores we know of to purchase all of their 3122 Hy-Mark recorders. When Chen gets there with the modified recorders he can have him return one of these recorders to each store, but not until I give him a call to take it back. That way, no one else can buy the recorder by mistake."

Royce listened but had a question, "We have four recorders and we only need two, why the extras?"

Jan smiled, "Good question Royce. Those are just in case there are any other stores that carry 3122 recorders that we don't know about, and also something might go wrong with the plan. It's all about backup; extra dominoes."

Chen put the recorders in the box and headed out the door. Chen put the recorders in his pickup and he drove off. Jan went off into the bedroom to change into a business suit and came back out wearing a blonde wig. She put the recorders in the canvas bag and nodded to Royce, "Okay, let's go." She and Royce walked out of the house. Jan carried her recorders out and got in the passenger side of Royce's vehicle. Royce got in the driver's side and they started to drive. Jan said, "Royce we need to stop at the printers on the way. I need to have some business cards made. After all, the vice president of sales for the Hy-Mark Corporation needs to have a business card to flash around."

Royce chuckled, "Maybe her chauffeur needs a business card too?"

Jan smiled and laughed, "Yeah, right. Oh and we need to leave our COM's here, I don't want anybody tracking us."

The drive to the printer shop and the Sheridan airport hotel, fortunately, encountered light traffic.

Royce stopped in front of the hotel and let Jan out. She went up to the front desk and pulled out a business card and handed it to the desk clerk.

"I'm Sarah Gold of Hy-Mark Corporation and I'd like to speak to one of your patrons, Dale Parsons."

The clerk checked the computer screen and dialed a number and spoke. He listened for a reply and hung up. He nodded to Jan, "Mr. Parsons said that you can come up, he's in room 413."

Jan said, "Thank you. If it's not too much trouble I would also like you to speak to another patron, Ellie Hemenway, and ask if she will meet me also. If you can give me her room number it will save me a trip back down to the desk."

The clerk looked at the business card again and relented. He checked the computer screen again, and dialed another number. He spoke for a minute and then returned.

"Ms. Hemengway is in 512." Jan smiled at the clerk and took out a fifty dollar bill and handed it to the clerk.

"Thank you for your assistance."

Jan turned and went to the elevator and pressed the call button.

She got to the fourth floor she went directly to room 413 and knocked. The door opened and Jan nodded, handed Parsons her business card, "Thank you for seeing me Mr. Parsons. I'm Sarah Gold with Hy-Mark Corporation and I have a business proposition for you, may I come in?"

Parsons studied Jan and seemed receptive and allowed her in. She went over to the table and sat down and placed her bag on the table. Parsons followed her and sat also.

Parsons asked, "Ms. Gold, you have a proposition for me?"

"Yes Mr. Parsons. My company is aware that you have been chosen as one of the witnesses to the conversation with the alien.

And we would like to offer you, at no cost, the state-of-the-art 3122 Hy-Mark Media Pro, to record that conversation. We will promote your use of our product, using your name and the Pittsburgh Gazette, to forever be a part of history."

Parsons studied the offer momentarily, "So, you're giving me the recorder and promoting my name and Pittsburgh Gazette's name without any strings attached?"

Jan applied, "The only string attached is that you allow us to use your names in our company promotion as the first recording of the alien conversation. We do not need a copy of the recording we only wish to use it as a promotional opportunity."

Parsons nodded tentatively, "I don't see a downside to this, and I'm sure the Gazette will agree to this."

Jan said, "Actually Mr. Parsons, you can work that out with your boss, I'm just here to give you this opportunity and you may take it or not, but the recorder is yours and if you use it the promotion will take place."

Jan reached in and took out the recorder out of the bag and slid it over to Parsons, as a deal closing gesture. She stood up and held out her hand and Parsons stood also and shook her hand.

Jan said, "You have my business card and my personal number. If you have any problems or any questions call me directly and I will take care of any situation that may arise."

Jan reached in her pocket and took out a $1000 bill and handed it to Parsons.

"This is just a little something from me to you."

She pressed it into his hand, "Thank you for your time Mr. Parsons, Hy-Mark Corporation thanks you also."

She picked up her bag, stood up and turned and walked toward the door.

Parsons was obviously taken aback and followed her to the door. He watched the door close behind her.

Jan smiled proudly as he headed for the elevator and pressed the call button. The elevator door opened and she stepped in and proceeded to the fifth floor. The door opened and she looked at the direction for room numbers on the wall and turned to the left and proceeded down to room 512 and knocked on the door.

Jan spoke loudly through the door, "Ms. Hemenway I'm Sarah Gold from Hy-Mark Corporation and I have a proposal for you."

There was a short pause and a voice from behind the door responded, "I'm sorry you are who?"

Jan repeated, "Ms. Hemenway, I'm Sarah Gold from Hy-Mark Corporation and I have a business proposal for you."

The door opened slowly and Hemenway assessed her visitor, "What kind of proposal?"

Jen's handed her a business card, "It's a business proposition that you will probably want to hear. May I come in?"

Ms. Hemengway scrutinized the business card and cautiously said, "All right, come inside."

Jan stepped in and went over to a table and Hemenway followed. Jan asked, "May I sit?"

Hemenway nodded. Jan sat her bag on the table and sat down. Ms. Hemenway eased her way into a chair.

Jan began, "I represent Hy-Mark Corporation and we are aware that you have been selected to witness the conversation with the alien." Jan pulled the recorder out of the bag and placed it in the center of the table.

"My company wants to give you this 3122 Hy-Mark Media Pro, free of charge, in hopes that you will use it to record the conversation. Should you do so, we would like to use your name and Austin Express in a promotion in representing our recorder as the device used to document this historical event. We do not require a copy of the conversation.

Your acknowledgment that you used our recorder in the promotion is all that's necessary."

Hemenway thought for a while, "So, you're giving me the recorder and if I use it, I will agree that you can use my name and Austin Express in a promotion for your company?"

Jan nodded, "Yes ma'am, no strings attached or other conditions apply."

Jan stood and picked up her empty bag and held her hand out for a handshake. Hemenway looked at the recorder and stood and shook Jan's hand.

Jan added, "So, I hope you will use this at the event. If you have any problems with the product or any questions you have my business card with my personal number." She reached in her pocket and pulled out a $1000 bill and pressed it into Hemengway's hand, "This is just a little something from me to you. Thank you for listening."

Jan stepped away and headed toward the door. She opened the door and turned, "Thank you again Ms. Hemengway."

Jan stepped out of the door.

THE GATHERING STORM

FBI director Pepper Martin made his way down the hallway and opened the door to the situation room. He was surprised to see the president sitting on the side of the table rather than at the head of the table. He walked over to the left side of the table across from the president and chose a seat. He nodded to the president, "Good morning Mr. President."

Tsirch smiled, "Good morning director Martin."

Gordon Noel, the president's economic advisor and Alice Riley the UN ambassador were the next to arrive. They too were surprised at the president's seating choice. Each expressed their greetings to the president, "Good morning Mr. President."

Tsirch continued to smile, "Good morning Gordon and Madame Ambassador."

Gordon chose a seat on the left side of the table to the left of Martin. The ambassador made her way to the president side of the table two seats to his right.

The vice president was speaking with DOD General, Walter Porter, as they got off the elevator.

"Walter, are you sure about the threat assessment?"

Porter replied, "Yes sir, DHS, Van Hook and Secret Service Director Potter received the same Intel, and I passed it on to domestic security commander, Narkiewicz."

Richard nodded, "Okay, we'll see if either Martin or Silver has anything else on their radar."

Richard opened the door to the situation room and stood while assessing the seating arrangements. He smiled and noticed Tsirch sitting on the side of the table and patting the table top to his left while looking at Richard. Richard smiled and dutifully went over to the seat as directed.

Still standing he said, "Good morning Mr. President, trying to stay out of the hot seat?" He nodded to the empty seat at the head of the table. Tsirch smiled and replied softly, "Waiting to see who takes it."

Richard sat down and General Porter said, "Good morning Mr. President." and took a seat to Richard's left. The president replied, "Good morning Walter." Tsirch leaned forward and looked around Richard and said to the General, "You could have picked better company to arrive with."

Porter shrugged, "He said if we came in together he'd buy me breakfast… a man's got eat." He smiled.

Richard chuffed, "I think I'm being set up."

The CIA director, Jack Silver, was next to come in the door, followed by the Secretary of State, Marilyn Richter. Both of the entrants too, perused the seating arrangements and Silver went to a seat across from the president and Marilyn promptly went to the seat at the head of the table. Silver nodded to Tsirch, "Mr. President." and sat down. Marilyn did her bidding to the president in a succinct tone, "Good morning Mr. President." as she sat down.

Tsirch acknowledged Silver, "Good morning director."

He nodded to Marilyn and responded, "And a pleasant morning to you, Madam Secretary."

Marilyn smiled and stifled a chuckle.

The COM monitors on the walls behind both sides of the table displayed the same screen. The images that populated the screens were that of Julia Van Hook, DHS Secretary; Commander Narkiewicz and Lieutenant Smithy, Domestic Security; Secret Service director, Annice Potter; Attorney General, Jerry Jameson and Captain Mark Narkiewicz.

Tsirch was looking over some files on his VPC that sat in front of him on the table. He looked around the room and up at the COM screen and began the session, "Welcome to all of you, I'd like to begin with any input about security threats, either foreign or domestic.

General Porter, I understand there has been a wide array of threats from various disruptive groups. Do you have any updates?"

Porter looked down at his notes on the table, "Yes, Mr. President, the group Segr8 is at the top of the list to perpetrate violent acts to disrupt the planned communication event at Hat Creek. Distinctive chatter on the social media platform, FlashCom, has been echoed on the fringe sources and dark media access points, that an explosive attempt will be made either by air and/or ground assault. Homeland security has developed identical intelligence profiles regarding Segr8 and it has connected the subversive group Anti-Adam as a partner in the threat."

Tsirch looked up at the screen, "Commander Narkiewicz, have you or Lieutenant Smithy been able to drill down on any specifics as to the method of delivery?"

Edward answered, "The Lieutenant advised me that the COM-taps, authorized by the FBI under the terrorist act are specific as to a likely air assault, but Intel concerning a secondary method appears to be shrouded deep underground."

Edward turned to Brie for further explanation, "Lieutenant, can you expand on this?"

Brie nodded, "The Intel from local law enforcement and FBI are unanimous in the assessment of a 'highly-likely threat'. However there are conflicting modes of delivery that include simultaneous air and ground assault. The concerning portion of the Intel is that the attack will come from the inside."

Richard's brows drooped as he asked, "Are you trying to say that someone within the group may be complicit in the assault?"

Brie grimaced, "I'm sorry, but I can only give you the bread-crumbs that I have followed. I realize that all the players at Hat Creek are above reproach and have absolutely no reason to sabotage such a historic event, but the information we have gathered does not seem to rest in hyperbole."

Director Martin interceded, "Mr. Vice President, I've been working closely with the Lieutenant and Secret Service director Potter and we can only verify that the assessment of the threat is real but the method of delivery and actors involved are disjointed and inconclusive, at best."

Director Potter inserted her perspective, "Mr. Vice President, I concur with director Martin and domestic security. We have gone over the credentials of Secret Service, local law enforcement, FBI and the included National Guard personnel and they all have 100 percent of our confidence in their allegiance.

Richard leaned back in his chair in thought.

Tsirch changed course, "Secretary Van Hook, what is Homeland experiencing with the public's overall acceptance of the upcoming conversation with the aliens?"

Julia nodded, "Mr. President, the mood of the people is overall positive, but it seems they want to be included in the conversation."

UN Ambassador Riley echoed the sentiment, "Mr. President, there is no shortage of concern that the US has a secret agenda by limiting the world's access to the conversation."

Tsirch nodded, "Am I to understand that the public and the world are displeased with the lack of transparency in our handling of the access to the conversation?

Riley and Van Hook both nodded in agreement, Riley replied, "Yes, Mr. President; that is exactly what we are saying."

Gordon Noel added his observation, "Mr. President, as your economic advisor, I'd like to point out that sentiment in the stock market lies precariously in a similar uncertainty."

Tsirch leaned back in his chair and thought. He looked over at Richard, "Mr. Vice President, as you are more versed in the alien conversation process, can you offer any suggestions that would not jeopardize safety and security?"

Richard leaned his head back and thought. Momentarily took a breath, "I believe we can make the conversation accessible, including video to all worldwide COM media, on perhaps a ten second or more delay for security purposes."

Tsirch thought for a moment, "Okay, if there is a delay for security purposes, what type of security breach might there be that would necessitate a pause or redaction in conversation?"

Richard smiled broadly, "Hell, Mr. President; that would be your call."

Tsirch chuffed.

There was an abundance of snickering heard among the participants.

Tsirch smiled, "Okay, Madam Ambassador, director Van Hook, Mr. Noel and," Tsirch looked over at Richard, "Mr. Vice President, would that be acceptable?"

The collective heads nodded and Richard stated, "Again Mr. President, it's your call."

Tsirch took a breath, "Okay, so be it." He turned his head toward Richard, smiling, "I'll leave it to you Mr. Vice President to work out the details."

The President looked around the room, "Director Silver, are there any new developments on the world front?"

Silver nodded, "There have been reports of further terrorist attacks from the Islamic state, Indonesian FATA, the Filipine Asian Terrorist Anarchist, on SETI sites and bio-safety labs specifically in South Africa, Australia, Myanmar, China, India and even now in the Middle East. NIS director Brown related that those factions are making connections to our own domestic security disruption groups; the Hi-Hangers, Silkmates, Segr8 and Anti-Adam in an attempt to coordinate their attacks."

Tsirch looked around the room, "I welcome anybody's input and insight on the logic or reasoning for their dissension."

Marilyn Richter adjusted her position chair and spoke, "Mr. President, if I may be so bold, as to offer my observation,"

Tsirch smiled and interrupted, "Madam Secretary, I've known you to be nothing but bold, but please give us your perspective."

The secretary had a snarl mixed in her smile, "Thank you Mr. President, your support is always welcomed." She took a short breath, "I've spent a fair amount of time interacting with heads of state, members of Congress and the Senate, trying to get a consensus of thought about how our contact with aliens has affected their lives. Additionally, I've engaged with those of the younger and middle age groups, to compare their thoughts and concerns about our alien contact. One of my assessments centers on the suddenness of our confirmed contact with the aliens, for as you know it has been less than six weeks since our discovery of extraterrestrials. We, in our daily forum, have been pressed to deal with the fallout, both positive and negative. Certainly, we are trying to make decisions based on incomplete data, and that in itself presents a dilemma. I've realized that I haven't taken the time to personally assess my feelings. I am ambivalent in my excitement in the discovery of alien life and also in the uncertainty of the future. I've spent my career dealing with solutions to situations or conflicts between people. But I find myself lacking in the ability to solve a conflict within oneself."

The audience had been listening closely and brought silent introspection and agreement.

Lieutenant Smithy disturbed the silence, "Mr. President if I may…"

Tsirch nodded, "Certainly Lieutenant, it's an open discussion."

Brie continued, "Listening to the Secretary's observation, I realize also, that I have been too busy doing my job to process what actual contact with aliens means to me. In my quiet moments I can hardly contain the excitement I feel when I think of all the questions that might be answered. But I can't help but wonder; what if I don't like the answers to my queries. To the secretary's point, uncertainty is a glaring issue of concern."

After short reflection Richard spoke, "I must confess, that I also have felt the pressure of decision-making, but for us in these roles, we, fortunately are able to press on. Unfortunately, we are yet faced with those who see the aliens as a threat to their religion, personal security and their future, because they refuse to deal with reality. For them, the process of reasonability of thought and facing the truth; is not one of their choices. Sadly, many of them choose to blindly hide behind violence as their only option to disguise their fears."

Tsirch listened and paused, "What I gleaned from your words is that we should take time to process our reaction to what the alien reality represents. But *OUR* reality is; that we do not control time. Perhaps we need to trust the religious shepherds to guide those who would listen and to seek philosophers to offer personal insight for the others who ponder. Meanwhile, we are tasked to steward this ship and navigate a course to avoid the obstacles that might sink it."

Edward inserted his stance, "To your point Mr. President, do we have any limitations in our efforts to maneuver along the constitutional guarantees of privacy and freedom of speech? The COM–taps authorized under the terrorist act only cover those targets that have a prior history of threats or illegal acts. There are private third-party contact considerations that could lead to corroboration of threats. Additionally, there are business entities that may be involved in planning, but we are not sure about the legality of pursuing those records."

Tsirch smiled, "That's why we have an Attorney General at our disposal. Mr. Jameson, would you care to weigh in on this subject?"

Jerry half nodded and simulated wiping sweat from his forehead, "Finally, a question of substance for me to answer instead of a philosophical or psychological interrogatory. So… Commander; if there are business entities that can be connected to proven actors; you can certainly pursue their COM records and files. As far as private individuals, if you can articulate the facts of their involvement, I'm sure that any competent JAG officer can lead you through the pitfalls. I can tell you that you, the president," nodding to Tsirch, "have assured my office that you will not stand in the way in the prevention of any terrorist act. That includes the suspension of subsection 3 of the terrorist act, by your Executive Order and its approval by both houses of Congress."

The Commander nodded, "Thank you Mr. Attorney General."

Tsirch smiled and scanned the room and the COM screen. Richard leaned over and whispered in his ear, "Renny, don't let Mark off the hook."

Tsirch looked up at the screen and focused on Mark Narkiewicz, "Captain Narkiewicz, don't let your brother steal your thunder, you must have something to offer the group."

Mark smiled and chuffed, "And here I thought I could skate through the intellectual exchange without embarrassing myself."

Mark took a short breath, "Actually, I'd like to offer a discourse of a more nonthreatening leaning. At this point, I'm sure that all of you have had the occasion to listen to both recordings of the alien conversations. I'd like to point out to you some of the less obvious, but important, biological implications of the diffusions and the mind-bending concepts of physics and time presented by the aliens. As I am not a biological scientist nor am I an astrophysicist, I do feel qualified to explain the importance of the alien's contributions in more practical terms." Mark took another short breath, "As for the 'diffusions', the waves sent by the aliens contain biological, micro-biological, inert, organic and inorganic materials infused in algae and Archaea microbes that are inexplicably shrouded with metallic particles."

Several of the listeners smiled and chuckled, while one comment was heard, "Well that certainly explains it."

Mark smiled, "Yeah, that's what I thought when I first heard this explanation, until I heard the resulting impact on our environment. This diffusion has significantly increased our ozone layer, reduced our carbon footprint and is absorbing the toxins in our lakes and oceans. Furthermore, there seems to be a modification in the lunar atmosphere, showing indications that the diffusions interactions with the lunar surface could be producing a hydrogen and oxygen compound similar to water. Further research as to other effects is ongoing."

Mark's audience seemed contained by thought. He continued, "Now for the physics portion of enlightenment… Our world's great minds, and I use great minds in quotation marks, are in a quantum physics disarray. They have no explanation of: how the diffusions were delivered; how the communications are accomplished in real time; how the holograms appear in specific and so many locations; or how quantum mechanics acceleration is even possible. The alien intelligence; seemingly at a distance of 4.3 years away traveling at the speed of light, have the answers to these questions." Mark took a deep breath, "I don't know about you, but I have unending questions begging for answers from such an advanced civilization. At the same time I suffer from trepidation: Why us? Why now? What do they want?" Mark paused and settled into his seat, "That being said, personally, I am totally invested in a positive outcome in our contact with the aliens."

Edward nodded slowly in agreement, "Well brother Mark, I see you got the lion's share of analytics from our parents. If we could only get the detractors to see the alien situation through your eyes, we might not be facing the violence we have encountered."

Tsirch sighed, "Well Commander, it hasn't been for a lack of trying to put that message out there. But, as the vice president alluded to, there are those who use violence to hide their fears, which is why we have the military and law enforcement to protect the reasonable."

Tsirch looked down at his the VPC and saw the screen flashing. He looked back up at his audience, "Okay, are there any other concerns that we need to address, as I have a meeting scheduled with several ministers of defense?"

General Porter leaned forward looking around Richard, "You might need to remind your vice president that he owes me a breakfast, and not from the vending machine."

Tsirch feigned a surprised look.

"The vice president is not cheap, in fact I think he'll probably buy everybody breakfast." Tsirch looked over at Richard with a grin.

Richard nodded his head, "Of course I'm buying breakfast; everyone follow me to the presidential dining room."

Richard smiled and nodded to Porter, "and the General here will be gracious enough to leave a big tip."

Pepper Martin stood up and announced, "Boy, am I hungry."

Richard looked at Tsirch and returned a grin.

Tsirch chuckled, looked up at the COM screen, "Those of you on the COM, remember the vice president owes you a breakfast." Tsirch picked up his VPC, stood up and was the first out of the room.

Puzzle Pieces Or Dominos

Corporal Rousan, thirty feet up on the light pole was adjusting the mount bracket on the solar security cam. He spoke into his headset, "How's that Johnson?"

Agent Ron Johnson was in the living room portion of his double wide, unit one, watching the COM screen that displayed eight individual feeds of cameras, five of which were active.

He answered Rousan on the desk mic, "That should do it, thanks Rousan."

Rousan secured his tools on his belt and easily used the foot spikes on the pole to descend to the ground.

*****

In the housing unit, Johnson used a joystick to manipulate the active camera feeds, testing their range of view. Agent Rayner leaned around the corner of the room, "Ron, breakfast is ready."

Ron nodded and stood up and walked around the corner to the kitchenette. Agent Grayson was sliding fried eggs out of the skillet onto a plate in front of agent Rayner.

"Here you go Anji, sunny-side up."

Anji replied, "Thanks Marnie."

Ron walked around the table and sat in front of the plate of eggs. The three consumers busied themselves, collecting potatoes and bacon to add to their plates of eggs.

Ron said, "We have five cameras working, thanks to 'wonder guy' Rousan, he sure knows his shit."

Anji asked, "Yes he does. How did you stumble on him?"

Ron replied, "I was talking to Lieutenant Carlson yesterday and lamenting that I was pressed for time in placement of security cameras around the units. She suggested that I recruit guardsmen Corporal Rousan to assist me. I said I'd give it a shot. I tracked Rousan down and he said he'd be glad to help, adding, he loved this technical shit, rather than welding and plumbing."

Marnie added, "Yep, networking pays off every time."

Rousan walked around to the front of unit two and knocked on the door.

Shortly the door opened and R.A. smiled, "Good morning Corporal; how may I help you?"

Rousan replied, "I'd like to check your security monitor to see if it's getting all of the camera feeds."

R.A. opened the door wider, "Of course."

Rousan walked by R.A. and went into the den where the monitor was and sat down. He used a joystick to select each camera feed. Soon he was satisfied with the results and got up, "Thank you sir, everything seems to be working fine. If you have any problems let me know. The three other camera feeds will be available within a couple of hours."

R.A. smiled, "Corporal Rousan is in it?"

Rousan replied, "Yes sir."

R.A. put his hand on Rousan's shoulder, "Son, thank you and call me R.A., please."

Rousan nodded, "Certainly, Mr. R.A.."

R.A. smiled as Rousan turned and headed toward the door, opened it and left.

Dom was coming down the hallway when she saw the door close. She asked, "Who was that?"

R.A. said, "That was Corporal Rousan he was checking the security monitor camera feeds. He said that five were working and the other three would be active within a couple hours."

Dom replied, "Oh, sorry I missed him, Amir and I found him to be well versed in electronics." Amir walked up and caught the last part of the conversation, "Who are you talking about?"

Dom said, "Corporal Rousan, he was just here checking the security camera feeds."

Amir nodded saying, "Yes, he is quite versed in electronics."

R.A. asked, "I was just going to fix some breakfast, are you two hungry?"

Amir said, "Yes, I'm just going to head to the kitchen and see what we can fix."

R.A. replied, "Well, let's go see what we got in the cupboards."

Dom and Amir headed toward the kitchen followed by R.A. who added as he was walking, "I didn't expect you two to be up this early."

Dom shrugged, "Why do you say that?"

R.A. said, "You two seemed to be up pretty late last night."

Dom glanced at Amir and half smiled, "Did we keep you up? We were talking, but I didn't think we were talking too loud."

R.A. shook his head, "No, you weren't talking too loud; I was just hypersensitive with the lack of vehicle traffic noise. I live near a well-traveled road."

Amir looked at Dom and took a tentative breath added, "Sorry, we'll try to be respectful of your sensitivity."

R.A. replied, "There's no need for concern, I found my recorder that I normally use to play sleep sounds. That should quell my hypersensitivity."

Dom glanced at Amir and half smiled.

R.A. covered a knowing smile from Dom and Amir hoping his explanation of a solution was sufficient to cover his deceit.

*****

The desk clerk at the Sheraton Hotel dialed the number to Dale Parsons' room.

"Mr. Parsons, there is a car here to pick you up." The clerk waited for a response and disconnected the call. She dialed a different number, "Ms. Hemenway, there is a car out front to pick you up." Again, the clerk waited for a response and hung up.

Parsons was the first out of the elevator at the lobby floor. He made his way, rolling his luggage, toward the hotel exit.

The automatic door opened and he stepped out onto the sidewalk. He nodded to the doorman, "I'm Mr. Parsons, is there a car for me?"

The doorman nodded, "Yes sir, the limo on the left."

He walked toward the limousine and the chauffeur asked, "You must be Dale Parsons; I'm here to take you to the airport. May I take your luggage?"

Parsons nodded, "Thank you."

The chauffeur opened the passenger door, collected Parsons' luggage and placed it in the opened trunk of the limo and made his way to close the door behind Mr. Parsons. Shortly, Ellie Hemenway exited the hotel and she also was absorbed into the limousine. The midmorning traffic to the airport was unusually heavy. Parsons and Hemenway engaged in pleasant conversation concerning their chance selection to attend the alien encounter at Hat Creek. Eventually the conversation focused on the mutual encounter with Sarah Gold of Hy-Mark Corporation.

Ellie offered her observation, "So, it seems that I don't see a downside to the promotional offer. It's a great opportunity for Austin Express and for me personally."

Dale nodded and agreed, "She explained the advantages and it is too good to pass up. Being a part of history is exciting enough, but the added notoriety and publicity can put us in the upper echelon of reporters and journalists."

Ellie smiled, "I assume she added the thousand dollar bonus to you also."

Dale nodded, "Yeah, I was sold when she gave me the 3122 Hy-Mark Media Pro, with no strings attached. But, the extra thousand dollars doesn't hurt."

Ellie wandered, "I was trying to see what kind of scam this would turn out to be, but my bosses said to go for it."

Dale agreed, "Yep, my editor said basically the same thing. Even if she is blowing smoke, there is no downside."

*****

Brad Stevens was on the final approach at the Fall River Mills airport. Vo Chen watched out the window of the Beechcraft King Air as it made a safe landing. Stevens taxied back to hanger 3, where Josh Frazier waited in a pickup truck. Stevens brought the plane to a stop and shut down the engines. He stepped back into the cabin and opened up the drop-down door exposing the stairway. Chen unbuckled his seatbelt and picked up his oversized suitcase and walked down the stairway onto the tarmac. Frazier drove up close to the plate and stopped. He got out of the truck and met Chen as he got down to the bottom of the stairs. Frazier put out his hand and Chen received the handshake.

"You must be Chen, I'm Josh, welcome to God's country."

Chen smiled, "Yeah, I caught the mountains and trees from the air. There's a lot of open space here."

Josh looked down at the suitcase, "You want some help with that precious cargo?"

Chen nodded, "Sure, I was a little nervous sitting next to a suitcase full of explosives. I know that Wheeler said that it won't explode unless it's ignited with something, but that didn't make me rest any easier."

Josh agreed, "Yeah, I don't blame you, I'd be concerned too." Josh reached down and grabbed the handle of the suitcase and sat it down carefully in the back of his pickup and strapped it in.

"Okay, let's get this payload to the farm. We'll have some lunch and wait for Wheeler's call."

Chen replied, "That sounds good to me."

They both got into the pickup and left the airport.

*****

Mike Mitchell and Security One, Darcy Blaine, were inside the drone hanger admiring a new addition to their drone fleet, a state-of-the-art Skyhawk drone. Mike was explaining to Darcy the charging process and the enhanced sensors and upgraded camera system.

Mike said, pointing to the charging apparatus, "Once it is completely charged, it can stay aloft for fifteen hours. After that the drone will use a self-homing system and land itself near the charging station. Additionally it can carry up to twenty pounds of payload and has an electrical plug in if the payload needs it. Certainly the added weight and electrical use does cut down the flight time, but only twenty percent for the weight factor and the electrical use will reduce the time one-half-hour for every kilowatt used."

Corporal Rousan was walking up toward the hanger, carrying a solar security system he was going to attach to the power pole above the hanger. As he walked by the hanger an excited grin appeared on his face. He interrupted Mike and Darcy's conversation saying, "Wow, that's a new Skyhawk, you mind if I take a look?"

Mike smiled, "You know about drones?"

Rousan nodded, "Yes, I grew up flying drones with my mom, we had a great time."

Mike stood up and extended a handshake and Rousan received it. Darcy had a wide smile and offered a handshake also. Rousan received her smile and responded in kind while softly shaking her hand. Mike offered, "I'm Mike Mitchell and this is Darcy Blaine, one of our security staff."

Rousan replied, "I'm Corporal Rousan, I'm part of the National Guard construction brigade, but I've been conscripted by agent Johnson to assist in setting up the added security cameras."

Darcy replied, "Is that so? Mike and I were just going over our new security addition, but apparently already know about the Skyhawk.

Rousan replied, "Yes, I've read all I could about them, but there little bit out of my price range, to own one."

Mike added, "That's for sure, if it wasn't for the presidential boost in our security budget, I'd have to get along with our old stand-bys. We have two Alpha drones that we rotate every six hours."

Rousan said, "Well, while I'm here I'd be glad to help out with the drones. And by the way, are you going to incorporate the drone camera feed into the security monitors?"

Mike replied, "I didn't know we could, you can do that?"

Rousan replied, "Certainly, I just need the frequency specs of the drones, but of course the monitors won't be able to fly the drones, they would only be used for surveillance monitoring."

Mike nodded, "Okay, if you can do that that would be great." Mike looked at his watch, "Well, I have meeting, but I'll leave you and Darcy here with the Skyhawk manual, so you can get it up and running and set up the security protocols for the camera feeds."

Rousan nodded, "Okay, thank you Mr. Mitchell."

Mike smiled, "Just call me Mike."

Rousan smiled, "Thank you, Mike."

Mike walked away and Darcy said, "So, Corporal Rousan, you must be a techie."

Rousan smiled, "Yeah, I'm going to school part-time for degree in electronics."

He hunched his shoulders slightly, leaned toward her, "You can call me Bashir."

Darcy smiled and held out her hand again and Bashir gladly accepted another handshake.

Suddenly their handshake was lavished with tongue licks from a friendly dog. Bashir was taken slightly by surprise, but reached down and clasped his hands around the friendly face, "Well, who is this?" The dog accepted the petting and wiggled slightly and wagged her tail with pleasure.

Darcy added her hands to the head and rubbed the sides of the dog, "Oh, this is Sophie. She has the run of the complex; she's liable to show up anywhere. She belongs to Kyle Arlitz the owner of the Herford RV Park, about a mile west of here."

Bashir asked, "What breed of dog is she?"

Darcy explained, "She's supposed to be an Aussiedor but I think her mom was Australian Shepherd and her dad just came from a good neighborhood."

Bashir smiled, "Well, she seems like a great dog."

Darcy said, "Yes, and she's really curious too and she sniffs and licks everything."

Darcy and Bashir finished greeting their friend and began to set up the Skyhawk and the other drones. When they finished Darcy contacted Mike via radio, to let him know the Skyhawk was operational. Mike took control remotely and the Skyhawk taxied off. Once the Skyhawk was in the air, Bashir watched admiringly as it glided around. He took a deep breath, "Okay, Darcy, I should set up the rest of the security cams before I get fired."

Darcy smiled, "No, you're too good at your job to get fired."

He smiled, "Do you work here every day?"

She replied, "Well, lately, my partner and I, Juan Gozier, Security Two, have been staying in our camp trailers by the river, working twelve hour shifts each. But, since the attempted bombing of the site we are pretty much here twenty-four seven, until more security is hired."

Bashir listened, "I see; we are bivouacked here until we finish this job. But, I hope I see you again while we're here"

Darcy smiled, "I'd like that too, but you can always stop by my camp trailer."

He smiled, "I'll do that."

Bashir picked up his tool belt and put it on. He also picked up security cam and walked over to the power pole and started to climb it."

*****

Chen sat at Frazier's kitchen table finishing up his ham sandwich and potato chips. Josh pushed the bag of potato chips over toward Chen, "Here Chen have some more chips."

Chen nodded, "Yeah, I think I will." as he reached for the bag and put some more chips on his plate.

So, Josh, how many of those recorders did you have to buy?"

Josh replied, "I bought three from Buy Mart in Redding and two from Barrett's Office Supply in Bella Vista. There was a Buy Mart, in Bella Vista, but it was sold out."

Chen asked, "How much did that set you back?"

Josh replied, "A little over 17 grand, but I got a promotional five percent discount at Buy Mart."

Chen replied, "I guess Jan will have to cough that up when you see her."

Josh said, "No, I'll just take back what I don't use and get a refund. And besides, we owe Jan for all that she does for us and we have a 'big bucks' state Senator covering our operating expenses."

Chen asked, "Oh yeah, who is it?"

Josh replied, "I don't know and I know better than to ask."

*****

Ellie Hemenway took in the view of the farmland from the window of the C-40 Clipper, as it circled the Sacramento airport. Dale Parsons also had a window seat behind Ellie. He asked, "Is this your first time in Sacramento?"

Ellie replied, "Yes, I've flown into LA but never to Sacramento. How about you, you ever been here?"

Dale replied, "No, I've flown into Oakland, but this is my first trip to Sacramento."

The military transport settled to earth and taxied to the west and of the runways and stopped. A Sergeant came over to the passengers, "Ms. Hemenway and Mr. Parsons you may depart the port doors when they open and I will escort you to the next leg of your journey."

Ellie said, "Thank you Sergeant."

Dale added, "Yes, thank you Sergeant."

The pair of passengers collected their luggage and following the Sergeant they made their way down the stairway to the tarmac.

Sergeant directed them toward a waiting helicopter with its engine still running. The pilot climbed out of the cockpit and met his two passengers.

He pulled out his COM and compared the pictures of his passengers to their faces and said loudly over the noise of the engine, "Good afternoon, Ms. Hemenway and Mr. Parsons, I am your pilot, Chip Barker, he pointed to the chopper, "I'll help you get in the cockpit and put your luggage in and then I will take you to Hat Creek. Hopefully we will have a smooth flight."

They both nodded and he assisted them one at a time getting onto the chopper and then he secured their seatbelts. He picked up their luggage and rolled them around to the other side and placed them inside and closed all the doors.

He returned to the cockpit and pointed to the headsets and signaled them to place the headsets on their ears.

He put his headset on and spoke to his passengers, "Again, welcome aboard I hope you enjoy your flight, it will take about two hours."

*****

At the FBI office in Redding, agent Frank Knox was going over reports of wire transfers and suspicious purchases that they could link to any of the subversive groups in the area.

Agent Robin Lane was comparing shipping bills of lading, factory deliveries and flight manifests with the names or company names used by known terrorists that may be linked in any way to employees or friends or family of anyone connected to the Hat Creek SETI site.

Robin shook her head and leaned away from the screen she was watching, "Frank, I'm going over all of the old reports and the new reports and I still can't find any connection to anyone at the SETI site."

She paused and stated, "I wonder if the chatter about an attack coming from within, is a diversion, and the attack is coming like it did before, from the outside."

Frank looked over at her nodded, "That would be my guess, except that Smithy said that her source was adamant about the attempt coming from within the complex."

Robin took a deep breath, "Okay, how about we trade jobs and take a look at each other's work with new eyes?"

Frank nodded in agreement, "Okay, why don't we just change places instead of re-delivering our reports to our COM's?"

Robin sighed and stood up and walked over to Frank's chair and waited for him to get up. Frank looked up at Robin, "What?"

Robin responded, "What, what? Get up and go sit in my chair."

Frank frowned, "No, I like my chair, I'll just roll around to your side."

Robin smiled and grimaced at the same time and reached down and took the back of Frank's chair and rolled him around to her side, while he was still in the chair. Then she reached down and grabbed her chair and rolled it to where Frank's chair was.

She exulted, "You spoiled shithead." Then she sat abruptly down in her chair. They stared at each other for a moment and then both began to laugh.

Frank said still laughing, "I think we need a break. I'm going to get something from the cafeteria; you want to bring you back something?"

Robin smiled, "Yeah; whiskey straight up."

Frank scrunched a disbelieving look at her. She noticed his expression, "Okay, how about coffee and a roll?"

Frank stood up and began to walk, "Really, and a roll too? Aren't you watching your weight?"

Robin smiled, shook her head and without looking up gave Frank 'the finger'.

Frank smiled and continued out of the office.

Robin looked at the report on the screen and then looked down at the paper reports on the desk and shuffled through a couple of pages. She took a short breath and reached for her COM, but remembered it was still on her side of the desk. She got up and went over and picked up her COM and selected Lieutenant Smithy as a contact. She waited for a connection as she went back over to the other side of the desk. Momentarily, Lieutenant Smithy answered, "Good afternoon agent Lane."

Robin responded looking down at the image on her COM, "Good afternoon Lieutenant. We've been going over our reports again and again, and we've yet to come up with any viable connection between the staff at the SETI site and any subversives. Are you certain that your source said that the attack was coming from within the complex?"

Brie took a short breath, "Hold on, let me get my notes and read you exactly what was said."

Robin rolled her head around and flexed her shoulders and neck while she waited. Brie came back on the COM, "Okay, this is what was said, exactly..."

"The explosion will take place from within the complex."

Robin listened carefully and repeated the words to herself, "The explosion will take place from within the complex."

She tilted her head slightly back and thought.

Brie watched her as she thought, "So, does that change anything?"

Robin took a short breath and stated, "What if the explosive device isn't at the site yet?"

Frank walked in to the office and heard Robin's statement. He asked, "What are you saying, the device isn't on-site yet?"

Robin replied, "That might be what we are missing."

She turned to Frank, "Brie said that the source said and I quote, "The explosion will take place from within the complex."

That may mean that the device is not there yet."

Frank nodded slowly and agreed, "Okay, now we just have to find out what, if anything new, is coming into the complex."

Brie added her thoughts, "Maybe it's not what is coming in but who?"

Robin combined the thoughts, "How about who, is bringing what in."

Frank added Brie to his COM and began, "How about we start with the date of the source's contact, and work forward from there. Who's coming in, or has arrived that is new since that date and what is coming in or has been delivered since that date?"

Brie nodded, "Okay, let me check things on my end."

Her fingers blazed over her keyboard as she gathered information. Her COM screen changed several times as she worked her magic. Momentarily she spoke, "Okay, the timeline suggests that the warning came in about six hours after the press conference announcing the timeline of the alien conversation at Hat Creek. Since then two new players have been added to the mix, the two reporters selected by lottery to attend the conversation; Dale Parsons and Ellie Hemenway."

Frank entered some keystrokes on his computer and pulled up the data on Parsons and Hemenway. He was scanning through the data as he spoke, "Yes, we've checked out the offender database, the NCIC, the Crime Data Explorer, CDE, and even involved the Criminal Justice Information Services (CJIS), and haven't come up with any red flags. As you know the White House vetted all of the reporters who applied for the lottery selection prior to their being accepted."

Robin added, "We've checked their bank accounts and even their families' accounts and acquaintances and came up with nothing suspicious. They both signed a full background check authorization and a waiver authorization to monitor their calls, emails and social media since their selection and, other than them contacting their family and their publishers there has been nothing unusual about their contacts."

Frank also added, "We're trying to check in with the DC agent at their hotel, but his government issued COM malfunctioned and he switched to his personal COM. He's currently on his way back from Sacramento where he handed off the surveillance to the helicopter pilot. He's going to check in when he gets to back to DC."

Robin pulled up a different screen on her computer, "As far as our usual suspects are concerned, we followed Josh Frazier to the Fall River Mills airport and he picked up an unknown Asian male who arrived on a Beechcraft King air and they went back to Frazier's farm."

Brie asked, "Where'd the aircraft fly in from?"

Robin replied, "We don't know but, I have the tail number."

Brie smiled, "Okay, give it to me." as she moved to a different screen.

"November 71284692."

Brie entered the numbers and came up with an answer, "That plane is registered to Brad Stevens a known collaborator with Segr8. He keeps the aircraft at Wilson airfield in Virginia."

Brie busied her fingers on the keyboard, "I checked for a flight manifest, but since it's a private aircraft, none was filed." She continued with more strokes on the keyboard, "I'm trying to pull up the closed circuit camera at Wilson airfield to see if I can get an ID on facial recognition of the passenger."

Frank chuckled, "You can do that? And I thought the FBI had a lot of tools."

Brie smiled as she continued searching the screen, "Yes, the Attorney General has given us clearance directly from the president."

Frank commented, "Talk about having friends in high places."

Brie was fast forwarding through the video of the closed circuit TV and finally came up with a usable face. She applied the facial recognition software to the video and came up with a name.

"Okay, I got a possible name of the passenger. It looks like his name is Vo Chen, a known associate of Segr8 and of the local leader of Segr8, Royce Pyle."

Robin exclaimed, "Now we're getting somewhere. Segr8 is our target, but how does that connect anyone at the SETI site?"

Frank asked, "LT, does Chen have any special expertise; perhaps explosives."

Brie moved back to her original screen and entered some keystrokes. She looked at the results, "No, he's a low-level grunt."

Robin asked, "That begs the question; how does a low-level grunt fit into a high-level plan to blow up a SETI site? Certainly none of these players will be allowed to even get close to the site."

Frank said, "Yeah, but we're missing a major piece. Where is our explosive expert, Jan Wheeler? She's gotta play a major part of the plan, but we haven't seen her for several days."

Brie looked over at another screen that was flashing and orange light. She said, "Okay guys, I'll check on Wheeler for you, but I've got to attend to something. I'll get back to you. I'll send you all the info I have so far."

Frank nodded, "Okay, thanks, do what you gotta do LT."

Brie's image left their COM screens.

THE BEST LAID PLANS...
NO COINCIDENCES

Chip Barker moved the radio switch on the panel of the Huey and spoke, "How about it Hat Creek; you have a copy on Huey One?"

A reply came over the radio, "Sure do Chip, this is Mike. I've been expecting your transmission."

"Copy that Mike, I'm three minutes out with two on board."

Mike replied, "I read you, I'll have security one pick you up at the landing site."

Chip flipped the toggle switch on the radio to intercom and spoke to his passengers, "Okay you two, we'll be landing in a couple minutes."

Parsons and Hemenway smiled at each other as they took in the view from the helicopter.

On the ground, Darcy was on her four-wheeler, when Mike advised her that she was to pick up passengers at the heliport. She turned the four-wheeler around and headed toward the SETI office and parked next to an SUV. She got off the four-wheeler, got in the SUV and headed toward the parking lot.

Chip maneuvered the Huey gracefully and sat it down near the end of the parking lot. Darcy watched the Huey approach and parked the SUV a short distance away. Chip shut down the engine of the Huey and stepped out of the cockpit. He went around to the other side and helped Parsons and Hemengway out of helicopter. Once they were out he went around to the other side of the Huey and took out their luggage. Darcy got out of the SUV and headed toward her guests. She held out her hand and shook each of their hands and said somewhat loudly over the sound of the engine noise, "Hi, I'm Darcy. Welcome to the Hat Creek SETI site. Why don't we move over to the SUV and get away from the noise?"

The two nodded and followed Darcy to the SUV. Chip was already carrying their luggage to the SUV. He went around to the back and opened up the hatchback and placed the luggage inside and closed the lift-gate. He turned and headed back toward the Huey.

When Darcy and her guests got to the SUV the noise from the Huey was subsiding. Darcy said, "You must be Mr. Parsons and Ms. Hemengway. Again, I want to welcome you to Hat Creek."

Ellie smiled, "This is so exciting; the helicopter ride and being here."

Dale nodded, "Yes, I agree it's been a little overwhelming."

Darcy replied, "Well, I hope you enjoy your stay. You have to realize that this event will be a first for everyone."

Dale and Ellie smiled.

Darcy opened the rear passenger door of the SUV, "Well, let's get you two down to the complex."

Dale motioned for Ellie to enter first and then followed her inside and closed the door. Darcy got in the driver seat and waited for Chip to come back. Shortly Chip arrived carrying a backpack and got in the SUV. Darcy started the SUV and drove it a short distance up to the complex and parked. Darcy exited the SUV and opened the rear passenger door and the pair stepped out. Darcy closed the door, "Okay, let's head inside and introduce you to everyone."

Dale nodded, "Thank you."

Ellie added, "Yes, thank you."

Chip was already out the vehicle and was the first to the complex door and opened it. Ellie and Dale went in first, followed by Darcy and Chip.

Mike was still in the security office checking the progress of the security cam installations. He checked the screen and found all eight security cameras were operational. And he noticed that Rousan had also linked the video feeds from the drones. The Skyhawk and Alpha drone were active, while Beta drone was being recharged. She looked over at her COM screen and saw an incoming COM alert notice. She stepped over and saw the icon of Lieutenant Smithy. She selected the icon and Smithy's image appeared.

"Good afternoon Lieutenant, how goes your day?" Mike asked, Brie replied, "It's going okay Mike, but I need you to implement another security protocol."

Mike said, "Sure, lay it on me LT."

Brie said, "I've sent a portable multi-scan unit to your guard shack and I need someone to pick it up."

Mike nodded, "Okay, I'll have it picked up right away, but what am I supposed to do with it?"

Brie responded, "The FBI and our office are trying to counter a possible threat to your site. We feel that the tip about the threat coming from within the complex was misread and we believe that the explosive device was not on grounds at the time the tip was received. We are thinking that any explosive device would not have been on grounds until after 0200 hours today."

Mike listened and absorbed the information. He paused and thought, "So, we need to check everything that has been delivered since 2 AM, correct?"

Brie added, "Not just anything that came in but anyone who came in since then."

Mike thought, "I'll check with Lieutenant Carlson about deliveries but the only new arrivals are the reporters who just came in."

Brie said, "Well, then you need to scan the reporters and whatever they brought with them in addition to the deliveries."

Mike paused, "Oh, I guess I'll have to scan our pilot Chip and his Huey also."

Brie nodded, "Yes; that would also fall under the protocol."

Mike said, "Okay, I know Chip won't have a problem with that, in fact you probably want to help."

Brie added, "That doesn't mean that we aren't continuing our standard security process. You guys are extremely important to us."

Mike replied, "We appreciate everything you're doing to keep this place safe."

Brie nodded, "Of course, you're welcome. Be safe."

Brie's image disappeared from his COM.

Mike immediately picked up radio mic and keyed the lever. "Security two, Gozier, control."

Mike waited patiently for a response. The weight was short.

"Go for Gozier."

"I need you to 10-20 the guard shack and pick up a portable multi-scanner and bring it to the complex."

Gozier replied, "Copy that, enroute."

Mike stepped out of the security office and looked down the walkway and saw Chip talking to the new arrivals. He waved at chip to come to him. Chip excused himself and came over to Mike.

Chip asked, What's up Mike?"

Mike began, "We have an added security protocol. Juan is going to bring us a portable multi-scanner. We need to scan everything and everyone that has arrived since 0200 hrs. The FBI and DCS believed that an explosive device might have been delivered after that time. So, if you want to help when Juan gets here with the scanner we need to check the new arrivals, their personal effects, you and your personal effects and your Huey." Mike put his hand on Chip's shoulder, "You know I don't suspect you of anything, but we can take no chances."

Chip smiled, "Mike, after surviving two IED's, I am the last one to skip a security protocol."

Mike replied, "I knew you would see it that way."

Chip said, "How about if I keep an eye on our new arrivals until the scanner gets here and we can start with them?"

Mike said, "That's a good idea. I'll track down Lieutenant Carlson and give her a rundown while I wait for Juan to arrive with the scanner."

Chip nodded, "Copy that." He went back over to keep an eye on the two new visitors.

Mike turned and picked up the two-way radio and keyed the mic.

"Lieutenant Carlson, Mitchell."

The reply was rather quick, "This is Carlson."

Mike replied, "What's your 20?"

Carlson replied, "I'm in the electrical room."

Mike answered, "Copy. Standby; coming to you."

Carlson said, "10–4 Mike."

Mike went down the hallway and out the complex door he went around the building and headed toward the electrical room. He came across Corporal Rousan tossing a ball for his new friend, Sophie. Mike chuckled on seeing Sophie and called her to him, "Sophie, where you been girl?" Sophie came to Mike who ruffled her fur playfully.

Rousan smiled, "She's been hanging around me helping me put the security cams up."

Mike said, "I see she found her ball, I thought she'd lost it."

Rousan said, "Yes, he came over and dropped it in front of me. So I guessed that she wanted to play."

Mike smiled, "Oh, I want to thank you for setting up the video feeds on the drones."

Rousan replied, "That's no problem, it was fun."

Mike nodded, "Why don't you come with me. I've got to talk to the Lieutenant about a new security alert."

Rousan partially snapped to attention on hearing the word Lieutenant.

He replied, "Of course I will, sir."

Mike replied, "It's just us, Corporal, call me Mike."

Rousan smiled and followed Mike. Sophie happily tagged along with the ball in her mouth.

They walked together around the fenced in power grid and went into the electrical room. Lieutenant Carlson was checking the power levels for the backup generators. Carlson shook Mike's hand and Rousan snapped a salute to the Lieutenant. Carlson saluted back to the Corporal, "At ease Corporal, no need to stand on ceremony here; let's just get this job done."

She turned to Mike, "So, Mike, what's up?"

Mike replied, "Lieutenant Smithy, at the DSC implemented a new security protocol. I have security 1, Gozier, picking up a multi-scan from the guard shack. Her sources previously believed that an explosive device was already on grounds, but she found that it's more likely that the device may have been delivered after 0200 hours, today, and that any deliveries or personnel arriving after that time should be scanned."

Carlson nodded, "We only had one delivery today and that was at 0800 hrs; It was 500 gallons of fuel transferred into our tank, which is certainly an explosive, but totally expected. The delivery truck came and went. No other personnel have arrived since yesterday."

Mike nodded, "Okay, I know you're on top of things, but I just want to keep you advised of any changes."

Carlson said, "Of course, we have to stay on the same page."

Mike started to turn away but stopped, "Oh, I want to thank you for loaning us Corporal Rousan to assist in setting up the security cameras." He looked at Rousan, "If you can spare the Corporal, I'd like to use him as part of the new security protocol team."

Carlson smiled, looked at Rousan, "I believe the Corporal would be quite pleased to assist you. His electronics specialist skills have been underused as a welder and plumber."

Lieutenant asked Rousan, "What say you Corporal?"

Rousan smiled and snapped a salute, "Thank you, sir. It will be my pleasure to assist Mr. Mitchell."

Carlson replied, "I thought so. You are so assigned Corporal."

Mike said, "Thank you LT." He turned and nodded to Rousan and they left the electrical room.

*****

Corporal Rich Lester was sitting at the desk in the guard shack when he heard an engine noise getting closer. He looked out the window and saw Corporal Vern Moya eyeing the tree line where the noise was coming from. Soon from around the edge of the tree line a four-wheeler slid around the trees and tossing dirt up against the guard shack it slid to a stop. Moya backed away avoiding the rush of dirt and laughed, "What the shit are you doing Gozier? Someday you're going to plow right through the wall of the shack."

Lester got up, "It's okay Vern, then we'll have reason to shoot him, for destruction of government property."

Moya replied, "Hell no, that's too much paperwork."

Rich replied, "Not if we bury his ass in the orchard in an unmarked grave."

Juan sat stoically on the four-wheeler, impervious to their verbal assaults. Juan smiled, "You lazy bastards can barely get off your asses, let alone dig a hole."

Moya looked at Lester, "You know he's right Rich, we could just douse him with gasoline and light him on fire."

Juan got off the bike and fist bumped Moya.

"Mike said you have a multi-scan for me to pick up."

Lester went in to the corner of the shack and picked up the multi-scan and brought it outside. Juan looked at the unit and noticed it had two handles and was larger than he expected.

"Wow, that's not the standard hand-scanner. I guess that's why they call it a multi-scan."

Juan retrieved it from Lester with two hands and set it in the basket in the rear of the four–wheeler.

Moya stated, "Yes, it's a special scanner it can detect drugs, explosives and other contraband. It also has an infrared screen display."

Lester went back into the shack and picked up another apparatus and brought it out to Gozier.

"Don't forget the charger and extra battery pack; it won't be much good without it."

Juan grabbed the charger and battery pack from Lester and placed it in the basket with the scanner. He nodded to Rich and Vern and got back on the bike started it up.

"Okay, thanks guys, I'll catch you in a bit." He spun the bike and kicked up a little more dirt toward the guard shack and headed toward the SETI site.

Moya said, as he simulated drawing a bead on the fleeing target, "Rich, hand me the rifle, I think I can pick him off at 100 yards."

Lester shook his head, "No way, I'm not filling out a negligent discharge report."

Juan continued merrily on his way.

*****

Mike and Rousan were coming around the side of the building just as Juan arrived at the complex with the multi-scanner.

Juan stopped his ATV and eased off the seat. Mike and Rousan walked up to him and Juan said, "Okay, I picked up the package as requested." He stepped to the rear of the ATV and reached in the basket and took out the multi-scanner.

"It's a lot bigger than I thought it would be."

Mike looked at the device and took it from Juan.

"Yes, it is different from a normal scanner."

Rousan smiled, "Yes, it has a lot of bells and whistles. It's the top-of-the-line in portable scanners. It scans for drugs, explosives and can be programmed for various orders, even dead bodies. Additionally it has an infrared image display screen."

Juan smiled looked at Rousan, "Well, I didn't know we had a living and breathing operations manual present."

Rousan smiled back and held out his hand for Juan to shake. Juan shook his hand and Mike grinned, "Juan this is Corporal Rousan. He is part of the National Guard construction crew, as an electronics specialist, and apparently he is well-versed in his field."

Juan nodded shaking Rousan's hand, "That's an understatement, Mike. I'm Juan Gozier, security two for the SETI complex. It's a pleasure to meet you."

Rousan replied, "You must be Darcy's partner, she spoke of you earlier today."

Juan replied, "Yep, she's my partner in crime."

Sophie brushed her nose against Juan's hand giving it a lick. Juan reached down and rubbed Sophie's head and neck vigorously with both hands.

"Sophie; how you doing girl?"

Rousan replied, "She's been helping me put up security cameras."

Juan added, "Yeah, she helps me on my security rounds too."

Mike was still looking at the scanner and said to Rousan, "Well, since you're the expert…why don't you show us how to operate this piece of equipment?" He handed the scanner to Rousan.

Rousan nodded, "Okay what do you want to scan first?"

Mike said, "Wait here, I've got to go in and get our guests and Chip." He turned and went inside the complex.

Rousan powered on the scanner and showed Juan how it scanned his ATV. The screen display showed an infrared image of the bike and frame and a digital display identified metal, fuel odor, rubber and leather.

Juan shook his head in amazement, "Wow, I wouldn't be surprised if it could tell you manufacturer of the bike."

Rousan smiled, "No, but it can pick up your finger prints off the bike."

Juan laughed, "You're shittin' me!"

Rousan grinned, touched a couple of pressure sensors on the screen and moved the scanner over the seat of the ATV and held it still. Momentarily, various smudges and fingerprints were detected. Rousan said, "Now, I can upload the prints to a server and get an ID if they're in the system."

Juan replied, "Holy crap, that's awesome."

Mike came back out of the complex with Chip and the new visitors. He turned to Chip, "How about we show our visitors our new security tool?"

Chip nodded, "Go for it Mike."

Mike looked at Rousan, "Okay Corporal; do your thing."

Rousan looked at Chip, "Just stand still for a moment."

Chip assumed the position and Rousan scanned Chip's body from his feet to his head. He showed Mike the results on the screen and digital display. Mike looked at the screen, "Okay Chip, it says you're alive and you have a metal plate in your left arm."

Chip smiled, "That's some scanner."

Mike looked at the visitors, "As I explained inside, we have a new security protocol since we received a bomb threat. This multi-scanner is an added security measure.

Mike looked at Dale Parsons, "Mr. Parsons do you mind?"

Parsons nodded and stepped over and stood still.

Rousan asked Mike, "Here Mike you try it." as he handed him the scanner. Mike tentatively grabbed the scanner by both handles and scanned Parsons as Rousan had shown him on Chip. When the scan was complete Mike looked at the displays, "Mr. Parsons, thank you. You're clear."

Ellie Hemenway stepped forward, "Okay my turn."

She stood still and waited to be scanned. Mike completed the scan, "Now we need to scan your luggage and then scan the SUV and we also need to scan Chips Huey; and that may take a while to do."

Chip went over to the passenger side of the SUV and took out his backpack and brought it over and set it on a table.

He looked at Mike, "Okay, do your thing."

Mike smiled, handed the scanner to Rousan, "Here you go, you're the expert; you do the scans."

Sophie was observing the scan process and decided to assist by sniffing Chip's backpack as it was being scanned.

Rousan turned to Parsons, "Mr. Parsons is it?"

Parsons replied, "Yes."

"I'm Corporal Rousan, would you mind getting your luggage, so I can scan it?"

Chip interrupted, "I'll go get their luggage and bring it to you."

Rousan nodded, "Thank you, sir."

Chip turned to Rousan and held out his hand, "I'm Chip Barker, the Huey pilot."

Rousan shook his hand, "Glad to meet you sir."

Chip replied, "It's just Chip, please."

Rousan said, "Of course, thank you Chip."

Chip went to the SUV and retrieved the two suitcases. He set one on the ground and one on the table. He asked, "Who's suitcase is this?" as he pointed to the one on the table.

Ellie replied, "That would be mine."

Rousan scanned the case slowly and checked the displays on the scanner.

Rousan said, "I noticed an electronic device in the suitcase, would you mind taking it out for me?"

Ellie nodded, "Of course." She unzipped the suitcase and pulled out the 3122 Hy-Mark Media Pro and set it on the table. Sophie put her paws on the table and leaned over and sniffed the recorder.

Rousan gently pulled her down to the ground. He looked at the recorder, "Wow, that's a great recorder, you must really like it."

Ellie smiled, "I've only had it since yesterday; it was given to me specifically for documenting the alien conversation."

Rousan replied, "Well, this will certainly do anything you wanted to; it's a top-of-the-line media recorder."

Rousan took the scanner and ran it over the recorder. He looked at the display on the scanner, "Okay, it's good."

She kept the recorder out of the suitcase and zipped it up.

Rousan set the suitcase aside and picked up the other suitcase and scanned it also. Again he paused and asked Parsons to take out the electronic device out of his suitcase.

Dale smiled and said as he opened the suitcase, "It's the same recorder that Ellie has; we were both given one for this event."

He took the recorder out and placed it on the table.

Again Sophie put her paws on the table and curiously sniffed the recorder. Rousan smiled and eased her off the table, "She sure is interested in these recorders."

Rousan scanned the recorder with the same result. Dale also kept his recorder out of the suitcase and zipped it up.

Chip picked up both the suitcases and looked at Dale and Ellie, "Do you want me to take these inside for you?"

Ellie said, "It's not necessary, I won't need them till tonight."

Dale also replied, "The same for me all I need is the recorder. I won't need my suitcase until I get to the hotel."

Chip stated, "Well, I'll leave the suitcases on the table until we finish scanning the SUV, and I'll place them back inside it."

Chip added, "The SETI director said that there was a change in procedures and that you can start recording and broadcasting whenever you want. It will be coordinated with our cameras already inside. The feed will be picked up by our COM-SAT, edited and rebroadcast with a ten second delay. Ellie and Dale gleefully picked up their recorders and proceeded inside the complex.

Darcy was talking to Mike, when she happened to look out the window and saw Rousan and Juan outside. She excused herself and stepped out of the building and walked up to the table.

"What are you two up to out here?" She asked, "Juan, are you trying to corrupt the Corporal here?"

Juan smiled, "No, I'm just absorbing his technical expertise."

Darcy noticed the multi-scanner, "Is that the new scanner?"

Juan replied, "Yes, it's quite the unit. Rousan was just showing some of the things it can do. The only thing he can't do is make breakfast, and I'm not so sure that it couldn't order it if push came to shove."

Rousan smiled, "Would you like ham and eggs or a Denver omelet?"

Juan looked over at Darcy and then back it Rousan who was smiling and realized he was joking.

Rousan's face turned serious and he said, "Really Juan, I can order breakfast."

Juan's face was confused, "I was joking, are you serious you can order breakfast with that thing?"

Rousan shrugged his shoulders and answered as he pulled out his personal COM, "No, but I can use my COM." Rousan chuckled.

Juan shook his head and laughed.

"Okay, you got me, but for that you owe me a lunch."

Chip had been listening to the ploy and laughed along with the others. He took a breath, "Okay let's get the rest of this scanning done so I can use my chopper."

Rousan smiled and picked up the multi-scanner and headed toward the SUV.

*****

Agent Knox was scanning through files on his COM screen searching wire transfers, business transactions and individual purchases for any suspicious activity. He studied the file for moment and wrote down some information on a notepad. He went back to the screen and pulled up some more files. Agent Rayner was also checking communication records of Segr8 players and their family, their COM's, personal messages, texts and social media interactions using an NCIC algorithm. As they were searching both of their COM screen displayed the flashing icon of Lieutenant Smithy. Anji caught Frank's attention, "Smithy is calling." Robin answered the COM call, "Lieutenant, what's new?" Frank joined the call also.

Brie noticed both Frank and Robin were on her screen.

"I wanted to get back to you about Jan Wheeler, she is in DC and was pinged at a location near the residence of Royce Pyle. And it also showed Chen was in an electronics store in Richmond. Perhaps you can use your sources to find out what he purchased, since that's in your wheelhouse."

Frank said, "That rings a bell, it seems that Josh Frazier also shopped at an electronics store in Redding. I'll try to see what he purchased and I'll see if I can track Chen's purchase also."

Robin added, "By the way, our agent Hank Becerra got back to us regarding his stakeout at the Sheridan where the journalists were staying. He said that both Parsons and Hemenway had a visitor from Hy-Mark Corporation."

Brie asked, "Did you get a name of the visitor?"

Robin replied, "Yes, he said he didn't see her but, her business card has her name as Sarah Gold. I checked her out on their site and she does work for Hy-Mark in the sales department. I'll try to contact Parsons and Hemenway to see what she wanted."

*****

Eve was looking out the window of the plane taking in the majestic view of what was left of the snowpack of the Sierra Nevada Mountains bordering California and Nevada. Her personal COM buzzed and she reached in her purse and pulled it out. She looked at the screen and selected Richard's flashing icon.

"Good afternoon Mr. Vice President."

Richard's image appeared on her COM. He smiled as he answered, "And the same to you Ms. Walker. Are you enjoying your flight?"

She looked blankly out the window, "Oh, just taking in the sights."

Richard looked at another screen said, "I see you are over the Sierras."

She smiled and she replied, "You know you can get charged with stalking and since I'm over the California border you could get several years for that offense."

He settled back into his chair, "As long as it's several years with you; that would be acceptable."

She shook her head, "Well, aren't you the romantic."

Richard smiled and took a short breath, "Actually, I think I know a judge that could add other charges and extend my sentence."

Eve sucked in on her cheek, "I know you didn't call just to harass me, so Mr. VP, state your purpose."

Richard stifled a chuckle, "I can't get anything past you. Okay, just wanted to give you a heads up on a new security protocol. It seems that the explosive device that was said to have already been placed at the SETI site, is not there yet. Everything and everyone that has arrived since 0200 hours today, is being scanned for security purposes. And unfortunately that does include you, even though you are a VIP."

Eve shrugged her shoulders, "That's no big deal; I'm used to being scrutinized as an attorney and journalist."

Richard smiled, "Well, I just went to let you know the process and that I wish you weren't going to be put in harm's way. I know that it's your choice to follow through with documenting our contact with the aliens, but that doesn't mean that I don't worry about you."

Eve nodded and sighed, "Yes I know, but I'm sure that the security procedures of the entire United States government will prevail in the prevention of an attack on the SETI site."

Richard listened to her sound-bite, "That sounded like a prepared statement you would give during an interview. However, I know you have your fears just as I have mine; I just want you to be safe."

Eve took a short breath, "I know you do, so try not to worry. I'll see you when I get back."

Richard nodded, "Okay, I love you."

He smiled, "I love you too."

*****

Rousan and Chip finished scanning the Huey with the multi-scanner. Chip checked his watch, "Whoa, I gotta get in the air, I have to pick up Evelyn Walker in Sacramento and bring her back here."

Rousan thought, "Evelyn Walker, isn't that the vice presidents…"

Chip nodded and interrupted saying, "Yes, that's her."

Rousan said, "I heard a lot about her and I look forward to meeting her."

Chip replied, "I haven't met her either, but I understand that she is intelligent, personable, well-liked and it doesn't hurt that she's good looking."

Rousan nodded, "Well, at any rate I look forward to meeting all of those attributes."

Chip smiled, reached down to pet Sophie, went over to the Huey, got in and fired it up. After it got up to speed, he lifted off and away it went.

Rousan went over to an ATV and picked up the multi-scan off the ground and secured it in the basket in the rear of the ATV.

He got on and started it up and drove it across the parking lot and a short distance up to SETI complex and parked it. Sophie happily ran beside him. He got off the ATV and said to Sophie, "Okay girl, you keep an eye on things." He went inside the complex and looked for Juan. He followed voices coming from the break room and found Darcy in Juan sitting at a table talking to R.A.. Darcy's face lit up as Rousan came up to the table. Rousan noticed her smile and said to Juan, "I parked your ATV outside and the multi-scan is in the basket."

Juan nodded, "Thanks, but Darcy and I were talking to Mike and we told him we had an extra ATV and that you could use mine and I'll use the other one. That way we wouldn't have to shuffle the use of the ATV."

Rousan nodded, "That works for me, by the way, where is Mike? I have to check in with him."

Darcy said, "He's down the hall in the security office. I'll take you to see him." She stood up and started down the hall with Rousan following. Juan grinned as he saw them leave. He got up also and followed them out of the break room.

R.A. watched the group leave and got up and followed voices to the other end of the hallway. He came upon Parsons and Hemenway talking to Amir and Dom at their workstation. They were both using their recorders to video Amir and Dom at their workstation.

Ellie said, So this is where the magic happened; your first contact with the alien, Adam."

Dom nodded, "Yes, and I am still in a daze after all this time."

Amir added, "Yes, it seems like a lifetime ago and yet it seems like only yesterday."

R.A. made himself known, "You know, you are in the presence of history and we all are fortunate to have the opportunity to witness and record it for posterity."

Dale and Ellie both heard R.A.'s voice and immediately turned their videos on him. Ellie added her commentary, "And this is the world renowned Doctor 'Gemo. I'm sure that we could fill eons of recordings on your life alone."

Dale added, "Could you step over here and stand next to Dom and Amir so we can complete the trifecta?"

Ellie added following R.A. with her video, "Yes please let's get this shot for everybody to see."

R.A. graciously succumbed to their request and went over and stood by Amir and Dom, placing his hands on their shoulders.

R.A. stood for a short time while they recorded the event, "Actually, you're forgetting an important documentation."

Dale asked, "What documentation?"

R.A. smiled, "If you will hand me your recorders, I would like to video both of you, as you are also a part of history."

They both tentatively handed the recorders to R.A. who turned the recorders toward Dale and Ellie. He urged them, "Okay, now it's your turn to say something."

Dale and Ellie were somewhat shy but took the opportunity in stride. They put their arms around each other's shoulders and Dale said, "I'm Dale Parsons representing the Pittsburgh Gazette and this is…" He looked over at Ellie and she said, "I'm Ellie Hemenway of the Austin Express."

R.A. added his voice to the video, "And they are here to document history in the making."

R.A. said, "Now you're officially a part of history." R.A. looked at their recorders, "I noticed you weren't using the wireless eye viewer and earpiece. They allow you to see and hear what you're recording."

Dale said with surprise, "Oh, we have an even used that yet, I guess we should get it out and try it."

R.A. replied, "Yes, it makes it easier to focus in on everything without having to look into the viewfinder on the recorder."

Ellie replied, "Yes, will have to make use of it."

R.A. turned the video once again toward the group, "Okay everyone smile and welcome to Hat Creek."

Dom and Amir leaned their heads together and smiled.

*****

The C-40 rolled to a stop and its engines began to shut down. Agent Danielle Alton unbuckled her seatbelt and looked up and down the aisle before getting up. She adjusted her service weapon in her holster and retrieved her carry-on off the seat next to her. She walked up the aisle and leaned down to speak to Eve.

"Excuse me Ms. Walker; if you'll stay on the plane while I check out the exit and the stairway, I depreciated it."

Eve nodded, "Certainly Danielle, I'll just get my things and wait by the exit."

Danielle nodded, "Thank you."

She turned and headed toward the exit door.

Eve unbuckled her seatbelt and stood up. She picked up her carry-on and purse and followed Danielle down the aisle.

Danielle waited for the door to open and scanned the stairway in front of her. She took a step out the exit and looked side to side.

She looked out on the tarmac and saw her destination; Chip Barker's Huey. She scanned the area around the Huey. She turned back to Eve, "Okay ma'am we can leave now, would you like some help with your carry-on?"

Eve shook her head, "No thank you, I got it."

Danielle walked down the stairway and waited for Eve at the bottom. Again she looked side to side maintained a half-step in front of Eve as they approached the Huey. Chip saw them coming and stepped out of the cockpit. As they got close he reached in and pulled out his ID and held it in front of him next to his face. Danielle saw Chip displayed his ID and pulled out her ID and did the same. As they met they both compared the IDs with the faces.

She asked, "What is your name?"

Chip replied, "I'm your pilot Chip Barker."

Danielle replied, "I'm agent Danielle Alton, you have a code word for me?"

Chip replied, "Avocado."

Danielle smiled and put her ID away, "Thank you Mr. Barker, let's get this package in the air."

Chip nodded and went over to Eve, "Ms. Walker, I'm Chip Barker, would you like me to take your satchel?"

Eve shook her head and declined, "No thank you Chip, I can handle it."

Chip replied, "Very well, let me help you in."

He escorted her over to the cockpit and had her put her foot on a step and helped her in. He secured her seatbelt and reached up and grabbed a headset and handed it to her. She placed the headset on her head and smiled.

"Thank you."

Chip went around to the other side and was going to assist agent Alton into the cockpit but she had already found her seat and had buckled it up and placed her headset on her head. Chip smiled and went back around and got in the cockpit and put his headset on. He turned the toggle switch on the panel to intercom mode.

"Okay ladies, welcome aboard you'll have a couple of hours to enjoy the view and if you wish, some conversation. Thank you for flying air Barker."

Liftoff was smooth as the craft swayed to the sky.

They reached cruising altitude and Chip started some conversation, "Ms. Walker, have you flown in a helicopter before?"

Eve replied, "Yes I have, I made the same trip a couple weeks ago, but you weren't my pilot."

Chip answered, "Oh, you must've flown with Jessie; he took a couple of my flights while I was in Panama."

Eve said, "Perhaps so I didn't catch his name, but I was a little nervous at the time, that being my first flight in a chopper."

Chip replied, "That's understandable. How about you agent Alton, it's probably not your first trip in a Huey."

Danielle smiled, "You are correct Mr. Barker; I flew with Delta squad in Israel for ten months."

Chip laughed, "Well, perhaps you should be flying this rig instead of me."

Danielle shook her head, "No, I'm fine where I am I've had enough airtime. I prefer my feet on the ground."

Chip smiled, "Copy that, especially when bullets are flying."

Danielle chuckled and nodded.

The rest of the flight enlisted pleasant conversation and convenient stories among the trio. The SETI complex was just coming into view. Chip reached over and switched the toggle to radio mode, "Hat Creek, you got your ears on? Barker's on your radar"

Mike was in the break room when he heard the radio squawk. He stood up and went around the corner and down the hallway. He went over to the radio, picked up the mic and keyed it.

Chip started to repeat his transmission but stopped when he heard Mike's voice.

"Copy that, Chip. It's about time you got your sorry ass back here."

Chip laughed and replied with a touch of sarcasm, "Yeah Mike, it'll be good to see you too. Thanks for the warm welcome. We'll be there in three, with two on board."

Mike responded, "Copy that, I'll set three extra plates at the table."

Chip smiled and gently guided his craft safely to the ground.

Sophie was well out of the way watching the Hilo as it touched down. She saw chip in the cockpit and playfully ran around the chopper several times.

The SUV made its way across the parking lot. Sophie spotted it and bolted across the grass toward the parking lot, stalking its larger prey. The SUV made a partial circle and parked near the Huey. Rousan got out of the SUV, carrying the multi-scanner and walked over to the chopper. Sophie sauntered to his side and sat down. Danielle was already out of the Huey and on the ground carrying her canvas bag. Chip made his way out of the cockpit and went to help Eve out of the Huey. She was partway out when chip got to her. He helped her get the rest of the way out. She grabbed her satchel and walked over to the SUV.

Rousan set the multi-scanner on the ground went up to agent Alton and extended his hand to her and she shook it.

"I'm Corporal Rousan with the National Guard, welcome."

Danielle replied, "I'm agent Danielle Alton with the Secret Service, I'm Ms. Walker's security, good to meet you."

Rousan stepped over to Eve and extended his hand and she shook it.

"I'm Corporal Rousan, you must be Evelyn Walker; it's a pleasure to meet you."

Eve replied, "Thank you, Corporal, and you may call me Eve."

Rousan scrunched his face, "I'm sorry ma'am, I hesitate to be so presumptive as to call you by your first name."

Eve shook her head somewhat, "Corporal; am I to assume that because of my relationship with the vice president you feel that it would be inappropriate to call me by my first name?" She smiled and joked, "I'm surprised you didn't salute me."

She chuckled and continued, "Corporal, what's your first name?"

Rousan was taken aback but replied, "Bashir, ma'am."

She held out her hand again and shook his hand, "Bashir I'm Eve."

Rousan nodded, "Yes ma'am, Eve."

She smiled, "Well, that's a start, thank you."

Sophie made herself known by coming up and sniffing and licking Eve's hand. At first Eve was surprised but looked down and saw Sophie panting. She reached down and pet Sophie's head, "Who's this pretty thing?"

Chip replied, "That's Sophie, she's part of the family and usually obnoxious."

Eve stated, "Well she seems pretty sweet."

Bashir addressed both Eve and Danielle, "If you don't mind before we get in the vehicle I need to do a scan of your person and your possessions."

Eve nodded, "Yes, I'm aware of the new protocol."

Eve handed Bashir her satchel and he took it over to the SUV and set the satchel on the hood. He turned the multi-scanner on and scanned her satchel. He looked at the screen on the scanner, "Ma'am, could you remove the electronic device in your satchel for me?"

Eve reached down and unzipped the satchel and pulled out her recorder and set it on the hood of the vehicle. Bashir noticed the recorder and remarked, "That's the same recorder that Dale and Ellie have, the 3122 Hy-Mark media Pro."

Eve replied, "Is that so, these are great recorders."

Sophie stretched up to the hood and sniffed the recorder.

She laughed, "Bashir, is this your version of a PET scan?"

Bashir smiled and eased her off the hood and away from the recorder. He scanned the recorder and gave it back to Eve. She put the recorder back in her satchel.

Bashir asked, "Could you stand still for a moment while I scan you?"

She did asked and he completed the scan of her person. Danielle stepped forward and handed Rousan her bag, "Corporal you will find two forty millimeter magazines in my bag and you will also discover a weapon on my person."

Rousan said, "Understood."

He performed the scan as needed, detected the magazines and weapon, "Thank you, ma'am"

Chip walked up, "My turn." as he stood for a scan.

Sophie added her presence and stood next to Chip.

Bashir smiled and scanned Chip as procedure dictated, and performed a cursory scan on Sophie.

When he finished he said, "We can scan the Huey again later. But right now let's get our guests to the complex."

Bashir waved them to the SUV and they each took a seat inside.

He drove through the parking lot and up to the complex and parked the vehicle. Sophie arrived first and was waiting.

Perry Edmonds was watching out the window of the complex waiting for his new arrivals. He saw the SUV approach and called to Mike, "Hey Mike, they're here now."

Perry stepped outside and Mike followed behind. They waited for their guests to get out of the vehicle. Rousan quickly exited and was trying to get to the door before Eve opened it, but that intent failed. Eve opened the door and was already out of the car. She grabbed her satchel and closed the door. Danielle got out of the SUV and went over and stood next to Eve. Perry smiled as he walked up to Eve and offered both of his hands to clasp Eve's outstretched hand.

"It's good to see you again Ms. Walker."

Eve nodded and smiled, "Yes, it's becoming a pleasurable habit showing up here." She turned to Mike and shook his hand, "and you Mike, it's good to see you also."

She gestured to Danielle, "Mike Mitchell and Perry Edmonds, I like to introduce you to agent Danielle Alton my security companion."

Mike and Perry each shook her hand, Mike said, "It's a pleasure to meet you, welcome to Hat Creek."

Perry added his greeting, "Yes agent Alton; welcome."

Danielle replied, "Thank you, it's good to meet you both."

She scanned the area, "This is quite a complex, I didn't expect it to be so expansive; with this many units."

Eve looked around also added her comment, "Yes, you've added a lot of buildings since the last time I was here."

Perry smiled, "Yes, the units have only been here a couple of days. The new security protocols have practically made this site a fortress."

Eve added, "Yes, Richard said, uh…" stopping her thoughts, she continued, "or rather the vice president said that there was a lot of changes here considering the recent attack and threats of more attacks."

Agent Johnson stepped out of the complex and noticed agent Alton. A broad smile came on his face and he hurried over to her. Gave her a hug, "Danielle, I heard you were coming, it's great to see you again. Anji and I were happy to hear you were assigned as Ms. Walker's security. Anji will be happy to see you."

Danielle replied smiling, "Yes, I heard you two were here and I was glad to get this assignment."

Eve witnessed Danielle and Ron's reunion and commented, "I'm glad that you have friends here Danielle, it should make your jobs a lot easier; backing each other up."

Danielle said, "Without a doubt, it will make things easier."

Ron walked over to Eve and held out his hand, "Ms. Walker, I'm Ron Johnson, one of the Secret Service agents assigned the complex."

Eve took his hand and shook it, "It's good to meet you agent Johnson."

Ron smiled and turned to Danielle and said in a mock professional tone, "Okay, agent, let me take you inside and show you the layout and then will go see Anji."

Danielle looked over at Eve, "Ms. Walker, I'm sure you'll have ample protection, with so many agents falling all over each other. I'll go inside and check out the complex and then survey the grounds. Meanwhile, I'll leave you in the hands of Mr. Edmonds and Mr. Mitchell."

Perry shook his head, "Agent Alton, I'll call you Danielle if you call us Mike and Perry."

Danielle nodded, "Okay Perry that's a deal."

She peeled off as Ron directed her inside the complex.

Perry turned to Eve, "Well, I guess you want to reunite with Dom and Amir."

Eve nodded, "Yes, and I also can't wait to meet the legendary Doctor 'Gemo."

Perry's face showed surprise, "That's right you've never met the famous Doctor, but he will be upset if you don't call him R.A. instead of Doctor 'Gemo."

Eve nodded, "Duly noted. Let's do this."

Perry nodded and led her in.

Once inside, Perry pointed to Eve's satchel, "Would you like me to put your purse and bag in the break room, as that's where we will hold the COM meeting?"

Eve handed her satchel to Perry, "You can take this, but I'll keep my purse, thank you."

He nodded, took her satchel and went toward the break room.

She knew the way to Dom and Amir's station and headed that direction. Dom, Amir, R.A., Parsons and Hemenway were yet engaged in conversation. Eve eased her way between Dom and Amir as they were seated facing away from her. She leaned down and put her head between them and grabbed them by the shoulders and squeezed them in a hug, "Hey you two celebrities, you got time to say hello?"

Dom and Amir swiveled their heads side to side to get a look at the intruder. Eventually they were able to see that it was Eve. They both smiled and struggled out of their seats to give Eve a joint hug. Dom said, "Oh, Eve this is great."

Amir joined in, "Wow, yes, this is great."

Eve said feigning disappointment, "So, you couldn't wait to speak to Adam again and didn't invite me?"

Dom laughed, "Well, as you know Adam has his own schedule."

Eve nodded, "Well maybe this time we can all be a part of history."

She turned to Parsons and Hemenway and offered a handshake.

"I'm Evelyn Walker and you must be Dale Parsons and Ellie Hemenway, the lucky lottery winners."

Ellie shook her hand eagerly, "Well, Ms. Walker, I've admired your work from afar and it's great to meet you in person."

Dale stole the handshake from Ellie, "I can echo that, you are an exceptional journalist."

Eve said, "Well, as fellow journalists, we are all on equal footing today. I know that my expectations are beyond description."

R.A. was standing quietly observing the interactions. Eve took a slow breath and smiled at him. R.A. returned the smile and held out his hand and was met by Eve's hand. She started with a deliberate inquiring tone, "So you are Sal's friend, and also Richard's friend. I haven't had the pleasure to meet you. I'm Evelyn Walker, but I would prefer you to call me, Eve. And I understand that you prefer to be called; R.A.." she paused and continued as she held his hand, "So, R.A.," she paused again and partially bowed her head and continued, "It is an extreme pleasure and honor to meet you."

R.A. silently watched her dissertation and he parsed a smile.

He slowly pulled Eve close to him and gave her a gentle hug. He released his hug, "Now I know what Richard sees in you and understand what Sal has told me about you. You surpass all my expectations."

Amir watched the interaction, chuckled, "Talk about a mutual admiration, this is it."

Both Dale and Ellie were capturing this entire meeting on their recorders.

Eve broke from her solemn portrayal and with somewhat of an animated tone, said, "Yes, R.A. it is good to meet you. Richard and Sal told me a bunch of stories about you and I can't wait for you to issue your disclaimer and denials."

R.A. smiled, "Then, I guess you are open to my reciprocating version of their prevarications and issue my own accounts of their activities."

He smiled, "I look forward to every morsel."

Eve turned and noticed the recorders Dale and Ellie were using. She stated, "I see you are using the same recorder I use. There isn't anything that I can't do with the media options and quality of recording it delivers."

Dale nodded, "Yes, we are finding that out. We each received one as a promotional gift specifically for this occasion."

Eve added, "Well, we should all have exceptional results with our recordings of this event." Eve paused, "As a matter of fact I have to get my recorder and connected it as well as connect your recorders to the SAT-COM, so we can start broadcasting this event to the world."

Murphy's Law......
Sophie By A Nose

J an Wheeler was intently watching the pre-broadcast events from The Hat Creek SETI site on the monitor. She saw that both Parsons and Hemenway were simultaneously broadcasting the event with that of Evelyn Walker's. Royce came out of the kitchen and sat down next to her on the sofa. He watched with her for a few moments, "Did you know they were going to broadcast the alien thing?"

Jan replied, "Yes, but I didn't think it was going to be live. They must've caved in to public outcry. Anyway, the celebration is going to be short-lived as I've got to set the dominoes in motion."

She picked up her personal COM and entered some numbers. She went over to her VPC and activated it. She entered some more keystrokes and said aloud, "Okay, it's show time."

She pressed the enter key on the keyboard.

Back at Hat Creek, Dale and Ellie were recording various aspects of the activities and people when their recorders stopped functioning.

Ellie noticed hers first, as her eyepiece and ear bud stopped working. She looked at the view finder on her recorder and it also was dark. She pressed the reset button and there was no response. Ellie looked over at Dale and he was trying to get his recorder to reboot, also with no success. Ellie went to locate Mike and found him in the security room. She went up to him, "Mike; is there some problem with the broadcast feed that has disabled our recorders?"

Mike looked down at the broadcast monitor and shook his head, "No, I'm getting a live feed broadcast also from the COM-SAT. Why do you ask?"

She showed him that her recorder was not recording. He pushed the on off switch on the recorder expecting it to function properly. However, he had the same result that Ellie had. It was not working. Ellie said, "I think Dale is having the same problem."

Mike said, "Well let's go see what's going on."

They went out of the office and went down the hallway to where Dale was. Dale was also having problems with his recorder. Mike tried to restart his recorder with negative results. Mike stood and thought for a moment, "This is strange that both of you recorders stop working at the same time. Let me see if my resident electronics wizard can come up with a solution."

He took them back into the security office and keyed the two-way radio mic.

"Security one or security two, this is control."

Darcy responded, "This is security one."

Mike asked, "Do you have a location on Corporal Rousan?"

Darcy answered, "Affirmative, Rousan is here."

Mike replied, "Can you have him 10-20 the complex?"

Darcy replied, "Copy that, he is nodding affirmative as we speak. I will send him to you ASAP."

Mike replied, "Copy."

Mike turned to Ellie and Dale, "I have a guy that might help us out."

Ellie reached into her purse, "You know; I have the business card of the representative that gave us the recorders. She said to call her if we had any problems. I'll call her and see what she can do."

Mike said, "Well, it can't hurt, give her a call."

Ellie dialed the number on the card.

Back in DC at Royce Pyle's residence, Jan answered the call.

"This is Sarah Gold, may I help you?"

Ellie replied, "Yes, this is Ellie Hemengway, you said to call that there was a problem with the recorder."

Jan replied, "Of course, Ellie, what is your problem?"

"My recorder and Mr. Parsons recorder both stopped working."

Jan replied, "Oh My, I'm sorry to hear that, where are you?"

Ellie replied, "We are at Hat Creek, for the alien contact event."

Jan said, "Okay, let me check the local suppliers and I'll have two ready for you to pick up." Jan put the call hold.

Ellie replied, "Okay I'll wait."

Jan waited a several seconds and re-connected the call, "Okay, I'll have two units ready for pickup or delivery at Buy Mart electronics in Redding or at Barrett's Office supply in Bella Vista, what would you prefer?"

Ellie said, "Okay, hold on let me check to see which is best way to get them here."

Jan said, "Okay, I will hold."

Ellie said to Mike, "The representative said that she could have two recorders available for delivery or pickup at Buy Mart electronics in Redding or at Barrett's Office supply in Bella Vista. Which do you prefer?"

Mike thought for a moment, "Actually, I can get my pilot to go pick them up in Bella Vista. That would only take about fifteen minutes each way, so a half-hour and your back in business."

Ellie agreed and got back on the call with Jan, "Okay, we'll pick them up in Bella Vista at Barrett's Office Supply."

Jan replied, "That would be fine, they'll be ready."

Ellie replied, "Thank you very much for your service."

Jan replied, "It's my pleasure to serve you Ms. Hemengway."

Jan disconnected the call and called Josh Frazier who was waiting in a car between Buy Mart electronics in Redding and Barrett's Office Supply in Bella Vista.

Josh answered the phone, "Hello, it's about time you called, where do I go and how many units?"

Jan replied, "Take two units to Bella Vista and tell them you are with Hy-Mark Corporation and you will pay for the cost of the units so our customers can pick them up."

Josh said, "Okay we're on our way."

Josh started up his car and said to Chen sitting next to him, "Okay Chen, it's time to push over a domino."

Chen replied, "I love these dominoes."

Josh looked over his shoulder to check the traffic, pulled out and headed down the road. They were only fifteen minutes from Bella Vista.

*****

Mike saw Chip in the break room and went over to him, "Chip I need you to take your chopper to Barrett's Office Supply in Bella Vista and pick up two of those recorders that Dale and Ellie were using. Apparently something went wrong with theirs and the company is giving them a replacement."

Chip replied, "Okay Mikey; your wish is my command."

Mike shook his head, "Chip, you're crazy."

Chip said, "I'll take Juan with me, he can go into the store for me. It's a little hard to park a Huey on the street."

Mike said, "That's a good idea, I'll tell him to meet you at the chopper."

Chip nodded and left the complex.

Mike got on the two-way radio, "Security two, control."

Juan replied, "Go for security two."

Mike replied, "I need you to meet Chip at his Huey and go with him to pick up some recorders at Barrett's Office Supply in Bella Vista." Juan replied joyfully, "Copy that. Can't wait to ride in the Hilo."

*****

Josh arrived at Barrett's office supply and parked his car. He turned to Chen, "Okay Chen, we practiced what you're supposed to say and do, several times. Are you sure you can do this?"

Chen replied, "Yes, I think so, but I don't understand why you can't take them in."

Josh explained once again, "For one thing, I'm the one that purchased all of the other recorders, and it would be suspicious if I showed up and was recognized, now, bringing to recorders back to the store."

Chen nodded, took a breath to convince himself, "Okay, I can do this." Chen opened the door, grabbed the two recorders, stepped out the car and headed toward the store.

Josh shook his head as he watched Chen going to the store. Chen went up to the counter, "Could I speak to your manager?"

The clerk said, "I'm the assistant manager, may I help you?"

Chen replied, "I'm with Hy-Mark media Corporation and I have two customers that need a replacement of our product, a 3122 Hy-Mark Media Pro, that have malfunctioned. They are sending someone to pick them up at this store. I understand that you do not have the product in stock, but I have two units here that you can give them. My company will pay for the units as a customer service." Chen placed the units on the counter.

The clerk was somewhat surprised at the request, "I'll have to check our cost of the units so I'll know how much you need to pay."

Chen replied, "That's okay; our company will reimburse you for the retail cost plus tax."

The clerk thought for a moment, "Okay, who are the customers and when are they coming?"

Chen replied, "Their names are Parsons and Hemengway, but someone will be picking them up for them. They should be here within the hour."

The clerk wrote the names down and rang up the price of the two units.

"That will be $8922.13."

Chen pulled out nine $1000 bills and handed them to the clerk. The clerk was totally surprised.

"You're paying cash?"

Chen replied, "Yes, you do take cash don't you?" The clerk was obviously flustered but replied, "Yes, I guess I do." He took the money and rang up the tender amount and offered Chen the change. Chen shook his head, "You know you've been so good about this, you keep the change. Thank you very much." Chen turned and left the store. The clerk shook his head in disbelief.

Chen went back out to the car and got in. Josh asked, "So, how'd it go?"

Chen had a 'pleased with himself' smile on his face and replied, "Piece of cake."

Josh said, "Okay, now we got to wait for them to pick 'em up."

Chen asked, "Do we know who is picking it up?

Just replied, "No, but we'll see them when they come out of the store with the recorders."

*****

Rousan came into the complex and went over to the security office looking for Mike. Mike was talking to Ellie and Dale about their recorders. Rousan walked up to Mike, "You wanted to see me Mike?"

Mike replied, "Yes, we have a strange situation."

Rousan shrugged his shoulders, "How can I help?"

Mike began, "Ellie and Dale's recorders were working just fine until about twenty minutes ago. Then they both shut down at the same time."

Rousan asked, "Were they connected to the Internet?"

Mike said, "Apparently they were on the same grid as the COM-SAT, and all of the other COM-SAT configurations are active. Now what's even stranger is that Eve has the same recorder model number, and it is working fine."

Rousan stopped and thought for a moment going over the probabilities. He picked up one of the recorders and examined it, pressing buttons and pressure switches. He turned to Mike, Do you have a set of small screwdrivers and wrenches, and possibly 1211 tester?"

Mike replied, "I have the tools and a 1613 system analyzer."

Rousan grinned widely, "Wow, that's better than what I expected. Could you get those for me?"

Mike replied, "Sure, be right back."

Rousan examined the outer portions of recorder looking for damage. He saw no damage. Mike came back with the necessary tools and placed them on the table. Rousan smiled and went to work.

*****

Chip and Juan were five minutes away from the office supply in Bella Vista. Chip was concerned with power lines and tall trees as he navigated the Bella Vista shopping area. He got on the radio and requested clearance to land.

"Redding air control, this is Huey 1713, I'm requesting permission to land in an open area near the Bella Vista shopping center on McArthur Road."

The answer came back, "Huey 1713, your request to land is denied, per the implementation of the Domestic Security Act."

Hearing that the air traffic controller flatly denied the request, Chip shook his head, "Well, I'll have to find a plan B."

Juan smiled, "Give me your COM and I'll get you clearance to land."

Chip said, "It's in the center console."

Juan looked down and picked up Chip's COM and used a voice search, "DSC: Cheyenne Mountain."

The images of Edward Narkiewicz and Brie Smithy showed on the screen. He selected Brie's image. Shortly the contact was made, "Lieutenant Smithy DSC, may I help you."

Juan replied, "LT, this is Gozier, I need your help."

Brie replied, "Hey Sergeant, what can I do for you?"

Juan replied, "I'm in a Huey, with Chip Barker near Bella Vista California. We need your help to get clearance from ATC for an emergency landing."

Brie replied, "Copy that, what's the Huey's number?"

Chip replied, "Huey: 1713."

Brie replied, "Copy, Huey 1713. Standby." She went to a keyboard and pulled up the contact for air traffic controller in the area. She initiated an open channel, "This is Lieutenant Smithy at Domestic Security Command in Cheyenne, Wyoming; I need immediate clearance for Huey 1713 piloted by Chip Barker to land at his chosen destination."

The controller on the other hand the conversation replied, "Yes Lieutenant, I will do as ordered."

She came back to Juan, "I guess you heard that transmission, so you should be good to go. I'll stay connected until you complete your mission."

Chip reinitiated contact with ATC, "Redding air traffic control, this is Chip Barker in Huey 1713 requesting clearance to land in a vacant lot across from Barrett's Office supply in Bella Vista."

The controller replied, "Yes, Huey 1713, you have clearance to land at your discretion."

Chip replied, "Roger, initiating landing procedures now. Thank you for your assistance, Barker out."

Chip chuckled, "That's a neat trick you pulled off, Sergeant."

Juan replied, "It helps to have friends in high places."

Chip hovered over the Bella Vista shopping center and found a safe landing zone. Carefully avoiding any power lines and structures, he set down safely. He looked at Juan, "Okay, soldier; go get 'em."

Juan hopped out of the chopper and jogged to the store. He went inside and up to the counter. He waited for a customer to finish their purchase and asked the clerk, "I'm here to pick up two recorders for Mr. Parsons and Ms. Hemengway; I was told that you would have them here."

The clerk said, "Yes, I was told you were coming. I have them in the back room."

The clerk turned and went to the back room and quickly returned with the recorders. He handed them to Juan, "Okay, just sign this receipt and they're all yours."

The clerk put the receipt on the counter

Juan picked up a pen and signed the receipt. He scooped up the recorders and headed back to the chopper. He hopped in, fastened his seatbelt, put his headset on and gave chip a 'thumbs up'."

Chip nodded and reactivated his COM call to Brie, "Thanks LT, we picked up the packages and we're on our way back. Thank you for your assistance."

Brie replied, "Always a pleasure to help you guys out."

Juan added his comment, "Okay LT, thanks again saving the day."

Brie said, "No problem Sergeant; be safe."

Chip ended the COM and put the pedal to the metal and they were off.

Frazier and Chen watched the show unfold and Frazier opened his COM and contacted Jan Wheeler.

Jan answered, "Okay, is it done?"

Josh said, "It's done, now what?"

Jan said, "Okay, do exactly as I tell you. I need you to pull out the remote microphone out of the holder on each of the other recorders and cut the cord so that the microphone is not connected. If you do not disconnect it, the recorder will explode when I send the signal to the other two units."

Josh looked at Chen and gritted his teeth. He said, "Oh boy, we gotta hurry back to the house and cut the cords on those other microphones off; we left the other recorders at the house. We have to get back before Jan sends the signal to detonate the explosives."

Chen twisted his face with worry as they drove away.

*****

After Lieutenant Smithy finished his COM with Chip something jogged an important memory. She pulled up her COM screen and selected agent Lane's icon.

Agent Lane was in the office sorting out some folders and files on her screen when Brie's icon flashed on her screen. She answered the COM, "LT, did you miss us so soon."

Brie smiled, "I always miss you guys but, I think I've got some sort of connection to your suspects."

Robin said, "Okay, what you got?"

Brie asked, "Did you mention something about purchases at an electronics store?"

Robin reached down and shuffled through some papers on her desk but, didn't find what she was looking for. She said, "Hold on LT, I've got to check some other reports on Frank's desk."

Robin started to get up, but she saw Frank come back in the office.

"Oh good, Frank your back I need your help?"

Frank replied with a chuckle, "What else is new?"

Robin shook her head, "Frank, I'm serious; the LT is on a COM and may have a lead for us."

Frank nodded and walked over to his desk and joined in on the COM with Robin and Brie, "Okay, tell me what you need."

Brie replied, "I was asking about any purchases in an electronics store. I think one of you mentioned that earlier."

Frank looked over some pages on his desk and retrieved one of them, "Yes, Vo Chen shopped at and electronics store near DC and Josh Frazier shopped in Redding and Bella Vista."

Brie continued, "Well, I just got off a COM with the Huey pilot at Hat Creek, Chip Barker, and he was at Barrett's Office Supply in Bella Vista picking up something there. I was wondering if Frazier shopped there also."

Robin shook her head, "That's too much of a coincidence to ignore. Thanks LT, this may be the break we need to stop the attack. We'll have to check this out. I'll let you know what shakes out, thanks again."

Brie replied, "I hope this helps, I'll talk to you later."

Brie's image disappeared from the screen.

Frank looked over at Robin, "What in hell are they up to?"

Robin sat thinking, "Why don't you check out the purchases at the electronics stores in DC and in the Redding area and I'll call Mike at Hat Creek and see if he has anything that can help."

Frank nodded, "Okay; the answer is here somewhere."

Robin engaged her COM and selected Mike Mitchell's image.

Mike, recognized Robin's image, promptly answered, "Agent Lane how can I help you?"

Robin said, "Perhaps we can help each other; I'm trying to make a connection with some suspects here in Redding and I'd like to know what your pilot was doing in Bella Vista."

Mike took a deep breath, "Well, where do I begin? First, Chip went to pick up two multi-media recorders to replace those belonging to Mr. Parsons and Ms. Hemengway, which suspiciously malfunctioned at the same time."

Robin thought for a moment, "Do you know why they malfunctioned?"

Mike replied, "So far, no. But I happen to have an electronics guru checking it out."

Robin asked, "Okay may I speak to your guru?"

Mike said, "Sure, I'll put him on." Mike stepped over to Rousan, who was working on the recorders, "Rousan, I have agent Lane from the FBI office in Redding, she would like to talk to you."

Rousan nodded, "Okay."

He stepped over in front of the COM monitor, "Agent Lane, Mike said you wish to talk to me."

Robin said, "Yes I'm trying to unravel some coincidences. Mike said you are assessing a problem with some multimedia recorders."

Rousan replied, "Yes, I think I found the problem, but it may be a little difficult to explain."

Robin replied, "Well, I'm no genius, but I'll try to follow along. Could you try to explain it to me?"

Rousan nodded, "It seems that the microphones on the recorders have been modified by placing a voltage regulator, microchip and a diode in sequence that allowed a signal when sent to the microchip that would increase the voltage in the diode and cause it to fail. I'm correcting that now."

Robin listened, "So, basically somebody altered the microphone so that they can stop it from working. Is that right?"

Rousan smiled, "Well agent, you cut to the chase very quickly."

Robin smiled, "Thank you for the compliment but perhaps you can answer another question."

Rousan nodded, "I'll try."

Robin asked, "How would such a signal, be sent?"

Rousan replied, "You mean; could the signal be sent by a radio transmission, or phone call?"

Robin replied, "What I'm asking is, however the signal could be sent, would it have to be within a certain distance from the recorders for the signal to be received?"

Rousan sighed, "Perhaps I can best answer this way, the signal would be a Wi-Fi signal and since we are using the COM-SAT broadband it could be sent from anywhere in the world."

Robin scrunched her face at his response, "Do you know where these recorders came from?"

Rousan shrugged, "I'll have to let you talk to one of the owners of the recorder."

He called over to Ellie, "Ellie could you step over to the COM screen, an FBI agent would like to talk to you."

Ellie stepped over to the screen and saw Robin's image, "Yes, this is Ellie Hemenway. You wish to talk to me?"

Robin replied, "Yes Ms. Hemenway, I'd like to know where you purchased the recorder."

Ellie replied, "I did not purchase it; Mr. Parsons and I were given the recorders to record the alien conversation."

Robin asked, "Can you tell me who gave them to you?"

Ellie replied, "Sure, Sarah Gold, from Hy-Mark Corporation, came to our hotel and gave them to us as a promotion for her company to record this event."

Robin furled her brow in thought. She knew there was a puzzle but where do the pieces go.

She asked, "So, why did you decide to have someone pick up new recorders?"

Ellie replied, "When the recorders malfunctioned, I called Ms. Gold about the recorders and she said that she would replace them. She said we could get new ones at a store close to here; Mike knew which store was the closest."

Robin asked, "Did she tell you which store to go to?"

Ellie replied, "Yes, but I don't remember perhaps Mike can tell you."

Robin said, "Okay, but before I talked to Mike can you tell me what number you called to reach Ms. Gold and what Ms. Gold looked like?"

Ellie pulled the business card out of her purse, "The number is 999-142-7368. And as far as her looks goes, she was about five foot three, with medium length blonde hair, probably a wig, she looked to be in her 40s. Oh, and she had a snake bracelet on her wrist."

Robin took a breath, "Okay Ms. Hemengway, you been more than helpful. Thank you for your cooperation. I'll speak to Mike if it's okay."

Ellie motioned for Mike to step over to the COM.

Robin saw him step in the view, "Mike, what stores were mentioned that would have the recorders?"

Mike replied, "They said, the Buy Mart electronics in Redding and Barrett's Office Supply in Bella Vista."

Robin smiled, "Okay thank you Mike you been very helpful. Be safe."

Mike replied, "With your help, I hope we will."

Robin nodded and disconnected the COM and said to herself, "If you only knew."

Robin kicked back in her chair and let out a yelp. Frank looked over from his side of the desk, "What the hell was that about?"

Robin said, "I just got a piece of the puzzle but I've got to find the other pieces. We need to get hold of the pilot from Hat Creek, right now. Can you get Lieutenant Smithy on a COM and have her contact the pilot Chip Barker; tell him he may have explosives on board. I've got a check the offender database to see if I'm right."

*****

Rousan was adjusting the settings on the 1613 analyzer and attached the test clip at the base of the microchip. He looked at the scope on the analyzer and moved the test clip to the voltage regulator and sighed. He removed the test clip and set it down on the table. He took the front part of the cover of the microphone and secured it in the base cover. Turned it over and put in two screws and secured the microphone covers together. He reached over and pressed the power button and the recorder came alive. Ellie was watching the process, as was Dale. Rousan smiled, "Okay, both of them are working now. I don't know why the microchip was placed in that circuit but, it was totally unnecessary."

Ellie picked up her working recorder, "I can't thank you enough Rousan you saved our day."

Dale reached over and hugged Rousan, "How can I ever thank you?"

Rousan replied, "No need, I loved every minute of the challenge."

Mike patted him on the shoulder, "Son, if you want to finish your schooling up here, I will gladly pay for it."

Rousan smiled and blushed, "I can't let you do that, I prefer to make my own way in life. But I will come and work for you when I finish."

Mike shook his hand, "That's a done deal."

*****

Chip and Juan were enjoying the last leg of their flight, recounting some pleasant war stories. A transmission on the radio interrupted their current version of the truth.

"Huey 1713, DSC Command."

Chip picked up the radio mic and responded, "DSC Command, do you have traffic for Huey 1713?"

"Roger that, this is Commander Narkiewicz, you have been requested to contact agent Frank Knox at the FBI Redding office, ASAP."

Chip replied, "Huey 1713; copies. Thank you."

Chip wondered aloud, "I wonder what the FBI wants."

Juan replied, "Well it's gotta be important if it's the FBI."

Chip said, "Yeah, I'll call him when we set down."

The chopper was buffered by a slight wind, but Chip held it steady and smoothly inserted the Hilo into the LZ. As the engine wound down their faithful friend, Sophie came bouncing up trying to get to the occupants. Chip started the shutdown process of the Huey. Juan jumped out the cockpit and ran over to the SUV at the edge of the parking. He picked up the multi-scanner out of the passenger side and placed it on the hood of the vehicle and went back to the Huey. Juan reached in the cockpit and took out the recorders. Sophie became hyper and began sniffing and licking the recorders incessantly. Juan laughed as her antics and rubbed her head and ruffled her fur. Juan walked back to the SUV with Sophie still pawing and tugging on the recorders.

Chip noticed his COM alert was flashing with Mike's icon and he answered it.

"Hey Chip, this is Mike. Just thought I let you know that Rousan worked his magic on the recorders and they're both working. So, we won't need the other ones."

Chip replied, "Well, we just got back with the recorders, but since you don't need them, what we do with them?"

Mike replied, "Well, I guess we'll just have extra super expensive media recorders as backup."

Chip replied, "Okay, but," Chip looked around for Juan and didn't see him.

He continued his conversation with Mike, "Oh, I was looking for Juan, but I guess he's already taken the recorders to the SUV. I'll tell them that we don't need them."

Mike added, "By the way, did you get the message that the FBI wanted to talk to you?"

Chip replied, "Yeah, I got the message, wonder what it's about."

Mike said, "I'm not sure but they were certainly concerned about the recorders you picked up."

Chip said, "Okay, I guess I'll contact the FBI and see what agent Knox wants."

He searched for FBI and located agent Knox. He selected the icon and began the COM.

Knox answered, "This is agent Knox."

Chip said, "This is Chip Barker, I was told you need to talk to me."

Frank looked at his notes, "I understand you picked up some electronic multi-recorders from Barrett's Office Supply, is that correct?"

Chip replied, "Yes I did."

Frank asked, "Is there anything suspicious about their packaging?"

Chip replied, "No, I didn't notice anything different."

Frank asked, "Where are you, exactly?"

Chip replied, "Well, I am at the Hat Creek SETI site in a field at the end of the parking lot."

Frank replied, "I suspect the recorders contain explosive materials, I suggest that you don't disturb the packages as much as possible. I don't know how they can be detonated, but I would assume that an explosion is imminent. I suggest you leave the area."

Chip had a flashback of the two IED explosions he had survived.

*****

Jan was watching the broadcast from Hat Creek. She saw that Parsons and Hemengway had resumed using their recorders. She smiled and said to Royce, "Well, I guess they picked up the recorders from the electronics store. I see they're both recording everything they see."

Royce asked, "When are you going to send the signal to blow it up?"

Jan continued to smile, "I'm waiting for just the right time so I can do as much damage as possible and take out as many of those assholes I can."

*****

The Gala at the Hat Creek SETI site was in full swing. The Secret Service agents, Darcy and Rousan were all seated at a table outside, watching the event on a large COM screen. Since there were three recorders sending signals to the COM-SAT broadband, the media production supervisor was piecing every camera view as possible. The planned ten to thirty second delay in the broadcast of the event turned into an approximate forty-five second to one minute delay. Thus the viewers of the media broadcast were able to absorb almost every aspect of the event. As expected contact time grew near, the scheduled participants began to crowd into the break room. The group included Dale Parsons, Ellie Hemenway, director Perry Edmonds, assistant director Mike Mitchell, Doctor 'Gemo in the course Dominique and Amir. Evelyn Walker was there as the main documentarian of the event.

*****

As they all began to settle into their seats, a big smile came over Jan's face sitting safely on the couch far away from the SETI site. She reached to the laptop on the coffee table and entered some keystrokes. She watched intently at the screen and selected an icon resembling an explosive. Her finger hovered over the icon and with a smile; she eagerly touched the screen. She looked back up at the monitor that was broadcasting the event, and concern grew on her face, as broadcast was still showing.

She exclaimed, "What the hell; it is supposed to explode!"

She reached down to the laptop and fervently touched the explosive icon several more times. She looked back up at the monitor with anger on her face. Suddenly she saw the video transmission of the broadcast turned to static. Jan took a big sigh of relief at seeing the static on the monitor.

Jan said, "For a minute there I thought we had failed."

*****

At Hat Creek the group sitting in the makeshift observation room, heard and felt the pressure from an explosion not too far from them. The agents outside, including Darcy and Rousan saw and heard the blast coming from beyond the parking lot.

It seemed that they all started to move as a unit running toward the explosion. Those with weapons had drawn them anticipating an altercation. Danielle and Marnie suddenly stopped and Danielle said, "You guys go ahead; we'll stay here in case that is a diversion."

The collective inside the building were trying to digest the explosion they heard. Mike and Perry got up from their seats and hurried their way out to the front of the unit. They saw Danielle and Marnie standing by the table looking toward the end of the parking lot. Mike asked, "Where did that explosion come from?"

235

Marnie replied pointing toward the parking lot, "He came from the other side of the parking lot, Ron, Anji, Darcy and Rousan just left to go check it out."

Mike asked, "Have you seen Chip or Juan?"

Marnie replied, "No, but we saw them land just a little bit ago."

Mike's face showed some stress as he took a deep breath.

Back inside the complex, Eve was recording the reaction of the group and turned the camera on herself and spoke to the production manager, Harlan Crow, "Harlan, we had an explosion on grounds not too far from us. You probably should advise the viewers that there will be a delay in your programming."

Eve heard Harlan's response on her earpiece, "Okay, Ms. Walker, I'll discontinue the feed and advise the viewers of the situation. I'll wait until you get back to me."

Although the feed was stopped, Eve continued to record everything that she was seeing. She panned the room, capturing the occupants and turned and went out of the break room and headed outside. She continued to record as events unfolded and made her way outside just behind Mike and Perry's exit.

*****

Back in DC, Jan was watching the feed as a program note displayed on the screen. The note read, "We are sorry for the interruption but there has been an incident at the SETI site and we will keep you advised with updates as we receive them."

Seeing the message, Jan was somewhat confused.

Royce asked, "What do you think is going on?"

Jan replied, "I'm not sure but if there was an explosion then how would they get that information unless someone at the site gave it to them. They all should be dead."

*****

At the Redding FBI office Frank awaited a response on his COM.

Robin asked, "Frank, what's going on?"

Frank replied, "I'm not sure I was talking to Chip about the packages possibly containing explosives, and then there was silence, but the COM was still open. A couple of minutes later I heard an explosion, but the COM is still active."

Robin replied, "Well, it doesn't sound good, but at least the COM is still active, so there's still hope for a good outcome."

Frank nodded and sighed and continued to listen.

*****

Ron, Anji, Darcy and Rousan ran past the SUV and noticed the scanner was still on the hood. They saw Sophie locked inside but no one else. They ran up to the Huey that was still intact. They looked inside and the cockpit was empty. They looked around the area and saw fire and smoke coming from the tree line some distance away. Something caught Rousan's eye. He sighed and took a deep breath and began to smile. Ron and Anji also saw the vision.

Juan and Chip were walking toward them, laughing with their arms around each other's shoulders. As they got closer, the emergency responders, believing they understood what had just happened, began to applaud.

Frank was still listening to his open COM and began to hear voices getting closer. At the same time, he the radio on the Huey came alive, "Huey 1713, DSC Command please respond."

Chip and Juan met the group and they all began laughing. Ron said, "Don't tell me you guys did what I thought you did."

Juan replied, "I don't know what you thought we did, but I can tell you, this guy Chip is one crazy son-of-a-bitch."

Chip replied, smiling, "Juan, you call me crazy? I wasn't the one running with two explosives."

Anji asked while laughing, "Okay, you guys going to let us in on this."

The Huey radio blared again, "Huey 1713, DSC Command, please respond."

Chip heard the radio call, "I'll have to let Juan lie to you first, I gotta take this radio transmission."

He went around to the cockpit and stepped inside. He picked up the radio mic and keyed it. He also saw his COM still on the seat with an open connection. He picked up the COM and spoke into the radio mic and the COM at the same time.

"Frank, I'm sorry I had to leave but I got DSC Command on the radio and I talking to both of you."

He took a breath, "DSC Command, Huey 1713 advises emergency avoided. Frank, thank you for letting us know about the explosives."

Colonel Narkiewicz responded, "Okay Chip, message received. Be safe. DSC Command, out."

Frank listened to the radio transmission and waited for Chip to come back on the line.

Chip put the radio mic back in its holder, "I'm back Frank; again, thank you for letting us know, you saved our bacon." Chip thought, "Actually, our bacon could have been 'well done' without you."

Frank said, "You should be thanking Robin also; she's the one that set things in motion. I think everybody did a great job today. I'll let you go and take a breath; I'll talk to you later."

Chip replied, "Yeah, give Robin a big kiss for me."

Robin was listening to the conversation and Frank saw her stare at him.

Frank laughed, "I'll leave that to you two, bye."

Chip closed out the COM and put it in his pocket. He got out of the cockpit and went around to the crew. He interrupted the conversations, "I don't know what kind of lies Juan's been telling you, but why don't we go back to the complex where we can explain everything to everyone."

*****

Eve was recording everyone's reaction to the explosion, when she saw the group getting closer to the complex. She focused the lens on the returnees. Harlan the production supervisor was in Eve's earpiece, "Ms. Walker, you are a magnet for drama. You keep videoing and I'll try to piece things together so we can resume the broadcast."

So, What Happened Was...

The responders returned back to the SETI complex and were sitting around several tables.

Chip began, "When Frank told me that the recorders may have explosives in them, I re-lived the two IED's that almost took me out. I didn't know where Juan was, so I dropped my COM in the seat and jumped out of the cockpit. I called out for Juan and he didn't respond. I recall seeing him with Sophie and I didn't see her either. I called out for Juan again and also called Sophie's name. Sophie probably heard me or I just happened to hear her bark. Her bark came from the parking lot area. By this time I was practically hyperventilating with the thought of a bomb going off. I ran like hell toward the parking lot and saw Juan at the SUV."

Juan held up his hand to stop the conversation. He said, "Okay, I've got to add some context at this point. When I got back to the SUV, I almost had to fight Sophie to keep hold of the recorders. She was pawing and biting at the packages. I set the recorders on the hood of the SUV. I thought I could use some practice with this highly technical scanner. I finally figured out how to turn it on. Some lights flashed, and I thought I was good to go. I looked at the many switches and buttons that had icons on them and selected what I thought was a proper setting. Sophie reached up and pulled one of the packages down to the ground, so I set the scanner back on the hood and picked up the recorder. Sophie wouldn't leave them alone so, I corralled her and stuffed her in the SUV and closed the door. She started barking which might be what Chip said he heard. Anyway, I picked up the scanner and moved it over the package and some red lights flashed quickly on the screen. I thought I'd broke it but, when I moved it away from the package the red lights stop flashing, but I noticed the digital display said, 'C-4'. Now, I'm no tech wizard, but I can fuckin' read."

The group began to laugh and Juan joined them for a moment and then continued, "Of course, I almost shit my pants," Chip pushed Juan's shoulder, leaned over to him as if to smell him and interjected, "Yep, I think he actually did."

Juan shook his head, "Will you let me finish my part of the story?" He paused then continued, "I dealt enough with C-4 in the service and knew that the scanner was probably correct, because as much as the package had been dropped, if it had a balance switch or something like that it would have gone off already, so it must have a timer or a detonation receiver in it." He paused, "So, for a moment, I thought about tossing them away from me, but I probably couldn't have thrown them far enough. So I picked up both recorders and began running for the tree line."

Chip put his hand over Juan's mouth, "Okay, I got it from here." He smiled and began, "So, I was running toward the SUV and then I saw Juan running toward me with the recorders. I waited for him to get close to me, expecting him to stop. I saw he wasn't stopping, so I turned and ran with him. I told him as we ran together, that the packages might have explosives in them. As he continued running he yelled, "No shit Sherlock, why you think I'm running?"

So asked him, "Okay, but where are you going?" He said, "I going to take them over to the tree line." So, I told him to give me one of those and we'll go together.

Juan said, still running, "You crazy? If these are bombs, you don't need to blow your ass up too."

So I reached down and took one of the packages from him, and we began to run together. When we got to the tree line we stopped and, for some reason, set the packages down gently.

Juan laughed, "Yeah, it doesn't make sense but we did."

Chip continued, "So, I out ran his sorry ass back to the chopper."

Juan said, "You lying piece of shit, you couldn't out run my mother."

Chip smiled, "Actually, when we got far enough away, we slowed to a walk and began laughing."

Juan said, "And that's when the explosives went off. It knocked us to the ground, but we were okay."

Danielle had been listening, "Chip, you survived two IED's what made you think you'd survive another one?"

Chip replied, "Well, I guess I thought, 'third time's a charm'."

Rousan interjected, "Chip you know that, the idiom, 'third time's a charm', in this case would imply that you wouldn't survive the third one. But, I guess, it makes for a good story anyway."

*****

Frank was busy reviewing CCTV footage in Bella Vista and Redding. Robin had the NCIC and offender database logos on her screen. Frank leaned back in his chair, took a breath, "Well, I've gone through the CCTV footage looking for Josh Frazier's presence at Buy Mart electronics or Barrett's office Supply, in the past four days. I found that he made purchases at both the Buy Mart stores and at Barrett's Office supply. I'm waiting for the managers to send me the receipts of his purchases."

Robin said, "And I've gone through NCIC and the offender database looking for verification that Jan Wheeler wears a snake brace-let. I recall that when I asked Ellie Hemenway about the Hy-Mark representative, she said that she wore a snake bracelet and was proba-bly wearing a blonde wig and was in her 40s. I made some calls to the Hy-Mark Corporation to find out if their representative Sarah Gold was the one that contacted Parsons and Hemenway at their hotel and to get her work profile. If I can connect Jan Wheeler to that ruse, I can probably get a search warrant for almost everything."

Frank said, "Do you think we can pull prints off of the record-ers, I know a lot of people have touched them?"

Robin replied, "At this point that would be a very long shot."

Frank paused, "You know, I'm having trouble getting CCTV and receipts from electronics stores in the DC area, near Royce Pyle's house. Do you think that Brie could cut through some red tape for us?"

Robin replied, "Well, if she can't, she'll probably know somebody who can."

Frank nodded and opened up his COM and pulled up Brie Smithy's icon, and selected it. After a short pause, Lieutenant Smithy's image appeared on the COM screen.

Frank said, "Well, Lieutenant, it looks like a catastrophe was avoided thanks to you."

Brie replied, "It's more like that you and Robin had more of a major role in this operation than I did."

Robin joined in on the COM, "Actually LT, if we hadn't all been working for the same goal, things might've turned out a lot different."

Brie said, "Yes, we all had a hand in this. See how well we work together."

Frank replied, "Well maybe you can lend us a hand again."

Brie replied, "Frankie my boy, what can I do for you?"

Frank asked, "Do you think you could get me access to purchases at electronics stores in the DC area?"

Brie said, "What are you looking for?"

Frank replied, "We're trying to make a connection between Jan Wheeler and purchases of the recorders that were modified into IEDs."

The Lieutenant reached down to a keyboard and entered some keystrokes, "I'm switching your COM to my other supercomputer, so I can get any information you want."

Frank said, "Well, okay; see if you can find out what my wife is getting me for Father's Day."

The COM screen flashed and Brie's image reappeared. She said, "I can't do that, she swore me to secrecy, however, using this computer, I can tell you if your mom has a birthmark."

Frank smiled incredulously, "Really, I don't suppose you'd have a picture of it."

Brie laughed, "Seriously, if there is a picture of it I can get it. That's how powerful this machine is. If it's out there in any digital format, I can get anything on this quantum computer."

Robin replied, "If you're serious we have a list for you."

Brie replied, "Okay, bring it on. I'm ready."

*****

Josh and Chen were breathing deeply, each drinking a beer as they leaned back on the sofa. They were looking down at the coffee table at the two recorders and the microphones that they had severed from the recorders. On the wall in front of them was a COM monitor.

Chen asked, "I wonder how close we were to getting blown up?"

Josh slowly shook his head, "I don't know but I'm sure it was real close, judging from the program note on the screen that the broadcast had been interrupted."

Chen asked, "Shouldn't we be getting a call from Jan, so we can all celebrate?"

Josh looked down at his watch, "Yeah, she should be calling us pretty quick."

*****

Jan's eyes were fixed to the COM screen and her brows drooped with worry. The notice on the screen, "Broadcast temporarily interrupted", was the cause for her concern.

"What the fuck's going on?" She shouted, Royce was sitting next to her, "Isn't that a good thing; that the broadcaster has been interrupted? Wouldn't that mean that the bombs went off?"

Jan scowled, "The bombs may have exploded, but there should be a blank screen or static on the screen. The broadcast producer wouldn't have been able to post the notice unless they had some information about why the video feed was stopped."

Royce said, "Well, the broadcast has been stopped and that's good enough for me."

Jan took a breath, "No, that's not good enough for me. There's something wrong."

*****

Lieutenant Smithy was still on the COM with Frank and Robin.

Robin looked at the screen, "LT, do you have Sarah Gold's profile from Hy-Mark yet?"

Brie smiled, "Yes, I just got it. Here it is."

Robin looked at the information that flashed on her screen. She read it carefully and slapped the desk exclaiming, "Yes, I knew it. It says here that Sarah Gold is twenty-seven years old and is on maternity leave. So that lends me to believe that, Jan Wheeler impersonated her to gain access to Parsons and Hemenway. Also the offender database says that Jan Wheeler wears a snake bracelet."

Frank added, "But, that's not enough to get a warrant unless we can connect her to the purchase of the recorders in DC. Nor can we connect her to the recorders that blew up, or the recorders that Parsons and Hemenway have."

Brie thought for a moment, "Well, I think there is way to get the evidence you need, and if it's not enough, I think that DSC can use the new terrorism act to at least get a warrant for cause." Brie paused and continued, "However, I think I've got a way to get the evidence from the recorders."

Frank scrunched his face, "Okay; I'm listening."

Brie replied, "Just hold on the sec."

She moved her hands to a different keyboard and battered the keys and looked up at the COM. She selected the icon for Mike Mitchell. Shortly his image appeared and Brie asked, "Mike, can I speak to Corporal Rousan?"

Mike replied, "Sure; he's right here." Mike looked over at Rousan and waved him to the COM.

Rousan stood in front of the COM and saw the Lieutenant.

"Yes, Lieutenant, what can I do for you?"

Brie replied, "I need you to get the multi-scan and see if you can pull the prints off of the recorders that Parsons and Hemingway have."

Rousan nodded, "Yes LT, I can do that but, I won't be able to separate the data."

Brie replied, "That's okay Corporal, you just get me the data and I'll do the rest."

Rousan replied, "Yes ma'am, right away."

He went over to the table and put on some latex gloves.

Rousan went out of the office and into the break room where the group had gathered for the event.

He went over to Dale and Ellie, "May I borrow your recorders for a few moments; I need to scan them for evidence in the explosion."

Both Dale and Ellie reluctantly handed over the recorders to Rousan. Rousan picked up a tray off the counter and had them place the recorders on it, careful not to add any fingerprints to the recorders. He carried the tray with the recorders on it, outside and set them on a table.

He went over to the ATV and picked up the multi-scanner out of the basket and set it on the table.

He placed the recorders in various positions as he scanned them for fingerprints. He looked at the display and was satisfied that he had covered the entire surface of both of the recorders. He picked up the recorders and took them inside and handed them back to Dale and Ellie. He said, "Here are your recorders, thank you for loaning them to me."

Bill smiled and Ellie said, "That's okay, we were glad to help."

Rousan went back outside and picked up the multi-scanner and brought it back inside to the security office. He went over to the COM and saw that the Lieutenant was still waiting. He asked, "Okay Lieutenant, I scanned the recorders for prints, but I'll have to get a COM connector cable from Mike to upload them."

Brie replied, "Okay Corporal I'll wait."

Rousan turned to Mike, "Mike, do you have a COM connector cable that I can use?"

Mike dropped his brows and thought, "Yes, think I have one."

He walked over to a drawer and rustled through it. He finally came up with a cable and brought it to Rousan.

Rousan nodded, "Thank you."

He connected the cable to the output on the multi-scanner and then to the input on the COM. He looked up at Brie, "Are you ready to receive Lieutenant?"

Brie smiled, "Ready, Corporal."

Rousan activated the send button and the data was delivered.

Brie entered some keystrokes and a file icon appeared on her screen. She selected the icon and entered some more keystrokes on the keyboard. She moved back over to the COM screen on her super-computer and entered some keystrokes. The file icon appeared on that screen and she transferred it to a waiting icon.

Frank and Robin were waiting for Brie's return to their COM screen.

Brie greeted them, "Okay, I have the fingerprint data from the recorders and I'm processing it now, it should be done in a few seconds."

Robin said, "A few seconds… I was thinking at least an hour to process it."

Brie smiled, looked at her screen, "Well think again, the data is ready and I'm sending it to you now."

The data file popped up on Robin and Frank's COM screens. They both opened it at about the same time. Robin looked at the screen, "I didn't know you could sort them and match them with our database."

Frank exclaimed, "Yahoo, look at that. We have a match with Jan Wheeler and Vo Chen, in addition to Parsons and Hemenway."

Robin replied, "We've got our smoking gun, now for the warrants."

Brie replied, "I've got good news. I anticipated that you would need warrants and the Commander already signed off on electronic warrants. You should have those in a few seconds, and I'm sending one to DC and I'll have your agent Hank Becerra execute the warrants for Jan Wheeler and Royce Pile. You can do the honors of picking up Frazier and Chen."

Frank replied, "Wow, this is sweet. You really do magic things Lieutenant."

Robin added, "If you're ever in Northern California, let us know. We owe you a couple of dinners."

Brie replied, "I look forward to that. You guys take care."

Brie's image left the screen.

Robin looked over at Frank, "Well partner, shall we gather a posse and go collect our miscreants?"

Frank replied, "That sounds like a deal to me. But I still wonder if the Lieutenant knows what my wife is getting me for Father's Day."

Robin smiled, "Frank, you're such a shithead."

*****

Agents Knox and Lane pulled up behind the Sheriff's patrol unit that was parked on Cassel Road. Deputies Ariza and Wallace saw them approach and got out of their unit. Frank and Robin stepped out of their vehicle and met them on the side of the road.

"Well, we're going to have to stop meeting like this." Robin said, as she shook Kerrie's hand. Wallace shook Robin's hand also, "Any time we can take down Josh Frazier, we can meet as often as you like." Frank shook both of their hands, "Bart, I thought you would get tired of hanging with Kerrie, but I guess he'll do until they hook you up with a better partner."

Ariza smiled, "I could say the same to Robin about you."

Robin shook her head and smiled, "Now that we have addressed our pleasantries, you guys want to do some work?"

Kerrie smiled, "So, what has our favorite criminal been up to?"

Frank replied, "We connected Frazier and a new partner in crime, Vo Chen, to the explosion near the SETI site."

Wallace said, "Yeah, we heard about the explosion, was anyone hurt?"

Frank said, "Luckily, some quick thinking and fast running by Chip Barker and Corporal Rousan, took the IED's away from the target to the tree line, and they cleared the area before they exploded."

Kerrie replied, "Wow; that must've been scary. We know Barker but haven't met the Corporal yet. Rousan is it?"

Robin replied, "Yes, is a real sharp Guardsman. Hopefully you guys will meet him sometime."

Kerrie replied, "Sounds like a cool dude."

Frank said, "So, down to business, did you get eyes on Frazier at his house?"

Bart replied, "We saw movement in the house and Frazier's car is there, so it's a good bet that they are there."

Frank nodded, "Okay, Kerrie, find a place that you can cover us with your long gun, and Bart do you have a battering ram?"

Bart nodded. Frank continued, "Okay, bring that. You and I and Robin will try to sneak up to the house. I don't believe that Frazier and Chen are normally armed and since they're not expecting us; I doubt they would have set any explosives around even if they knew how. Robin, if you'll do the honors of announcing our entry; then Bart can take the door down and we can take care of business."

The partial evening darkness, offered some concealment to their movement. Kerrie gave a high sign when he got into position. The trio ferreted their way to the front door. Kerrie kept an eye on the windows for any suspicious movement. The voices and television noise coming from inside created some sense of opportunity. Frank nodded to Robin, who yelled out; "FBI."

Bart pounded the door with the ram and they made entry.

Frank burst through followed by Robin both with their guns drawn and they were followed in by Bart, also with his weapon drawn.

Chen and Frazier were sitting at the kitchen table and were taken totally by surprise. They both complied with orders to get on the floor. They were placed in restraints, searched and escorted outside on to the porch by Bart. Robin and Frank secured the rest of the house and found the two unexploded recorders.

*****

Meanwhile, in DC, agent Hank Becerra headed up a SWAT team and an ordinance disposal unit at the residence of Royce Pyle, in the DC area. Both Royce and Jan Wheeler were taken into custody and a search of the premises, revealed several pounds of C-4 and presumptive bomb making materials. On hearing the news, Frank and Robin immediately opened a COM to Hank.

Robyn waited patiently until Becerra's icon changed to his image.

"Hank, congratulations, I hear you gathered up the primary Kingpin in the attempted bombing of the Hat Creek SETI site."

Hank replied, "Not only that, we collected data from her COM and computers that will probably lead to the arrest of several higher-ups in Segr8. Your pal, Lieutenant Smithy at the DSC is some cookie. She and the commander cut through a lot of barriers to make that happen."

Frank added, "Yes I agree, but there were a lot of other players involved in this takedown. If you get a chance you might give a shout out to the Huey pilot, Chip Barker, Sergeant Juan Gozier and Corporal Bashir Rousan at the Hat Creek SETI site. Without them the complex would have been toast."

Hank replied, "I'll be sure to contact them and include them in my report." Hank paused and continued, "Okay, I've got reports to file and I'm sure you also have some to file. So thanks for the COM and if you're ever in DC look me up."

Robin replied, "That's for sure and the same goes for you if you're ever in NorCal. Be safe."

The COM's went dark.

How Can We Help?
We Drink Water.

Darcy and Juan, along with a new temporarily assigned security assistant Corporal Rousan, were patrolling the perimeter of the SETI site. Agents Johnson, Rayner, and Grayson were roving the grounds in heightened awareness due to the recent attempted attack.

Mike was in the security office monitoring the Alpha drones in the newly added Skyhawk drone. He picked up the two-way mic and stated, "All security; check-in."

The response was rather quick with a short pause between each announcement, "Security one, check... Security two, check... Security three, check."

Mike continued, "Agent Johnson; status."

Ron heard the call and responded, "Johnson, 10-8."

Mike said, "Base copies, agent Rayner; status."

Anji replied, "Rayner, 10-8."

Mike said once again, "Base copies, Grayson, status."

Marnie replied, "Grayson, 10-8."

Mike replied, "Base copies."

Mike put the mic back on the table he turned to Danielle, standing next to him and smiling said, "Agent Alton; what's your status?"

Darlene returned the smile and acting coy, replied, "Why Mr. Mitchell, are you asking me if I'm single?"

Mike seemed to be flustered at her question and stuttered a response, "I'm...uh, I wasn't..."

Darlene smiled and chuffed, "It's okay Mike, just trying to lighten the mood. But to answer your question; I'm also 10-8 and also single."

Mike chuckled, "Okay Ms. Alton, I owe you one."

Darlene laughed and turned and walked back toward the break room. She went in and took a seat away from the other occupants.

Perry Edmonds was fine tuning the COM screen that displayed Richard and Sal's icons and a countdown clock with nine minutes and forty-two seconds on its display.

R.A. sat with his VPC perched in front of him with a collective of images of his scientific think tank. He had an ear-bud connected to his VPC. Dom and Amir sat patiently awaiting the show. Dale and Ellie were making use of their special access to the occasion, by recording everything they could. Eve, no stranger to documenting important events was stealthily covering details that only her trained eye could catch. Perry selected the icons of Sal and Richard on the COM screen and their images appeared.

Perry asked, "Mr. Vice President, Doctor Uschin; are you receiving my COM?"

Richard replied, "Yes, I have a connection."

Sal responded, "I also have a live feed."

Perry replied, "Okay, we're all standing by."

Richard asked, "I know we spoke before, but are you sure that everyone is okay? That attack must have been rather unnerving."

Perry replied, "Well, there was some stress due to the explosion, but it seems that this pending contact with Adam is quelling any fears and concerns of this group."

Richard scanned his monitor and saw all the smiles and excitement on the faces of the group.

He saw Tsirch's image pop-up on his screen and responded, "Mr. President, glad you could make it."

Tsirch smiled, "What? And miss being part of history and let you upstage me?"

Richard shrugged, "That never changes."

Tsirch smiled, "Careful Mr. VP, you're already on thin ice."

Richard chuckled, "It's good to see you're in a good mood for once, Mr. President."

Sal shook his head as he absorbed their banter, "Now boys, behave yourselves, or no pony rides after the meeting."

Eve listened to the exchange on the monitor and shook her head.

*****

Mike picked up a two-way radio off of the table and left the security office and made his way into the break room to join the gathering.

All eyes were on the countdown display on the COM screen, and each second was privately counted down in the minds of the participants.

Perry stood quietly and ceremoniously, enunciated the last ten seconds as if he were conducting an orchestra. He marked the last second with a pronounced gesture of his hands.

Pale anticipation overcame the onlookers. Mike spoke first, "This is the humans on earth; awaiting contact from our friend; Adam."

The ensuing silence was disturbing and yet anticipated. At long last the wait was over.

"This is Adam. Am I speaking to the representative of humans on earth?"

Perry smiled sheepishly, "No, this is Perry Edmonds; I am just a facilitator of our conversation. There are several others present who are honored to speak with you."

Adam replied, "Thank you for your explanation; I will add your audible characteristics to my database. If you will ask the other participants to give me their name, I will add them also, so I may respond to their questions directly."

Perry shrugged his shoulders and looked at the group and waited for someone to join the dialogue.

Dom began, "Adam, this is Dominique Soul."

Adam replied, "Yes, Ms. Soul, I have your vocal pattern already in my database as well as those of Mr. Hadad and Doctor 'Gemo. If there are others present, please have them speak their names also."

Perry pointed to Ellie, who hesitated to speak, but Perry nodded in approval.

Ellie swallowed, "This is Ellie Hemenway."

Adam replied, "It's a pleasure to meet you Ms. Hemenway."

Perry pointed to Dale, who unnecessarily stood, "My name is Dale Parsons."

Adam responded, "Also a pleasure to meet you Mr. Parsons."

Dale smiled and sat back down.

Mike pointed to Danielle.

"I'm Danielle Alton."

"Thank you Ms. Alton, I note a sense of confidence in your voice."

Danielle shrugged her shoulders.

Eve took her turn without a prompt, "I am Evelyn Walker."

Adam replied, "Thank you Ms. Walker it's a pleasure to finally hear your voice. Congratulations on your notoriety."

Eve's face showed curiosity as she replied, "Thank you, Adam."

Perry nudged Mike stated, "My name is Mike Mitchell."

Adam replied, "It's a pleasure Mr. Mitchell."

Perry looked up at the COM screen, "There are three others were not physically present, but may yet take part in the conversation."

Perry waited for Tsirch, Sal or Richard to speak. Richard took the initiative, "My name is Richard Natás."

Adam replied, "Yes, it's a pleasure to meet you Mr. Vice President."

Richard added, "You know who I am?"

Adam replied in an almost jestful tone, "Of course Mr. Vice President, I listen to the news."

Richard smiled and Sal shook his head, "Hello Adam, I'm Sal."

Adam responded, "Thank you. Do you prefer Doctor Uschin or Sal?"

Sal replied, "I see you've done your homework, Adam."

Adam replied, "Yes, Doctor Uschin, I try to keep my database updated."

Sal smiled and replied, "Sal will be fine, Adam."

Tsirch added his introduction, "I'm Tsirch Ren Lang; Adam, it's a pleasure to finally meet you."

Adam replied, "Thank you Mr. President for joining the conversation and thank you for the leadership you've shown in maintaining stability in your difficult times."

Tsirch replied, "I guess you do read the news, Adam."

Adam replied, "Yes indeed Mr. President."

Perry tied up the introductions, "Adam, that should be all that are at this meeting."

Adam replied, "Thank you Mr. Edmonds. If I may, I'd like to start this discourse with an opening statement."

Perry replied, "Of course you may, Adam."

Adam began, "I've come to realize that the discovery of extraterrestrial life has caused the people of Earth, concern about our reason for contact and our intentions. Our primary reason for contacting Earth is the same reason that we have contacted other life forms; we are curious. Our intent is also very basic; we wish to learn and share information, and to get an answer to one question: How can we help?"

Sal responded to Adam's opening foray, "Adam, regardless of the relatively small number of our species that have issues with our mutual contact; the results of your engagement, so far, has been to our benefit. The 'diffusion' events you delivered have decreased our carbon footprint and increased our ozone layer. Additionally, the increase in water purification and nitrogen in our soil is still being evaluated. So, my friend, in my estimation your controlling question has been answered."

Adam replied, "We are pleased with your evaluation, Sal."

R.A. dug into Adam's premise, "You alluded to other life forms you've contacted; how many other life forms have you contacted?"

Adam responded, "We have had ongoing efforts to contact other species, just as you have; so far the number that are able to effectively respond, is less than 100."

R.A. followed up, "By ability to effectively respond; that indicates what?"

Adam said, "The standard would be in their ability to carry on a comprehensive digital or audio exchange, similar to what we have been doing."

Dominique required further comment, "Am I to understand that the other life forms lack the ability to communicate?"

Adam took exception, "On the contrary, our assumption is that we lack the ability to communicate on their level; it's possible that their abilities are beyond our abilities."

Amir tossed his hat in the ring, "Can you relate to us what your search or contact criteria would involve?"

Adam said, "To answer that I will offer a short explanation of our contact capabilities."

Amir responded, "Yes please, continue."

Adam explained, "As you are aware, our contact capability is virtually instantaneous; however we cannot presume that other life forms have the same capability. It is possible that they do not communicate in a similar process that we are using. Since we are searching for carbon-based entities that have access to an environment containing water, we cannot presume that intelligence only exists in our reality."

Sal punched back in, "If I'm reading you correctly, you have the capability to scan other environments, such as planets, and categorize them in some sort of phylum."

Adam replied, "Yes Sal, that could be a general description, however, as an example; we have a plant on our planet we call a Kaiap, that can respond to the direction of a sound or voice and reply by using tentacles to tap on its leaves. And the tapping varies depending on the type and pitch of the noise: it also recognizes specific sounds and responds accordingly. We are humbled by and respect its capability and only perform our version of an autopsy when we are certain of its demise. So you understand that we hesitate to dismiss a lack of communication as a lack of intelligence. It's entirely possible that that life form simply refuses to communicate with us."

Tsirch listened to the exchange and empathetically swallowed and offered, "Adam, it's inconceivable that anyone could see your species as a threat; given the explanation you just delivered. However, as our conversation is being broadcast worldwide, I would like to offer this thought to those who would do violence in response to hearing the truth; for the more you hear the truth the more your denial is confirmed."

Adam responded, "Thank you Mr. President."

R.A. changed course, "Adam, my data indicates that you have communicated with and delivered a 'diffusion' to the planet we call Wolf 1061c, why did you send them a 'diffusion' or did they ask for one?"

Adam explained, "The Wolf 'diffusion', while similar to that was sent to earth, was modified to induce a corrective imbalance in their ecosystem. Their planet suffered an asteroid impact that increased the hydrogen sulfide content of their troposphere. The 'diffusion' was sent in response to a distress signal from the planet and fortunately the biosphere is now protected."

Sal interjected, "The query I have is; why a 'diffusion' was sent to the earth and why was there a second diffusion?"

Adam responded, "It is somewhat embarrassing to admit, but the first diffusion was sent by mistake. Some of our technicians overreacted to some of your broadcasts that expressed a desire to repair your ozone layer and to revitalize the earth's soil. They took that as a request for assistance and sent the 'diffusion': So for that I apologize. As for the second 'diffusion', it was sent to modify inert materials, sent in the first 'diffusion', that could have possibly expanded your biosphere. That has been corrected."

Dominique smiled and summarized, "So, Adam you are simply responding to an, SOS?"

Adam paused for a moment and replied, "Yes, Ms. Soul, that appears to be one explanation."

Amir added, "It seems, Adam, that altruism is one of your planets virtues."

Adam's pause was longer this time, "Sadly Mr. Hadad, I wish that were totally true. As I mentioned before, our reason for making contact with other life forms is to learn from them and to share information. It seems that your planet may have something to benefit us both."

R.A.'s brows dropped as he replied, "So, you do want something from us."

Adam explained, "I assure you it is nothing nefarious. Since making contact, we are becoming more aware that your technology may be advanced enough to participate in a joint venture."

Richard quipped, "Mr. President, I think he wants you to get out your checkbook."

Adam upped his game.

"There is the humor that I've heard about from you Mr. Vice President."

Richard replied, "And you, Adam, that's not a bad retort for an alien."

Richard could almost hear Adam smile.

R.A. interrupted, "Okay you two, business first, drinks later. Adam, what do you have in mind?"

Adam continued, "It may take some doing, but we would like to propose that earth create a way-station to receive genetic material."

R.A. pressed his face and thought, "But, you already have the capability of sending organic material, how would this be different?"

Adam explained, "Our scientists, as scientist are prone to be, wish to expand their knowledge through experimentation. While we can send materials through space to designated locations we have yet dared to send a life form through the process.

They have postulated, that a receiving station would be necessary to ensure 100 percent success of a life form transportation."

Richard said, "I'm no scientist but I think you're saying you want us to build a contraption to receive one of your inhabitants."

Adam replied, "Mr. Vice President, your choice of the word 'contraption' is interesting."

Eve laughed and entered the conversation, "And you said you were no scientist."

Although they weren't in the same room Richard and Eve exchanged a stare.

Tsirch laughed, "Yep, you're right Richard, I gotta get out my checkbook; or better yet, round up some investors."

Sal engaged his concerns, "I hate to be a wet blanket in this discussion, but given the technical data you have provided that would enable us to create our own connection portal, we have yet to construct even a feasible computer generated model. I am not sure that we have the materials or the technology to do as you ask."

Adam took exception, "I understand your concern, Sal, but having scanned your periodic table and taken inventory of your current skills of construction and your availability of materials, we believe that the project is totally within your capabilities. As a matter of fact, the 'contraption', as your vice president would call it, is there is similar to what you call a Faraday cage."

Richard responded with exception, "Adam; thank you for exposing my scientific knowledge."

Adam seemed to understand Richard's implication.

"I'm sorry Mr. Vice President but that was too good to pass up."

Sal added, "I thought that was a pretty good retort, Adam?"

Richard looked at Sal and responded, "Et tu, Brute?"

Sal smiled.

Adam surprisingly responded, "I assume that that quote was made out of friendship."

Richard replied, "Yes Adam, we are friends, and I believe you are beginning to understand our kind too well."

Adam replied, "It's a work in progress."

Sal reengaged in the task at hand, "Adam, if you think we are capable of building such container, then perhaps the world's scientists can collaborate in such a venture."

Tsirch interjected, "As the world is listening, I would expect a quorum to reply shortly and support of building such a structure."

R.A. inserted his suggestion, "I'm sure that if you send the construction plans, Dominique and Amir can decipher and deliver them to the appropriate entrepreneurs."

Amir added, "Yes, we can translate them into whichever language and format that is necessary."

Tsirch opened up his query, "Adam, on behalf of our inhabitants; should we complete this construction and the delivery is successful, what would be the endgame in such an endeavor?"

Adam responded, "Our hope is that one of our inhabitants could successfully integrate into your society so that we may learn from each other. The caveat, for the individual selected to make the journey, would be the likelihood of never returning home; unless the individual finds the means and resources to create a transportation device to return home."

Tsirch replied, "I understand your dilemma and this requires further discussion among our people as well as your inhabitants. I for one support the proposal, but I am only one vote."

Adam replied, "I agree Mr. President, we have many things to discuss."

R.A. reacquired the discussion, "While we have you available, we have other questions."

Adam replied, "Of course, how can I help?"

R.A. began, "While we saw your hologram, we noticed that your physicality is practically identical to ours. The questions that arise relate to your environment, society, history and beliefs."

Adam replied, "Since we had a limited amount of time to participate in such a discussion, I anticipated such interrogatories, and I prepared an audio data file that will attempt to answer many of those inquiries. I have sent them to Mr. Hadad and Ms. Soul, so they may translate them and deliver them to your inhabitants.

Dom interrupted, "Adam, I have one question that one of our citizens, TylerRudolph asked and I assured him that I would ask it."

Adam replied, "Certainly Ms. Soul."

Dom asked, "What do aliens drink?"

Adam replied, "We drink water."

Start Spreading The News

A week after the Hat Creek event, the nations appeared to coalesce in efforts to construct a transport platform to receive an alien visitor. In the same vein the disruptive groups were honing their skills to counter every aspect of alien insertion into their lives.

The morning broke and found Eve sitting at her desk in a newly converted 'bedroom to office' in the Vice President's residence. She was on a conference COM with Bill Parsons and Ellie Hemenway.

"Okay, Dale and Ellie, do you have any corrections or additions to the file I sent yesterday?"

Ellie replied, "Are you sure you want to share the byline with us? Most of this video and reporting is your work."

Eve shook her head, "Are you kidding, your, off-the-cuff and ex parte additions, are what makes this documentary so valuable. Your straight to the point questions during the interviews were just what makes the delivery so interesting. You asked questions that everyone who wasn't there, wanted to ask."

Dale replied, "That's because we didn't understand anything about the aliens."

Eve smiled and chuckled, "That's why you two are such good reporters; you dig for the answers regardless of where it takes you."

Ellie replied, "Well, I had to watch the entire documentary twice to remember what; was a blur at the time."

Eve replied, "Ellie my dear, every interview I've done, is a blurred memory until I watch or listen to what I reported and was said." Dale added, "One of the things that I felt curious about, was Adam's secrecy regarding their contact with other alien life forms."

Ellie responded, "I believe that Adam explained that he wanted to protect the identity and location to prevent unwanted interference in the lives of their alien partners."

Eve replied, "Exactly Ellie; you recall that Adam asked if it would be okay if we were contacted by other aliens if they so chose. That is their way of protecting their partners."

Dale replied, "Yes, now I do recall. I guess I'm still processing the whole event."

Eve smiled, "Dale, I'm still processing the last four weeks, and I wake up each morning wondering if what has happened, did happen."

Eve scanned her VPC screen and closed some files. She looked back at Dale and Ellie's images on her screen, "Okay, as far as I'm concerned the ball is in your court. The story is yours to file."

Ellie asked, "What do you think, Dale, are we ready to leap forward?"

Dale nodded, "It's a go for me. Let's do it."

She smiled and responded, "Okay you two, but be prepared for the onslaught of both adulation and degradation. And I suggest you take advantage of the government security that was offered."

Ellie replied, "Yes, both of us have accepted their services."

Eve smiled and nodded, "Okay, take care."

The images disappeared from Eve's monitor.

She disengaged her VPC, stood up and placed it in her jacket pocket. She walked out of her office down the hall and went into the kitchen. Shari, was wiping down the counter and she noticed Eve come in.

"Would you like something to drink Ms. Walker?"

Eve smiled, "Shari, remember it's Eve, not Ms. Walker, and I will have some coffee if it's not too much trouble."

Shari replied, "I'm sorry Ms. Walker, I cannot disrespect your relative position with the vice president. I must insist on calling you Ms. Walker, at least until your status changes."

Shari became somewhat embarrassed and continued, "And if you don't mind me saying, hopefully your status may be upgraded to Mrs. vice president."

It was Eve's turn to be somewhat embarrassed, "Shari, I realize my relationship with the vice president has been on the fast track; albeit a wonderful fast track, but given the events of the past month, I've come to realize that the future can always change." Eve put her hand on Shari shoulder, "But, thank you for your support. I'll be in the dining room."

Shari smiled, "Of course, Ms. Walker."

Eve left the kitchen and went into the dining room and sat down. She looked up at the monitors and pressed some buttons on the controller. She spoke to the COM.

"COM, show news icons."

Several news service icons displayed on the screen.

Eve said, "Open icon, one and six to medium view."

The news services she requested opened on a split screen view. She reached down and increased the volume on the controller.

Shari came into the dining room and set a cup of coffee on the table in front of Eve. Eve said, "Thank you Shari." Eve settled back into her chair and smiled as she reflected on the passionate night before.

Eve sat naked, astraddle of Richard's waist as he lay on the bed. She leaned up, off of his chest as they gripped each other's hands. Her head arched back in passion, she leaned forward with a sigh and smile. Richard took a deep breath and let go of her hands and pulled her back down on his body.

*****

The light from an electrical pole outside the modular filtered through the blinds in the window and bathed the room in soft light. Amir's eyes opened slowly from a peaceful slumber. The ceiling gradually came into focus. A soft smile pulled his face to one side where Dominique lay on his arm. His other arm reached to softly cradle her bare shoulders and he pulled himself onto his side and let his hand slide to caress her soft breasts and nipples. He continued on down to her ribs and pulled himself easily upon her. Dom felt her awakening body responding to Amir's caress.

Their smiles combined and fell into gentle kisses. Amir snuggled his face into the nape of her neck and kissed it gently. He leaned up to see her face and said very softly, "Good morning."

She smiled and replied in the same soft voice, "Good morning to you."

She turned her head to the side and looked at the clock.

Quietly she said, "Morning? It's only 4:30."

Amir smiled and quietly said, "I know but I want to get an early start on this."

Dom replied, "Start on what."

He replied quietly, "This."

He eased down on her with a passionate kiss and infused his body into her body.

*****

Morning had broken and R.A. and Marnie were collaborating on breakfast preparations. R.A. retrieved four plates out of the cabinet and placed them on the table next to the necessary utensils. He scanned the table and decided it was time to awaken their roommates. He began to walk out of the kitchen to the hallway and said to Marnie, "Okay, I'm gonna rouse the sleepy heads."

He walked over to Amir's door and knocked.

"Amir, are you awake?"

Dom's voice answered from inside, "Yes, come in."

R.A. complied and opened the door. He saw Dom sitting on the bed in a robe, brushing her slightly damp hair. Not at all surprised at seeing her in Amir's bedroom he said, "I was going to tell you and Amir that breakfast was ready."

Dom replied casually, "Amir is still in the shower, but we should be along shortly." Dom smiled, "Thank you R.A.."

R.A. nodded and closed the door and went back to the kitchen.

Marnie was plating the bacon, "Well, are they hungry?"

R.A. grinned, "Most likely."

Marnie looked at R.A. curiously, "What you mean most likely?"

R.A. replied, "Well, I knocked on Amir's door and Dom said 'come in'. And I told her breakfast was ready and while she was brushing her still damp hair, she said Amir was still in the shower and they would be out shortly. So, it depends on which appetite they yet have a need to satisfy."

Marnie looked at R.A., smiled with raised brows and uttered a long, "Ohhhh."

*****

R.A., Dom and Amir came into the complex and settled into the break room, after having consumed their breakfast. Perry was on the COM with Sal's image and numerous icons representing audio only COM participants. They sat down at a table with Mike and listened to the current conversation. Sal saw them come in and sit down, "Good morning, R.A., Dom and Amir, I have a gang of contemporaries going over the status of alien communications and the development of the transport platform. I'll read you the list so you'll know who we're talking to."

Sal picked up a paper and began reading, "We have Lucas and Mark, Cory and Jo from Johannesburg and Honrí Foster, at the VLA and our esteemed think tank; Marie Barrett, Jubal Jung, Carmen Hafed and Aldo Karloff."

R.A. replied, "I dare not try to respond to each of you, so I will collectively say 'good morning', from Dom, Amir and myself and accept your collective salutations."

R.A. paused, "So, what is the status, Sal?"

Sal replied, "So far it's only good news. It appears that the COM-SAT system has been updated and all of the satellites are capable of receiving and responding to the alien conversations. All of the audio transmissions and data streams have been made available to all those with signal array capabilities. We are not sure how Adam has pulled it off, but apparently he can simultaneously correspond with any and all conversations. Additionally, I have tapped our system into Adam's data stream, thus it's likely that he is listening to our transmission and could likely respond at any time."

Dom replied in surprise, "This is Dominique; this is incredibly wonderful news. This means that we can all have access to the data stream and continue working jointly to construct the transport receiving platform. Amir and I will immediately get to work translating the blueprints and directions into each language."

A voice came over the COM, "This is Carmen Hafed; I agree, our workers have been struggling with the previous translations and we have been waiting for responses to specific diagram materials. This will greatly increase our rate of productivity and hopefully one or several of the devices currently under construction will be successful."

Perry added, "This is Perry Edmonds; if any of you have any problems but the translation data, please contact me and we will respond as soon as possible."

Another voice was heard, "This is Jubal Jung; I'm happy to report that our crew has completed a platform and is currently running computer simulations. If anyone requires assistance, we will be happy to help."

A voice replied, "Aldo Karloff thanks you and will contact you shortly, Jubal."

Yet another voice entered conversation, "Cory and Jo, this is Honrí; if you can give me a side channel, I'd appreciate it."

A response was heard, "This is Jo; Cory and I have a side channel open. Thanks to everyone."

Sal noticed that Marie Barrett's icon was yet active. He asked, "Marie; are you still there?"

The voice responded, "Yes Sal, I was just going over the current data from the Alphas and it seems that the new matrix opened up a new avenue to build the transport device. I'll see if I can catch up with you at the VLA."

Sal responded, "Okay, I should be there tomorrow."

Marie replied, "Alright, I'll see you then. Later everybody."

Most of the audio icons left the COM screen and that left only Lucas and Mark as participants. As the others left, Lucas and Mark's images appeared on the monitor. R.A. responded on seeing their faces on the screen.

"Wow, I haven't seen your two ugly mugs for quite a while."

Lucas replied, "Mark, it appears that R.A. is looking in a mirror; talk about the pot calling the kettle black."

Mark replied, "Yeah, I saw a picture ID of him when he pretended to be a derelict at the VLA."

Lucas replied, "Actually, I think he was better looking then."

Sal interrupted, "Are you guys quite done? I believe Lucas has an announcement."

R.A. replied, "Don't tell me, Ari is finally leaving your sorry ass."

Lucas replied, "Thanks for your confidence, you old curmudgeon, but, no, I would like to invite everyone, to the girls' birthday party."

R.A. replied, "I can't think of a better occasion to attend. It will be my honor."

Mike replied, "Okay, count me in."

Perry added, "Me too."

Dom and Amir turned to each other smiling and Dom grabbed Amir's hand, "Amir and I would love to attend."

The lingering hand contact of Amir and Dom did not go unnoticed.

Lucas smiled, "Okay, we'll send you the details, and I hope you like pizza."

Two Birds Out Of Hand

In his office in Moscow, FSB agent Yuri Damyan was scanning the satellite tracking monitor, when he noticed two heat signature blips sporadically showing up on his map. Realizing that someone was trying to cloak some type of rocket engine, he opened up a COM and selected the familiar icon, and waited for a response. Momentarily, the image of Edward Narkiewicz displayed on his screen.

Yuri greeted Edward, "Commander Narkiewicz this is Yuri Damyan." Edward replied, "Yes, Yuri, of course. I remember you from the Balkans situation. How is your brother Liev?"

Yuri replied, "He is recovering well, thank you for asking."

Edward added, "He's a brave soul, stopping that mass shooting attempt."

Yuri replied smiling, "Yes, but he still says he's lucky that the gunman's weapon jammed just at the right time and he just took one bullet."

Edward continued, "Perhaps so, but it was quick thinking on his part. Give him my regards."

Yuri replied, "I shall do so, but I'm afraid I have a situation that you may be able to assist me with."

Edward asked, "Of course, whatever you need."

Yuri said, "I have two signatures on my satellite COM indicating high heat engines, most likely rocket engines, coming from the Kotlon Island near St. Petersburg in the Gulf of Finland. The problem is we have no testing or launching facilities of that nature on the island. Additionally, it appears that someone is trying to jam or cloak the heat signatures, as they appear intermittently."

Edward said, "That does sound suspicious you want me to check our satellites view of the island?"

Yuri replied, "That would be extremely helpful if you could do so."

Edward replied, "Okay, give me a moment."

Edward looked over at Brie, "Brie, I need you to check satellites, Foster and Rachel over St. Petersburg. And focus in on Kotlon Island. We're looking for excessive heat signatures; possibly from rocket engines."

Brie nodded and stepped over to a different keyboard and worked her magic. The COM screen displayed the infrared view of the island. Brie responded, "I can verify high heat signatures on the north end of the island."

Edward said to Yuri, "Yuri, heat signatures are verified do you want me to patch you in?"

Yuri was surprised, "You can do that?"

Edward replied, "No, but my Lieutenant can, stand by."

Brie heard the conversation and immediately patched the COM screen into Yuri's COM.

Yuri saw the display change.

Edward asked, "Yuri, you see the view. I can give you control if you want."

Yuri said, "You can do that?"

Edward replied, "No; but my Lieutenant can."

Edward nodded to Brie and she surrendered control of the satellites.

Yuri studied the screen and manipulated the images of the island. He zoomed in on the heat signatures and his face showed concern. He reached over and picked up a radio COM and pressed a red button.

A voice responded, "Commander Novikov."

Yuri said, "Commander, I have a red notice."

Novikov replied, "I'm engaging now. Location?"

Yuri said, "Kotlon Island."

Novikov replied, "Two minutes from Levashovo."

Yuri swallowed and began waiting. He entered the coordinates and Novikov relayed them to the pilot.

Shortly a voice replied

"Captain Bela Sidorova; at your service."

Yuri said, "Captain, investigate heat signatures at the coordinates given."

"Dah." was the response.

Several seconds later an urgent voice crackled, "I have two birds in the air… following."

Yuri asked, "Trajectory?"

"Vertical, I repeat, vertical." The Captain responded urgently.

Edward was watching the COM screen and Brie followed it also. Brie entered some keystrokes and instantly matched the trajectory to two satellites. Edward saw trajectory also and said to Yuri, "Yuri the targets are satellites, suggest removal."

Yuri said to the pilot, "Captain; engage targets."

Captain Sidorova replied, "Dah."

The MiG-31 FoxHound climbed to the sky, released two missiles to intercept and continued to follow. Edward followed the plane on the screen and saw that it was still chasing the targets getting dangerous close to a blast radius. He spoke into the COM with urgency. He said, "Disengage; dammit; disengage."

As the targets exploded, they disappeared from the radar.

Edward took a big sigh of relief when he saw the aircraft returning back to earth.

Edward asked Yuri, "Why didn't the pilot disengage after she fired the missiles?"

Yee replied, "I cannot tell you perhaps you can ask her I'll patch you in."

Edward replied, "Yes I'd appreciate that."

A voice came over the COM, "This is Captain Sidorova."

Edward asked, "Captain, this is Commander Narkiewicz at the DSC, I was wondering why you waited so long to disengage from the targets after you fired your missiles."

The captain responded, "Sir, I only wished to ensure that the targets were destroyed, and I remained engaged until they were destroyed. I would not accept failure."

Edward replied, "Thank you Captain, you're a credit to the service."

The captain replied simply, "Dah."

Edward spoke in a relieved voice.

"Yuri, that is one brave pilot."

Yuri replied, also relieved, "Dah."

Edward smiled and nodded to Brie, "Lieutenant; excellent job."

Yuri added, "Now I understand you and your Lieutenants' capabilities. Lieutenant, thank you."

Brie joined the conversation, "Dah."

Yuri and Edward smiled.

*****

Tsirch was going over some paperwork in the Oval Office, when the COM notice flashed and he looked up and saw General Porter's icon on the screen. He accepted the COM, "General Porter, how can I help you?"

Porter responded, "I just got a report from DSC that FSB agent Yuri Damyan contacted Commander Narkiewicz and asked for some assistance with satellite surveillance. There were two missiles launched from Kotlan Island in the Gulf of Finland. It appears the targets were two satellites above Russia. A MiG-31 FoxHound piloted by a Captain Bela Sidorova was sent to intercept the missiles and she successfully destroyed the missiles. Agent Damyan sent some of his agents to the island where the missiles were launched and discovered some FATA and Segr8 associates trying to leave the island."

Tsirch paused and absorbed the information, "Have we been able to back trace any communications and get a connection to anyone stateside or in Myanmar?"

Porter responded, "Negative Mr. President but curiously there was a brief connection made from Taipei."

Tsirch cocked his head in thought. After a moment Tsirch replied, "Taiwan? That's a pretty big stretch, for Segr8. It has to be a FATA connection."

Porter replied, "I agree, but DSC is running down the COM links anyway, just as a precaution."

Tsirch replied, "That's a good idea. By the way, can you send the pilot a big 'thank you' from the president?"

Porter replied, "I certainly will, Mr. President."

Tsirch asked, "Do you have anything else for me, General?"

Porter responded, "No sir, just the one report."

Tsirch replied, "Thank you General. Have a good day."

Tsirch ended the COM.

HIDDEN DECEIT

Jubal Jung was going over a checklist on a clipboard with Ayan Ping at the newly created transport project construction site at the Nangang Exhibition Center in Taipei.

Ayan asked, "Aren't you getting excited? We're the first to build a platform and everyone is asking for our design."

Jubal smiled, "Ayan, of course I'm excited, but not just because we are the first to build the platform, but more so what it represents. Don't you realize what an amazing opportunity we have to receive an actual alien; what we can learn from them?"

Ayan replied somewhat ashamed, "Of course I realize that, but it is yet such an honor to be the first."

Jubal shook his head, "You realize also that this project would not be possible had the Taiwan Space Agency not received unsuspected support from Beijing. To have this project advance so quickly is a testament to the dedication of our people. It's only been a week since Adam requested assistance in building a transport receiving enclosure and every science agency and foundation has been fast at work in completing the project. Although it wasn't a race, everyone took it as such."

Ayan said, "Of course, but I also realize that our senior engineer, Hua Na, gave us a leg up on its construction, as she had created a similar device based on a Faraday cage. But, as I said, it is yet such an honor to be the first."

Jubal shook his head dismissively, "Have you seen that new assistant Hayato; I need him to pick up some parts at the electronics shop?"

Ayan replied, "Yes, I saw him a couple of hours ago working on the fusion chamber."

Jubal scrunched his face, "He was working on the fusion chamber? He doesn't have clearance for that area."

Jubal set the clipboard on the table, turned and went down the stairs toward the fusion chamber with Ayan following. As he went down the last flight of stairs he sensed something wrong. The power cage door was open and the circuit breaker, inside the cage, was in the on position. Jubal quickly shut the breaker off and closed the power cage door and locked it. He looked inside the control room and saw the panel had been smashed with some sort of ax or hammer. The monitors were broken and someone had attempted to enter the fusion chamber by breaking the lock and the keyboard sensor. He turned to Ayan, "Go upstairs and get on the COM and tell security we need to find Hayato."

Ayan nodded and went up the stairs. Jubal went over to the plated glass viewing port of the fusion chamber, and looked in. He shook his head and hurried over to a security vault and entered a code on the keyboard and pressed his hand on the palm print reader.

The vault opened and he reached in and turned a lever. He stepped back out and went over to the fusion chamber door which was now open. He went inside and noticed the ignition cell had been the depleted due to the circuit being left on.

Jubal went back out and closed the fusion chamber door and went out of the control room and locked it behind him. He proceeded up the stairs to the office. Ayan was still on the COM with security. He turned to Jubal, "Security has video of Hayato leaving the center forty minutes ago. Someone picked him up out front in a gray minivan and I have the license plate number. I wrote it down here."

He pointed to a tablet. Jubal took the tablet and wrote down 'Hayato Singh' on the tablet also.

Jubal both smiled and grimaced. He went over to the COM and entered some keystrokes. The screen lit up and he selected Sal Uschin's icon. Seconds later Sal's image appeared on the screen.

Sal saw Jubal's image and started to speak but was interrupted, as Jubal spoke first.

"Sal, I need your help."

Sal noticed the sense of urgency, "Okay, tell me what you need."

Jubal said, "Someone sabotaged our project and I need to see if you can have your friend at the DSC track him down."

Sal took a short breath, "Let me patch us into the DSC."

The screens flickered and Edward Narkiewicz image appeared.

Edward noticed the dual images, "Sal, and isn't it Jubal, also?"

Jubal took charge, "Yes commander and I need your urgent assistance. Someone sabotaged my transport platform and I have a name and license plate number."

Edward looked over at Brie and pointed two fingers to the screen. Brie understood Edward's gesture and joined the COM.

Edward said, "Okay Jubal give me the name and license plate."

Jubal replied, "Hayato Singh and here is his name and license plate." He showed the information on the tablet to the COM screen and continued, "He left the Nangang Exhibition Center in Taipei, forty minutes ago in this vehicle." Brie saw the information and entered it into her computer.

In less than ten seconds Hayato's information was on the screen as well as the vehicle ownership and address. Brie entered some more keystrokes in and satellite tracking was following the vehicle on the screens.

Edward was running his own information on his computer and shared the results with the group.

"Hayato has a connection to FATA and Segr8."

He entered some more keystrokes, "And Taipei police are receiving a BOLO as we speak."

Jubal finally took a breath, "Thank you, Sal and Commander; I just couldn't let this guy get away."

Edward replied, "You have to include Lieutenant Smithy in your thanks. She is par-excellence at her job."

Jubal smiled, "Well, then a super 'thank you' to Lieutenant Smithy."

Brie only smiled and did not respond.

Edward smiled, "Is there anything else we can do for you, Jubal?"

Jubal replied, "No thank you. You've done more than I expected."

Edward replied, "No problema, I'll leave you two to catch up."

Edward's image left the COM screen.

Jubal said, "Thank you again, Sal, for your help."

Sal asked, "You said the project was sabotaged; how badly was it damaged?"

Jubal replied, "I'm not sure, but it appears that the control panel and screens were smashed with a sledgehammer or something. And they tried to gain entry into the fusion chamber, but failed to do so. However, the standby circuitry for the ignition cell was severed and the cell depleted. Fortunately, all of that can be repaired and it will only set us back a couple of days."

Sal responded, "I feel sorry for you and your crew, I know you were ready for a test run."

Jubal replied, "Yes, but our crew will persevere."

Sal said, "Yes, your dedication to the project is well known. I'm certain that if there's anything you need, there will be no shortage of assistance."

Jubal said, "Thank you. I need to relate the events to the staff and began repairs. Thank you so much for your assistance."

Sal replied, "Just remember that everyone is here if you need anything."

Jubal nodded and disappeared from the COM.

Just Another Party

Thomas Ren Lang came out of the shower and went into the locker room and opened up his locker. He sat down next to his best friend, Jason Hill, and they both began to get dressed.

Jason said, "I don't know about you but I rather run the 440 against the other guys than to run against you in the mile."

Thomas smiled, "Jason, it doesn't matter who you run against, you'd still come in first."

Jason replied shaking his head, "Maybe Tommy boy, but I have to run my ass off because you have no quit in you. I have to push myself to the limit every time."

Thomas laughed, "That's why I like running against you, because even if I come in second I'm pretty sure that I won't wind up in third place. Your spirit of competition is second to none, and that buddy, is what I feed on."

Thomas playfully punched Jason on the shoulder, "That's why you're the DC Track Star at Sidwell Friends School and being your friend makes me feel important."

Jason laughed aloud, "Oh, what a bunch of shit: being the president's son isn't important enough?"

Thomas smiled and said soberly, "You know that I struggle with being treated special because of who I am."

Jason sighed, "Yeah, I know. We've had this conversation before, and I keep telling you that, everyone that I know; respects you for the person that you are, and not for who your father is."

Thomas smiled and finished getting dressed. As they walked out of the locker room Thomas asked, "Jason, you're still coming to the pizza birthday party, aren't you?"

Jason replied, "Of course. I've only met the girls a couple of times, but they are always such a joy to be around. I can have my dad drop me off."

Thomas replied, "Why don't you give me a call at about, 3:30. I may come down early and pick you up."

Jason chuffed, "You want to drag an entourage of Secret Service agents to pick me up."

Thomas smiled, "Actually, I think I can talk my cousin Jenny into driving me down and picking you up."

Jason was surprised, "Without a gang of Secret Service… that would be a first."

Thomas replied, "Well, my dad trusts her implicitly and I think I can pull it off. So call me when you get ready."

Jason nodded and exchanged a fist bump with Thomas, "Okay, I'll give you a call."

Thomas said, "Okay buddy." and left the locker room.

Another classmate; Arthur, was sitting across from Jason as they finished getting dressed.

He turned, "Wow, I've never seen Thomas without at least three Secret Service agents around him. It's highly unusual that his dad would trust him without them."

Jason nodded, "Yeah, but we'll see what happens."

Jason left the locker room and Arthur walked out behind him and stopped outside the door. He took out his COM and dialed a number, and waited for an answer. He looked around to see if anyone was listening, "Hey, this is Arthur, you asked me to let you know if Thomas was going to be without Secret Service agents and I think that opportunity has come."

*****

The party was shaping up to be a gathering of Who's Who. Aside from Lucas and Ari and the twins; Sal and Congresswoman Walsh, R.A., Dominique, Amir, Mark Narkiewicz, Perry, Michael, the vice president and Eve and Thomas Ren Lang were filling out the dance card. Of course their corresponding agents were also in attendance; Johnson, Rayner, Grayson, Gordon, Alton and Jennifer Natás. Thomas and Richard's standard protocol of agents and the prior sweep of the area sealed the entire area from unauthorized intruders.

As the adults mingled in the open dining area, Angela and Nicole were totally involved with their playmates from school in the playroom of the pizza parlor. Thomas went into the playroom and yelled, "Where are my birthday girls?"

Nicole heard his voice and called out to Angela, "Angela, Thomas is here."

Smiles overwhelmed their faces and they came running to Thomas and their hugs push them all to the floor in laughter. Thomas gathered his composure, "Okay, okay. You guys win; I give."

Angela replied, "You can't give we won't let you."

And they continue to wrestle.

Thomas chuckled, "I'm going to need some help, I'm gonna go get Jason so we can have a fair fight."

Nicole said, "Okay, but it's no fair tickling; got it?"

Thomas smiled and set up and held up his crossed fingers, "Okay, I promise, no tickling."

Angela grabbed his crossed fingers and said smiling, "No; promise; no tickling."

Thomas relented. He uncrossed his fingers, "I promise."

Thomas began to struggle slightly, "Okay let me up. I gotta go."

The girls released their holds on his arms and legs and Thomas got up.

He went out the door of the playroom and went over to Jennifer, "Did you clear it with dad; that we could pick up Jason?"

Jennifer replied, "Well, partially, I have to have another agent go with us. Agent Gordon will take another vehicle."

Thomas nodded and smiled, "Thank you, Cousin Jenny."

Jennifer replied, "Okay, straight down and straight back."

Thomas nodded. Jennifer put her arm around his shoulder and they walked outside.

Agent Gordon was waiting next to her vehicle and Jennifer and Thomas came out the building. She tapped her ear-com, "This is Overwatch, Racehorse is on the move."

Jennifer opened the passenger door to the vehicle and Thomas got in. She scanned the area and walked around to the driver's side and got in. She started the car and said in her ear-com, "This is Horizon, I have racehorse."

Darlene got in her vehicle and followed Jennifer down the street. The drive was only fifteen minutes to Jason's father's business, Bob Hill construction, located in a business park. Jennifer pulled up to the entrance and Darlene stopped her vehicle at the curb across the street.

Jennifer and Thomas got out of the car. Jennifer touched her ear-com, "Racehorse is out of the vehicle."

They walked toward the office. Mr. Hill and Jason came out of his office and Mr. Hill walked over to Jennifer and offered his hand.

As they were meeting, Darlene noticed a plumbing supply van come down the street and slow down perceptively as it passed Jennifer and Thomas. She noted two individuals in the front seat and they took an unusual interest in the meeting.

Darlene spoke into her ear-com, "This is Overwatch, I have a light-colored Capital Plumbing van, license plate, 1032526. Requesting identification."

Jennifer heard Darlene's comments and covertly turned to look at the van also, then turned back to greet Mr. Hill.

"Hello, I'm Bob Hill."

Jennifer replied, shaking his hand, "I'm glad to meet you, Mr. Hill, I'm Jennifer." She turned and shook Jason's extended hand, "You must be the Track Star, Jason; Thomas has said such good things about you."

The suspicious van continued its slow speed to the end of the street. It stopped at the stop sign and waited longer than necessary to make a left turn.

Jason replied, "Well, the president must think a lot of you, bringing him down here without the normal Secret Service protection."

Jennifer confessed, "Well actually, I AM with the Secret Service and there is another agent across the street for backup."

Bob Hill looked curiously at Jennifer, "I thought you looked familiar, you're Jennifer Natás the vice president's daughter."

Jennifer nodded, "Guilty as charged."

Jason said, "Thomas said you were his cousin; how's that work?"

Jennifer smiled, "We are not actually related, but our families have been friends since our dads' college days. Thomas has always called me, 'cousin' Jenny and he calls my dad, 'uncle' Richard."

Bob replied, "Well, that sort of explains it."

Jennifer nodded and as she scanned the area, said, "Okay, it was nice to meet you but we're sort of exposed out here and we have to go."

Bob waved, "Okay, thank you. Jason; call me when you get ready to come home."

Jason replied as he walked toward the car, "Okay dad, later."

Jennifer spoke into her ear-com, "Racehorse is returning to the vehicle."

They returned to the vehicle and Jason and Thomas got in the rear passenger seat. Darlene drove up next to their vehicle and nodded to Jennifer. Darlene continued down the street and turned left at the corner. Jennifer followed her to the corner and made a left turn also. They drove past numerous blocks of business addresses and came to the main exit of the business park. Darlene stopped at the stop sign and waited for the previously noted plumbing supply van, stopped at the stop sign, to proceed from the left. The van waved her on. Darlene declined and waved the van to proceed, not wanting to place a vehicle between her vehicle and Jennifer's vehicle. Jennifer saw the interaction between Darlene and the van driver. The driver of the van curiously began to make a slow right turn. As Darlene made a right turn, the van abruptly pulled between Darlene and Jennifer's vehicles. Jennifer's reaction was instantaneous; she checked her rearview mirror and put the vehicle in reverse.

She yelled at Thomas and Jason, "Get down on the floorboard."

Thomas and Jason immediately ducked. There was a vehicle coming up behind Jennifer and there was no room to back around it. Jennifer spoke into her ear-com, "This is Horizon, 1033; Racehorse in danger; immediate assistance requested."

She stopped her vehicle, rolled down the window, drew her weapon and stepped out and crouched behind the door. She quickly looked at the vehicle behind her and didn't see it as a threat. She turned her attention back to the van. Darlene spoke into her earcom, "This is Overwatch, 1033; backup ASAP."

As she spoke, she quickly made a complete U-turn and drove her vehicle and stopped in between the van and Jennifer's vehicle. Darlene stepped out of her vehicle and drew her weapon and pointed it at the van.

The driver of the van saw both weapons pointed at him, and he and the passenger raised their hands while still in the vehicle. Darlene yelled to the van, "Driver, turn you vehicle off and step out of the van with your hands raised and face away from me."

The driver did as directed.

Jennifer kept an eye on the van while quickly scanning a 360 view of the area for any other threats, and settled back aiming toward the van.

Darlene directed the van driver, "Walk back toward me and kneel on the ground and put your hands behind your head and don't move." The driver did as directed. Darlene again called to the van, "Passenger in the van, come out with your hands raised and face away from me."

Passenger complied with her directions. Darlene continued, "Walk back toward me and kneel on the ground, put your hands behind your head and don't move."

One more occupant came out of the van and submitted to Darlene's orders.

Jennifer realized that she could not leave her protection assignment to assist Darlene. Within two minutes the local PD and Sheriff arrived and secured scene.

Darlene and Jennifer holstered their weapons and Darlene came over to Jennifer. Jason and Thomas set up in their seats.

Jason said to Thomas with a nervous laugh, "You sure know how to show a guy a good time."

Thomas shook his head, "Well, this wasn't my plan."

Jennifer said to Darlene, "I felt so useless not being able to help you with the van."

Darlene replied, "I know what you mean, but your primary objective was protecting the son of the POTUS at all cost."

Darlene and Jennifer waited for the FBI to arrive.

Three other Secret Service agents arrived and gathered up the suspects and relieved Darlene and Jennifer. They got back into their vehicles and drove back to the pizza party.

*****

As they walked in the door it was apparent that the party had been put on hold pending the outcome of the incident.

Angela and Nicole came running up to Thomas and Jason.

Angela said, "I was scared for you, don't do this again."

Thomas took a deep sigh, "I think we've had enough excitement for today." He paused, looking at Jason, "I'm ready for pizza; how about you Jason?"

Jason replied, "Yeah, show me the way."

The girls led them into the pizza parlor.

Richard came over to Darlene and Jennifer, "It appears that you two stopped an attempted kidnapping the president's son."

Darlene shook her head, "I wasn't exactly sure what was going on, the crew didn't become aggressive, and they complied with all my orders."

Richard replied, "Well, they did have weapons but, fortunately, chose not to use them.

Jennifer asked, "Do we know who was behind it?"

Richard replied, "We're still trying to put all the pieces together but it appears that it was orchestrated by the Anti-Adam faction." Richard continued, "Apparently, they didn't expect Secret Service to be with Thomas. Their plan was to kidnap Thomas and force the president to stop the alien invasion, as they call it."

Darlene said, "Well, I suppose we're lucky it wasn't Segr8, we might've had a different result."

Richard nodded and put his arms around Jennifer and Darlene's shoulders and asked, "So, very special agents; how was your day?"

Prelude To History

In the weeks since, in what they now call, 'The Revelation', when Adam suggested the construction of a transport platform; there had been major changes, worldwide, in the scientific community in solving the challenge. At least four platforms had been constructed to offer options for Adam to choose from:

Jubal Jung at the Nangang Exhibition Center; Honrí Foster and Marie Barrett at the VLA in New Mexico; Aldo Karloff in collaboration at the SETI site in Johannesburg with Cory and Jo James; and of course Hat Creek, all constructed a platform using various technologies.

A thirty by thirty prefab COM center was constructed just off of the edge of the parking lot near the SETI site. Rousan and Mike were finishing connecting a backup generator outside of the COM center.

Mike said, "Now all we need to do is install the automatic power transfer cable to the generator."

Bashir nodded, "Yeah, it's pretty much plug-and-play from here on. I'll go get it out of the ATV."

He walked over to get the cable and saw Darcy driving up on her ATV. Bashir smiled, "So, Darcy are you keeping the bad guys away?"

Darcy smiled, "So far we've chased off two foxes and the vicious possum."

Bashir smiled, "I guess that's not as exciting as tracking down explosives."

Darcy replied, "No but I can do without that kind of excitement." She smiled, "You have time to take a break?"

Bashir replied, "Sure, Mike and I were just finishing up. Let me take this power cable over and plug it in."

Bashir grabbed the cable and went back over to the generator and plugged the cable in to the generator and into the wall.

He asked Mike, "Mike, you need anything else?"

Mike noticed Darcy, "Nope, that's it, thank you,"

Bashir said, "No problem. Let me know when we need to check the circuits in the platform."

Mike nodded, "Will do."

Mike went inside the COM center and went over to the wall and flipped a switch. A green light display and Mike smiled. He made his way around several tables and chairs lined up in the COM center and flipped another switch on the wall. Another green light displayed. He reached and flipped another switch and four monitors attached to the walls lit up. Once again Mike smiled. He turned and went out of the COM center and headed toward the SETI complex.

He got to the door at the same time Carmen Hafed arrived at the door. Mike said, "Hey, Carmen, glad to see you made it back."

Carmen replied, "It's good to be back, but all we have to do now, is wait."

Mike nodded and opened the door to allow Carmen to enter first. Mike added, "I think some of the guys are in the break room."

Mike followed Carmen toward the break room and Carmen went inside but Mike continued on to the security office.

Perry was talking to agents Johnson and Rayner when he saw Carmen come into the break room. Perry shook Carmen's hand, "Carmen, good to see you back."

He turned to Ron and Anji, "Carmen Hafed, you remember agents Johnson and Rayner?"

Carmen shook both their hands, "Yes, it's a pleasure to see you again."

Ron and Anji both nodded.

Ron replied, "Thank you Professor."

Anji replied, "Yes, good to see you again."

Perry asked Carmen, "Why don't we go out to the COM center and wait there?"

Carmen replied, "Certainly, sounds like a plan."

Carmen nodded to Ron and Anji and followed Perry out of the room. Mike entered the break room as they were leaving. He asked Ron and Anji, "Are Dom and Amir eating in their unit or are they coming here to eat?"

Anji replied, "Marnie said they were still in their unit when she and R.A. left."

Mike offered a wrinkle smiled, "Okay, I'll let them fend for themselves."

Anji smiled, "Or fend off each other."

Ron smiled and playfully slapped Anji's arm, "Hey!"

Anji shrugged and smiled, "Well!"

Mike shook his head and smiled, "Okay I'm going out to the COM center. Are you guys coming?"

Ron nodded, "Just finishing our coffee and we're heading that way."

Mike turned and walked out of the break room and as he left the complex he saw R.A. and Sal sitting at a station in the complex.

R.A. was looking at the screen searching through some data files. Sal was sitting next to him when he got a notice on his VPC. He took it out of his pocket and activated it. He saw his lab associate Eric Mimilis was calling. He answered the call, "Eric buddy, what's up?"

Eric looked serious.

"Sal you know those skin samples that Adam sent in one of the trial transports?"

Sal replied with concern, "Yes, is there something wrong? Are they contaminated? Do we need to shut down the lab?"

Eric shook his head, "No, Sal, it's nothing serious but the DNA results are perplexing."

Sal asked, "Okay, what about them?"

Eric replied, "Well, I'm still working on them but I'll send the data to you when Susan and I finish analyzing them."

Sal replied, "Okay, I'll wait till I get it. You be safe. Thank you."

Sal disconnected the call. R.A. heard the conversation, "I wonder what that's about."

Sal replied, "I guess will find out when I get them."

R.A. stood up, "Well, I guess we better head on over to the COM center."

Sal stood also and followed R.A. out of the complex and over to the COM center. Marnie and Jennifer were standing outside the COM center watching the skies.

As Sal and R.A. got close to the COM center they heard the roar of two F-35 jets crisscrossing the skies. Sal turned to R.A., "Well, I know what those jets signify."

R.A. asked, "And what is that?"

Sal replied, "We're about to get a visit from Marine One."

Jennifer heard Sal's response, "Yep, POTUS and friends are coming to town."

Sal and R.A. continued on inside and found a couple of seats at one of the tables. Perry was busy setting up the COM screens that were attached to the walls. Mike was outside talking to the standby paramedics who were assigned there as a precaution, in case something went wrong during the transport. Mike saw the jets fly by. He reached for his two-way radio mic attached to his shirt and keyed it up.

"Security two, Gozier, base."

Juan Gozier answered, "Go for security two."

Mike said, "I need you to pick up the passenger bus from the secret service and drive it down to the end of the parking lot to pick up our new arrivals."

Juan replied, "Copy that, security two out."

*****

Dominique and Amir sat next to each other at the kitchen table in their unit, finishing up their tuna salad sandwiches and mushroom soup. They both looked up when they heard the jets circling about. Amir looked back down at Dom and reached over and placed his hand on Dom's hand, "I can't think of anyone I'd rather be sharing this life with than with you."

Dom smiled, "That's very sweet of you to say. I cherish every day with you, Amir, and I so enjoy our spontaneous interludes."

Amir replied, "You, Dom, make every day worthwhile."

Dom took a slow breath, "Well, I guess we had better join our friends and begin our next adventure."

Amir replied dramatically, "Yes, let us go forth."

Dom smiled and shook her head. They got up and placed their empty dishes in the sink and ran some water into them.

They turned to each other, embraced and kissed gently at first and then with more passion, and then ended up separating with a gentle peck. They each checked their pockets for their VPCs and proceeded out the door. They made their appearance at the COM center and found seats next to Sal and R.A..

******

Juan pulled the bus up to the end of the parking lot; stopped it, opened the front and rear side doors, and waited. A Secret Service agent, who was with him, got out of the bus and stood by the door. Juan's wait was not very long as he heard heavy rotor blades of two aircraft a Chinook helicopter and Marine One encroaching. The Chinook landed first a safe distance away and Marine One hovered, temporarily, and eased down to the ground close by.

The attendants of the aircraft deployed the stairways and the passengers began to depart.

Some media personnel quickly departed the Chinook and began documenting the arrival. Noticeably absent from the media entourage was Evelyn Walker. As the engines wound down the first off of Marine One was the president and his wife, Vicki, followed by Thomas. Chief of Staff, Joel Mack followed him immediately down the stairway and quickly came over to the bus. The secret service agent acknowledged him and they both waited for the president.

Juan stood at attention as the president made his way to the bus. The president helped the First Lady on and Juan said, "Welcome Madam First Lady." The president followed her up the steps and Juan said, "Welcome aboard Mr. President."

Tsirch recognized Juan's obvious military stand at attention, "You served didn't you son?"

Juan replied, "Yes, Mr. President; Crew Chief, Sergeant Gozier, 2nd Cav."

Tsirch replied, "Oh, yes, and weren't you the one who took down the hang glider."

Juan replied, "Yes sir."

Tsirch offered his hand and Juan took it. Tsirch said, "Our nation thanks you, Sergeant."

Juan replied, "Thank you Mr. President."

Tsirch gave him a salute and Juan instinctively responded although he was in civilian clothes. Thomas followed the president up the steps. Juan greeted Thomas and waited for the other passengers to get on the bus. Johnny Walsh, Vice President Natás, Evelyn Walker, agents Danielle Alton and Darlene Gordon and Chief of Staff, Joel Mack, made their way aboard. The media and other passengers entered in the rear side door.

When everyone was aboard Juan closed the doors, started the bus and drove the short distance to the COM center.

Juan parked the bus and the passengers began to depart.

Michael and Perry waited for the President, First Lady and Thomas, at the entrance to the COM center. Perry approached the president and shook his hand, "Mr. President, I'm Perry Edmonds the co-director at Hat Creek, and this is co-director Michael Mitchell." The president shook Mike's hand and Perry continued, "I'm sorry for the accommodations, but we were not sure that you would be coming."

Tsirch replied, "There is no need to apologize for anything Mr. Edmonds, as we are on Adams timetable. And besides it's not my show."

Perry looked around, "I guess you can sit anywhere you want Mr. President."

Tsirch laughed, "Thank you Mr. Edmonds I think we'll be just fine."

Tsirch, the First Lady and Thomas, gradually made their way pressing flesh and making conversation through the crowd and settled one table away from R.A., Sal, Dom and Amir. Richard and Eve found seating nearby, and Congresswoman Walsh eased in next to Sal.

Although they were still on the job the corresponding agents at Hat Creek were rendered superfluous, considering the throng of Secret Service that arrived with the president and his entourage. Jennifer, Darlene, Marnie and the other agents mingled at will. As a possible time of activation of the transport platform got closer, Sal decided to take charge of the event.

He went over to a table and picked up a microphone and walked toward the front of the COM center.

He began to speak, "Ladies and gentlemen, may I have your attention please."

The crowd wasn't unusually loud and they settled down rather quickly. Sal waited for the lull.

He started, "I'm sure you realize why we're all here," he paused and smiled, "at least I know why I'm here."

The crowd delivered sporadic laughter.

"This event, if it does occur, is likely to be the most historic and unprecedented event in human history. The untold number of people that made this event possible truly boggles the mind. We have biological scientists, astronauts, pilots, astrophysicist, astronomers, politicians, military personnel, FBI and CIA agents, local law enforcement, military and special forces from Russia, China, Africa, Southeast Asia and Australia, who all came together to combat the divisive groups that would have destroyed this opportunity. There also civilians who surrendered their time with their families to gather and document seemingly meaningless information that eventually brought us to realize the truth."

Sal looked over at Dom and Amir and smiled, "I wouldn't ordinarily single out any particular person to ascribe the turning point of our discovery of alien intelligence, but I will make an exception. I would like to recognize astronomers and space scientists Dominique Soul and Amir Hadad."

He pointed toward Amir and Dom, "Could you both please come forward and be recognized?"

Sal led the applause. Dom and Amir sat stoically not wanting to get up. R.A. and Richard stood and urged them to stand. Dom and Amir exchanged glances at each other and smiled.

Eventually they succumbed to the growing applause and stood.

Sal continued to urge them to come up.

"Amir and Dom please come up."

Tsirch stood and clapped enthusiastically. Dom saw the president standing and applauding. She slowly grabbed Amir's hand and let him to Sal. When they got to the front Sal handed them the microphone. Dom took the microphone and quickly handed it to Amir. The crowd chuckle at the gesture. Amir looked around, "This is embarrassing; not for being urged to speak, but for being singled out for something that I had no control over. I realize that someone, if not me, would have eventually made the connection that the aliens were trying to contact us."

He looked over Dom, "But I can say if there is someone to give credit to for the discovery of Adam, it is my personal heroine, Ms. Dominique Soul."

Dom listened and shook her head; she needed to change the perspective. She took the mic from Amir. She said quickly, "No, no. Yes I was the first to speak to Adam, but there would be no, 'first contact' there would be no 'transport platform' if YOU," she swept her hand to the crowd, "did not want to believe that there is other life out there." She became more animated, "If you had let the dissidents and reality deniers, keep you from following your need to explore, to imagine, to dream and to wonder what is 'out there'" she paused, "and what life is about." She slowed her pace, "No, YOU," gesturing toward the crowd, "are the heroes for embracing and defending the truth."

Dom slowly handed the mic to Sal. She looked at Amir and he put his arm around her shoulders and tucked her head to his shoulder. The gathering responded with the raucous applause.

Dom and Amir smiled shyly as they made their way back to their seats through a congratulatory crowd.

Tsirch looked over at the transport platform and stood up. He casually walked over to get a closer look. Michael saw him inspecting the platform and went over to him.

"Mr. President, are you familiar with the technology that went into the construction of this transport platform?"

Tsirch shrugged, "I've been briefed on its construction and seen various designs, but I must admit I'm intrigued by the concept of transporting anything from a distance light years away, almost instantaneously. I know there have been test runs where materials have been delivered, but until you actually see it happen, it all seems like it's a fantasy."

Mike nodded and smiled, "Well you're not alone with those thoughts Mr. President. I'm a space scientist, physicist and astronomer and I've watched this project develop, but yet even after having witnessed the instantaneous delivery of materials and physically held them, I too question the reality."

Tsirch nodded and walked around the platform, taking in its seemingly simple design.

"So, this looks like an oversized elevator except that it has a large amount of glass on its sides.' Tsirch smiled, "Can you give me a more technical description?"

Mike nodded, "Of course, sir. The 'elevator', as you described it, is seven by seven feet square and twelve feet in height. Theoretically, the alien's sending source is powered by fusion reaction that uses a collider type of beam to somehow transform its target; in this case a life form, into some type of particle form that is held in state by what we can best understand as a containment carrier. The more incredible part of the process is trying to understand how the aliens use time as a wave and combining their use of quantum mechanics acceleration to jump from the top of each wave of time instantaneously."

Tsirch was trying to follow the logic and appeared to be waiting for a reasonable explanation.

"Well, okay. Let's pretend I understand that; and then what happens?"

Mike smiled, "Well, Mr. President I guess the alien magicians haven't it seen fit to show us their secret, at least one that we understand." Mike took a breath, "However, our part in the process is to generate a signal at a specified frequency to draw the beam or ionic state, and catch it with our transport platform." Mike took another breath, "We have used the alien's fusion power design to stabilize the frequency. When the transport is completed and the alien's remote sensors determined that it is sufficiently stable in the platform, the containment carrier releases it to the platform."

Mike raised his brows and looked at Tsirch, "It's that simple, Mr. President."

Tsirch thought for a moment and gripped his forehead with his hand, "Okay, now I understand." He smiled, looked at Mike and chuckled, "I think I'll go back to my seat and see if I can find a stiff drink."

Mike smiled, "Of course, Mr. President."

Sal saw the president walk away from Michael and he went up to Mike.

"What were you saying to the president?"

Mike smiled, "I was explaining the transport process to him and, strangely, I think he understood."

Sal half smiled and showed an incredulous look, "Really?"

Welcome Adam

Richard was talking to R.A. when Sal came up to them, "R.A., I just got a note from the other transport sites, they want to talk to us inside."

R.A. nodded, "Okay, let's go." He looked at Richard, "You want to come with us and see what's up?"

Richard nodded, "Sure, I'll tag along."

The three got up from the table and walked toward the exit of the COM center.

Johnny saw them leaving and turned to Eve, "I wonder where the guys are going."

Eve looked at her watch, "I don't know but, they better be back soon, it's getting close to crunch time."

Johnny looked at Eve, "I thought you would be front and center with the media documenting the entire event."

Eve sighed, "I thought it was about time to give my protégé a chance to get her feet wet, and this is no better time to have a baptism by fire."

Johnny smiled, "You and I are of the same mind. I've been delegating some of my work to my Chief of Staff."

Eve looked across the room to the president's table, "How about we go check in with Vicki and Thomas?"

Johnny stood up, "Okay, I'm game."

Eve got up and led the way across the room. Halfway there, Mike and Carmen approached Johnny. Mike seemed a little stressed, "Do you know where Sal is?"

Johnny said, "Yes, he and R.A. and Richard went out together a moment ago. Is there a problem?"

Mike sighed, "I hope not but if you see him tell him we need to see in the complex."

Johnny nodded, "Okay, I'll tell him."

Mike and Carmen began walking out at the entrance and turned toward the complex. Mike looked toward the complex and saw R.A. going in the door. Mike tapped Carmen on the arm, "There they are, going inside."

They both hurried toward the complex.

Sal, R.A. and Richard went into the break room and Sal turned on the COM. Three icons showed on the screen; Marie Barrett, Jubal Jung and the combination of Cory and Jo. Mike and Carmen came into the break room and Mike took a short breath, "There you are; we've been looking for you. We got a message from Jubal to contact him."

Sal nodded, "Yes, I got a message too. Let's see what this is about."

All three icons change to images. Sal asked, "Okay we got the message, what's going on?"

Jubal the first to reply, "We are not sure what's going on but all three of our transport platforms are acting strangely. It seems that there is some type of power surge that causes transport beam send an image and then it seems to pull it back."

Marie added, "Each of us have experienced this type of interference before, but they all happen at separate times. It seems that there is a problem stabilizing the transport."

Jo chimed in, "We've theorized that there is a problem with the frequency stabilization and we've been checking the each of our frequencies to see if they match."

Jubal summarize their question, "We have sent you our frequency setting to see if it is the same as yours."

Sal nodded, "Okay, let me go back to my station and see what our settings are. I'll be back in a moment."

Sal got up and went out of the break room and around the corner. He went down the hall and sat down at his station and activated his COM. He also noticed a pending data message from Eric. He entered some keystrokes and a keyboard and the frequency setting from the other three sites displayed on the screen. He entered some more keystrokes and his frequency setting displayed on the screen. He leaned back in the chair in surprise. He entered some keystrokes and got up and went back toward the break room.

When he got to the break room and went to the keyboard and entered some keystrokes. The frequencies displayed on the screen.

"Hey guys; my frequency does not match your frequencies. Why did Adam give us different frequencies?"

The think tank collective went silent in thought.

Marie ticked her head back and started to speak but held her tongue. Jubal broke the silence, "Okay, Sal, is your transport powered up?"

Sal looked at R.A.

"No, we were waiting until about ten minutes before the scheduled."

Jo smiled, "Well, maybe that's the problem; it's possible that the Alphas primary transport unit is having a problem sending the signal to three different platforms."

Sal shrugged, "That could be the problem but my question is; why is my frequency different than your three frequencies?"

R.A. offered his observation, "If I'm not mistaken, I understand that your three platforms are built on the same design created by Jubal's technician, Hua Na. Is that right?"

Apparently a light went on and illuminated the problem.

Sal shook his head, "Okay, we might can solve this problem if two of you three want to shut down your platform and let the other one received the package."

Carmen offered her opinion, "For me I realize we all worked hard in our projects but it appears that since the platform was based on Hua Na's design that Jubal and his crew should have the first shot."

Marie acquiesced, "As much as the disappointment would be I tend to agree."

Jo was temporarily away from the screen and came back.

"I was talking to Cory and Aldo and they came to the same conclusion; Hua Na deserves the credit."

R.A. added a fly to the ointment, "While I appreciate all your attempts at magnanimity, we yet have to address our initial reason for building several platforms."

Sal nodded, "R.A. is correct; due to the alignment of everything in between our planets, Adam realized that in order for the transport to succeed, it would be advantageous to have several location options of the receiving platform."

Sal leaned his head to his chest and raised it back up, "So, there are some options we might consider. Option number one: Our platform and one of yours can be powered on at the same time. Option number two: Our platform and one of your platforms can alternate powering on to give you each a chance at receiving our package. Or, option number three: one of you keeps your power on and the others turn their power off." Sal paused, "Any choice we make only gives us two opportunities to receive the package."

Jubal took a couple deep breaths, "Sal, would you mind if we three confer in a side channel?"

Sal shrugged his shoulders and looked at R.A. and Carmen, "Sure, you can do that."

Joel replied, "Thank you will get back shortly."

Richard looked at R.A., Sal, Mike and Carmen, "Well, this is quite a situation."

Sal nodded and remembered his message from Eric. As the others talk amongst themselves, he took his VPC out and activated it. He opened up the data message and read it carefully, twice.

He sat quietly in thought.

His introspection was broken by the activation of the COM screen.

Jubal smiled, "We had a discussion about the options, but we have fourth option."

Sal nodded, "Okay, we'd like to hear it."

Jubal sighed, "Since there is no urgency to receive our visitor, we've decided that although any of us greatly appreciate the honor of receiving our first visitor from another planet, we've decided that history should be written reflecting the original contact and receiving of the first visitor from another planet should rest with the Hat Creek SETI site."

Sal ticked his head to one side, "While we appreciate your decision there is still a chance that one of you might receive visitor instead of us."

Jubal smiled, "My dear Doctor Uschin, you don't understand. We choose not to power our platforms up and give you a singular opportunity at receiving our visitor."

Sal thought for a moment, "You realize that is possible that we may not be able to receive visitor at this time."

Jubal nodded, "Yes, we discussed that possibility and decided that at this time the first opportunity should rest with Hat Creek."

Sal leaned back in his chair, "Okay, if that's your decision, we will respect it and if the visit doesn't take place now we will make other choices together."

Jubal nodded, "Thank you we will be watching and cheering for all mankind."

The images disappeared from the screen.

Richard looked at Sal, "That was a great gesture they made.

It epitomizes our humanity."

They sat quietly for a moment and R.A. stood up.

"Okay, we have a visitor to meet."

The group followed R.A. out to the COM center and they returned to their seats except for Sal.

Sal peeled off and went over to Perry and told him about the decision of the other sites. Perry listened and nodded and went over to the power switch on the platform and engaged it. Anticipation filled the air.

Sal opened up his VPC and looked at the data message once more. He leaned over to R.A. and showed him the message. R.A. shook his head, "Are you sure this DNA sequencing of the Alphas is accurate?"

Sal sighed, "Well, soon will have a live breathing sample to compare it to."

The platform began to flicker and an image slowly materialized into a life form. Slowly it moved its head and body. At last, to the amazement, wonderment and fascination of mankind there stood proof that we are not alone. Above the platform flashed a large sign reading in broad letters:

WELCOME ADAM.

ABOUT THE AUTHOR

Terol McCullar actively perused his twenty-six year career as a California Correctional Officer and Sergeant Instructor known as T-Mac. The dichotomy of witnessing both good times and turmoil and having lived through the 1950s and 1960s and his passion for the law and teaching has helped mold his intrinsic belief in self-efficacy. His latent passion as an author has flourished into three previous works: HOGGS I and II and S.I.C.Q. SOS a sequel to S.I.C.Q. is his latest offering and he has started the next sequel, DNA:ALIEN LEGACY and the next addition to the HOGGS series.

The author yet acknowledges the undying support of his wife Tricia, daughters Angela and Marnie, and a growing list of great friends.

9 781778 390999